Charles Dudley Warner

Studies in the South and West

with comments on Canada

Charles Dudley Warner

Studies in the South and West
with comments on Canada

ISBN/EAN: 9783337190040

Printed in Europe, USA, Canada, Australia, Japan

Cover: Foto ©Andreas Hilbeck / pixelio.de

More available books at **www.hansebooks.com**

STUDIES

IN THE

SOUTH AND WEST

WITH COMMENTS ON CANADA

BY

CHARLES DUDLEY WARNER
AUTHOR OF "THEIR PILGRIMAGE" ETC.

NEW YORK AND LONDON

HARPER & BROTHERS PUBLISHERS

PREFATORY NOTE.

To **Henry M. Alden,** *Esq., Editor of* **Harper's Monthly:**

My dear Mr. Alden,—It was at your suggestion that these Studies were undertaken; all of them passed under your eye, except "Society in the New South," which appeared in the *New Princeton Review.* The object was not to present a comprehensive account of the country South and West—which would have been impossible in the time and space given—but to note certain representative developments, tendencies, and dispositions, the communication of which would lead to a better understanding between different sections. The subjects chosen embrace by no means all that is important and interesting, but it is believed that they are fairly representative. The strongest impression produced upon the writer in making these Studies was that the prosperous life of the Union depends upon the life and dignity of the individual States.

C. D. W

CONTENTS.

SOUTH AND WEST.

I.

IMPRESSIONS OF THE SOUTH.

IN 1885.

IT is borne in upon me, as the Friends would say, that I ought to bear my testimony of certain impressions made by a recent visit to the Gulf States. In doing this I am aware that I shall be under the suspicion of having received kindness and hospitality, and of forming opinions upon a brief sojourn. Both these facts must be confessed, and allowed their due weight in discrediting what I have to say. A month of my short visit was given to New Orleans in the spring, during the Exposition, and these impressions are mainly of Louisiana.

The first general impression made was that the war is over in spirit as well as in deed. The thoughts of the people are not upon the war, not much upon the past at all, except as their losses remind them of it, but upon the future, upon business, a revival of trade, upon education, and adjustment to the new state of things. The thoughts are not much upon politics either, or upon offices ; certainly they are not turned more in this direction than the thoughts of people at the North are. When we read a despatch which declares that there is immense dissatisfaction throughout Arkansas because offices are not dealt out more liberally to it, we may know that the case is exactly what it is in, say, Wisconsin — that a few political managers are grumbling, and that the great body of the people are indifferent, perhaps too indifferent, to the distribution of offices.

Undoubtedly immense satisfaction was felt at the election of Mr. Cleveland, and elation of triumph in the belief that now the party which had been largely a non-participant in Federal affairs would have a large share and weight in the administration. With this went, however, a new feeling of responsibility, of a stake in the country, that manifested itself at once in attachment to the Union as the common possession of all sections. I feel sure that Louisiana, for instance, was never in its whole history, from the day of the Jefferson purchase, so consciously loyal to the United States as it is to-day. I have believed that for the past ten years there has been growing in this country a stronger feeling of nationality—a distinct American historic consciousness — and nowhere else has it developed so rapidly of late as at the South. I am convinced that this is a genuine development of attachment to the Union and of pride in the nation, and not in any respect a political movement for unworthy purposes. I am sorry that it is necessary, for the sake of any lingering prejudice at the North, to say this. But it is time that sober, thoughtful, patriotic people at the North should quit representing the desire for office at the South as a desire to get into the Government saddle and ride again with a " rebel " impulse. It would be, indeed, a discouraging fact if any considerable portion of the South held aloof in sullenness from Federal affairs. Nor is it any just cause either of reproach or of uneasiness that men

who were prominent in the war of the rebellion should
be prominent now in official positions, for with a few
exceptions the worth and weight of the South went
into the war.   It would be idle to discuss the question
whether the masses of the South were not dragooned
into the war by the politicians; it is sufficient to recognize the fact that it became practically, by one
means or another, a unanimous revolt.

One of the strongest impressions made upon a
Northerner who visits the extreme South now, having
been familiar with it only by report, is the extent to
which it suffered in the war.   Of course there was
extravagance and there were impending bankruptcies
before the war, debt, and methods of business inher-
ently vicious, and no doubt the war is charged with
many losses which would have come without it, just
as in every crisis half the failures wrongfully accuse
the crisis.   Yet, with all allowance for these things,
the fact remains that the war practically wiped out
personal property and the means of livelihood.   The
completeness of this loss and disaster never came
home to me before.   In some cases the picture of the
ante bellum civilization is more roseate in the minds
of those who lost everything than cool observation of
it would justify.   But conceding this, the actual disaster needs no embellishment of the imagination.   It
seems to me, in the reverse, that the Southern people
do not appreciate the sacrifices the North made for
the Union.   They do not, I think, realize the fact that
the North put into the war its best blood, that every
battle brought mourning into our households, and
filled our churches day by day and year by year with
the black garments of bereavement ; nor did they

ever understand the tearful enthusiasm for the Union
and the flag, and the unselfish devotion that underlay
all the self-sacrifice. Some time the Southern people
will know that it was love for the Union, and not
hatred of the South, that made heroes of the men
and angels of renunciation of the women.

Yes, say our Southern friends, we can believe that
you lost dear ones and were in mourning; but, after
all, the North was prosperous; you grew rich; and
when the war ended, life went on in the fulness of
material prosperity. We lost not only our friends
and relatives, fathers, sons, brothers, till there was
scarcely a household that was not broken up, we lost
not only the cause on which we had set our hearts,
and for which we had suffered privation and hardship, were fugitives and wanderers, and endured the
bitterness of defeat at the end, but our property was
gone, we were stripped, with scarcely a home, and the
whole of life had to be begun over again, under all
the disadvantage of a sudden social revolution.

It is not necessary to dwell upon this or to heighten
it, but it must be borne in mind when we observe the
temper of the South, and especially when we are looking for remaining bitterness, and the wonder to me is
that after so short a space of time there is remaining
so little of resentment or of bitter feeling over loss
and discomfiture. I believe there is not in history
any parallel to it. Every American must take pride
in the fact that Americans have so risen superior to
circumstances, and come out of trials that thoroughly
threshed and winnowed soul and body in a temper
so gentle and a spirit so noble. It is good stuff that
can endure a test of this kind.

A lady, whose family sustained all the losses that were possible in the war, said to me—and she said only what several others said in substance—" We are going to get more out of this war than you at the North, because we suffered more. We were drawn out of ourselves in sacrifices, and were drawn together in a tenderer feeling of humanity ; I do believe we were chastened into a higher and purer spirit."

Let me not be misunderstood. The people who thus recognize the moral training of adversity and its effects upon character, and who are glad that slavery is gone, and believe that a new and better era for the South is at hand, would not for a moment put them-selves in an attitude of apology for the part they took in the war, nor confess that they were wrong, nor join in any denunciation of the leaders they followed to their sorrow. They simply put the past behind them, so far as the conduct of the present life is concerned. They do not propose to stamp upon memories that are tender and sacred, and they cherish certain senti-ments which are to them loyalty to their past and to the great passionate experiences of their lives. When a woman, who enlisted by the consent of Jeff Davis, whose name appeared for four years upon the rolls, and who endured all the perils and hardships of the conflict as a field-nurse, speaks of " President " Davis, what does it mean? It is only a sentiment. This heroine of the war on the wrong side had in the Ex-position a tent, where the veterans of the Confederacy recorded their names. On one side, at the back of the tent, was a table piled with touching relics of the war, and above it a portrait of Robert E. Lee, wreath-ed in immortelles. It was surely a harmless shrine.

On the other side was also a table, piled with fruit and cereals—not relics, but signs of prosperity and peace—and above it a portrait of Ulysses S. Grant. Here was the sentiment, cherished with an aching heart maybe, and here was the fact of the Union and the future.

Another strong impression made upon the visitor is, as I said, that the South has entirely put the past behind it, and is devoting itself to the work of rebuilding on new foundations. There is no reluctance to talk about the war, or to discuss its conduct and what might have been. But all this is historic. It engenders no heat. The mind of the South to-day is on the development of its resources, upon the rehabilitation of its affairs. I think it is rather more concerned about national prosperity than it is about the great problem of the negro—but I will refer to this further on. There goes with this interest in material development the same interest in the general prosperity of the country that exists at the North—the anxiety that the country should prosper, acquit itself well, and stand well with the other nations. There is, of course, a sectional feeling—as to tariff, as to internal improvements—but I do not think the Southern States are any more anxious to get things for themselves out of the Federal Government than the Northern States are. That the most extreme of Southern politicians have any sinister purpose (any more than any of the Northern "rings" on either side have) in wanting to "rule" the country, is, in my humble opinion, only a chimera evoked to make political capital.

Illustrations in point as to the absolute subsidence of hostile intention (this phrase I know will sound

queer in the South), and the laying aside of bitterness
for the past, are not necessary in the presence of a
strong general impression, but they might be given in
great number. I note one that was significant from
its origin, remembering, what is well known, that
women and clergymen are always the last to experience subsidence of hostile feeling after a civil war.
On the Confederate Decoration Day in New Orleans
I was standing near the Confederate monument in
one of the cemeteries when the veterans marched in
to decorate it. First came the veterans of the Army
of Virginia, last those of the Army of Tennessee, and
between them the veterans of the Grand Army of the
Republic, Union soldiers now living in Louisiana. I
stood beside a lady whose name, if I mentioned it,
would be recognized as representative of a family
which was as conspicuous, and did as much and lost
as much, as any other in the war—a family that would
be popularly supposed to cherish unrelenting feelings.
As the veterans, some of them on crutches, many of
them with empty sleeves, grouped themselves about
the monument, we remarked upon the sight as a
touching one, and I said: "I see you have no address
on Decoration Day. At the North we still keep up
the custom." "No," she replied; "we have given it
up. So many imprudent things were said that we
thought best to discontinue the address." And then,
after a pause, she added, thoughtfully: "Each side did
the best it could ; it is all over and done with, and
let's have an end of it." In the mouth of the lady
who uttered it, the remark was very significant, but
it expresses, I am firmly convinced, the feeling of the
South.

Of course the South will build monuments to its heroes, and weep over their graves, and live upon the memory of their devotion and genius. In Heaven's name, why shouldn't it? Is human nature itself to be changed in twenty years?

A long chapter might be written upon the dis-likeness of North and South, the difference in education, in training, in mental inheritances, the misapprehensions, radical and very singular to us, of the civilization of the North. We must recognize certain historic facts, not only the effect of the institution of slavery, but other facts in Southern development. Suppose we say that an unreasonable prejudice exists, or did exist, about the people of the North. That prejudice is a historic fact, of which the statesman must take account. It enters into the question of the time needed to effect the revolution now in progress. There are prejudices in the North about the South as well. We admit their existence. But what impresses me is the rapidity with which they are disappearing in the South. Knowing what human nature is, it seems incredible that they could have subsided so rapidly. Enough remain for national variety, and enough will remain for purposes of social badinage, but common interests in the country and in making money are melting them away very fast. So far as loyalty to the Government is concerned, I am not authorized to say that it is as deeply rooted in the South as in the North, but it is expressed as vividly, and felt with a good deal of fresh enthusiasm. The "American" sentiment, pride in this as the most glorious of all lands, is genuine, and amounts to enthusiasm with many who would in an argument glory in their rebellion. " We had more loyalty to our States than you had," said one lady, "and we have transferred it to the whole country."

But the negro ? Granting that the South is loyal enough, wishes never another rebellion, and is satisfied to be rid of slavery, do not the people intend to keep the negroes practically a servile class, slaves in all but the name, and to defeat by chicanery or by force the legitimate results of the war and of enfranchisement ? This is a very large question, and cannot be discussed in my limits. If I were to say what my impression is, it would be about this : the South is quite as much perplexed by the negro problem as the North is, and is very much disposed to await developments, and to let time solve it. One thing, however, must be admitted in all this discussion. The Southerners will not permit such Legislatures as those assembled once in Louisiana and South Carolina to rule them again. " Will you disfranchise the blacks by management or by force ?" " Well, what would you do in Ohio or in Connecticut ? Would you be ruled by a lot of ignorant field-hands allied with a gang of plunderers ?"

In looking at this question from a Northern point of view we have to keep in mind two things : first, the Federal Government imposed colored suffrage without any educational qualification — a hazardous experiment ; in the second place, it has handed over the control of the colored people in each State to the State, under the Constitution, as completely in Louisiana as in New York. The responsibility is on Louisiana. The North cannot relieve her of it, and it cannot interfere, except by ways provided in the Constitution. In the South, where fear of a legislative domination has gone, the feeling between the two races is that of amity and mutual help. This is, I think, especially true in Louisiana. The Southerners never have forgotten the loyalty of the slaves during the war, the security with which the white families dwelt in the midst of a black population while all the white men were absent in the field ; they often refer to this. It touches with tenderness the new relation of the races. I think there is generally in the South a feeling of good-will towards the negroes, a desire that they should develop into true manhood and womanhood. Undeniably there are indifference and neglect and some remaining suspicion about the schools that Northern charity has organized for the negroes. As to this neglect of the negro, two things are to be said: the whole subject of education (as we have understood it in the North) is comparatively new in the South ; and the necessity of earning a living since the war has distracted attention from it. But the general development of education is quite as advanced as could be expected. The thoughtful and the leaders of opinion are fully awake to the fact that the mass of the people must be educated, and that the only settlement of the negro problem is in the education of the negro, intellectually and morally. They go further than this. They say that for the South to hold its own—since the negro is there and will stay there, and is the majority of the laboring class—it is necessary that the great agricultural mass of unskilled labor should be transformed, to a great extent, into a class of skilled labor, skilled on the farm, in shops, in factories, and that the South must have a highly diversified industry. To this end they want industrial as well as ordinary schools for the colored people.

It is believed that, with this education and with diversified industry, the social question will settle itself, as it does the world over. Society cannot be made or unmade by legislation. In New Orleans the street-cars are free to all colors; at the Exposition white and colored people mingled freely, talking and looking at what was of common interest.

We who live in States where hotel-keepers exclude Hebrews cannot say much about the exclusion of negroes from Southern hotels. There are prejudices remaining. There are cases of hardship on the railways, where for the same charge perfectly respectable and nearly white women are shut out of cars while there is no discrimination against dirty and disagreeable white people. In time all this will doubtless rest upon the basis it rests on at the North, and social life will take care of itself. It is my impression that the negroes are no more desirous to mingle socially with the whites than the whites are with the negroes. Among the negroes there are social grades as distinctly marked as in white society. What will be the final outcome of the juxtaposition nobody can tell; meantime it must be recorded that good-will exists between the races.

I had one day at the Exposition an interesting talk with the colored woman in charge of the Alabama section of the exhibit of the colored people. This exhibit, made by States, was suggested and promoted by Major Burke in order to show the whites what the colored people could do, and as a stimulus to the latter. There was not much time—only two or three

months—in which to prepare the exhibit, and it was
hardly a fair showing of the capacity of the colored
people. The work was mainly women's work—em-
broidery, sewing, household stuffs, with a little of the
handiwork of artisans, and an exhibit of the progress
in education; but small as it was, it was wonderful
as the result of only a few years of freedom. The
Alabama exhibit was largely from Mobile, and was
due to the energy, executive ability, and taste of the
commissioner in charge. She was a quadroon, a widow, a woman of character and uncommon mental and
moral quality. She talked exceedingly well, and with
a practical good-sense which would be notable in anybody. In the course of our conversation the whole
social and political question was gone over. Herself
a person of light color, and with a confirmed social
prejudice against black people, she thoroughly identified herself with the colored race, and it was evident
that her sympathies were with them. She confirmed
what I had heard of the social grades among colored
people, but her whole soul was in the elevation of her
race as a race, inclining always to their side, but with
no trace of hostility to the whites. Many of her best
friends were whites, and perhaps the most valuable
part of her education was acquired in families of social distinction. "I can illustrate," she said, "the
state of feeling between the two races in Mobile by
an incident last summer. There was an election coming off in the City Government, and I knew that the
reformers wanted and needed the colored vote. I
went, therefore, to some of the chief men, who knew
me and had confidence in me, for I had had business
relations with many of them [she had kept a fashion-

able boarding-house], and told them that I wanted the
Opera-house for the colored people to give an entertainment and exhibition in. The request was extraordinary. Nobody but white people had ever been admitted to the Opera-house. But, after some hesitation
and consultation, the request was granted. We gave
the exhibition, and the white people all attended. It
was really a beautiful affair, lovely tableaux, with
gorgeous dresses, recitations, etc., and everybody was
astonished that the colored people had so much taste
and talent, and had got on so far in education. They
said they were delighted and surprised, and they liked
it so well that they wanted the entertainment repeated
—it was given for one of our charities—but I was too
wise for that. I didn't want to run the chance of destroying the impression by repeating, and I said we
would wait a while, and then show them something
better. Well, the election came off in August, and
everything went all right, and now the colored people
in Mobile can have anything they want. There is the
best feeling between the races. I tell you we should
get on beautifully if the politicians would let us alone.
It is politics that has made all the trouble in Alabama
and in Mobile." And I learned that in Mobile, as in
many other places, the negroes were put in minor official positions, the duties of which they were capable
of discharging, and had places in the police.

On " Louisiana Day " in the Exposition the colored
citizens took their full share of the parade and the
honors. Their societies marched with the others, and
the races mingled on the grounds in unconscious equality of privileges. Speeches were made, glorifying the
State and its history, by able speakers, the Governor

among them; but it was the testimony of Democrats of undoubted Southern orthodoxy that the honors of the day were carried off by a colored clergyman, an educated man, who united eloquence with excellent good-sense, and who spoke as a citizen of Louisiana, proud of his native State, dwelling with richness of allusion upon its history. It was a perfectly manly speech in the assertion of the rights and the position of his race, and it breathed throughout the same spirit of good-will and amity in a common hope of progress that characterized the talk of the colored woman commissioner of Mobile. It was warmly applauded, and accepted, so far as I heard, as a matter of course.

No one, however, can see the mass of colored people in the cities and on the plantations, the ignorant mass, slowly coming to moral consciousness, without a recognition of the magnitude of the negro problem. I am glad that my State has not the practical settlement of it, and I cannot do less than express profound sympathy with the people who have. They inherit the most difficult task now anywhere visible in human progress. They will make mistakes, and they will do injustice now and then; but one feels like turning away from these, and thanking God for what they do well.

There are many encouraging things in the condition of the negro. Good-will, generally, among the people where he lives is one thing; their tolerance of his weaknesses and failings is another. He is himself, here and there, making heroic sacrifices to obtain an education. There are negro mothers earning money at the wash-tub to keep their boys at school and in college. In the South-west there is such a call for

colored teachers that the Straight University in New
Orleans, which has about five hundred pupils, cannot
begin to supply the demand, although the teachers,
male and female, are paid from thirty-five to fifty
dollars a month. A colored graduate of this school a
year ago is now superintendent of the colored schools
in Memphis, at a salary of $1200 a year.

Are these exceptional cases ? Well, I suppose it is
also exceptional to see a colored clergyman in his sur-
plice seated in the chancel of the most important white
Episcopal church in New Orleans, assisting in the
service; but it is significant. There are many good
auguries to be drawn from the improved condition of
the negroes on the plantations, the more rational and
less emotional character of their religious services,
and the hold of the temperance movement on all
classes in the country places.

2

II.

SOCIETY IN THE NEW SOUTH.

THE American Revolution made less social change in the South than in the North. Under conservative influences the South developed her social life with little alteration in form and spirit—allowing for the decay that always attends conservatism—down to the Civil War. The social revolution which was in fact accomplished contemporaneously with the political severance from Great Britain, in the North, was not effected in the South until Lee offered his sword to Grant, and Grant told him to keep it and beat it into a ploughshare. The change had indeed been inevitable, and ripening for four years, but it was at that moment universally recognized. Impossible, of course, except by the removal of slavery, it is not wholly accounted for by the removal of slavery ; it results also from an economical and political revolution, and from a total alteration of the relations of the South to the rest of the world. The story of this social change will be one of the most marvellous the historian has to deal with.

Provincial is a comparative term. All England is provincial to the Londoner, all America to the Englishman. Perhaps New York looks upon Philadelphia as provincial; and if Chicago is forced to admit that Boston resembles ancient Athens, then Athens, by the Chicago standard, must have been a very provincial city. The root of provincialism is localism, or a condition of being on one side and apart from the general movement of contemporary life. In this sense, and compared with the North in its absolute openness to every wind from all parts of the globe, the South was provincial. Provincialism may have its decided advantages, and it may nurture many superior virtues and produce a social state that is as charming as it is interesting, but along with it goes a certain self-appreciation, which ultracosmopolitan critics would call Concord-like, that seems exaggerated to outsiders.

The South, and notably Virginia and South Carolina, cherished English traditions long after the political relation was severed. But it kept the traditions of the time of the separation, and did not share the literary and political evolution of England. Slavery divided it from the North in sympathy, and slavery, by excluding European emigration, shut out the South from the influence of the new ideas germinating in Europe. It was not exactly true to say that the library of the Southern gentleman stopped with the publications current in the reign of George the Third, but, well stocked as it was with the classics and with the English literature become classic, it was not likely to contain much of later date than the Reform Bill in England and the beginning of the abolition movement in the North. The pages of *De Bow's Review* attest the ambition and direction of Southern scholarship—a scholarship not much troubled by the new problems that were at the time rending England and the North. The young men who still went abroad to be educated brought back with them the traditions and flavor of the old England and not the spirit of

the new, the traditions of the universities and not the
new life of research and doubt in them. The conservatism of the Southern life was so strong that the
students at Northern colleges returned unchanged by
contact with a different civilization. The South met
the North in business and in politics, and in a limited
social intercourse, but from one cause and another for
three-quarters of a century it was practically isolated,
and consequently developed a peculiar social life.

One result of this isolation was that the South was
more homogeneous than the North, and perhaps more
distinctly American in its characteristics. This was
to be expected, since it had one common and over-
mastering interest in slavery, had little foreign ad-
mixture, and was removed from the currents of commerce and the disturbing ideas of Reform. The
South, so far as society was concerned, was an agricultural aristocracy, based upon a perfectly defined
lowest class in the slaves, and holding all trade, commerce, and industrial and mechanical pursuits in true
mediæval contempt. Its literature was monarchical,
tempered by some Jeffersonian, doctrinaire notions of
the rights of man, which were satisfied, however, by
an insistence upon the sovereignty of the States, and
by equal privileges to a certain social order in each
State. Looked at, then, from the outside, the South
appeared to be homogeneous, but from its own point
of view, socially, it was not at all so. Social life in
these jealously independent States developed almost
as freely and variously as it did in the Middle Ages
in the free cities of Italy. Virginia was not at all
like South Carolina (except in one common interest),
and Louisiana—especially in its centre, New Orleans

—more cosmopolitan than any other part of the South by reason of its foreign elements, more closely always in sympathy with Paris than with New York or Boston, was widely, in its social life, separated from its sisters. Indeed, in early days, before the slavery agitation, there was, owing to the heritage of English traditions, more in common between Boston and Charleston than between New Orleans and Charleston. And later, there was a marked social difference between towns and cities near together—as, for instance, between agricultural Lexington and commercial Louisville, in Kentucky.

The historian who writes the social life of the Southern States will be embarrassed with romantic and picturesque material. Nowhere else in this levelling age will he find a community developing so much of the dramatic, so much splendor and such pathetic contrasts in the highest social cultivation, as in the plantation and city life of South Carolina. Already, in regarding it, it assumes an air of unreality, and vanishes in its strong lights and heavy shades like a dream of the chivalric age. An allusion to its character is sufficient for the purposes of this paper. Persons are still alive who saw the prodigal style of living and the reckless hospitality of the planters in those days, when in the Charleston and Sea Island mansions the guests constantly entertained were only outnumbered by the swarms of servants; when it was not incongruous and scarcely ostentatious that the courtly company, which had the fine and free manner of another age, should dine off gold and silver plate; and when all that wealth and luxury could suggest was lavished in a princely magnificence that was almost barbaric in its profusion. The young men were educated in England; the young women were reared like helpless princesses, with a servant for every want and whim; it was a day of elegant accomplishments and deferential manners, but the men gamed like Fox and drank like Sheridan, and the duel was the ordinary arbiter of any difference of opinion or of any point of honor. Not even slavery itself could support existence on such a scale, and even before the war it began to give way to the conditions of our modern life. And now that old peculiar civilization of South Carolina belongs to romance. It can never be repeated, even by the aid of such gigantic fortunes as are now accumulating in the North.

The agricultural life of Virginia appeals with scarcely less attraction to the imagination of the novelist. Mr. Thackeray caught the flavor of it in his "Virginians" from an actual study of it in the old houses, when it was becoming a faded memory. The vast estates—principalities in size—with troops of slaves attached to each plantation; the hospitality, less costly, but as free as that of South Carolina; the land in the hands of a few people; politics and society controlled by a small number of historic families, intermarried until all Virginians of a certain grade were related—all this forms a picture as feudal-like and foreign to this age as can be imagined. The writer recently read the will of a country gentleman of the last century in Virginia, which raises a distinct image of the landed aristocracy of the time. It devised his plantation of six thousand acres with its slaves attached, his plantation of eighteen hundred acres and slaves, his plantation of twelve hundred acres and

slaves, with other farms and outlying property; it
mentioned all the cattle, sheep, and hogs, the riding-
horses in stables, the racing-steeds, the several coaches with the six horses that drew them (an acknowl-
edgment of the wretched state of the roads), and so
on in all the details of a vast domain. All the slaves
are called by name, all the farming implements were
enumerated, and all the homely articles of furniture
down to the beds and kitchen utensils. This whole
structure of a unique civilization is practically swept
away now, and with it the peculiar social life it produced. Let us pause a moment upon a few details of
it, as it had its highest development in Eastern Virginia.

The family was the fetich. In this high social caste
the estates were entailed to the limit of the law, for
one generation, and this entail was commonly religiously renewed by the heir. It was not expected that
a widow would remarry; as a rule she did not, and
it was almost a matter of course that the will of the
husband should make the enjoyment of even the entailed estate dependent upon the non-marriage of the
widow. These prohibitions upon her freedom of
choice were not considered singular or cruel in a
society whose chief gospel was the preservation of
the family name.

The planters lived more simply than the great seaboard planters of South Carolina and Georgia, with
not less pride, but with less ostentation and show.
The houses were of the accepted colonial pattern,
square, with four rooms on a floor, but with wide
galleries (wherein they differed from the colonial
houses in New England), and sometimes with addi-

tions in the way of offices and lodging-rooms. The
furniture was very simple and plain—a few hundred
dollars would cover the cost of it in most mansions.
There were not in all Virginia more than two or
three magnificent houses. It was the taste of gentlemen to adorn the ground in front of the house
with evergreens, with the locust and acanthus, and
perhaps the maple-trees not native to the spot ; while
the oak, which is nowhere more stately and noble
than in Virginia, was never seen on the lawn or the
drive-way, but might be found about the "quarters,"
or in an adjacent forest park. As the interior of the
houses was plain, so the taste of the people was simple in the matter of ornament—jewellery was very
little worn ; in fact, it is almost literally true that
there were in Virginia no family jewels.

So thoroughly did this society believe in itself and
keep to its traditions that the young gentleman of the
house, educated in England, brought on his return
nothing foreign home with him—no foreign tastes, no
bric-à-brac for his home, and never a foreign wife.
He came back unchanged, and married the cousin he
met at the first country dance he went to.

The pride of the people, which was intense, did not
manifest itself in ways that are common elsewhere—
it was sufficient to itself in its own homespun independence. What would make one distinguished elsewhere was powerless here. Literary talent, and even
acquired wealth, gave no distinction; aside from family and membership of the caste, nothing gave it to
any native or visitor. There was no lion-hunting, no
desire whatever to attract the attention of, or to pay
any deference to, men of letters. If a member of so-

ciety happened to be distinguished in letters or in scholarship, it made not the slightest difference in his social appreciation. There was absolutely no encouragement for men of letters, and consequently there was no literary class and little literature. There was only one thing that gave a man any distinction in this society, except a long pedigree, and that was the talent of oratory—that was prized, for that was connected with prestige in the State and the politics of the dominant class. The planters took few newspapers, and read those few very little. They were a fox-hunting, convivial race, generally Whig in politics, always orthodox in religion. The man of cultivation was rare, and, if he was cultivated, it was usually only on a single subject. But the planter might be an astute politician, and a man of wide knowledge and influence in public affairs. There was one thing, however, that was held in almost equal value with pedigree, and that was female beauty. There was always the recognized "belle," the beauty of the day, who was the toast and the theme of talk, whose memory was always green with her chivalrous contemporaries; the veterans liked to recall over the old Madeira the wit and charms of the raving beauties who had long gone the way of the famous vintages of the cellar.

The position of the clergyman in the Episcopal Church was very much what his position was in England in the time of James II. He was patronized and paid like any other adjunct of a well-ordered society. If he did not satisfy his masters he was quietly informed that he could probably be more useful elsewhere. If he was acceptable, one element of his popularity was that he rode to hounds and could tell a good story over the wine at dinner.

The pride of this society preserved itself in a certain high, chivalrous state. If any of its members were poor, as most of them became after the war, they took a certain pride in their poverty. They were too proud to enter into a vulgar struggle to be otherwise, and they were too old to learn the habit of labor. No such thing was known in it as scandal. If any breach of morals occurred, it was apt to be acknowledged with a Spartan regard for truth, and defiantly published by the families affected, who announced that they accepted the humiliation of it. Scandal there should be none. In that caste the character of women was not even to be the subject of talk in private gossip and innuendo. No breach of social caste was possible. The overseer, for instance, and the descendants of the overseer, however rich, or well educated, or accomplished they might become, could never marry into the select class. An alliance of this sort doomed the offender to an absolute and permanent loss of social position. This was the rule. Beauty could no more gain entrance there than wealth.

This plantation life, of which so much has been written, was repeated with variations all over the South. In Louisiana and lower Mississippi it was more prodigal than in Virginia. To a great extent its tone was determined by a relaxing climate, and it must be confessed that it had in it an element of the irresponsible — of the "after us the deluge." The whole system wanted thrift and, to an English or Northern visitor, certain conditions of comfort. Yet everybody acknowledged its fascination; for there

was nowhere else such a display of open-hearted hospitality. An invitation to visit meant an invitation
to stay indefinitely. The longer the visit lasted, if it
ran into months, the better were the entertainers
pleased. It was an uncalculating hospitality, and
possibly it went along with littleness and meanness,
in some directions, that were no more creditable than
the alleged meanness of the New England farmer.
At any rate, it was not a systematized generosity.
The hospitality had somewhat the character of a new
country and of a society not crowded. Company was
welcome on the vast, isolated plantations. Society
also was really small, composed of a few families, and
intercourse by long visits and profuse entertainments
was natural and even necessary.

This social aristocracy had the faults as well as the
virtues of an aristocracy so formed. One fault was
an undue sense of superiority, a sense nurtured by isolation from the intellectual contests and the illusion-
destroying tests of modern life. And this sense of
superiority diffused itself downward through the mass
of the Southern population. The slave of a great
family was proud; he held himself very much above
the poor white, and he would not associate with the
slave of the small farmer; and the poor white never
doubted his own superiority to the Northern " mud-
sill "—as the phrase of the day was. The whole life
was somehow pitched to a romantic key, and often
there was a queer contrast between the Gascon-like
pretension and the reality—all the more because of a
certain sincerity and single-mindedness that was unable to see the anachronism of trying to live in the
spirit of Scott's romances in our day and generation.

But with all allowance for this, there was a real basis for romance in the impulsive, sun-nurtured people, in the conflict between the two distinct races, and in the system of labor that was an anomaly in modern life. With the downfall of this system it was inevitable that the social state should radically change, and especially as this downfall was sudden and by violence, and in a struggle that left the South impoverished, and reduced to the rank of bread-winners those who had always regarded labor as a thing impossible for themselves.

As a necessary effect of this change, the dignity of the agricultural interest was lowered, and trade and industrial pursuits were elevated. Labor itself was perforce dignified. To earn one's living by actual work, in the shop, with the needle, by the pen, in the counting-house or school, in any honorable way, was a lot accepted with cheerful courage. And it is to the credit of all concerned that reduced circumstances and the necessity of work for daily bread have not thus far cost men and women in Southern society their social position. Work was a necessity of the situation, and the spirit in which the new life was taken up brought out the solid qualities of the race. In a few trying years they had to reverse the habits and traditions of a century. I think the honest observer will acknowledge that they have accomplished this without loss of that social elasticity and charm which were heretofore supposed to depend very much upon the artificial state of slave labor. And they have gained much. They have gained in losing a kind of suspicion that was inevitable in the isolation of their peculiar institution. They have gained freedom of thought and action in all the fields of modern endeavor, in the industrial arts, in science, in literature. And the fruits of this enlargement must add greatly to the industrial and intellectual wealth of the world.

Society itself in the new South has cut loose from its old moorings, but it is still in a transition state, and offers the most interesting study of tendencies and possibilities. Its danger, of course, is that of the North—a drift into materialism, into a mere struggle for wealth, undue importance attached to money, and a loss of public spirit in the selfish accumulation of property. Unfortunately, in the transition of twenty years the higher education has been neglected. The young men of this generation have not given even as much attention to intellectual pursuits as their fathers gave. Neither in polite letters nor in politics and political history have they had the same training. They have been too busy in the hard struggle for a living. It is true at the North that the young men in business are not so well educated, not so well read, as the young women of their own rank in society. And I suspect that this is still more true in the South. It is not uncommon to find in this generation Southern young women who add to sincerity, openness and frankness of manner; to the charm born of the wish to please, the graces of cultivation; who know French like their native tongue, who are well acquainted with the French and German literatures, who are well read in the English classics—though perhaps guiltless of much familiarity with our modern American literature. But taking the South at large, the schools for either sex are far behind those of the North both in discipline and range. And this is especially to be regretted, since the higher education is an absolute necessity to counteract the intellectual demoralization of the newly come industrial spirit.

We have yet to study the compensations left to the South in their century of isolation from this industrial spirit, and from the absolutely free inquiry of our modern life. Shall we find something sweet and sound there, that will yet be a powerful conservative influence in the republic? Will it not be strange, said a distinguished biblical scholar and an old-time antislavery radical, if we have to depend, after all, upon the orthodox conservatism of the South? For it is to be noted that the Southern pulpit holds still the traditions of the old theology, and the mass of Southern Christians are still undisturbed by doubts. They are no more troubled by agnosticism in religion than by altruism in sociology. There remains a great mass of sound and simple faith. We are not discussing either the advantage or the danger of disturbing thought, or any question of morality or of the conduct of life, nor the shield or the peril of ignorance— it is simply a matter of fact that the South is comparatively free from what is called modern doubt.

Another fact is noticeable. The South is not and never has been disturbed by "isms" of any sort. "Spiritualism" or "Spiritism" has absolutely no lodgement there. It has not even appealed in any way to the excitable and superstitious colored race. Inquiry failed to discover to the writer any trace of this delusion among whites or blacks. Society has never been agitated on the important subjects of grahambread or of the divided skirt. The temperance question has forced itself upon the attention of deeply drinking communities here and there. Usually it has been treated in a very common-sense way, and not as a matter of politics. Fanaticism may sometimes be a necessity against an overwhelming evil; but the writer knows of communities in the South that have effected a practical reform in liquor selling and drinking without fanatical excitement. Bar-room drinking is a fearful curse in Southern cities, as it is in Northern; it is an evil that the colored people fall into easily, but it is beginning to be met in some Southern localities in a resolute and sensible manner.

The students of what we like to call "progress," especially if they are disciples of Mr. Ruskin, have an admirable field of investigation in the contrast of the social, economic, and educational structure of the North and the South at the close of the war. After a century of free schools, perpetual intellectual agitation, extraordinary enterprise in every domain of thought and material achievement, the North presented a spectacle at once of the highest hope and the gravest anxiety. What diversity of life! What fulness! What intellectual and even social emancipation! What reforms, called by one party Heaven-sent, and by the other reforms against nature! What agitations, doubts, contempt of authority! What wild attempts to conduct life on no basis philosophic or divine! And yet what prosperity, what charities, what a marvellous growth, what an improvement in physical life! With better knowledge of sanitary conditions and of the culinary art, what an increase of beauty in women and of stalwartness in men! For beauty and physical comeliness, it must be acknowledged (parenthetically), largely depend upon food.

It is in the impoverished parts of the country, whether South or North, the sandy barrens, and the still vast regions where cooking is an unknown art, that scrawny and dyspeptic men and women abound—the sallow-faced, flat-chested, spindle-limbed.

This Northern picture is a veritable nineteenth-century spectacle. Side by side with it was the other society, also covering a vast domain, that was in many respects a projection of the eighteenth century into the nineteenth. It had much of the conservatism, and preserved something of the manners, of the eighteenth century, and lacked a good deal the so-called spirit of the age of the nineteenth, together with its doubts, its isms, its delusions, its energies. Life in the South is still on simpler terms than in the North, and society is not so complex. I am inclined to think it is a little more natural, more sincere in manner though not in fact, more frank and impulsive. One would hesitate to use the word unworldly with regard to it, but it may be less calculating. A bungling male observer would be certain to get himself into trouble by expressing an opinion about women in any part of the world; but women make society, and to discuss society at all is to discuss them. It is probably true that the education of women at the South, taken at large, is more superficial than at the North, lacking in purpose, in discipline, in intellectual vigor. The aim of the old civilization was to develop the graces of life, to make women attractive, charming, good talkers (but not too learned), graceful, and entertaining companions. When the main object is to charm and please, society is certain to be agreeable. In Southern society beauty, physical beauty, was and is much thought of, much talked of. The "belle" was an institution, and is yet. The belle of one city or village had a wide reputation, and trains of admirers wherever she went—in short, a veritable career, and was probably better known than a poetess at the North. She not only ruled in her day, but she left a memory which became a romance to the next generation. There went along with such careers a certain lightness and gayety of life, and now and again a good deal of pathos and tragedy.

With all its social accomplishments, its love of color, its climatic tendency to the sensuous side of life, the South has been unexpectedly wanting in a fine-art development—namely, in music and pictorial art. Culture of this sort has been slow enough in the North, and only lately has had any solidity or been much diffused. The love of art, and especially of art decoration, was greatly quickened by the Philadelphia Exhibition, and the comparatively recent infusion of German music has begun to elevate the taste. But I imagine that while the South naturally was fond of music of a light sort, and New Orleans could sustain and almost make native the French opera when New York failed entirely to popularize any sort of opera, the musical taste was generally very rudimentary; and the poverty in respect to pictures and engravings was more marked still. In a few great houses were fine paintings, brought over from Europe, and here and there a noble family portrait. But the traveller to-day will go through city after city, and village after village, and find no art-shop (as he may look in vain in large cities for any sort of book-store except a news-room); rarely will see an etching or a fine

engraving; and he will be led to doubt if the taste
for either existed to any great degree before the war.
Of course he will remember that taste and knowledge
in the fine arts may be said in the North to be recent
acquirements, and that, meantime, the South has been
impoverished and struggling in a political and social
revolution.

Slavery and isolation and a semi-feudal state have
left traces that must long continue to modify social
life in the South, and that may not wear out for a
century to come. The new life must also differ from
that in the North by reason of climate, and on account
of the presence of the alien, *insouciant* colored race.
The vast black population, however it may change,
and however education may influence it, must remain
a powerful determining factor. The body of the
slaves, themselves inert, and with no voice in affairs,
inevitably influenced life, the character of civilization, manners, even speech itself. With slavery ended, the Southern whites are emancipated, and the influence of the alien race will be other than what it
was, but it cannot fail to affect the tone of life in the
States where it is a large element.

When, however, we have made all allowance for
difference in climate, difference in traditions, total
difference in the way of looking at life for a century,
it is plain to be seen that a great transformation is
taking place in the South, and that Southern society
and Northern society are becoming every day more
and more alike. I know there are those, and Southerners, too, who insist that we are still two peoples,
with more points of difference than of resemblance—
certainly farther apart than Gascons and Bretons.

This seems to me not true in general, though it may
be of a portion of the passing generation. Of course
there is difference in temperament, and peculiarities
of speech and manner remain and will continue, as
they exist in different portions of the North—the accent of the Bostonian differs from that of the Phila-
delphian, and the inhabitant of Richmond is known
by his speech as neither of New Orleans nor New
York. But the influence of economic laws, of common political action, of interest and pride in one country, is stronger than local bias in such an age of inter-
communication as this. The great barrier between
North and South having been removed, social assimi-
lation must go on. It is true that the small farmer
in Vermont, and the small planter in Georgia, and the
village life in the two States, will preserve their strong
contrasts. But that which, without clearly defining,
we call society becomes yearly more and more alike
North and South. It is becoming more and more difficult to tell in any summer assembly—at Newport,
the White Sulphur, Saratoga, Bar Harbor—by physiognomy, dress, or manner, a person's birthplace.
There are noticeable fewer distinctive traits that
enable us to say with certainty that one is from the
South, or the West, or the East. No doubt the type
at such a Southern resort as the White Sulphur is
more distinctly American than at such a Northern
resort as Saratoga. We are prone to make a good
deal of local peculiarities, but when we look at the
matter broadly and consider the vastness of our territory and the varieties of climate, it is marvellous
that there is so little difference in speech, manner,
and appearance. Contrast us with Europe and its va-

rious irreconcilable races occupying less territory. Even little England offers greater variety than the United States. When we think of our large, widely scattered population, the wonder is that we do not differ more.

Southern society has always had a certain prestige in the North. One reason for this was the fact that the ruling class South had more leisure for social life. Climate, also, had much to do in softening manners, making the temperament ardent, and at the same time producing that leisurely movement which is essential to a polished life. It is probably true, also, that mere wealth was less a passport to social distinction than at the North, or than it has become at the North ; that is to say, family, or a certain charm of breeding, or the talent of being agreeable, or the gift of cleverness, or of beauty, were necessary, and money was not. In this respect it seems to be true that social life is changing at the South ; that is to say, money is getting to have the social power in New Orleans that it has in New York. It is inevitable in a commercial and industrial community that money should have a controlling power, as it is regrettable that the enjoyment of its power very slowly admits a sense of its responsibility. The old traditions of the South having been broken down, and nearly all attention being turned to the necessity of making money, it must follow that mere wealth will rise as a social factor. Herein lies one danger to what was best in the old régime. Another danger is that it must be put to the test of the ideas, the agitations, the elements of doubt and disintegration that seem inseparable to " progress," which give Northern

society its present complexity, and just cause of
alarm to all who watch its headlong career. Fulness
of life is accepted as desirable, but it has its dangers.

Within the past five years social intercourse between North and South has been greatly increased.
Northerners who felt strongly about the Union and
about slavery, and took up the cause of the freedman,
and were accustomed all their lives to absolute free
speech, were not comfortable in the post-reconstruc-
tion atmosphere. Perhaps they expected too much
of human nature—a too sudden subsidence of suspicion and resentment. They felt that they were
not welcome socially, however much their capital and
business energy were desired. On the other hand,
most Southerners were too poor to travel in the
North, as they did formerly. But all these points
have been turned. Social intercourse and travel are
renewed. If difficulties and alienations remain they
are sporadic, and melting away. The harshness of
the Northern winter climate has turned a stream of
travel and occupation to the Gulf States, and par-
ticularly to Florida, which is indeed now scarcely a
Southern State except in climate. The Atlanta and
New Orleans Exhibitions did much to bring people
of all sections together socially. With returning
financial prosperity all the Northern summer resorts
have seen increasing numbers of Southern people
seeking health and pleasure. I believe that during
the past summer more Southerners have been travelling and visiting in the North than ever before.

This social intermingling is significant in itself, and
of the utmost importance for the removal of lingering misunderstandings. They who learn to like each

other personally will be tolerant in political differences, and helpful and unsuspicious in the very grave
problems that rest upon the late slave States.   Differences of opinion and different interests will exist, but
surely love is stronger than hate, and sympathy and
kindness are better solvents than alienation and criticism.   The play of social forces is very powerful in
such a republic as ours, and there is certainly reason
to believe that they will be exerted now in behalf of
that cordial appreciation of what is good and that
toleration of traditional differences which are necessary to a people indissolubly bound together in one
national destiny.   Alienated for a century, the society
of the North and the society of the South have something to forget but more to gain in the union that
every day becomes closer.

III.

NEW ORLEANS.

THE first time I saw New Orleans was on a Sunday morning in the month of March. We alighted from the train at the foot of Esplanade Street, and walked along through the French Market, and by Jackson Square to the Hotel Royal. The morning, after rain, was charming; there was a fresh breeze from the river; the foliage was a tender green; in the balconies and on the mouldering window-ledges flowers bloomed, and in the decaying courts climbing-roses mingled their perfume with the orange; the shops were open; ladies tripped along from early mass or to early market; there was a twittering in the square and in the sweet old gardens; caged birds sang and screamed the songs of South America and the tropics; the language heard on all sides was French or the degraded jargon which the easy-going African has manufactured out of the tongue of Bienville. Nothing could be more shabby than the streets, ill-paved, with undulating sidewalks and open gutters green with slime, and both stealing and giving odor; little canals in which the cat, become the companion of the crawfish, and the vegetable in decay sought in vain a current to oblivion; the streets with rows of one-story houses, wooden, with green doors and batten window-shutters, or brick, with the painted stucco peeling off, the line broken often by an edifice of two stories, with gal-

leries and delicate tracery of wrought - iron, houses
pink and yellow and brown and gray — colors all
blending and harmonious when we get a long vista of
them and lose the details of view in the broad artistic
effect. Nothing could be shabbier than the streets,
unless it is the tumble-down, picturesque old market,
bright with flowers and vegetables and many-hued
fish, and enlivened by the genial African, who in the
New World experiments in all colors, from coal black
to the pale pink of the sea-shell, to find one that suits
his mobile nature. I liked it all from the first; I lingered long in that morning walk, liking it more and
more, in spite of its shabbiness, but utterly unable to
say then or ever since wherein its charm lies. I suppose we are all wrongly made up and have a fallen
nature; else why is it that while the most thrifty and
neat and orderly city only wins our approval, and
perhaps gratifies us intellectually, such a thriftless,
battered and stained, and lazy old place as the French
quarter of New Orleans takes our hearts?

I never could find out exactly where New Orleans
is. I have looked for it on the map without much
enlightenment. It is dropped down there somewhere
in the marshes of the Mississippi and the bayous and
lakes. It is below the one, and tangled up among the
others, or it might some day float out to the Gulf and
disappear. How the Mississippi gets out I never
could discover. When it first comes in sight of the
town it is running east; at Carrollton it abruptly turns
its rapid, broad, yellow flood and runs south, turns
presently eastward, circles a great portion of the city,
then makes a bold push for the north in order to
avoid Algiers and reach the foot of Canal Street, and

encountering there the heart of the town, it sheers off again along the old French quarter and Jackson Square due east, and goes no one knows where, except perhaps Mr. Eads.

The city is supposed to lie in this bend of the river, but it in fact extends eastward along the bank down to the Barracks, and spreads backward towards Lake Pontchartrain over a vast area, and includes some very good snipe-shooting.

Although New Orleans has only about a quarter of a million of inhabitants, and so many only in the winter, it is larger than Pekin, and I believe than Philadelphia, having an area of about one hundred and five square miles. From Carrollton to the Barracks, which are not far from the Battle-field, the distance by the river is some thirteen miles. From the river to the lake the least distance is four miles. This vast territory is traversed by lines of horse-cars which all meet in Canal Street, the most important business thoroughfare of the city, which runs north-east from the river, and divides the French from the American quarter. One taking a horse-car in any part of the city will ultimately land, having boxed the compass, in Canal Street. But it needs a person of vast local erudition to tell in what part of the city, or in what section of the home of the frog and crawfish, he will land if he takes a horse-car in Canal Street. The river being higher than the city, there is of course no drainage into it; but there is a theory that the water in the open gutters does move, and that it moves in the direction of the Bayou St. John, and of the cypress swamps that drain into Lake Pontchartrain. The stranger who is accustomed to closed

sewers, and to get his malaria and typhoid through
pipes conducted into his house by the most approved
methods of plumbing, is aghast at this spectacle of
slime and filth in the streets, and wonders why the
city is not in perennial epidemic ; but the sun and the
wind are great scavengers, and the city is not nearly
so unhealthy as it ought to be with such a city government as they say it endures.

It is not necessary to dwell much upon the external
features of New Orleans, for innumerable descriptions
and pictures have familiarized the public with them.
Besides, descriptions can give the stranger little idea
of the peculiar city.   Although all on one level, it is
a town of contrasts.   In no other city of the United States or of Mexico is the old and romantic preserved in such integrity and brought into such sharp
contrast to the modern.   There are many handsome
public buildings, churches, club-houses, elegant shops,
and on the American side a great area of well-paved
streets solidly built up in business blocks.   The Square
of the original city, included between the river and
canal, Rampart and Esplanade streets, which was once
surrounded by a wall, is as closely built, but the
streets are narrow, the houses generally are smaller,
and although it swarms with people, and contains the
cathedral, the old Spanish buildings, Jackson Square,
the French Market, the French Opera-house, and other
theatres, the Mint, the Custom-house, the old Ursuline
convent (now the residence of the archbishop), old
banks, and scores of houses of historic celebrity, it is
a city of the past, and specially interesting in its picturesque decay.   Beyond this, eastward and northward extend interminable streets of small houses, with

now and then a flowery court or a pretty rose garden, occupied mainly by people of French and Spanish descent. The African pervades all parts of the town, except the new residence portion of the American quarter. This, which occupies the vast area in the bend of the river west of the business blocks as far as Carrollton, is in character a great village rather than a city. Not all its broad avenues and handsome streets are paved (and those that are not are in some seasons impassable), its houses are nearly all of wood, most of them detached, with plots of ground and gardens, and as the quarter is very well shaded, the effect is bright and agreeable. In it are many stately residences, occupying a square or half a square, and embowered in foliage and flowers. Care has been given lately to turf-culture, and one sees here thick-set and handsome lawns. The broad Esplanade Street, with its elegant old-fashioned houses, and double rows of shade trees, which has long been the rural pride of the French quarter, has now rivals in respectability and style on the American side.

New Orleans is said to be delightful in the late fall months, before the winter rains set in, but I believe it looks its best in March and April. This is owing to the roses. If the town was not attached to the name of the Crescent City, it might very well adopt the title of the City of Roses. So kind are climate and soil that the magnificent varieties of this queen of flowers, which at the North bloom only in hot-houses, or with great care are planted out-doors in the heat of our summer, thrive here in the open air in prodigal abundance and beauty. In April the town is literally embowered in them ; they fill door-yards and gardens,

they overrun the porches, they climb the sides of the
houses, they spread over the trees, they take possession of trellises and fences and walls, perfuming the
air and entrancing the heart with color.   In the outlying parks, like that of the Jockey Club, and the
florists' gardens at Carrollton, there are fields of them,
acres of the finest sorts waving in the spring wind.
Alas! can beauty ever satisfy? This wonderful spectacle fills one with I know not what exquisite longing.
These flowers pervade the town, old women on the
street corners sit behind banks of them, the florists'
windows blush with them, friends despatch to each
other great baskets of them, the favorites at the theatre and the amateur performers stand behind high
barricades of roses which the good-humored audience
piles upon the stage, everybody carries roses and
wears roses, and the houses overflow with them. In
this passion for flowers you may read a prominent
trait of the people. For myself I like to see a spot
on this earth where beauty is enjoyed for itself and
let to run to waste, but if ever the industrial spirit
of the French-Italians should prevail along the litto-
ral of Louisiana and Mississippi, the raising of flowers for the manufacture of perfumes would become
a most profitable industry.

New Orleans is the most cosmopolitan of provincial
cities. Its comparative isolation has secured the development of provincial traits and manners, has preserved the individuality of the many races that give
it color, morals, and character, while its close relations
with France—an affiliation and sympathy which the
late war has not altogether broken—and the constant
influx of Northern men of business and affairs have

given it the air of a metropolis. To the Northern
stranger the aspect and the manners of the city are
foreign, but if he remains long enough he is sure to
yield to its fascinations, and become a partisan of it.
It is not altogether the soft and somewhat enervating
and occasionally treacherous climate that beguiles
him, but quite as much the easy terms on which life
can be lived. There is a human as well as a climatic
amiability that wins him. No doubt it is better for a
man to be always braced up, but no doubt also there
is an attraction in a complaisance that indulges his
inclinations.

Socially as well as commercially New Orleans is in
a transitive state. The change from river to railway
transportation has made her levees vacant ; the shipment of cotton by rail and its direct transfer to ocean
carriage have nearly destroyed a large middle-men
industry ; a large part of the agricultural tribute of
the South-west has been diverted; plantations have
either not recovered from the effects of the war or
have not adjusted themselves to new productions, and
the city waits the rather blind developments of the
new era. The falling off of law business, which I
should like to attribute to the growth of common-
sense and good-will is, I fear, rather due to business
lassitude, for it is observed that men quarrel most
when they are most actively engaged in acquiring
each other's property. The business habits of the
Creoles were conservative and slow ; they do not
readily accept new ways, and in this transition time
the American element is taking the lead in all enterprises. The American element itself is toned down
by the climate and the contagion of the leisurely hab-

its of the Creoles, and loses something of the sharpness and excitability exhibited by business men in all
Northern cities, but it is certainly changing the social
as well as the business aspect of the city. Whether
these social changes will make New Orleans a more
agreeable place of residence remains to be seen.

For the old civilization had many admirable qualities. With all its love of money and luxury and an
easy life, it was comparatively simple. It cared less
for display than the society that is supplanting it.
Its rule was domesticity. I should say that it had
the virtues as well as the prejudices and the narrow-
ness of intense family feeling, and its exclusiveness.
But when it trusted, it had few reserves, and its cordiality was equal to its *naïveté.* The Creole civilization differed totally from that in any Northern city;
it looked at life, literature, wit, manners, from altogether another plane; in order to understand the society of New Orleans one needs to imagine what
French society would be in a genial climate and in
the freedom of a new country. Undeniably, until
recently, the Creoles gave the tone to New Orleans.
And it was the French culture, the French view of
life, that was diffused. The young ladies mainly
were educated in convents and French schools. This
education had womanly agreeability and matrimony
in view, and the graces of social life. It differed not
much from the education of young ladies of the period elsewhere, except that it was from the French
rather than the English side, but this made a world
of difference. French was a study and a possession,
not a fashionable accomplishment. The Creole had
gayety, sentiment, spirit, with a certain climatic lan-

guor, sweetness of disposition, and charm of manner, and not seldom winning beauty; she was passionately fond of dancing and of music, and occasionally an adept in the latter; and she had candor, and either simplicity or the art of it. But with her tendency to domesticity and her capacity for friendship, and notwithstanding her gay temperament, she was less worldly than some of her sisters who were more gravely educated after the English manner. There was therefore in the old New Orleans life something nobler than the spirit of plutocracy. The Creole middle-class population had, and has yet, captivating *naïveté*, friendliness, cordiality.

But the Creole influence in New Orleans is wider and deeper than this. It has affected literary sympathies and what may be called literary morals. In business the Creole is accused of being slow, conservative, in regard to improvements obstinate and reactionary, preferring to nurse a prejudice rather than run the risk of removing it by improving himself, and of having a conceit that his way of looking at life is better than the Boston way. His literary culture is derived from France, and not from England or the North. And his ideas a good deal affect the attitude of New Orleans towards English and contemporary literature. The American element of the town was for the most part commercial, and little given to literary tastes. That also is changing, but I fancy it is still true that the most solid culture is with the Creoles, and it has not been appreciated because it is French, and because its point of view for literary criticism is quite different from that prevailing elsewhere in America. It brings our American and English contemporary authors, for instance, to comparison, not with each other, but with French and other Continental writers. And this point of view considerably affects the New Orleans opinion of Northern literature. In this view it wants color, passion; it is too self-conscious and prudish, not to say Puritanically mock-modest. I do not mean to say that the Creoles as a class are a reading people, but the literary standards of their scholars and of those among them who do cultivate literature deeply are different from those at the North. We may call it provincial, or we may call it cosmopolitan, but we shall not understand New Orleans until we get its point of view of both life and letters.

In making these observations it will occur to the reader that they are of necessity superficial, and not entitled to be regarded as criticism or judgment. But I am impressed with the foreignness of New Orleans civilization, and whether its point of view is right or wrong, I am very far from wishing it to change. It contains a valuable element of variety for the republic. We tend everywhere to sameness and monotony. New Orleans is entering upon a new era of development, especially in educational life. The Toulane University is beginning to make itself felt as a force both in polite letters and in industrial education. And I sincerely hope that the literary development of the city and of the South-west will be in the line of its own traditions, and that it will not be a copy of New England or of Dutch Manhattan. It can, if it is faithful to its own sympathies and temperament, make an original and valuable contribution to our literary life.

There is a great temptation to regard New Orleans through the romance of its past; and the most interesting occupation of the idler is to stroll about in the French part of the town, search the shelves of French and Spanish literature in the second-hand book-shops, try to identify the historic sites and the houses that are the seats of local romances, and observe the life in the narrow streets and alleys that, except for the presence of the colored folk, recall the quaint picturesqueness of many a French provincial town. One never tires of wandering in the neighborhood of the old cathedral, facing the smart Jackson Square, which is flanked by the respectable Pontalba buildings, and supported on either side by the ancient Spanish court-house, the most interesting specimens of Spanish architecture this side of Mexico. When the court is in session, iron cables are stretched across the street to prevent the passage of wagons, and justice is administered in silence only broken by the trill of birds in the Place d'Armes and in the old flower-garden in the rear of the cathedral, and by the muffled sound of footsteps in the flagged passages. The region is saturated with romance, and so full of present sentiment and picturesqueness that I can fancy no ground more congenial to the artist and the story-teller. To enter into any details of it would be to commit one's self to a task quite foreign to the purpose of this paper, and I leave it to the writers who have done and are doing so much to make old New Orleans classic.

Possibly no other city of the United States so abounds in stories pathetic and tragic, many of which cannot yet be published, growing out of the mingling of races, the conflicts of French and Spanish, the pres-

4

ence of adventurers from the Old World and the Spanish Main, and especially out of the relations between the whites and the fair women who had in their thin veins drops of African blood. The quadroon and the octoroon are the staple of hundreds of thrilling tales. Duels were common incidents of the Creole dancing assemblies, and of the *cordon bleu* balls—the deities of which were the quadroon women, "the handsomest race of women in the world," says the description, and the most splendid dancers and the most exquisitely dressed—the affairs of honor being settled by a midnight thrust in a vacant square behind the cathedral, or adjourned to a more French daylight encounter at "The Oaks," or "Les Trois Capalins." But this life has all gone. In a stately building in this quarter, said by tradition to have been the quadroon ball-room, but I believe it was a white assembly-room connected with the opera, is now a well-ordered school for colored orphans, presided over by colored Sisters of Charity.

It is quite evident that the peculiar prestige of the quadroon and the octoroon is a thing of the past. Indeed, the result of the war has greatly changed the relations of the two races in New Orleans. The colored people withdraw more and more to themselves. Isolation from white influence has good results and bad results, the bad being, as one can see, in some quarters of the town, a tendency to barbarism, which can only be counteracted by free public schools, and by a necessity which shall compel them to habits of thrift and industry. One needs to be very much an optimist, however, to have patience for these developments.

I believe there is an instinct in both races against mixture of blood, and upon this rests the law of Louisiana, which forbids such intermarriages; the time may come when the colored people will be as strenuous in insisting upon its execution as the whites, unless there is a great change in popular feeling, of which there is no sign at present; it is they who will see that there is no escape from the equivocal position in which those nearly white in appearance find themselves except by a rigid separation of races. The danger is of a reversal at any time to the original type, and that is always present to the offspring of any one with a drop of African blood in the veins. The pathos of this situation is infinite, and it cannot be lessened by saying that the prejudice about color is unreasonable; it exists. Often the African strain is so attenuated that the possessor of it would pass to the ordinary observer for Spanish or French; and I suppose that many so-called Creole peculiarities of speech and manner are traceable to this strain. An incident in point may not be uninteresting.

I once lodged in the old French quarter in a house kept by two maiden sisters, only one of whom spoke English at all. They were refined, and had the air of decayed gentlewomen. The one who spoke English had the vivacity and agreeability of a Paris landlady, without the latter's invariable hardness and sharpness. I thought I had found in her pretty mode of speech the real Creole dialect of her class. "You are French," I said, when I engaged my room.

"No," she said, "no, m'sieu, I am an American; we are of the United States," with the air of informing a stranger that New Orleans was now annexed.

"Yes," I replied, "but you are of French descent?"

"Oh, and a little Spanish."

"Can you tell me, madame," I asked, one Sunday morning, "the way to Trinity Church?"

"I cannot tell, m'sieu; it is somewhere the other side; I do not know the other side."

"But have you never been the other side of Canal Street?"

"Oh yes, I went once, to make a visit on a friend on New-Year's."

I explained that it was far uptown, and a Protestant church.

"M'sieu, is he Cat'olic?"

"Oh no; I am a Protestant."

"Well, me, I am Cat'olic; but Protestan' o' Cat'olic, it is 'mos' ze same."

This was purely the instinct of politeness, and that my feelings might not be wounded, for she was a good Catholic, and did not believe at all that it was "'mos' ze same."

It was Exposition year, and then April, and madame had never been to the Exposition. I urged her to go, and one day, after great preparation for a journey to the other side, she made the expedition, and returned enchanted with all she had seen, especially with the Mexican band. A new world was opened to her, and she resolved to go again. The morning of Louisiana Day she rapped at my door and informed me that she was going to the fair. "And"—she paused at the door-way, her eyes sparkling with her new project—"you know what I goin' do?"

"No."

"I goin' get one big bouquet, and give to the leader of the orchestre."

"You know him, the leader?"

"No, not yet."

I did not know then how poor she was, and how much sacrifice this would be to her, this gratification of a sentiment.

The next year, in the same month, I asked for her at the lodging. She was not there. "You did not know," said the woman then in possession—"good God! her sister died four days ago, from want of food, and madame has gone away back of town, nobody knows where. They told nobody, they were so proud; none of their friends knew, or they would have helped. They had no lodgers, and could not keep this place, and took another opposite; but they were unlucky, and the sheriff came." I said that I was very sorry that I had not known; she might have been helped. "No," she replied, with considerable spirit; "she would have accepted nothing; she would starve rather. So would I." The woman referred me to some well-known Creole families who knew madame, but I was unable to find her hiding-place. I asked who madame was. "Oh, she was a very nice woman, very respectable. Her father was Spanish, her mother was an octoroon."

One does not need to go into the past of New Orleans for the picturesque; the streets have their peculiar physiognomy, and "character" such as the artists delight to depict is the result of the extraordinary mixture of races and the habit of out-door life. The long summer, from April to November, with a heat continuous, though rarely so excessive as it oc-

casionally is in higher latitudes, determines the mode
of life and the structure of the houses, and gives a
leisurely and amiable tone to the aspect of people and
streets which exists in few other American cities.
The French quarter is out of repair, and has the air
of being for rent; but in fact there is comparatively
little change in occupancy, Creole families being re-
markably adhesive to localities. The stranger who
sees all over the French and the business parts of the
town the immense number of lodging-houses—some
of them the most stately old mansions — let largely
by colored landladies, is likely to underestimate the
home life of this city. New Orleans soil is so wet
that the city is without cellars for storage, and its
court-yards and odd corners become catch-alls of broken furniture and other lumber. The solid window-
shutters, useful in the glare of the long summer, give
a blank appearance to the streets. This is relieved,
however, by the queer little Spanish houses, and by
the endless variety of galleries and balconies. In one
part of the town the iron-work of the balconies is cast,
and uninteresting in its set patterns; in French-town
much of it is hand-made, exquisite in design, and gives
to a street vista a delicate lace-work appearance. I
do not know any foreign town which has on view so
much exquisite wrought-iron work as the old part of
New Orleans. Besides the balconies, there are re-
cessed galleries, old dormer-windows, fantastic little
nooks and corners, tricked out with flower-pots and
vines.

The glimpses of street life are always entertaining,
because unconscious, while full of character. It may
be a Creole court-yard, the walls draped with vines,

flowers blooming in hap-hazard disarray, and a group
of pretty girls sewing and chatting, and stabbing the
passer-by with a charmed glance. It may be a cotton
team in the street, the mules, the rollicking driver, the
creaking cart. It may be a single figure, or a group
in the market or on the levee—a slender yellow girl
sweeping up the grains of rice, a colored gleaner recalling Ruth; an ancient darky asleep, with mouth
open, in his tipped-up two-wheeled cart, waiting for a
job; the "solid South," in the shape of an immense
"aunty" under a red umbrella, standing and contem-
plating the river; the broad-faced women in gay ban-
dannas behind their cake-stands; a group of levee
hands about a rickety table, taking their noonday
meal of pork and greens; the blind-man, capable of
sitting more patiently than an American Congress-
man, with a dog trained to hold his basket for the
pennies of the charitable; the black stalwart vender
of tin and iron utensils, who totes in a basket, and
piled on his head, and strung on his back, a weight of
over two hundred and fifty pounds; and negro women
who walk erect with baskets of clothes or enormous
bundles balanced on their heads, smiling and "jaw-
ing," unconscious of their burdens. These are the familiar figures of a street life as varied and picturesque
as the artist can desire.

New Orleans amuses itself in the winter with very
good theatres, and until recently has sustained an excellent French opera. It has all the year round plenty of *cafés chantants*, gilded saloons, and gambling-
houses, and more than enough of the resorts upon
which the police are supposed to keep one blind eye.
" Back of town," towards Lake Pontchartrain, there is

much that is picturesque and blooming, especially in
the spring of the year—the charming gardens of the
Jockey Club, the City Park, the old duelling-ground
with its superb oaks, and the Bayou St. John with its
idling fishing-boats, and the colored houses and plantations along the banks—a piece of Holland wanting
the Dutch windmills. On a breezy day one may go
far for a prettier sight than the river-bank and esplanade at Carrollton, where the mighty coffee-colored
flood swirls by, where the vast steamers struggle and
cough against the stream, or swiftly go with it round
the bend, leaving their trail of smoke, and the delicate
line of foliage against the sky on the far opposite
shore completes the outline of an exquisite landscape.
Suburban resorts much patronized, and reached by
frequent trains, are the old Spanish Fort and the West
End of Lake Pontchartrain. The way lies through
cypress swamp and palmetto thickets, brilliant at certain seasons with *fleur-de-lis.* At each of these resorts
are restaurants, dancing-halls, promenade-galleries, all
on a large scale; boat-houses, and semi-tropical gardens
very prettily laid out in walks and labyrinths, and
adorned with trees and flowers. Even in the heat of
summer at night the lake is sure to offer a breeze, and
with waltz music and moonlight and ices and tinkling
glasses with straws in them and love's young dream,
even the *ennuyé* globe-trotter declares that it is not
half bad.

The city, indeed, offers opportunity for charming
excursions in all directions. Parties are constantly
made up to visit the river plantations, to sail up and
down the stream, or to take an outing across the lake,
or to the many lovely places along the coast. In the

winter, excursions are made to these places, and in summer the well-to-do take the sea-air in cottages, at such places as Mandeville across the lake, or at such resorts on the Mississippi as Pass Christian.

I crossed the lake one spring day to the pretty town of Mandeville, and then sailed up the Tchefuncta River to Covington. The winding Tchefuncta is in character like some of the narrow Florida streams, has the same luxuriant overhanging foliage, and as many shy lounging alligators to the mile, and is prettier by reason of occasional open glades and large moss-draped live-oaks and China-trees. From the steamer landing in the woods we drove three miles through a lovely open pine forest to the town. Covington is one of the oldest settlements in the State, is the centre of considerable historic interest, and the origin of several historic families. The land is elevated a good deal above the coast-level, and is consequently dry. The town has a few roomy old-time houses, a mineral spring, some pleasing scenery along the river that winds through it, and not much else. But it is in the midst of pine woods, it is sheltered from all "northers," it has the soft air, but not the dampness, of the Gulf, and is exceedingly salubrious in all the winter months, to say nothing of the summer. It has lately come into local repute as a health resort, although it lacks sufficient accommodations for the entertainment of many strangers. I was told by some New Orleans physicians that they regarded it as almost a specific for pulmonary diseases, and instances were given of persons in what was supposed to be advanced stages of lung and bronchial troubles who had been apparently cured by a few months' residence there; and invalids are, I believe, greatly benefited by its healing, soft, and piny atmosphere.

I have no doubt, from what I hear and my limited observation, that all this coast about New Orleans would be a favorite winter resort if it had hotels as good as, for instance, that at Pass Christian. The region has many attractions for the idler and the invalid. It is, in the first place, interesting; it has a good deal of variety of scenery and of historical interest; there is excellent fishing and shooting; and if the visitor tires of the monotony of the country, he can by a short ride on cars or a steamer transfer himself for a day or a week to a large and most hospitable city, to society, the club, the opera, balls, parties, and every variety of life that his taste craves. The disadvantage of many Southern places to which our Northern regions force us is that they are uninteresting, stupid, and monotonous, if not malarious. It seems a long way from New York to New Orleans, but I do not doubt that the region around the city would become immediately a great winter resort if money and enterprise were enlisted to make it so.

New Orleans has never been called a "strait-laced" city; its Sunday is still of the Continental type; but it seems to me free from the socialistic agnosticism which flaunts itself more or less in Cincinnati, St. Louis, and Chicago; the tone of leading Presbyterian churches is distinctly Calvinistic, one perceives comparatively little of religious speculation and doubt, and so far as I could see there is harmony and entire social good feeling between the Catholic and Protestant communions. Protestant ladies assist at Catholic fairs, and the compliment is returned by the society ladies of the Catholic faith when a Protestant good cause is to be furthered by a bazaar or a "pink tea." Denominational lines seem to have little to do with social affiliations. There may be friction in the management of the great public charities, but on the surface there is toleration and united good-will. The Catholic faith long had the prestige of wealth, family, and power, and the education of the daughters of Protestant houses in convent schools tended to allay prejudice. Notwithstanding the reputation New Orleans has for gayety and even frivolity—and no one can deny the fast and furious living of ante-bellum days—it possesses at bottom an old-fashioned religious simplicity. If any one thinks that "faith" has died out of modern life, let him visit the mortuary chapel of St. Roch. In a distant part of the town, beyond the street of the Elysian Fields, and on Washington Avenue, in a district very sparsely built up, is the Campo Santo of the Catholic Church of the Holy Trinity. In this foreign-looking cemetery is the pretty little Gothic Chapel of St. Roch, having a background of common and swampy land. It is a brown stuccoed edifice, wholly open in front, and was a year or two ago covered with beautiful ivy. The small interior is paved in white marble, the windows are stained glass, the side walls are composed of tiers of vaults, where are buried the members of certain societies, and the spaces in the wall and in the altar area are thickly covered with votive offerings, in wax and in *naïve* painting—contributed by those who have been healed by the intercession of the saints. Over the altar is the shrine of St. Roch—a cavalier, staff in hand, with his dog by his side, the faithful animal which accompanied this eighth-century philanthropist in his visitations to the plague-stricken people of Munich. Within the altar rail are rows of lighted candles, tended and renewed by the attendant, placed there by penitents or by seekers after the favor of the saint. On the wooden benches, kneeling, are ladies, servants, colored women, in silent prayer. One approaches the lighted, picturesque shrine through the formal rows of tombs, and comes there into an atmosphere of peace and faith. It is believed that miracles are daily wrought here, and one notices in all the gardeners, keepers, and attendants of the place the accent and demeanor of simple faith. On the wall hangs this inscription:

" O great St. Roch, deliver us, we beseech thee, from the scourges of God. Through thy intercessions preserve our bodies from contagious diseases, and our souls from the contagion of sin. Obtain for us salubrious air; but, above all, purity of heart. Assist us to make good use of health, to bear suffering with patience, and after thy example to live in the practice of penitence and charity, that we may one day enjoy the happiness which thou hast merited by thy virtues.

" St. Roch, pray for us.

" St. Roch, pray for us.

" St. Roch, pray for us."

There is testimony that many people, even Protestants, and men, have had wounds cured and been healed of diseases by prayer in this chapel. To this distant shrine come ladies from all parts of the city to make the " novena "—the prayer of nine days, with the offer of the burning taper—and here daily resort hundreds to intercede for themselves or their friends. It is believed by the damsels of this district that if

they offer prayer daily in this chapel they will have a
husband within the year, and one may see kneeling
here every evening these trustful devotees to the welfare of the human race. I asked the colored woman
who sold medals and leaflets and renewed the candles
if she personally knew any persons who had been mi-
raculously cured by prayer, or novena, in St. Roch.
"Plenty, sir, plenty." And she related many instances, which were confirmed by votive offerings on
the walls. "Why," said she, "there was a friend of
mine who wanted a place, and could hear of none,
who made a novena here, and right away got a place,
a good place, and " (conscious that she was making an
astonishing statement about a New Orleans servant)
" she kept it a whole year !"

"But one must come in the right spirit," I said.

"Ah, indeed. It needs to believe. You can't fool
God !"

One might make various studies of New Orleans:
its commercial life; its methods, more or less antiquated, of doing business, and the leisure for talk that
enters into it; its admirable charities and its mediæval
prisons; its romantic French and Spanish history, still
lingering in the old houses, and traits of family and
street life; the city politics, which nobody can explain, and no other city need covet; its sanitary condition, which needs an intelligent despot with plenty
of money and an ingenuity that can make water run
uphill; its colored population—about a fourth of the
city—with its distinct social grades, its superstition,
nonchalant good-humor, turn for idling and basking
in the sun, slowly awaking to a sense of thrift, chas-
tity, truth-speaking, with many excellent order-loving,

patriotic men and women, but a mass that needs moral training quite as much as the spelling-book before it can contribute to the vigor and prosperity of the city; its schools and recent libraries, and the developing literary and art taste which will sustain book-shops and picture-galleries; its cuisine, peculiar in its mingling of French and African skill, and determined largely by a market unexcelled in the quality of fish, game, and fruit—the fig alone would go far to reconcile one to four or five months of hot nights; the climatic influence in assimilating races meeting there from every region of the earth.

But whatever way we regard New Orleans, it is in its aspect, social tone, and character *sui generis;* its civilization differs widely from that of any other, and it remains one of the most interesting places in the republic. Of course, social life in these days is much the same in all great cities in its observances, but that of New Orleans is markedly cordial, ingenuous, warm-hearted. I do not imagine that it could tolerate, as Boston does, absolute freedom of local opinion on all subjects, and undoubtedly it is sensitive to criticism; but I believe that it is literally true, as one of its citizens said, that it is still more sensitive to kindness.

The metropolis of the South-west has geographical reasons for a great future. Louisiana is rich in alluvial soil, the capability of which has not yet been tested, except in some localities, by skilful agriculture. But the prosperity of the city depends much upon local conditions. Science and energy can solve the problem of drainage, can convert all the territory between the city and Lake Pontchartrain into a veritable garden, surpassing in fertility the flat environs of the city of Mexico. And the steady development of common-school education, together with technical and industrial schools, will create a skill which will make New Orleans the industrial and manufacturing centre of that region.

IV.

A VOUDOO DANCE.

There was nothing mysterious about it. The ceremony took place in broad day, at noon in the upper chambers of a small frame house in a street just beyond Congo Square and the old Parish prison in New Orleans. It was an incantation rather than a dance—a curious mingling of African Voudoo rites with modern "spiritualism" and faith-cure.

The explanation of Voudooism (or Vaudouism) would require a chapter by itself. It is sufficient to say for the purpose of this paper that the barbaric rites of Voudooism originated with the Congo and Guinea negroes, were brought to San Domingo, and thence to Louisiana. In Hayti the sect is in full vigor, and its midnight orgies have reverted more and more to the barbaric original in the last twenty-five years. The wild dance and incantations are accompanied by sacrifice of animals and occasionally of infants, and with cannibalism, and scenes of most indecent license. In its origin it is serpent worship. The Voudoo signifies a being all-powerful on the earth, who is, or is represented by, a harmless species of serpent (*couleuvre*), and in this belief the sect perform rites in which the serpent is propitiated. In common parlance, the chief actor is called the Voudoo —if a man, the Voudoo King ; if a woman, the Voudoo Queen. Some years ago Congo Square was the

scene of the weird midnight rites of this sect, as un-
restrained and barbarous as ever took place in the
Congo country. All these semi-public performances
have been suppressed, and all private assemblies for
this worship are illegal, and broken up by the police
when discovered. It is said in New Orleans that
Voudooism is a thing of the past. But the superstition remains, and I believe that very few of the colored people in New Orleans are free from it—that is,
free from it as a superstition. Those who repudiate
it, have nothing to do with it, and regard it as only
evil, still ascribe power to the Voudoo, to some ugly
old woman or man, who is popularly believed to have
occult power (as the Italians believe in the "evil-
eye"), can cast a charm and put the victims under a
spell, or by incantations relieve them from it. The
power of the Voudoo is still feared by many who are
too intelligent to believe in it intellectually. That
persons are still Voudooed, probably few doubt; and
that people are injured by charms secretly placed in
their beds, or are bewitched in various ways, is common
belief—more common than the Saxon notion that it
is ill-luck to see the new moon over the left shoulder.

Although very few white people in New Orleans
have ever seen the performance I shall try to describe, and it is said that the police would break it
up if they knew of it, it takes place every Wednesday
at noon at the house where I saw it ; and there are
three or four other places in the city where the rites
are celebrated sometimes at night. Our admission
was procured through a friend who had, I suppose,
vouched for our good intentions.

We were received in the living-rooms of the house

5

on the ground-floor by the "doctor," a good-looking
mulatto of middle age, clad in a white shirt with gold
studs, linen pantaloons, and list slippers. He had the
simple-minded shrewd look of a "healing medium."
The interior was neat, though in some confusion;
among the rude attempts at art on the walls was the
worst chromo print of General Grant that was probably ever made. There were several negroes about
the door, many in the rooms and in the backyard,
and all had an air of expectation and mild excitement.
After we had satisfied the scruples of the doctor, and
signed our names in his register, we were invited to
ascend by a narrow, crooked stair-way in the rear.
This led to a small landing where a dozen people
might stand, and from this a door opened into a
chamber perhaps fifteen feet by ten, where the rites
were to take place; beyond this was a small bedroom.
Around the sides of these rooms were benches and
chairs, and the close quarters were already well filled.

The assembly was perfectly orderly, but a motley
one, and the women largely outnumbered the men.
There were coal-black negroes, porters, and stevedores,
fat cooks, slender chamber-maids, all shades of complexion, yellow girls and comely quadroons, most of
them in common servant attire, but some neatly
dressed. And among them were, to my surprise, several white people.

On one side of the middle room where we sat was
constructed a sort of buffet or bureau, used as an altar.
On it stood an image of the Virgin Mary in painted
plaster, about two feet high, flanked by lighted candles and a couple of cruets, with some other small
objects. On a shelf below were two other candles,

and on this shelf and the floor in front were various offerings to be used in the rites—plates of apples, grapes, bananas, oranges ; dishes of sugar, of sugar-plums; a dish of powdered orris root, packages of candles, bottles of brandy and of water. Two other lighted candles stood on the floor, and in front an earthen bowl. The clear space in front for the dancer was not more than four or five feet square.

Some time was consumed in preparations, or in waiting for the worshippers to assemble. From conversation with those near me, I found that the doctor had a reputation for healing the diseased by virtue of his incantations, of removing "spells," of finding lost articles, of ministering to the troubles of lovers, and, in short, of doing very much what clairvoyants and healing mediums claim to do in what are called civilized communities. But failing to get a very intelligent account of the expected performance from the negro woman next me, I moved to the side of the altar and took a chair next a girl of perhaps twenty years old, whose complexion and features gave evidence that she was white. Still, finding her in that company, and there as a participant in the Voudoo rites, I concluded that I must be mistaken, and that she must have colored blood in her veins. Assuming the privilege of an inquirer, I asked her questions about the coming performance, and in doing so carried the impression that she was kin to the colored race. But I was soon convinced, from her manner and her replies, that she was pure white. She was a pretty, modest girl, very reticent, well-bred, polite, and civil. None of the colored people seemed to know who she was, but she said she had been there before. She told me, in course of the conversation, the name of the street where she lived (in the American part of the town), the private school at which she had been educated (one of the best in the city), and that she and her parents were Episcopalians. Whatever her trouble was, mental or physical, she was evidently infatuated with the notion that this Voudoo doctor could conjure it away, and said that she thought he had already been of service to her. She did not communicate her difficulties to him or speak to him, but she evidently had faith that he could discern what every one present needed, and minister to them. When I asked her if, with her education, she did not think that more good would come to her by confiding in known friends or in regular practitioners, she wearily said that she did not know. After the performance began, her intense interest in it, and the light in her eyes, were evidence of the deep hold the superstition had upon her nature. In coming to this place she had gone a step beyond the young ladies of her class who make a novena at St. Roch.

While we still waited, the doctor and two other colored men called me into the next chamber, and wanted to be assured that it was my own name I had written on the register, and that I had no unfriendly intentions in being present. Their doubts at rest, all was ready.

The doctor squatted on one side of the altar, and his wife, a stout woman of darker hue, on the other.

"*Commençons*," said the woman, in a low voice. All the colored people spoke French, and French only, to each other and in the ceremony.

The doctor nodded, bent over, and gave three sharp raps on the floor with a bit of wood. (This is the usual opening of Voudoo rites.) All the others rapped three times on the floor with their knuckles. Any one coming in to join the circle afterwards, stooped and rapped three times. After a moment's silence, all kneeled and repeated together in French the Apostles' Creed, and still on their knees, they said two prayers to the Virgin Mary.

The colored woman at the side of the altar began a chant in a low, melodious voice. It was the weird and strange "Dansé Calinda." A tall negress, with a bright, good-natured face, entered the circle with the air of a chief performer, knelt, rapped the floor, laid an offering of candles before the altar, with a small bottle of brandy, seated herself beside the singer, and took up in a strong, sweet voice the bizarre rhythm of the song. Nearly all those who came in had laid some little offering before the altar. The chant grew, the single line was enunciated in stronger pulsations, and other voices joined in the wild refrain,

"Dansé Calinda, boudoum, boudoum!
Dansé Calinda, boudoum, boudoum!"

bodies swayed, the hands kept time in soft patpatting, and the feet in muffled accentuation. The Voudoo arose, removed his slippers, seized a bottle of brandy, dashed some of the liquid on the floor on each side of the brown bowl as a libation, threw back his head and took a long pull at the bottle, and then began in the open space a slow measured dance, a rhythmical shuffle, with more movement of the hips than of the feet, backward and forward, round and round, but accelerating his movement as the time of the song quickened and the excitement rose in the room. The singing became wilder and more impassioned, a strange minor strain, full of savage pathos and longing, that made it almost impossible for the spectator not to join in the swing of its influence, while the dancer wrought himself up into the wild passion of a Cairene dervish. Without a moment ceasing his rhythmical steps and his extravagant gesticulation, he poured liquid into the basin, and dashing in brandy, ignited the fluid with a match. The liquid flamed up before the altar. He seized then a bunch of candles, plunged them into the bowl, held them up all flaming with the burning brandy, and, keeping his step to the maddening "Calinda," distributed them lighted to the devotees. In the same way he snatched up dishes of apples, grapes, bananas, oranges, deluged them with burning brandy, and tossed them about the room to the eager and excited crowd. His hands were aflame, his clothes seemed to be on fire ; he held the burning dishes close to his breast, apparently inhaling the flame, closing his eyes and swaying his head backward and forward in an ecstasy, the hips advancing and receding, the feet still shuffling to the barbaric measure.

Every moment his own excitement and that of the audience increased. The floor was covered with the débris of the sacrifice—broken candy, crushed sugarplums, scattered grapes—and all more or less in flame. The wild dancer was dancing in fire ! In the height of his frenzy he grasped a large plate filled with lump - sugar. That was set on fire. He held the burning mass to his breast, he swung it round, and

finally, with his hand extended under the bottom of
the plate (the plate only adhering to his hand by the
rapidity of his circular motion), he spun around like
a dancing dervish, his eyes shut, the perspiration pouring in streams from his face, in a frenzy. The flaming sugar scattered about the floor, and the devotees
scrambled for it. In intervals of the dance, though
the singing went on, the various offerings which had
been conjured were passed around—bits of sugar and
fruit and orris powder. That which fell to my share
I gave to the young girl next me, whose eyes were
blazing with excitement, though she had remained
perfectly tranquil, and joined neither by voice or
hands or feet in the excitement. She put the conjured sugar and fruit in her pocket, and seemed grateful to me for relinquishing it to her.

Before this point had been reached the chant had
been changed for the wild *canga*, more rapid in movement than the *chanson africaine:*

> "Eh! eh! Bomba, hen! hen!
> Canga bafio té
> Canga moune dé lé
> Canga do ki la
> Canga li."

At intervals during the performance, when the
charm had begun to work, the believers came forward into the open space, and knelt for "treatment."
The singing, the dance, the wild incantation, went on
uninterruptedly; but amid all his antics the dancer had
an eye to business. The first group that knelt were
four stalwart men, three of them white laborers. All
of them, I presume, had some disease which they had
faith the incantation would drive away. Each held a

lighted candle in each hand. The doctor successively extinguished each candle by putting it in his mouth, and performed a number of antics of a saltatory sort. During his dancing and whirling he frequently filled his mouth with liquid, and discharged it in spray, exactly as a Chinese laundryman sprinkles his clothes, into the faces and on the heads of any man or woman within reach. Those so treated considered themselves specially favored. Having extinguished the candles of the suppliants, he scooped the liquid from the bowl, flaming or not as it might be, and with his hands vigorously scrubbed their faces and heads, as if he were shampooing them. While the victim was still sputtering and choking he seized him by the right hand, lifted him up, spun him round half a dozen times, and then sent him whirling.

This was substantially the treatment that all received who knelt in the circle, though sometimes it was more violent. Some of them were slapped smartly upon the back and the breast, and much knocked about. Occasionally a woman was whirled till she was dizzy, and perhaps swung about in his arms as if she had been a bundle of clothes. They all took it meekly and gratefully. One little girl of twelve, who had rickets, was banged about till it seemed as if every bone in her body would be broken. But the doctor had discrimination, even in his wildest moods. Some of the women were gently whirled, and the conjurer forbore either to spray them from his mouth or to shampoo them.

Nearly all those present knelt, and were whirled and shaken, and those who did not take this "cure" I suppose got the benefit of the incantation by carrying away some of the consecrated offerings. Occasionally a woman in the whirl would whisper something in the doctor's ear, and receive from him doubtless the counsel she needed. But generally the doctor made no inquiries of his patients, and they said nothing to him.

While the wild chanting, the rhythmic movement of hands and feet, the barbarous dance, and the fiery incantations were at their height, it was difficult to believe that we were in a civilized city of an enlightened republic. Nothing indecent occurred in word or gesture, but it was so wild and bizarre that one might easily imagine he was in Africa or in hell.

As I said, nearly all the participants were colored people; but in the height of the frenzy one white woman knelt and was sprayed and whirled with the others. She was a respectable married woman from the other side of Canal Street. I waited with some anxiety to see what my modest little neighbor would do. She had told me that she should look on and take no part. I hoped that the senseless antics, the mummery, the rough treatment, would disgust her. Towards the close of the séance, when the spells were all woven and the flames had subsided, the tall, good-natured negress motioned to me that it was my turn to advance into the circle and kneel. I excused myself. But the young girl was unable to resist longer. She went forward and knelt, with a candle in her hand. The conjurer was either touched by her youth and race, or he had spent his force. He gently lifted her by one hand, and gave her one turn around, and she came back to her seat.

The singing ceased. The doctor's wife passed

round the hat for contributions, and the ceremony, which had lasted nearly an hour and a half, was over. The doctor retired exhausted with the violent exertions. As for the patients, I trust they were well cured of rheumatism, of fever, or whatever ill they had, and that the young ladies have either got husbands to their minds or have escaped faithless lovers. In the breaking up I had no opportunity to speak further to the interesting young white neophyte; but as I saw her resuming her hat and cloak in the adjoining room there was a strange excitement in her face, and in her eyes a light of triumph and faith. We came out by the back way, and through an alley made our escape into the sunny street and the air of the nineteenth century.

V

THE ACADIAN LAND.

IF one crosses the river from New Orleans to Algiers, and takes Morgan's Louisiana and Texas Railway (now a part of the Southern Pacific line), he will go west, with a dip at first southerly, and will pass through a region little attractive except to water-fowl, snakes, and alligators, by an occasional rice plantation, an abandoned indigo field, an interminable stretch of cypress swamps, thickets of Spanish-bayonets, black waters, rank and rampant vegetation, vines, and water-plants; by-and-by firmer arable land, and cane plantations, many of them forsaken and become thickets of undergrowth, owing to frequent inundations and the low price of sugar.

At a distance of eighty miles Morgan City is reached, and the broad Atchafalaya Bayou is crossed. Hence is steamboat communication with New Orleans and Vera Cruz. The Atchafalaya Bayou has its origin near the mouth of the Red River, and diverting from the Mississippi most of that great stream, it makes its tortuous way to the Gulf, frequently expanding into the proportions of a lake, and giving this region a great deal more water than it needs. The Bayou Teche, which is, in fact, a lazy river, wanders down from the rolling country of Washington and Opelousas, with a great deal of uncertainty of purpose, but mainly south-easterly, and parallel with the

Atchafalaya, and joins the latter at Morgan City. Steamers of good size navigate it as far as New Iberia, some forty to fifty miles, and the railway follows it to the latter place, within sight of its fringe of live-oaks and cotton-woods. The region south and west of the Bayou Teche, a vast plain cut by innumerable small bayous and streams, which have mostly a connection with the bay of Côte Blanche and Vermilion Bay, is the home of the Nova Scotia Acadians.

The Acadians in 1755 made a good exchange, little as they thought so at the time, of bleak Nova Scotia for these sunny, genial, and fertile lands. They came into a land and a climate suited to their idiosyncrasies, and which have enabled them to preserve their primitive traits. In a comparative isolation from the disturbing currents of modern life, they have preserved the habits and customs of the eighteenth century. The immigrants spread themselves abroad among those bayous, made their homes wide apart, and the traveller will nowhere find—at least I did not—large and compact communities of them, unalloyed with the American and other elements. Indeed, I imagine that they are losing, in the general settlement of the country, their conspicuousness. They still give the tone, however, to considerable districts, as in the village and neighborhood of Abbeville. Some places, like the old town of St. Martinsville, on the Teche, once the social capital of the region, and entitled, for its wealth and gayety, the Petit Paris, had a large element of French who were not Acadians.

The Teche from Morgan City to New Iberia is a deep, slow, and winding stream, flowing through a flat region of sugar plantations. It is very picturesque

by reason of its tortuousness and the great spreading
live - oak trees, moss - draped, that hang over it. A
voyage on it is one of the most romantic entertainments offered to the traveller. The scenery is peaceful, and exceedingly pretty. There are few conspicuous plantations with mansions and sugar-stacks of any
pretensions, but the panorama from the deck of the
steamer is always pleasing. There is an air of leisure
and "afternoon" about the expedition, which is heightened by the idle ease of the inhabitants lounging at
the rude wharves and landing-places, and the patience
of the colored fishers, boys in scant raiment and wom-
en in sun-bonnets, seated on the banks. Typical of
this universal contentment is the ancient colored man
stretched on a plank close to the steamer's boiler, ob-
livious of the heat, apparently asleep, with his spacious
mouth wide open, but softly singing.

"Are you asleep, uncle ?"

"No, not adzackly asleep, boss. I jes wake up,
and thinkin' how good de Lord is, I couldn't help
singin'."

The panorama is always interesting. There are
wide silvery expanses of water, into which fall the
shadows of great trees. A tug is dragging along a tow
of old rafts composed of cypress logs all water-soak-
ed, green with weeds and grass, so that it looks like a
floating garden. What pictures ! Clusters of oaks
on the prairie; a picturesque old cotton-press; a house
thatched with palmettoes; rice - fields irrigated by
pumps; darkies, field-hands, men and women, hoeing
in the cane-fields, giving stalwart strokes that exhibit
their robust figures ; an old sugar - mill in ruin and
vine-draped; an old begass chimney against the sky;

an antique cotton-press with its mouldering roof supported on timbers; a darky on a mule motionless on the bank, clad in Attakapas cloth, his slouch hat falling about his head like a roof from which the rafters have been withdrawn; palmettoes, oaks, and funereal moss; lines of Spanish-bayonets; rickety wharves; primitive boats; spider-legged bridges. Neither on the Teche nor the Atchafalaya, nor on the great plain near the Mississippi, fit for amphibious creatures, where one standing on the level wonders to see the wheels of the vast river steamers above him, apparently without cause, revolving, is there any lack of the picturesque.

New Iberia, the thriving mart of the region, which has drawn away the life from St. Martinsville, ten miles farther up the bayou, is a village mainly of small frame houses, with a smart court-house, a lively business street, a few pretty houses, and some old-time mansions on the bank of the bayou, half smothered in old rose gardens, the ground in the rear sloping to the water under the shade of gigantic oaks. One of them, which with its outside staircases in the pillared gallery suggests Spanish taste on the outside, and in the interior the arrangement of connecting rooms a French chateau, has a self-keeping rose garden, where one might easily become sentimental; the vines disport themselves like holiday children, climbing the trees, the side of the house, and revelling in an abandon of color and perfume.

The population is mixed—Americans, French, Italians, now and then a Spaniard and even a Mexican, occasionally a basket-making Attakapas, and the all-pervading person of color. The darky is a born fish-

erman, in places where fishing requires no exertion,
and one may see him any hour seated on the banks
of the Teche, especially the boy and the sun-bonneted
woman, placidly holding their poles over the muddy
stream, and can study, if he like, the black face in expectation of a bite. There too are the washer-women,
with their tubs and a plank thrust into the water,
and a handkerchief of bright colors for a turban.
These people somehow never fail to be picturesque,
whatever attitude they take, and they are not at all
self-conscious. The groups on Sunday give an interest to church-going—a lean white horse, with a
man, his wife, and boy strung along its backbone, an
aged darky and his wife seated in a cart, in stiff Sunday clothes and flaming colors, the wheels of the cart
making all angles with the ground, and wabbling and
creaking along, the whole party as proud of its appearance as Julius Cæsar in a triumph.

I drove on Sunday morning early from New Iberia
to church at St. Martinsville. It was a lovely April
morning. The way lay over fertile prairies, past fine
cane plantations, with some irrigation, and for a distance along the pretty Teche, shaded by great live-
oaks, and here and there a fine magnolia-tree; a country with few houses, and those mostly shanties, but a
sunny, smiling land, loved of the birds. We passed
on our left the Spanish Lake, a shallow, irregular
body of water. My driver was an ex-Confederate
soldier, whose tramp with a musket through Virginia
had not greatly enlightened him as to what it was all
about. As to the Acadians, however, he had a decided opinion, and it was a poor one. They are no
good. "You ask them a question, and they shrug

their shoulders like a tarrapin—don't know no more'n a dead alligator ; only language they ever have is 'no' and 'what?'"

If St. Martinsville, once the seat of fashion, retains anything of its past elegance, its life has departed from it. It has stopped growing anything but old, and yet it has not much of interest that is antique ; it is a village of small white frame houses, with three or four big gaunt brick structures, two stories and a half high, with galleries, and here and there a Creole cottage, the stairs running up inside the galleries, over which roses climb in profusion.

I went to breakfast at a French inn, kept by Madame Castillo, a large red-brick house on the banks of the Teche, where the live-oaks cast shadows upon the silvery stream. It had, of course, a double gallery. Below, the waiting-room, dining-room, and general assembly-room were paved with brick, and instead of a door, Turkey-red curtains hung in the entrance, and blowing aside, hospitably invited the stranger within. The breakfast was neatly served, the house was scrupulously clean, and the guest felt the influence of that personal hospitality which is always so pleasing. Madame offered me a seat in her pew in church, and meantime a chair on the upper gallery, which opened from large square sleeping chambers. In that fresh morning I thought I never had seen a more sweet and peaceful place than this gallery. Close to it grew graceful China-trees in full blossom and odor ; up and down the Teche were charming views under the oaks ; only the roofs of the town could be seen amid the foliage of China-trees ; and there was an atmosphere of repose in all the scene.

It was Easter morning. I felt that I should like to linger there a week in absolute forgetfulness of the world. French is the ordinary language of the village, spoken more or less corruptly by all colors.

The Catholic church, a large and ugly structure, stands on the plaza, which is not at all like a Spanish plaza, but a veritable New England "green," with stores and shops on all sides—New England, except that the shops are open on Sunday. In the church apse is a noted and not bad painting of St. Martin, and at the bottom of one aisle a vast bank of black stucco clouds, with the Virgin standing on them, and the legend, "*Je suis l'immaculée conception.*"

Country people were pouring into town for the Easter service and festivities — more blacks than whites — on horseback and in rickety carriages, and the horses were hitched on either side of the church. Before service the square was full of lively young colored lads cracking Easter-eggs. Two meet and strike together the eggs in their hands, and the one loses whose egg breaks. A tough shell is a valuable possession. The custom provokes a good deal of larking and merriment. While this is going on, the worshippers are making their way into the church through the throng, ladies in the neat glory of provincial dress, and high-stepping, saucy colored belles, yellow and black, the blackest in the most radiant apparel of violent pink and light blue, and now and then a society favorite in all the hues of the rainbow. The centre pews of the church are reserved for the whites, the seats of the side aisles for the negroes. When mass begins, the church is crowded. The boys, with occasional excursions into the vestibule to dip the finger

6

in the holy-water, or perhaps say a prayer, are still
winning and losing eggs on the green.

On the gallery at the inn it is also Sunday. The
air is full of odor. A strong south wind begins to
blow. I think the south wind is the wind of memory
and of longing. I wonder if the gay spirits of the
last generation ever return to the scenes of their rev-
elry? Will they come back to the theatre this Sunday night, and to the Grand Ball afterwards? The
admission to both is only twenty-five cents, including
gombo filé.

From New Iberia southward towards Vermilion
Bay stretches a vast prairie; if it is not absolutely
flat, if it resembles the ocean, it is the ocean when its
long swells have settled nearly to a calm. This prairie would be monotonous were it not dotted with
small round ponds, like hand-mirrors for the flitting
birds and sailing clouds, were its expanse not spotted
with herds of cattle, scattered or clustering like fishing-boats on a green sea, were it not for a cabin here
and there, a field of cane or cotton, a garden plot, and
were it not for the forests which break the horizon
line, and send out dark capes into the verdant plains.
On a gray day, or when storms and fogs roll in from
the Gulf, it might be a gloomy region, but under the
sunlight and in the spring it is full of life and color;
it has an air of refinement and repose that is very
welcome. Besides the uplift of the spirit that a wide
horizon is apt to give, one is conscious here of the
neighborhood of the sea, and of the possibilities of romantic adventure in a coast intersected by bayous,
and the presence of novel forms of animal and vegetable life, and of a people with habits foreign and

strange. There is also a grateful sense of freedom and expansion.

Soon, over the plain, is seen on the horizon, ten miles from New Iberia, the dark foliage on the island of Petite Anse, or Avery's Island. This unexpected upheaval from the marsh, bounded by the narrow, circling Petite Anse Bayou, rises into the sky one hundred and eighty feet, and has the effect in this flat expanse of a veritable mountain, comparatively a surprise, like Pike's Peak seen from the elevation of Denver. Perhaps nowhere else would a hill of one hundred and eighty feet make such an impression on the mind. Crossing the bayou, where alligators sun themselves and eye with affection the colored people angling at the bridge, and passing a long causeway over the marsh, the firm land of the island is reached. This island, which is a sort of geological puzzle, has a very uneven surface, and is some two and a half miles long by one mile broad. It is a little kingdom in itself, capable of producing in its soil and adjacent waters nearly everything one desires of the necessaries of life. A portion of the island is devoted to a cane plantation and sugar-works; a part of it is covered with forests; and on the lowlands and gentle slopes, besides thickets of palmetto, are gigantic live-oaks, moss-draped trees monstrous in girth, and towering into the sky with a vast spread of branches. Scarcely anywhere else will one see a nobler growth of these stately trees. In a depression is the famous salt-mine, unique in quality and situation in the world. Here is grown and put up the Tobasco pepper; here, amid fields of clover and flowers, a large apiary flourishes. Stones of some value for ornament are found.

Indeed, I should not be surprised at anything turning up there, for I am told that good kaoline has been discovered; and about the residences of the hospitable proprietors roses bloom in abundance, the China-tree blossoms sweetly, and the mocking-bird sings.

But better than all these things I think I like the view from the broad cottage piazzas, and I like it best when the salt breeze is strong enough to sweep away the coast mosquitoes—a most undesirable variety. I do not know another view of its kind for extent and color comparable to that from this hill over the waters seaward. The expanse of luxuriant grass, brown, golden, reddish, in patches, is intersected by a network of bayous, which gleam like silver in the sun, or trail like dark fabulous serpents under a cloudy sky. The scene is limited only by the power of the eye to meet the sky line. Vast and level, it is constantly changing, almost in motion with life; the long grass and weeds run like waves when the wind blows, great shadows of clouds pass on its surface, alternating dark masses with vivid ones of sunlight; fishing-boats and the masts of schooners creep along the threads of water; when the sun goes down, a red globe of fire in the Gulf mists, all the expanse is warm and ruddy, and the waters sparkle like jewels; and at night, under the great field of stars, marsh fires here and there give a sort of lurid splendor to the scene. In the winter it is a temperate spot, and at all times of the year it is blessed by an invigorating sea-breeze.

Those who have enjoyed the charming social life and the unbounded hospitality of the family who inhabit this island may envy them their paradisiacal home, but they would be able to select none others so worthy to enjoy it.

It is said that the Attakapas Indians are shy of this island, having a legend that it was the scene of a great catastrophe to their race. Whether this catastrophe has any connection with the upheaval of the salt mountain I do not know. Many stories are current in this region in regard to the discovery of this deposit. A little over a quarter of a century ago it was unsuspected. The presence of salt in the water of a small spring led somebody to dig in that place, and at the depth of sixteen feet below the surface solid salt was struck. In stripping away the soil several relics of human workmanship came to light, among them stone implements and a woven basket, exactly such as the Attakapas make now. This basket, found at the depth of sixteen feet, lay upon the salt rock, and was in perfect preservation. Half of it can now be seen in the Smithsonian Institution. At the beginning of the war great quantities of salt were taken from this mine for the use of the Confederacy. But this supply was cut off by the Unionists, who at first sent gunboats up the bayou within shelling distance, and at length occupied it with troops.

The ascertained area of the mine is several acres; the depth of the deposit is unknown. The first shaft was sunk a hundred feet; below this a shaft of seventy feet fails to find any limit to the salt. The excavation is already large. Descending, the visitor enters vast cathedral-like chambers; the sides are solid salt, sparkling with crystals; the floor is solid salt; the roof is solid salt, supported on pillars of salt left by the excavators, forty or perhaps sixty feet square. When the interior is lighted by dynamite the effect is superbly weird and grotesque. The salt is blasted by dynamite, loaded into cars which run on rails to the elevator, hoisted, and distributed into the crushers, and from the crushers directly into the bags for shipment. The crushers differ in crushing capacity, some producing fine and others coarse salt. No bleaching or cleansing process is needed; the salt is almost absolutely pure. Large blocks of it are sent to the Western plains for "cattle licks." The mine is connected by rail with the main line at New Iberia.

Across the marshes and bayous eight miles to the west from Petite Anse Island rises Orange Island, famous for its orange plantation, but called Jefferson Island since it became the property and home of Joseph Jefferson. Not so high as Petite Anse, it is still conspicuous with its crown of dark forest. From a high point on Petite Anse, through a lovely vista of trees, with flowering cacti in the foreground, Jefferson's house is a white spot in the landscape. We reached it by a circuitous drive of twelve miles over the prairie, sometimes in and sometimes out of the water, and continually diverted from our course by fences. It is a good sign of the thrift of the race, and of its independence, that the colored people have taken up or bought little tracts of thirty or forty acres, put up cabins, and new fences round their domains regardless of the travelling public. We zigzagged all about the country to get round these little enclosures. At one place, where the main road was bad, a thrifty Acadian had set up a toll of twenty-five cents for the privilege of passing through his premises. The scenery was pastoral and pleasing.

There were frequent round ponds, brilliant with lilies
and *fleurs-de-lis*, and hundreds of cattle feeding on the
prairie or standing in the water, and generally of a
dun-color, made always an agreeable picture. The
monotony was broken by lines of trees, by cape-like
woods stretching into the plain, and the horizon line
was always fine. Great variety of birds enlivened
the landscape, game birds abounding. There was the
lively little nonpareil, which seems to change its col-
or, and is red and green and blue, I believe of the
oriole family, the papabotte, a favorite on New Orleans tables in the autumn, snipe, killdee, the cherooke
(snipe?), the meadow-lark, and quantities of teal
ducks in the ponds. These little ponds are called
" bull-holes." The traveller is told that they are
started in this watery soil by the pawing of bulls,
and gradually enlarged as the cattle frequent them.
He remembers that he has seen similar circular ponds
in the North not made by bulls.

Mr. Jefferson's residence—a pretty rose-vine-covered
cottage—is situated on the slope of the hill, overlooking a broad plain and a vast stretch of bayou country.
Along one side of his home enclosure for a mile runs
a superb hedge of Chickasaw roses. On the slope
back of the house, and almost embracing it, is a magnificent grove of live-oaks, great gray stems, and the
branches hung with heavy masses of moss, which
swing in the wind like the pendent boughs of the
willow, and with something of its sentimental and
mournful suggestion. The recesses of this forest are
cool and dark, but upon ascending the hill, suddenly
bursts upon the view under the trees a most lovely
lake of clear blue water. This lake, which may be

a mile long and half a mile broad, is called Lake
Peigneur, from its fanciful resemblance, I believe, to
a wool-comber. The shores are wooded. On the isl-
and side the bank is precipitous; on the opposite
shore amid the trees is a hunting-lodge, and I believe
there are plantations on the north end, but it is in aspect altogether solitary and peaceful. But the island
did not want life. The day was brilliant, with a deep
blue sky and high-sailing fleecy clouds, and it seemed
a sort of animal holiday: squirrels chattered; cardinal-birds flashed through the green leaves; there
flitted about the red-winged blackbird, blue jays, red-
headed woodpeckers, thrushes, and occasionally a rain-
crow crossed the scene; high overhead sailed the
heavy buzzards, describing great aerial circles; and
off in the still lake the ugly heads of alligators were
toasting in the sun.

It was very pleasant to sit on the wooded point, enlivened by all this animal activity, looking off upon
the lake and the great expanse of marsh, over which
came a refreshing breeze. There was great variety
of forest-trees. Besides the live-oaks, in one small
area I noticed the water-oak, red-oak, pin-oak, the elm,
the cypress, the hackberry, and the pecan tree.

This point is a favorite rendezvous for the buzzards.
Before I reached it I heard a tremendous whirring in
the air, and, lo! there upon the oaks were hundreds
and hundreds of buzzards. Upon one dead tree, vast,
gaunt, and bleached, they had settled in black masses.
When I came near they rose and flew about with
clamor and surprise, momentarily obscuring the sunlight. With these unpleasant birds consorted in un-
clean fellowship numerous long-necked water-turkeys.

Doré would have liked **to introduce into one of** his
melodramatic pictures this helpless **dead tree, extend-**
ing its gray arms loaded with these black scavengers.
It needed the blue sky and **blue** lake to prevent **the**
scene from being altogether uncanny. I remember
still the harsh, croaking noise of the buzzards and the
water-turkeys when they were disturbed, and the flap-
ping of their funereal wings, and perhaps the alligators lying off in the lake noted it, for they grunted
and bellowed a response. But the birds sang merrily,
the wind blew softly ; there was the repose as of a
far country undisturbed by man, and a silvery **tone**
on the water and all the landscape that refined **the**
whole.

If **the** Acadians can anywhere be seen in the prosperity of their primitive simplicity, I fancy it is in
the parish of Vermilion, in the vicinity **of** Abbeville
and on the Bayou Tigre. Here, among the intricate
bayous that are their highways and supply them with
the poorer sort of fish, and the fair meadows on which
their cattle pasture, and where they grow **nearly ev-**
erything their simple habits require, they have **for**
over a century enjoyed a quiet existence, practically
undisturbed by the agitations of modern life, ignorant
of its progress. History makes their departure **from**
the comparatively bleak meadows of Grand Pré **a**
cruel hardship, if a political necessity. But they
made a very fortunate exchange. Nowhere else on
the continent could they so well have preserved their
primitive habits, or found climate and soil so suited
to their humor. Others have exhaustively set forth the
history and **idiosyncrasies of** this peculiar people ; **it**
is in my way only to tell what I saw on a spring day.

To reach the heart of this abode of contented and perhaps wise ignorance we took boats early one morning at Petite Anse Island, while the dew was still heavy and the birds were at matins, and rowed down the Petite Anse Bayou. A stranger would surely be lost in these winding, branching, interlacing streams. Evangeline and her lover might have passed each other unknown within hail across these marshes. The party of a dozen people occupied two row-boats. Among them were gentlemen who knew the route, but the reserve of wisdom as to what bayous and cutoffs were navigable was an ancient ex-slave, now a voter, who responded to the name of "Honorable"— a weather-beaten and weather-wise darky, a redoubtable fisherman, whose memory extended away beyond the war, and played familiarly about the person of Lafayette, with whom he had been on agreeable terms in Charleston, and who dated his narratives, to our relief, not from the war, but from the year of some great sickness on the coast. From the Petite Anse we entered the Carlin Bayou, and wound through it is needless to say what others in our tortuous course. In the fresh morning, with the salt air, it was a voyage of delight. Mullet were jumping in the glassy stream, perhaps disturbed by the gar-fish, and alligators lazily slid from the reedy banks into the water at our approach. All the marsh was gay with flowers, vast patches of the blue *fleur-de-lis* intermingled with the exquisite white spider-lily, nodding in clusters on long stalks; an amaryllis (pancratium), its pure half-disk fringed with delicate white filaments. The air was vocal with the notes of birds, the nonpareil and the meadow-lark, and most conspicuous of all the hand-

some boat-tail grackle, a blackbird, which alighted
on the slender dead reeds that swayed with his
weight as he poured forth his song. Sometimes the
bayou narrowed so that it was impossible to row with
the oars, and poling was resorted to, and the current
was swift and strong. At such passes we saw only
the banks with nodding flowers, and the reeds, with
the blackbirds singing, against the sky. Again we
emerged into placid reaches overhung by gigantic
live-oaks and fringed with cypress. It was enchant-
ing. But the way was not quite solitary. Numerous
fishing parties were encountered, boats on their way
to the bay, and now and then a party of stalwart men
drawing a net in the bayou, their clothes being deposited on the banks. Occasionally a large schooner
was seen, tied to the bank or slowly working its way,
and on one a whole family was domesticated. There
is a good deal of queer life hidden in these bayous.

After passing through a narrow artificial canal, we
came into the Bayou Tigre, and landed for breakfast
on a greensward, with meadow-land and signs of hab-
itations in the distance, under spreading live-oaks.
Under one of the most attractive of these trees, close
to the stream, we did not spread our table-cloth and
shawls, because a large moccason snake was seen to
glide under the roots, and we did not know but that
his modesty was assumed, and he might join the
breakfast party. It is said that these snakes never
attack any one who has kept all the ten commandments from his youth up. Cardinal-birds made the
wood gay for us while we breakfasted, and we might
have added plenty of partridges to our *menu* if we
had been armed.

Resuming our voyage, we presently entered the inhabited part of the bayou, among cultivated fields,
and made our first call on the Thibodeaux. They had
been expecting us, and Andonia came down to the
landing to welcome us, and with a formal, pretty
courtesy led the way to the house. Does the reader
happen to remember, say in New England, say fifty
years ago, the sweetest maiden lady in the village,
prim, staid, full of kindness, the proportions of the
figure never quite developed, with a row of small
corkscrew curls about her serene forehead, and all the
juices of life that might have overflowed into the life
of others somehow withered into the sweetness of her
wistful face ? Yes; a little timid and appealing, and
yet trustful, and in a scant, quaint gown ? Well, Andonia was never married, and she had such curls, and
a high-waisted gown, and a kerchief folded across her
breast; and when she spoke, it was in the language of
France as it is rendered in Acadia.

The house, like all in this region, stands upon blocks
of wood, is in appearance a frame house, but the walls
between timbers are of concrete mixed with moss,
and the same inside as out. It had no glass in the
windows, which were closed with solid shutters. Upon
the rough walls were hung sacred pictures and other
crudely colored prints. The furniture was rude and
apparently home-made, and the whole interior was as
painfully neat as a Dutch parlor. Even the beams
overhead and ceiling had been scrubbed. Andonia
showed us with a blush of pride her neat little sleep-
ing-room, with its souvenirs of affection, and perhaps
some of the dried flowers of a possible romance, and
the ladies admired the finely woven white counterpane

on the bed. Andonia's married sister was a large, handsome woman, smiling and prosperous. There were children and, I think, a baby about, besides Mr. Thibodeaux. Nothing could exceed the kindly manner of these people. Andonia showed us how they card, weave, and spin the cotton out of which their blankets and the jean for their clothing are made. They use the old-fashioned hand-cards, spin on a little wheel with a foot - treadle, have the most primitive warping-bars, and weave most laboriously on a rude loom. But the cloth they make will wear forever, and the colors they use are all fast. It is a great pleasure, we might almost say shock, to encounter such honest work in these times. The Acadians grow a yellow or nankeen sort of cotton which, without requiring any dye, is woven into a handsome yellow stuff. When we departed Andonia slipped into the door-yard, and returned with a rose for each of us. I fancied she was loath to have us go, and that the visit was an event in the monotony of her single life.

Embarking again on the placid stream, we moved along through a land of peace. The houses of the Acadians are scattered along the bayou at considerable distances apart. The voyager seems to be in an unoccupied country, when suddenly the turn of the stream shows him a farm-house, with its little landing-wharf, boats, and perhaps a schooner moored at the bank, and behind it cultivated fields and a fringe of trees. In the blossoming time of the year, when the birds are most active, these scenes are idyllic. At a bend in the bayou, where a tree sent its horizontal trunk half across it, we made our next call, at the house of Mr. Vallet, a large frame house, and evi-

dently the abode of a man of means. The house was
ceiled outside and inside with native woods. As usual
in this region, the premises were not as orderly as
those about some Northern farm-houses, but the interior of the house was spotlessly clean, and in its polish
and barrenness of ornament and of appliances of comfort suggested a Brittany home, while its openness
and the broad veranda spoke of a genial climate. Our
call here was brief, for a sick man, very ill, they said,
lay in the front room—a stranger who had been over-
taken with fever, and was being cared for by these
kind-hearted people.

Other calls were made—this visiting by boat recalls
Venice—but the end of our voyage was the plantation
of Simonette Le Blanc, a sturdy old man, a sort of pa-
triarch in this region, the centre of a very large family of sons, daughters, and grandchildren. The residence, a rambling story-and-a-half house, grown by
accretions as more room was needed, calls for no comment. It was all very plain, and contained no books,
nor any adornments except some family photographs,
the poor work of a travelling artist. But in front, on
the bayou, Mr. Le Blanc had erected a grand ball-
room, which gave an air of distinction to the place.
This hall, which had benches along the wall, and at
one end a high dais for the fiddlers, and a little counter
where the gombo filé (the common refreshment) is
served, had an air of gayety by reason of engravings
cut from the illustrated papers, and was shown with
some pride. Here neighborhood dances take place
once in two weeks, and a grand ball was to come off
on Easter-Sunday night, to which we were urgently
invited to come.

Simonette Le Blanc, with several of his sons, had returned at midnight from an expedition to Vermilion Bay, where they had been camping for a couple of weeks, fishing and taking oysters. Working the schooner through the bayou at night had been fatiguing, and then there was supper, and all the news of the fortnight to be talked over, so that it was four o'clock before the house was at rest, but neither the hale old man nor his stalwart sons seemed the worse for the adventure. Such trips are not uncommon, for these people seem to have leisure for enjoyment, and vary the toil of the plantation with the pleasures of fishing and lazy navigation. But to the women and the home-stayers this was evidently an event. The men had been to the outer world, and brought back with them the gossip of the bayous and the simple incidents of the camping life on the coast. "There was a great deal to talk over that had happened in a fortnight," said Simonette—he and one of his sons spoke English. I do not imagine that the talk was about politics, or any of the events that seem important in other portions of the United States, only the faintest echoes of which ever reach this secluded place. This is a purely domestic and patriarchal community, where there are no books to bring in agitating doubts, and few newspapers to disquiet the nerves. The only matter of politics broached was in regard to an appropriation by Congress to improve a cut-off between two bayous. So far as I could learn, the most intelligent of these people had no other interest in or concern about the Government. There is a neighborhood school where English is taught, but no church nearer than Abbeville, six miles away. I should not describe the population as fanatically religious, nor a church-going one except on special days. But by all accounts it is moral, orderly, sociable, fond of dancing, thrifty, and conservative.

The Acadians are fond of their homes. It is not the fashion for the young people to go away to better their condition. Few young men have ever been as far from home as New Orleans; they marry young, and settle down near the homestead. Mr. Le Blanc has a colony of his descendants about him, within hail from his door. It must be large, and his race must be prolific, judging by the number of small children who gathered at the homestead to have a sly peep at the strangers. They took small interest in the war, and it had few attractions for them. The conscription carried away many of their young men, but I am told they did not make very good soldiers, not because they were not stalwart and brave, but because they were so intolerably homesick that they deserted whenever they had a chance. The men whom we saw were most of them fine athletic fellows, with honest, dark, sun-browned faces; some of the children were very pretty, but the women usually showed the effects of isolation and toil, and had the common plainness of French peasants. They are a self-supporting community, raise their own cotton, corn, and sugar, and for the most part manufacture their own clothes and articles of household use. Some of the cotton jeans, striped with blue, indigo-dyed, made into garments for men and women, and the blankets, plain yellow (from the native nankeen cotton), curiously clouded, are very pretty and serviceable. Further than that their habits of living are simple, and their ways primitive, I saw few eccentricities. The peculiarity of this community is in its freedom from all the hurry and worry and information of our modern life. I have read that the gallants train their little horses to prance and curvet and rear and fidget about, and that these are called "courtin' horses," and are used when a young man goes courting, to impress his mistress with his manly horsemanship. I have seen these horses perform under the saddle, but I was not so fortunate as to see any courting going on.

In their given as well as their family names these people are classical and peculiar. I heard, of men, the names L'Odias, Peigneur, Niolas, Elias, Homère, Lemaire, and of women, Emilite, Ségoura, Antoinette, Clarise, Elia.

We were very hospitably entertained by the Le Blancs. On our arrival tiny cups of black coffee were handed round, and later a drink of syrup and water, which some of the party sipped with a sickly smile of enjoyment. Before dinner we walked up to the bridge over the bayou on the road leading to Abbeville, where there is a little cluster of houses, a small country store, and a closed drug-shop—the owner of which had put up his shutters and gone to a more unhealthy region. Here is a fine grove of oaks, and from the bridge we had in view a grand sweep of prairie, with trees, single and in masses, which made with the winding silvery stream a very pleasing picture. We sat down to a dinner—the women waiting on the table—of gombo filé, fried oysters, eggs, sweet-potatoes (the delicious saccharine, sticky sort), with syrup out of a bottle served in little saucers, and af-

7

terwards black coffee. We were sincerely welcome
to whatever the house contained, and when we departed the whole family, and indeed all the neighborhood, accompanied us to our boats, and we went away
down the stream with a chorus of adieus and good
wishes.

We were watching for a hail from the Thibodeaux.
The doors and shutters were closed, and the mansion
seemed blank and forgetful. But as we came opposite the landing, there stood Andonia, faithful, waving
her handkerchief. Ah me!

We went home gayly and more swiftly, current
and tide with us, though a little pensive, perhaps, with
too much pleasure and the sunset effects on the wide
marshes through which we voyaged. Cattle wander
at will over these marshes, and are often stalled and
lost. We saw some pitiful sights. The cattle vent-
uring too near the boggy edge to drink become in-
extricably involved. We passed an ox sunken to
his back, and dead; a cow frantically struggling in
the mire, almost exhausted, and a cow and calf, the
mother dead, the calf moaning beside her. On a cattle lookout near by sat three black buzzards surveying the prospect with hungry eyes.

When we landed and climbed the hill, and from
the rose-embowered veranda looked back over the
strange land we had sailed through, away to Bayou
Tigre, where the red sun was setting, we felt that we
had been in a country that is not of this world.

VI.

THE SOUTH REVISITED.

IN 1887.

In speaking again of the South in HARPER'S MONTHLY, after an interval of about two years, and as before at the request of the editor, I said, I shrink a good deal from the appearance of forwardness which a second paper may seem to give to observations which have the single purpose of contributing my mite towards making the present spirit of the Southern people, their progress in industries and in education, their aspirations, better known. On the other hand, I have no desire to escape the imputation of a warm interest in the South, and of a belief that its development and prosperity are essential to the greatness and glory of the nation. Indeed, no one can go through the South, with his eyes open, without having his patriotic fervor quickened and broadened, and without increased pride in the republic.

We are one people. Different traditions, different education or the lack of it, the demoralizing curse of slavery, different prejudices, made us look at life from irreconcilable points of view; but the prominent common feature, after all, is our Americanism. In any assembly of gentlemen from the two sections the resemblances are greater than the differences. A score of times I have heard it said, "We look alike, talk

alike, feel alike ; how strange it is we should have
fought!" Personal contact always tends to remove
prejudices, and to bring into prominence the national
feeling, the race feeling, the human nature common
to all of us.

I wish to give as succinctly as I can the general
impressions of a recent six weeks' tour, made by a
company of artists and writers, which became known
as the "Harper party," through a considerable portion of the South, including the cities of Lynchburg,
Richmond, Danville, Atlanta, Augusta (with a brief
call at Charleston and Columbia, for it was not intended to take in the eastern seaboard on this trip),
Knoxville, Chattanooga, South Pittsburg, Nashville,
Birmingham, Montgomery, Pensacola, Mobile, New
Orleans, Baton Rouge, Vicksburg, Memphis, Louisville. Points of great interest were necessarily omitted in a tour which could only include representatives of the industrial and educational development
of the New South. Naturally we were thrown more
with business men and with educators than with others ; that is, with those who are actually making the
New South ; but we saw something of social life,
something of the homes and mode of living of every
class, and we had abundant opportunities of conversation with whites and blacks of every social grade and
political affinity. The Southern people were anxious
to show us what they were doing, and they expressed
their sentiments with entire frankness ; if we were
misled, it is our own fault. It must be noted, however, in estimating the value of our observations, that
they were mainly made in cities and large villages,
and little in the country districts.

Inquiries in the South as to the feeling of the
North show that there is still left some misapprehension of the spirit in which the North sent out its
armies, though it is beginning to be widely understood that the North was not animated by hatred of
the South, but by intense love of the Union. On the
other hand, I have no doubt there still lingers in the
North a little misapprehension of the present feeling
of the Southern people about the Union. It arises
from a confusion of two facts which it is best to speak
of plainly. Everybody knows that the South is
heartily glad that slavery is gone, and that a new era
of freedom has set in. Everybody who knows the
South at all is aware that any idea of any renewal of
the strife, now or at any time, is nowhere entertained,
even as a speculation, and that to the women especially, who are said to be first in war, last in peace,
and first in the hearts of their countrymen, the idea
of war is a subject of utter loathing. The two facts
to which I refer are the loyalty of the Southern whites
to the Union, and their determination to rule in domestic affairs. Naturally there are here and there
soreness and some bitterness over personal loss and
ruin, life-long grief, maybe, over lost illusions—the
observer who remembers what human nature is wonders that so little of this is left—but the great fact is
that the South is politically loyal to the Union of the
States, that the sentiment for its symbol is growing
into a deep reality which would flame out in passion
under any foreign insult, and that nationality, pride
in the republic, is everywhere strong and prominent.
It is hardly necessary to say this, but it needs to be
emphasized when the other fact is dwelt on, namely,

the denial of free suffrage to the colored man. These two things are confused, and this confusion is the source of much political misunderstanding. Often when a Southern election "outrage" is telegraphed, when intimidation or fraud is revealed, it is said in print, "So that is Southern loyalty!" In short, the political treatment of the negro is taken to be a sign of surviving war feeling, if not of a renewed purpose of rebellion. In this year of grace 1887 the two things have no relation to each other. It would be as true to say that election frauds and violence to individuals and on the ballot-box in Cincinnati are signs of hatred of the Union and of Union men, as that a suppressed negro vote at the South, by adroit management or otherwise, is indication of remaining hostility to the Union. In the South it is sometimes due to the same depraved party spirit that causes frauds in the North—the determination of a party to get or keep the upperhand at all hazards; but it is, in its origin and generally, simply the result of the resolution of the majority of the brains and property of the South to govern the cities and the States, and in the Southern mind this is perfectly consistent with entire allegiance to the Government. I could name men who were abettors of what is called the "shotgun policy" whose national patriotism is beyond question, and who are warm promoters of negro education and the improvement of the condition of the colored people.

We might as well go to the bottom of this state of things, and look it squarely in the face. Under reconstruction, sometimes owing to a tardy acceptance of the new conditions by the ruling class, the State

governments and the municipalities fell under the
control of ignorant colored people, guided by un-
scrupulous white adventurers. States and cities were
prostrate under the heel of ignorance and fraud,
crushed with taxes, and no improvements to show for
them. It was ruin on the way to universal bankruptcy.
The regaining of power by the intelligent and the
property owners was a question of civilization. The
situation was intolerable. There is no Northern community that would have submitted to it; if it could
not have been changed by legal process, it would have
been upset by revolution, as it was at the South. Recognizing as we must the existence of race prejudice
and pride, it was nevertheless a struggle for existence.
The methods resorted to were often violent, and being sweeping, carried injustice. To be a Republican,
in the eyes of those smarting under carpet-bag government and the rule of the ignorant lately enfran-
chised, was to be identified with the detested carpet-
bag government and with negro rule. The Southern
Unionist and the Northern emigrant, who justly regarded the name Republican as the proudest they
could bear, identified as it was with the preservation
of the Union and the national credit, could not show
their Republican principles at the polls without personal danger in the country and social ostracism in
the cities. Social ostracism on account of politics
even outran social ostracism on account of participa-
tion in the education of the negroes. The very men
who would say, "I respect a man who fought for the
Union more than a Northern Copperhead, and if I
had lived North, no doubt I should have gone with
my section," would at the same time say, or think,

"But you cannot be a Republican down here now, for to be that is to identify yourself with the party here that is hostile to everything in life that is dear to us." This feeling was intensified by the memories of the war, but it was in a measure distinct from the war feeling, and it lived on when the latter grew weak, and it still survives in communities perfectly loyal to the Union, glad that slavery is ended, and sincerely desirous of the establishment and improvement of public education for colored and white alike.

Any tampering with the freedom of the ballot-box in a republic, no matter what the provocation, is dangerous; the methods used to regain white ascendancy were speedily adopted for purely party purposes and factional purposes; the chicanery, even the violence, employed to render powerless the negro and "carpet-bag" vote were freely used by partisans in local elections against each other, and in time became means of preserving party and ring ascendancy. Thoughtful men South as well as North recognize the vital danger to popular government if voting and the ballot-box are not sacredly protected. In a recent election in Texas, in a district where, I am told, the majority of the inhabitants are white, and the majority of the whites are Republicans, and the majority of the colored voters voted the Republican ticket, and greatly the larger proportion of the wealth and business of the district are in Republican hands, there was an election row; ballot-boxes were destroyed in several precincts, persons killed on both sides, and leading Republicans driven out of the State. This is barbarism. If the case is substantiated as stated, that in the district it was not a question of race ascendancy, but of party ascendancy, no fair-minded man in the South can do otherwise than condemn it, for under such conditions not only is a republican form of government impossible, but development and prosperity are impossible.

For this reason, and because separation of voters on class lines is always a peril, it is my decided impression that throughout the South, though not by everybody, a breaking up of the solidarity of the South would be welcome; that is to say, a breaking up of both the negro and the white vote, and the reforming upon lines of national and economic policy, as in the old days of Whig and Democrat, and liberty of free action in all local affairs, without regard to color or previous party relations. There are politicians who would preserve a solid South, or as a counterpart a solid North, for party purposes. But the sense of the country, the perception of business men North and South, is that this condition of politics interferes with the free play of industrial development, with emigration, investment of capital, and with that untrammelled agitation and movement in society which are the life of prosperous States.

Let us come a little closer to the subject, dealing altogether with facts, and not with opinions. The Republicans of the North protest against the injustice of an increased power in the Lower House and in the Electoral College based upon a vote which is not represented. It is a valid protest in law; there is no answer to it. What is the reply to it? The substance of hundreds of replies to it is that "we dare not let go so long as the negroes all vote together, regardless of local considerations or any economic problems what-

ever; we are in danger of a return to a rule of ignorance that was intolerable, and as long as you wave
the bloody shirt at the North, which means to us a
return to that rule, the South will be solid." The remark made by one man of political prominence was
perhaps typical: "The waving of the bloody shirt
suits me exactly as a political game; we should have
hard work to keep our State Democratic if you did
not wave it." So the case stands. The Republican
party will always insist on freedom, not only of political opinion, but of action, in every part of the Union;
and the South will keep "solid" so long as it fears, or
so long as politicians can persuade it to fear, the return of the late disastrous domination. And recognizing this fact, and speaking in the interest of no
party, but only in that of better understanding and of
the prosperity of the whole country, I cannot doubt
that the way out of most of our complications is in
letting the past drop absolutely, and addressing ourselves with sympathy and good-will all around to the
great economical problems and national issues. And
I believe that in this way also lies the speediest and
most permanent good to the colored as well as the
white population of the South.

There has been a great change in the aspect of the
South and in its sentiment within two years; or perhaps it would be more correct to say that the change
maturing for fifteen years is more apparent in a period
of comparative rest from race or sectional agitation.
The educational development is not more marvellous
than the industrial, and both are unparalleled in history. Let us begin by an illustration.

I stood one day before an assembly of four hundred

pupils of a colored college—called a college, but with a necessary preparatory department—children and well-grown young women and men. The buildings are fine, spacious, not inferior to the best modern educational buildings either in architectural appearance or in interior furnishing, with scientific apparatus, a library, the appliances approved by recent experience in teaching, with admirable methods and discipline, and an accomplished corps of instructors. The scholars were neat, orderly, intelligent in appearance. As I stood for a moment or two looking at their bright expectant faces the profound significance of the spectacle and the situation came over me, and I said : " I wonder if you know what you are doing, if you realize what this means. Here you are in a school the equal of any of its grade in the land, with better methods of instruction than prevailed anywhere when I was a boy, with the gates of all knowledge opened as freely to you as to any youth in the land—here, in this State, where only about twenty years ago it was a misdemeanor, punishable with fine and imprisonment, to teach a colored person to read and write. And I am brought here to see this fine school, as one of the best things he can show me in the city, by a Confederate colonel. Not in all history is there any instance of a change like this in a quarter of a century : no, not in one nor in two hundred years. It seems incredible."

This is one of the schools instituted and sustained by Northern friends of the South; but while it exhibits the capacity of the colored people for education, it is not so significant in the view we are now taking of the New South as the public schools. Indeed, next to the amazing industrial change in the South, nothing is so striking as the interest and progress in the matter of public schools. In all the cities we visited the people were enthusiastic about their common schools. It was a common remark, " I suppose we have one of the best school systems in the country." There is a wholesome rivalry to have the best. We found everywhere the graded system and the newest methods of teaching in vogue. In many of the primary rooms in both white and colored schools, when I asked if these little children knew the alphabet when they came to school, the reply was, " Not generally. We prefer they should not; we use the new method of teaching words." In many schools the youngest pupils were taught to read music by sight, and to understand its notation by exercises on the blackboard. In the higher classes generally, the instruction in arithmetic, in reading, in geography, in history, and in literature was wholly in the modern method.. In some of the geography classes and in the language classes I was reminded of the drill in the German schools. In all the cities, as far as I could learn, the public money was equally distributed to the colored and to the white schools, and the number of schools bore a just proportion to the number of the two races. When the town was equally divided in population, the number of pupils in the colored schools was about the same as the number in the white schools. There was this exception: though provision was made for a high-school to terminate the graded for both colors, the number in the colored high-school department was usually very small; and the reason given by colored and white teachers was that the colored children had not yet worked up to it. The colored people prefer teachers of their own race, and they are quite generally employed; but many of the colored schools have white teachers, and generally, I think, with better results, although I saw many thoroughly good colored teachers, and one or two colored classes under them that compared favorably with any white classes of the same grade.

The great fact, however, is that the common-school system has become a part of Southern life, is everywhere accepted as a necessity, and usually money is freely voted to sustain it. But practically, as an efficient factor in civilization, the system is yet undeveloped in the country districts. I can only speak from personal observation of the cities, but the universal testimony was that the common schools in the country for both whites and blacks are poor. Three months' schooling in the year is about the rule, and that of a slack and inferior sort, under incompetent teachers. In some places the colored people complain that ignorant teachers are put over them, who are chosen simply on political considerations. More than one respectable colored man told me that he would not send his children to such schools, but combined with a few others to get them private instruction. The colored people are more dependent on public schools than the whites, for while there are vast masses of colored people in city and country who have neither the money nor the disposition to sustain schools, in all the large places the whites are able to have excellent private schools, and do have them. Scarcely anywhere can the colored people as yet have a private school without white aid from somewhere. At the present rate of progress, and even of the increase of tax-paying ability, it must be a long time before the ignorant masses, white and black, in the country districts, scattered over a wide area, can have public schools at all efficient. The necessity is great. The danger to the State of ignorance is more and more apprehended; and it is upon this that many of the best men of the South base their urgent appeal for temporary aid from the Federal Government for public schools. It is seen that a State cannot soundly prosper unless its laborers are to some degree intelligent. This opinion is shown in little things. One of the great planters of the Yazoo Delta told me that he used to have no end of trouble in settling with his hands. But now that numbers of them can read and cipher, and explain the accounts to the others, he never has the least trouble.

One cannot speak too highly of the private schools in the South, especially of those for young women. I do not know what they were before the war, probably mainly devoted to "accomplishments," as most of girls' schools in the North were. Now most of them are wider in range, thorough in discipline, excellent in all the modern methods. Some of them, under accomplished women, are entirely in line with the best in the country. Before leaving this general subject of education, it is necessary to say that the advisability of industrial training, as supplementary to book-learning, is growing in favor, and that in some colored schools it is tried with good results.

When we come to the New Industrial South the change is marvellous, and so vast and various that I scarcely know where to begin in a short paper that

cannot go much into details. Instead of a South devoted to agriculture and politics, we find a South wide
awake to business, excited and even astonished at the
development of its own immense resources in metals,
marbles, coal, timber, fertilizers, eagerly laying lines
of communication, rapidly opening mines, building
furnaces, founderies, and all sorts of shops for util-
izing the native riches. It is like the discovery of a
new world. When the Northerner finds great founderies in Virginia using only (with slight exceptions)
the products of Virginia iron and coal mines ; when
he finds Alabama and Tennessee making iron so good
and so cheap that it finds ready market in Pennsylvania, and founderies multiplying near the great furnaces for supplying Northern markets; when he finds
cotton-mills running to full capacity on grades of
cheap cottons universally in demand throughout the
South and South-west; when he finds small industries,
such as paper-box factories and wooden bucket and
tub factories, sending all they can make into the
North and widely over the West; when he sees the
loads of most beautiful marbles shipped North; when
he learns that some of the largest and most important
engines and mill machinery were made in Southern
shops; when he finds in Richmond a "pole locomotive," made to run on logs laid end to end, and drag
out from Michigan forests and Southern swamps lumber hitherto inaccessible; when he sees worn-out highlands in Georgia and Carolina bear more cotton than
ever before by help of a fertilizer the base of which is
the cotton-seed itself (worth more as a fertilizer than
it was before the oil was extracted from it); when he
sees a multitude of small shops giving employment to

men, women, and children who never had any work of that sort to do before ; and when he sees Roanoke iron cast in Richmond into car-irons, and returned to a car-factory in Roanoke which last year sold three hundred cars to the New York and New England Railroad—he begins to open his eyes. The South is manufacturing a great variety of things needed in the house, on the farm, and in the shops, for home consumption, and already sends to the North and West several manufactured products. With iron, coal, timber contiguous and easily obtained, the amount sent out is certain to increase as the labor becomes more skilful. The most striking industrial development to-day is in iron, coal, lumber, and marbles; the more encouraging for the self-sustaining life of the Southern people is the multiplication of small industries in nearly every city I visited.

When I have been asked what impressed me most in this hasty tour, I have always said that the most notable thing was that everybody was at work. In many cities this was literally true: every man, woman, and child was actively employed, and in most there were fewer idlers than in many Northern towns. There are, of course, slow places, antiquated methods, easy - going ways, a - hundred - years - behind - the - time makeshifts, but the spirit in all the centres, and leavening the whole country, is work. Perhaps the greatest revolution of all in Southern sentiment is in regard to the dignity of labor. Labor is honorable, made so by the example of the best in the land. There are, no doubt, fossils or Bourbons, sitting in the midst of the ruins of their estates, martyrs to an ancient pride; but usually the leaders in business and enterprise bear names well known in politics and society. The nonsense that it is beneath the dignity of any man or woman to work for a living is pretty much eliminated from the Southern mind. It still remains true that the Anglo-Saxon type is prevalent in the South; but in all the cities the business sign-boards show that the enterprising Hebrew is increasingly prominent as merchant and trader, and he is becoming a plantation owner as well.

It cannot be too strongly impressed upon the public mind that the South, to use a comprehensible phrase, "has joined the procession." Its mind is turned to the development of its resources, to business, to enterprise, to education, to economic problems; it is marching with the North in the same purpose of wealth by industry. It is true that the railways, mines, and furnaces could not have been without enormous investments of Northern capital, but I was continually surprised to find so many and important local industries the result solely of home capital, made and saved since the war.

In this industrial change, in the growth of manufactures, the Southern people are necessarily divided on the national economic problems. Speaking of it purely from the side of political economy and not of politics, great sections of the South—whole States, in fact—are becoming more in favor of "protection" every day. All theories aside, whenever a man begins to work up the raw material at hand into manufactured articles for the market, he thinks that the revenue should be so adjusted as to help and not to hinder him.

Underlying everything else is the negro problem. It is the most difficult ever given to a people to solve.

8

It must, under our Constitution, be left to the States concerned, and there is a general hopefulness that time and patience will solve it to the advantage of both races. The negro is generally regarded as the best laborer in the world, and there is generally goodwill towards him, desire that he shall be educated and become thrifty. The negro has more confidence now than formerly in the white man, and he will go to him for aid and advice in everything except politics. Again and again colored men said to me, "If anybody tells you that any considerable number of colored men are Democrats, don't you believe him ; it is not so." The philanthropist who goes South will find many things to encourage him, but if he knows the colored people thoroughly, he will lose many illusions. But to speak of things hopeful, the progress in education, in industry, in ability to earn money, is extraordinary—much greater than ought to have been expected in twenty years even by their most sanguine friends, and it is greater now than at any other period. They are generally well paid, according to the class of work they do. Usually I found the same wages for the same class of work as whites received. I cannot say how this is in remote country districts. The treatment of laborers depends, I have no doubt, as elsewhere, upon the nature of the employer. In some districts I heard that the negroes never got out of debt, never could lay up anything, and were in a very bad condition. But on some plantations certainly, and generally in the cities, there is an improvement in thrift shown in the ownership of bits of land and houses, and in the possession of neat and pretty homes. As to morals, the gain is slower, but it is discernible, and exhibited in a growing public opinion against immorality and lax family relations. He is no friend to the colored people who blinks this subject, and does not plainly say to them that their position as citizens in the enjoyment of all civil rights depends quite as much upon their personal virtue and their acquiring habits of thrift as it does upon school privileges.

I had many interesting talks with representative colored men in different sections. While it is undoubtedly true that more are indifferent to politics than formerly, owing to causes already named and to the unfulfilled promises of wheedling politicians, it would be untrue to say that there is not great soreness over the present situation. At Nashville I had an interview with eight or ten of the best colored citizens, men of all shades of color. One of them was a trusted clerk in the post-office; another was a mail agent, who had saved money, and made more by an investment in Birmingham; another was a lawyer of good practice in the courts, a man of decided refinement and cultivation; another was at the head of one of the leading transportation lines in the city, and another had the largest provision establishment in town, and both were men of considerable property; and another, a slave when the war ended, was a large furniture dealer, and reputed worth a hundred thousand dollars. They were all solid, sensible business men, and all respected as citizens. They talked most intelligently of politics, and freely about social conditions. In regard to voting in Tennessee there was little to complain of; but in regard to Mississippi, as an illustration, it was an outrage that the dominant

party had increased power in Congress and in the
election of President, while the colored Republican
vote did not count. What could they do? Some
said that probably nothing could be done; time must
be left to cure the wrong. Others wanted the Federal Government to interfere, at least to the extent of
making a test case on some member of Congress that
his election was illegal. They did not think that
need excite anew any race prejudice. As to exciting
race and sectional agitation, we discussed this question : whether the present marvellous improvement
of the colored people, with general good-will, or at
least a truce everywhere, would not be hindered by
anything like a race or class agitation ; that is to say,
whether under the present conditions of education
and thrift the colored people (whatever injustice they
felt) were not going on faster towards the realization
of all they wanted than would be possible under any
circumstances of adverse agitation. As a matter of
policy most of them assented to this. I put this question : "In the first reconstruction days, how many
colored men were there in the State of Mississippi
fitted either by knowledge of letters, law, political
economy, history, or politics to make laws for the
State?" Very few. Well, then, it was unfortunate
that they should have attempted it. There are more
to-day, and with education and the accumulation of
property the number will constantly increase. In a
republic, power usually goes with intelligence and
property.

Finally I asked this intelligent company, every
man of which stood upon his own ability in perfect
self-respect, " What do you want here in the way of

civil rights that you have not?" The reply from one was that he got the respect of the whites just as he was able to command it by his ability and by making money, and, with a touch of a sense of injustice, he said he had ceased to expect that the colored race would get it in any other way. Another reply was—and this was evidently the deep feeling of all: "We want to be treated like men, like anybody else, regardless of color. We don't mean by this social equality at all; that is a matter that regulates itself among whites and colored people everywhere. We want the public conveyances open to us according to the fare we pay; we want privilege to go to hotels and to theatres, operas and places of amusement. We wish you could see our families and the way we live; you would then understand that we cannot go to the places assigned us in concerts and theatres without loss of self-respect." I might have said, but I did not, that the question raised by this last observation is not a local one, but as wide as the world.

If I tried to put in a single sentence the most widespread and active sentiment in the South to-day, it would be this: The past is put behind us; we are one with the North in business and national ambition: we want a sympathetic recognition of this fact.

VII.

A FAR AND FAIR COUNTRY.

Lewis and Clarke, sent out by Mr. Jefferson in 1804 to discover the North-west by the route of the Missouri River, left the town of St. Charles early in the spring, sailed and poled and dragged their boats up the swift, turbulent, and treacherous stream all summer, wintered with the Mandan Indians, and reached the Great Falls of the Missouri in about a year and a quarter from the beginning of their voyage. Now, when we wish to rediscover this interesting country, which is still virgin land, we lay down a railway-track in the spring and summer, and go over there in the autumn in a palace-car—a much more expeditious and comfortable mode of exploration.

In beginning a series of observations and comments upon Western life it is proper to say that the reader is not to expect exhaustive statistical statements of growth or development, nor descriptions, except such as will illustrate the point of view taken of the making of the Great West. Materialism is the most obtrusive feature of a cursory observation, but it does not interest one so much as the forces that underlie it, the enterprise and the joyousness of conquest and achievement that it stands for, or the finer processes evolved in the marvellous building up of new societies. What is the spirit, what is the civilization of the West? I have not the presumption to expect to an-

swer these large questions to any one's satisfaction—
least of all to my own—but if I may be permitted to
talk about them familiarly, in the manner that one
speaks to his friends of what interested him most in a
journey, and with flexibility in passing from one topic
to another, I shall hope to contribute something to a
better understanding between the territories of a vast
empire. How vast this republic is, no one can at all
appreciate who does not actually travel over its wide
areas. To many of us the West is still the West of
the geographies of thirty years ago; it is the simple
truth to say that comparatively few Eastern people
have any adequate conception of what lies west of
Chicago and St. Louis: perhaps a hazy geographical
notion of it, but not the faintest idea of its civilization
and society. Now, a good understanding of each other between the great sections of the republic is politically of the first importance. We shall hang together
as a nation ; blood, relationship, steel rails, navigable
waters, trade, absence of natural boundaries, settle
that. We shall pull and push and grumble, we shall
vituperate each other, parties will continue to make
capital out of sectional prejudice, and wantonly in-
flame it (what a pitiful sort of "politics" that is!),
but we shall stick together like wax. Still, anything
like smooth working of our political machine depends
upon good understanding between sections. And the
remark applies to East and West as well as to North
and South It is a common remark at the West that
"Eastern people know nothing about us ; they think
us half civilized ;" and there is mingled with slight
irritability at this ignorance a waxing feeling of superiority over the East in force and power. One would

not say that repose as yet goes along with this sense
of great capacity and great achievement; indeed, it
is inevitable that in a condition of development and
of quick growth unparalleled in the history of the
world there should be abundant self-assertion and
even monumental boastfulness.

When the Western man goes East he carries the
consciousness of playing a great part in the making
of an empire; his horizon is large; but he finds himself surrounded by an atmosphere of indifference or
non-comprehension of the prodigiousness of his country, of incredulity as to the refinement and luxury of
his civilization; and self-assertion is his natural defence. This longitudinal incredulity and swagger is
a curious phenomenon. London thinks New York
puts on airs, New York complains of Chicago's want
of modesty, Chicago can see that Kansas City and
Omaha are aggressively boastful, and these cities acknowledge the expansive self-appreciation of Denver
and Helena.

Does going West work a radical difference in a
man's character? Hardly. We are all cut out of
the same piece of cloth. The Western man is the
Eastern or the Southern man let loose, with his lead-
ing-strings cut. But the change of situation creates
immense diversity in interests and in spirit. One has
but to take up any of the great newspapers, say in St.
Paul or Minneapolis, to be aware that he is in another
world of ideas, of news, of interests. The topics that
most interest the East he does not find there, nor much
of its news. Persons of whom he reads daily in the
East drop out of sight, and other persons, magnates
in politics, packing, railways, loom up. It takes col-

umns to tell the daily history of places which have heretofore only caught the attention of the Eastern reader for freaks of the thermometer, and he has an opportunity to read daily pages about Dakota, concerning which a weekly paragraph has formerly satisfied his curiosity. Before he can be absorbed in these lively and intelligent newspapers he must change the whole current of his thoughts, and take up other subjects, persons, and places than those that have occupied his mind. He is in a new world.

One of the most striking facts in the West is State pride, attachment to the State, the profound belief of every citizen that his State is the best. Engendered perhaps at first by a permanent investment and the spur of self-interest, it speedily becomes a passion, as strong in the newest State as it is in any one of the original thirteen. Rivalry between cities is sharp, and civic pride is excessive, but both are outdone by the larger devotion to the commonwealth. And this pride is developed in the inhabitants of a Territory as soon as it is organized. Montana has condensed the ordinary achievements of a century into twenty years, and loyalty to its present and expectation of its future are as strong in its citizens as is the attachment of men of Massachusetts to the State of nearly three centuries of growth. In Nebraska I was pleased with the talk of a clergyman who had just returned from three months' travel in Europe. He was full of his novel experiences; he had greatly enjoyed the trip; but he was glad to get back to Nebraska and its full, vigorous life. In England and on the Continent he had seen much to interest him; but he could not help comparing Europe with Nebraska; and as for him, this was the substance of it: give him Nebraska every time. What astonished him most, and wounded his feelings (and there was a note of pathos in his statement of it), was the general foreign ignorance abroad about Nebraska—the utter failure in the European mind to take it in. I felt guilty, for to me it had been little more than a geographical expression, and I presume the Continent did not know whether Nebraska was a new kind of patent medicine or a new sort of religion. To the clergymen this ignorance of the central, richest, about-to-be-the-most-important of States, was simply incredible.

This feeling is not only admirable in itself, but it has an incalculable political value, especially in the West, where there is a little haze as to the limitations of Federal power, and a notion that the Constitution was swaddling-clothes for an infant, which manly limbs may need to kick off. Healthy and even assertive State pride is the only possible counterbalance in our system against that centralization which tends to corruption in the centre and weakness and discontent in the individual members.

It should be added that the West, speaking of it generally, is defiantly "American." It wants a more vigorous and assertive foreign policy. Conscious of its power, the growing pains in the limbs of the young giant will not let it rest. That this is the most magnificent country, that we have the only government beyond criticism, that our civilization is far and away the best, does not admit of doubt. It is refreshing to see men who believe in something heartily and without reserve, even if it is only in themselves. There is a tonic in this challenge of all time and history. A certain attitude of American assertion towards other powers is desired. For want of this our late representatives to Great Britain are said to be un-American; "political dudes" is what the Governor of Iowa calls them. It is his indictment against the present Minister to St. James that "he is numerous in his visits to the castles of English noblemen, and profuse in his obsequiousness to British aristocrats." And perhaps the Governor speaks for a majority of Western voters and fighters when he says that "timidity has characterized our State Department for the last twenty years."

By chance I begin these Western studies with the North-west. Passing by for the present the intelligent and progressive State of Wisconsin, we will consider Minnesota and the vast region at present more or less tributary to it. It is necessary to remember that the State was admitted to the Union in 1858, and that its extraordinary industrial development dates from the building of the first railway in its limits— ten miles from St. Paul to St. Anthony—in 1862. For this road the first stake was driven and the first shovelful of earth lifted by a citizen of St. Paul who has lived to see his State gridironed with railways, and whose firm constructed in 1887 over eleven hundred miles of railroad.

It is unnecessary to dwell upon the familiar facts that Minnesota is a great wheat State, and that it is intersected by railways that stimulate the enormous yield and market it with facility. The discovery that the State, especially the Red River Valley, and Dakota and the country beyond, were peculiarly adapted to the production of hard spring-wheat, which is the most desirable for flour, probably gave this vast region its first immense advantage. Minnesota, a prairie country, rolling, but with no important hills, well watered, well grassed, with a repellent reputation for severe winters, not well adapted to corn, nor friendly to most fruits, attracted nevertheless hardy and adventurous people, and proved specially inviting to the Scandinavians, who are tough and industrious. It would grow wheat without end. And wheat is the easiest crop to raise, and returns the greatest income for the least labor. In good seasons and with good prices it is a mine of wealth. But Minnesota had to learn that one industry does not suffice to make a State, and that wheat-raising alone is not only unreliable, but exhaustive. The grasshopper scourge was no doubt a blessing in disguise. It helped to turn the attention of farmers to cattle and sheep, and to more varied agriculture. I shall have more to say about this in connection with certain most interesting movements in Wisconsin.

The notion has prevailed that the North-west was being absorbed by owners of immense tracts of land, great capitalists who by the aid of machinery were monopolizing the production of wheat, and crowding out small farmers. There are still vast wheat farms under one control, but I am happy to believe that the danger of this great land monopoly has reached its height, and the tendency is the other way. Small farms are on the increase, practising a more varied agriculture. The reason is this : A plantation of 5000 or 15,000 acres, with a good season, freedom from blight and insects, will enrich the owner if prices are good ; but one poor crop, with low prices, will bankrupt him. Whereas the small farmer can get a living under the most adverse circumstances, and taking one year with another, accumulate something, especially if he varies his products and feeds them to stock, thus returning the richness of his farm to itself. The skinning of the land by sending away its substance in hard wheat is an improvidence of natural resources, which belongs, like cattle-ranging, to a half-civilized era, and like cattle-ranging has probably seen its best days. One incident illustrates what can be done. Mr. James J. Hill, the president of the Manitoba railway system, an importer and breeder of fine cattle on his Minnesota country place, recently gave and loaned a number of blooded bulls to farmers over a wide area in Minnesota and Dakota. The result of this benefaction has been surprising in adding to the wealth of those regions and the prosperity of the farmers. It is the beginning of a varied farming and of cattle production, which will be of incalculable benefit to the North-west.

It is in the memory of men still in active life when the Territory of Minnesota was supposed to be beyond the pale of desirable settlement. The State, except in the north-east portion, is now well settled, and well sprinkled with thriving villages and cities. Of the latter, St. Paul and Minneapolis are still a wonder to themselves, as they are to the world. I knew that they were big cities, having each a population nearly approaching 175,000, but I was not prepared to find them so handsome and substantial, and exhibiting such vigor and activity of movement. One of the most impressive things to an Eastern man in both of them is their public spirit, and the harmony with

which business men work together for anything which
will build up and beautify the city. I believe that
the ruling force in Minneapolis is of New England
stock, while St. Paul has a larger proportion of New
York people, with a mixture of Southern ; and I have
a fancy that there is a social shading that shows this
distinction. It is worth noting, however, that the
Southerner, transplanted to Minnesota or Montana,
loses the *laisser faire* with which he is credited at
home, and becomes as active and pushing as anybody.
Both cities have a very large Scandinavian population.
The laborers and the domestic servants are mostly
Swedes. In forecasting what sort of a State Minnesota is to be, the Scandinavian is a largely determining force. It is a virile element. The traveller is
impressed with the idea that the women whom he
sees at the stations in the country and in the city
streets are sturdy, ruddy, and better able to endure
the protracted season of cold and the highly stimulating atmosphere than the American-born women,
who tend to become nervous in these climatic conditions. The Swedes are thrifty, taking eagerly to
politics, and as ready to profit by them as anybody ;
unreservedly American in intention, and on the whole,
good citizens.

The physical difference of the two cities is mainly
one of situation. Minneapolis spreads out on both
sides of the Mississippi over a plain, from the gigantic
flouring-mills and the canal and the Falls of St. Anthony as a centre (the falls being, by-the-way, planked
over with a wooden apron to prevent the total wear-
ing away of the shaly rock) to rolling land and beautiful building sites on moderate elevations. Nature

has surrounded the city with a lovely country, diversified by lakes and forests, and enterprise has developed
it into one of the most inviting of summer regions.
Twelve miles west of it, Lake Minnetonka, naturally
surpassingly lovely, has become, by an immense expenditure of money, perhaps the most attractive summer resort in the North-west. Each city has a hotel
(the West in Minneapolis, the Ryan in St. Paul) which
would be distinguished monuments of cost and elegance in any city in the world, and each city has
blocks of business houses, shops, and offices of solidity
and architectural beauty, and each has many private
residences which are palaces in size, in solidity, and
interior embellishment, but they are scattered over
the city in Minneapolis, which can boast of no single
street equal to Summit Avenue in St. Paul. The most
conspicuous of the private houses is the stone mansion
of Governor Washburn, pleasing in color, harmonious
in design, but so gigantic that the visitor (who may
have seen palaces abroad) expects to find a somewhat
vacant interior. He is therefore surprised that the
predominating note is homelikeness and comfort, and
he does not see how a family of moderate size could
well get along with less than the seventy rooms (most
of them large) which they have at their disposal.

St. Paul has the advantage of picturesqueness of
situation. The business part of the town lies on a
spacious uneven elevation above the river, surrounded
by a semicircle of bluffs averaging something like two
hundred feet high. Up the sides of these the city
climbs, beautifying every vantage-ground with handsome and stately residences. On the north the bluffs
maintain their elevation in a splendid plateau, and

over this dry and healthful plain the two cities advance
to meet each other, and already meet in suburbs, colleges, and various public buildings. Summit Avenue
curves along the line of the northern bluff, and then
turns northward, two hundred feet broad, graded a
distance of over two miles, and with a magnificent
asphalt road-way for more than a mile. It is almost
literally a street of palaces, for although wooden structures alternate with the varied and architecturally interesting mansions of stone and brick on both sides,
each house is isolated, with a handsome lawn and ornamental trees, and the total effect is spacious and noble.
This avenue commands an almost unequalled view of
the sweep of bluffs round to the Indian Mounds, of
the city, the winding river, and the town and heights
of West St. Paul. It is not easy to recall a street and
view anywhere finer than this, and this is only one of
the streets on this plateau conspicuous for handsome
houses. I see no reason why St. Paul should not become, within a few years, one of the notably most
beautiful cities in the world. And it is now wonderfully well advanced in that direction. Of course the
reader understands that both these rapidly growing
cities are in the process of "making," and that means
cutting and digging and slashing, torn-up streets,
shabby structures alternating with gigantic and solid
buildings, and the usual unsightliness of transition and
growth.

Minneapolis has the State University, St. Paul the
Capitol, an ordinary building of brick, which will not
long, it is safe to say, suit the needs of the pride of
the State. I do not set out to describe the city, the
churches, big newspaper buildings, great wholesale

and ware houses, handsome club-house (the Minnesota
Club), stately City Hall, banks, Chamber of Commerce,
and so on. I was impressed with the size of the buildings needed to house the great railway offices. Nothing can give one a livelier idea of the growth and
grasp of Western business than one of these plain
structures, five or six stories high, devoted to the several departments of one road or system of roads,
crowded with busy officials and clerks, offices of the
president, vice - president, assistant of the president,
secretary, treasurer, engineer, general manager, general superintendent, general freight, general traffic,
general passenger, perhaps a land officer, and so on—
affairs as complicated and vast in organization and extensive in detail as those of a State government.

There are sixteen railways which run in Minnesota,
having a total mileage of 5024 miles in the State.
Those which have over two hundred miles of road in
the State are the Chicago and North-western, Chicago,
Milwaukee, and St. Paul, Chicago, St. Paul, Minneapolis, and Omaha, Minneapolis and St. Louis, Northern
Pacific, St. Paul and Duluth, and the St. Paul, Minneapolis, and Manitoba. The names of these roads give
little indication of their location, as the reader knows,
for many of them run all over the North-west like
spider-webs.

It goes without saying that the management of
these great interests—imperial, almost continental in
scope—requires brains, sobriety, integrity ; and one is
not surprised to find that the railways command and
pay liberally for the highest talent and skill. It is
not merely a matter of laying rails and running trains,
but of developing the resources—one might almost say

9

creating the industries — of vast territories. These
are gigantic interests, concerning which there is such
sharp rivalry and competition, and as a rule it is the
generous, large-minded policy that wins. Somebody
has said that the railway managers and magnates (I
do not mean those who deal in railways for the sake
of gambling) are the *élite* of Western life. I am not
drawing distinctions of this sort, but I will say, and
it might as well be said here and simply, that next to
the impression I got of the powerful hand of the railways in the making of the West, was that of the high
character, the moral stamina, the ability, the devotion
to something outside themselves, of the railway men
I met in the North-west. Specialists many of them
are, and absorbed in special work, but I doubt if any
other profession or occupation can show a proportionally larger number of broad-minded, fair-minded men,
of higher integrity and less pettiness, or more inclined
to the liberalizing culture in art and social life. Either dealing with large concerns has lifted up the
men, or the large opportunities have attracted men of
high talent and character; and I sincerely believe that
we should have no occasion for anxiety if the average
community did not go below the standard of railway
morality and honorable dealing.

What is the *raison d'être* of these two phenomenal
cities? why do they grow? why are they likely to
continue to grow? I confess that this was an enigma
to me until I had looked beyond to see what country
was tributary to them, what a territory they have to
supply. Of course, the railways, the flouring-mills,
the vast wholesale dry goods and grocery houses speak
for themselves. But I had thought of these cities as

on the confines of civilization. They are, however, the two posts of the gate-way to an empire. In order to comprehend their future, I made some little trips north-east and north-west.

Duluth, though as yet with only about twenty-five to thirty thousand inhabitants, feels itself, by its position, a rival of the cities on the Mississippi. A few figures show the basis of this feeling. In 1880 the population was 3740; in 1886, 25,000. In 1880 the receipts of wheat were 1,347,679 bushels; in 1886, 22,425,730 bushels ; in 1880 the shipments of wheat 1,453,647 bushels; in 1886, 17,981,965 bushels. In 1880 the shipments of flour were 551,800 bushels ; in 1886, 1,500,000 bushels. In 1886 there were grain elevators with a capacity of 18,000,000 bushels. The tax valuation had increased from $669,012 in 1880 to $11,773,-729 in 1886. The following comparisons are made : The receipt of wheat in Chicago in 1885 was 19,266,-000 bushels; in Duluth, 14,880,000 bushels. The receipt of wheat in 1886 was at Duluth 22,425,730 bushels; at Minneapolis, 33,394,450; at Chicago, 15,982,524; at Milwaukee, 7,930,102. This shows that an increasing amount of the great volume of wheat raised in north Dakota and north-west Minnesota (that is, largely in the Red River Valley) is seeking market by way of Duluth and water transportation. In 1869 Minnesota raised about 18,000,000 bushels of wheat; in 1886, about 50,000,000. In 1869 Dakota grew no grain at all ; in 1886 it produced about 50,000,000 bushels of wheat. To understand the amount of transportation the reader has only to look on the map and see the railway lines—the Northern Pacific, the Chicago, St. Paul, Minneapolis, and Omaha, the St.

Paul, Minneapolis, and Manitoba, and other lines, running to Duluth, and sending out spurs, like the roots of an elm-tree, into the wheat lands of the North-west.

Most of the route from St. Paul to Duluth is uninteresting; there is nothing picturesque except the Dalles of the St. Louis River, and a good deal of the country passed through seems agriculturally of no value. The approaches to Duluth, both from the Wisconsin and the Minnesota side, are rough and vexatious by reason of broken, low, hummocky, and swamp land. Duluth itself, with good harbor facilities, has only a strip of level ground for a street, and inadequate room for railway tracks and transfers. The town itself climbs up the hill, whence there is a good view of the lake and the Wisconsin shore, and a fair chance for both summer and winter breezes. The residence portion of the town, mainly small wooden houses, has many highly ornamental dwellings, and the long street below, following the shore, has many noble buildings of stone and brick, which would be a credit to any city. Grading and sewer-making render a large number of the streets impassable, and add to the signs of push, growth, and business excitement.

For the purposes of trade, Duluth, and the towns of Superior and West Superior, in Wisconsin, may be considered one port; and while Duluth may continue to be the money and business centre, the expansion for railway terminal facilities, elevators, and manufactures is likely to be in the Wisconsin towns on the south side of the harbor. From the Great Northern Elevator in West Superior the view of the other elevators, of the immense dock room, of the harbor and lake, of a net-work of miles and miles of terminal

tracks of the various roads, gives one an idea of gigantic commerce ; and the long freight trains laden with
wheat, glutting all the roads and sidings approaching
Duluth, speak of the bursting abundance of the tributary country. This Great Northern Elevator, belonging to the Manitoba system, is the largest in the
world; its dimensions are 360 feet long, 95 in width,
115 in height, with a capacity of 1,800,000 bushels,
and with facilities for handling 40 car-loads an hour,
or 400 cars in a day of 10 hours. As I am merely illustrating the amount of the present great staple of
the North-west, I say nothing here of the mineral,
stone, and lumber business of this region. Duluth
has a cool, salubrious summer and a snug winter climate. I ought to add that the enterprising inhabitants attend to education as well as the elevation of
grain ; the city has eight commodious school buildings.

To return to the Mississippi. To understand what
feeds Minneapolis and St. Paul, and what country
their great wholesale houses supply, one must take
the rail and penetrate the vast North-west. The famous Park or Lake district, between St. Cloud (75
miles north-west of St. Paul) and Fergus Falls, is too
well known to need description. A rolling prairie,
with hundreds of small lakes, tree fringed, it is a region of surpassing loveliness, and already dotted, as
at Alexandria, with summer resorts. The whole region, up as far as Moorhead (240 miles from St. Paul),
on the Red River, opposite Fargo, Dakota, is well settled, and full of prosperous towns. At Fargo, crossing the Northern Pacific, we ran parallel with the Red
River, through a line of bursting elevators and wheat

farms, down to Grand Forks, where we turned westward, and passed out of the Red River Valley, rising to the plateau at Larimore, some three hundred feet above it.

The Red River, a narrow but deep and navigable stream, has from its source to Lake Winnipeg a tortuous course of about 600 miles, while the valley itself is about 285 miles long, of which 180 miles is in the United States. This valley, which has astonished the world by its wheat production, is about 160 miles in breadth, and level as a floor, except that it has a northward slope of, I believe, about five feet to the mile. The river forms the boundary between Minnesota and Dakota; the width of valley on the Dakota side varies from 50 to 100 miles. The rich soil is from two to three feet deep, underlaid with clay. Fargo, the centre of this valley, is 940 feet above the sea. The climate is one of extremes between winter and summer, but of much constancy of cold or heat according to the season. Although it is undeniable that one does not feel the severe cold there as much as in more humid atmospheres, it cannot be doubted that the long continuance of extreme cold is trying to the system. And it may be said of all the North-west, including Minnesota, that while it is more favorable to the lungs than many regions where the thermometer has less sinking power, it is not free from catarrh (the curse of New England), nor from rheumatism. The climate seems to me specially stimulating, and I should say there is less excuse here for the use of stimulants (on account of "lowness" or lassitude) than in almost any other portion of the United States with which I am acquainted.

But whatever attractions or drawbacks this territory has as a place of residence, its grain and stock growing capacity is inexhaustible, and having seen it, we begin to comprehend the vigorous activity and growth of the twin cities. And yet this is the beginning of resources ; there lies Dakota, with its 149,100 square miles (96,596,480 acres of land), larger than all the New England States and New York combined, and Montana beyond, together making a belt of hard spring-wheat land sufficient, one would think, to feed the world. When one travels over 1200 miles of it, doubt ceases.

I cannot better illustrate the resources and enterprise of the North-west than by speaking in some detail of the St. Paul, Minneapolis, and Manitoba Railway (known as the Manitoba system), and by telling briefly the story of one season's work, not because this system is bigger or more enterprising or of more importance in the West than some others I might name, but because it has lately pierced a comparatively unknown region, and opened to settlement a fertile empire.

The Manitoba system gridirons north Minnesota, runs to Duluth, puts two tracks down the Red River Valley (one on each side of the river) to the Canada line, sends out various spurs into Dakota, and operates a main line from Grand Forks westward through the whole of Dakota, and through Montana as far as the Great Falls of the Missouri, and thence through the cañon of the Missouri and the cañon of the Prickly-Pear to Helena—in all about 3000 miles of track. Its president is Mr. James J. Hill, a Canadian by birth, whose rapid career from that of a clerk on the St.

Paul levee to his present position of influence, opportunity, and wealth is a romance in itself, and whose
character, integrity, tastes, and accomplishments, and
domestic life, were it proper to speak of them, would
satisfactorily answer many of the questions that are
asked about the materialistic West.

The Manitoba line west had reached Minot, 530
miles from St. Paul, in 1886. I shall speak of its extension in 1887, which was intrusted to Mr. D. C.
Shepard, a veteran engineer and railway builder of
St. Paul, and his firm, Messrs. Shepard, Winston &
Co.   Credit should be given by name to the men who
conducted this Napoleonic enterprise ; for it required
not only the advance of millions of money, but the
foresight, energy, vigilance, and capacity that insure
success in a distant military campaign.

It needs to be noted that the continuation of the
St. Paul, Minneapolis, and Manitoba road from Great
Falls to Helena, 98 miles, is called the Montana Central. The work to be accomplished in 1887 was to
grade 500 miles of railroad to reach Great Falls, to
put in the bridging and mechanical structures (by
hauling all material brought up by rail ahead of the
track by teams, so as not to delay the progress of the
track) on 530 miles of continuous railway, and to lay
and put in good running condition 643 miles of rails
continuously and from one end only.

In the winter of 1886–87 the road was completed
to a point five miles west of Minot, and work was
done beyond which if consolidated would amount to
about fifty miles of completed grading, and the mechanical structures were done for twenty miles west
from Minot. On the Montana Central the grading

and mechanical structures were made from Helena
as a base, and completed before the track reached
Great Falls. St. Paul, Minneapolis, and Duluth were
the primary bases of operations, and generally speaking all materials, labor, fuel, and supplies originated
at these three points ; Minot was the secondary base,
and here in the winter of 1886–87 large depots of supplies and materials for construction were formed.

Track-laying began April 2, 1887, but was greatly
retarded by snow and ice in the completed cuts, and
by the grading, which was heavy. The cuts were
frozen more or less up to May 15th. The forwarding
of grading forces to Minot began April 6th, but it
was a labor of considerable magnitude to outfit them
at Minot and get them forward to the work ; so that
it was as late as May 10th before the entire force was
under employment.

The average force on the grading was 3300 teams
and about 8000 men. Upon the track-laying, surfac-
ing, piling, and timber-work there were 225 teams
and about 650 men. The heaviest work was encountered on the eastern end, so that the track was
close upon the grading up to the 10th of June. Some
of the cuttings and embankments were heavy. After
the 10th of June progress upon the grading was very
rapid. From the mouth of Milk River to Great Falls
(a distance of 200 miles) grading was done at an
average rate of seven miles a day. Those who saw
this army of men and teams stretching over the
prairie and casting up this continental highway think
they beheld one of the most striking achievements of
civilization.

I may mention that the track is all cast up (even

where the grading is easy) to such a height as to relieve it of drifting snow ; and to give some idea of the character of the work, it is noted that in preparing it there were moved 9,700,000 cubic yards of earth, 15,000 cubic yards of loose rock, and 17,500 cubic yards of solid rock, and that there were hauled ahead of the track and put in the work to such distance as would not obstruct the track - laying (in some instances 30 miles), 9,000,000 feet (board measure) of timber and 390,000 lineal feet of piling.

On the 5th of August the grading of the entire line to Great Falls was either finished or properly manned for its completion the first day of September, and on the 10th of August it became necessary to remove outfits to the east as they completed their work, and about 2500 teams and their quota of men were withdrawn between the 10th and 20th of August, and placed upon work elsewhere.

The record of track laid is as follows : April 2d to 30th, 30 miles; May, 82 miles; June, 79.8 miles; July, 100.8 miles; August, 115.4 miles; September, 102.4 miles ; up to October 15th to Great Falls, 34.6 miles —a total to Great Falls of 545 miles. October 16th being Sunday, no track was laid. The track started from Great Falls Monday, October 17th, and reached Helena on Friday, November 18th, a distance of 98 miles, making a grand total of 643 miles, and an average rate for every working-day of three and one-quarter miles. It will thus be seen that laying a good road was a much more expeditious method of reaching the Great Falls of the Missouri than that adopted by Lewis and Clarke.

Some of the details of this construction and track-

laying will interest railroad men. On the 16th of July
7 miles and 1040 feet of track were laid, and on the
8th of August 8 miles and 60 feet were laid, in each
instance by daylight, and by the regular gang of
track-layers, without any increase of their numbers
whatever. The entire work was done by handling
the iron on low iron cars, and depositing it on the
track from the car at the front end. The method
pursued was the same as when one mile of track is
laid per day in the ordinary manner. The force of
track-layers was maintained at the proper number for
the ordinary daily work, and was never increased to
obtain any special result. The result on the 11th of
August was probably decreased by a quarter to a half
mile by the breaking of an axle of an iron car while
going to the front with its load at about 4 P.M. From
six to eight iron cars were employed in doing this day's
work. The number ordinarily used was four to five.

Sidings were graded at intervals of seven to eight
miles, and spur tracks, laid on the natural surface,
put in at convenient points, sixteen miles apart, for
storage of materials and supplies at or near the front.
As the work went on, the spur tracks in the rear were
taken up. The construction train contained box cars
two and three stories high, in which workmen were
boarded and lodged. Supplies, as a rule, were taken
by wagon-trains from the spur tracks near the front
to their destination, an average distance of one hundred miles and an extreme one of two hundred miles.
Steamboats were employed to a limited extent on the
Missouri River in supplying such remote points as
Fort Benton and the Coal Banks, but not more than
fifteen per cent. of the transportation was done by

steamers. A single item illustrating the magnitude of the supply transportation is that there were shipped to Minot and forwarded and consumed on the work 590,000 bushels of oats.

It is believed that the work of grading 500 miles of railroad in five months, and the transportation into the country of everything consumed, grass and water excepted, and of every rail, tie, bit of timber, pile, tool, machine, man, or team employed, and laying 643 miles of track in seven and a half months, from one end, far exceeds in magnitude and rapidity of execution any similar undertaking in this or any other country. It reflects also the greatest credit on the managers of the railway transportation (it is not invidious to mention the names of Mr. A. Manvel, general manager, and Mr. J. M. Egan, general superintendent, upon whom the working details devolved) when it is stated that the delays for material or supplies on the entire work did not retard it in the aggregate one hour. And every hour counted in this masterly campaign.

The Western people apparently think no more of throwing down a railroad, if they want to go anywhere, than a conservative Easterner does of taking an unaccustomed walk across country; and the railway constructors and managers are a little amused at the Eastern slowness and want of facility in construction and management. One hears that the East is antiquated, and does not know anything about railroad building. Shovels, carts, and wheelbarrows are of a past age; the big wheel-scraper does the business. It is a common remark that a contractor accustomed to Eastern work is not desired on a Western job.

On Friday afternoon, November 18th, the news was

flashed that the last rail was laid, and at 6 P.M. a special train was on the way from St. Paul with a double complement of engineers and train-men. For the first 500 miles there was more or less delay in avoiding the long and frequent freight trains, but after that not much except the necessary stops for cleaning the engine. Great Falls, about 1100 miles, was reached Sunday noon, in thirty-six hours, an average of over thirty miles an hour. A part of the time the speed was as much as fifty miles an hour. The track was solid, evenly graded, heavily tied, well aligned, and the cars ran over it with no more swing and bounce than on an old road. The only exception to this is the piece from Great Falls to Helena, which had not been surfaced all the way. It is excellent railway construction, and it is necessary to emphasize this when we consider the rapidity with which it was built.

The company has built this road without land grant or subsidy of any kind. The Montana extension, from Minot, Dakota, to Great Falls, runs mostly through Indian and military reservations, permission to pass through being given by special Act of Congress, and the company buying 200 feet road-way. Little of it, therefore, is open to settlement.

These reservations, naming them in order westward, are as follows: The Fort Berthold Indian reservation, Dakota, the eastern boundary of which is twenty-seven miles west of Minot, has an area of 4550 square miles (about as large as Connecticut), or 2,912,000 acres. The Fort Buford military reservation, lying in Dakota and Montana, has an area of 900 square miles, or 576,-000 acres. The Blackfeet Indian reserve has an area of 34,000 square miles (the State of New York has 46,-

000), or 21,760,000 acres. The Fort Assiniboin military reserve has an area of 869.82 square miles, or 556,684 acres.

It is a liberal estimate that there are 6000 Indians on the Blackfeet and Fort Berthold reservations. As nearly as I could ascertain, there are not over 3500 Indians (some of those I saw were Crees on a long visit from Canada) on the Blackfeet reservation of about 22,000,000 acres. Some judges put the number as low as 2500 to all this territory, and estimate that there was about one Indian to ten square miles, or one Indian family to fifty square miles. We rode through 300 miles of this territory along the Milk River, nearly every acre of it good soil, with thick, abundant grass, splendid wheat land.

I have no space to take up the Indian problem. But the present condition of affairs is neither fair to white settlers nor just or humane to the Indians. These big reservations are of no use to them, nor they to the reservations. The buffaloes have disappeared; they do not live by hunting; they cultivate very little ground; they use little even to pasture their ponies. They are fed and clothed by the Government, and they camp about the agencies in idleness, under conditions that pauperize them, destroy their manhood, degrade them into dependent, vicious lives. The reservations ought to be sold, and the proceeds devoted to educating the Indians and setting them up in a self-sustaining existence. They should be allotted an abundance of good land, in the region to which they are acclimated, in severalty, and under such restrictions that they cannot alienate it at least for a generation or two. As the Indian is now, he will neither work, nor keep clean, nor live decently. Close to, the Indian is not a romantic object, and certainly no better now morally than Lewis and Clarke depicted him in 1804. But he is a man; he has been barbarously treated; and it is certainly not beyond honest administration and Christian effort to better his condition. And his condition will not be improved simply by keeping from settlement and civilization the magnificent agricultural territory that is reserved to him.

Of this almost unknown country, pierced by the road west from Larimore, I can only make the briefest notes. I need not say that this open, unobstructed highway of arable land and habitable country, from the Red River to the Rocky Mountains, was an astonishment to me; but it is more to the purpose to say that the fertile region was a surprise to railway men who are perfectly familiar with the West.

We had passed some snow in the night, which had been very cold, but there was very little at Larimore, a considerable town ; there was a high, raw wind during the day, and a temperature of about 10° above, which heavily frosted the car windows. At Devil's Lake (a body of brackish water twenty-eight miles long) is a settlement three years old, and from this and two insignificant stations beyond were shipped, in 1887, 1,500,000 bushels of wheat. The country beyond is slightly rolling, fine land, has much wheat, little houses scattered about, some stock, very promising altogether. Minot, where we crossed the Mouse River the second time, is a village of 700 people, with several brick houses and plenty of saloons. Thence we ran up to a plateau some three hundred feet higher than the Mouse River Valley, and found a land more broken, and interspersed with rocky land and bowlders—the only touch of "bad lands" I recall on the route. We crossed several small streams, White Earth, Sandy, Little Muddy, and Muddy, and before reaching Williston descended into the valley of the Missouri, reached Fort Buford, where the Yellowstone comes in, entered what is called Paradise Valley, and continued parallel with the Missouri as far as the mouth of Milk River. Before reaching this we crossed the Big Muddy and the Poplar rivers, both rising in Canada. At Poplar Station is a large Indian agency, and hundreds of Teton Sioux Indians (I was told 1800) camped there in their conical tepees. I climbed the plateau above the station where the Indians bury their dead, wrapping the bodies in blankets and buffalo-robes, and suspending them aloft on crossbars supported by stakes, to keep them from the wolves. Beyond Assiniboin I saw a platform in a cottonwood-tree on which reposed the remains of a chief and his family. This country is all good, so far as I could see and learn.

It gave me a sense of geographical deficiency in my education to travel three hundred miles on a river I had never heard of before. But it happened on the Milk River, a considerable but not navigable stream, although some six hundred miles long. The broad Milk River Valley is in itself an empire of excellent land, ready for the plough and the wheat - sower. Judging by the grass (which cures into the most nutritious feed as it stands), there had been no lack of rain during the summer; but if there is lack of water, all the land can be irrigated by the Milk River, and it may also be said of the country beyond to Great Falls that frequent streams make irrigation easy, if there is scant rainfall. I should say that this would be the only question about water.

Leaving the Milk River Valley, we began to curve southward, passing Fort Assiniboin on our right. In this region and beyond at Fort Benton great herds of cattle are grazed by Government contractors, who supply the posts with beef. At the Big Sandy Station they were shipping cattle eastward. We crossed the Marias River (originally named Maria's River), a stream that had the respectful attention of Lewis and Clarke, and the Teton, a wilfully erratic watercourse in a narrow valley, which caused the railway constructors a good deal of trouble. We looked down, in passing, on Fort Benton, nestled in a bend of the Missouri ; a smart town, with a daily newspaper, an old trading station. Shortly after leaving Assiniboin we saw on our left the Bear Paw Mountains and the noble Highwood Mountains, fine peaks, snow-dusted, about thirty miles from us, and adjoining them the Belt Mountains. Between them is a shapely little pyramid called the Wolf Butte. Far to our right were the Sweet Grass Hills, on the Canada line, where gold-miners are at work. I have noted of all this country that it is agriculturally fine. After Fort Benton we had glimpses of the Rockies, off to the right (we had seen before the Little Rockies in the south, towards Yellowstone Park); then the Bird-tail Divide came in sight, and the mathematically Square Butte, sometimes called Fort Montana.

At noon, November 20th, we reached Great Falls, where the Sun River, coming in from the west, joins

10

the Missouri. The railway crosses the Sun River, and runs on up the left bank of the Missouri. Great Falls, which lies in a bend of the Missouri on the east side, was not then, but soon will be, connected with the line by a railway bridge. I wish I could convey to the reader some idea of the beauty of the view as we came out upon the Sun River Valley, or the feeling of exhilaration and elevation we experienced. I had come to no place before that did not seem remote, far from home, lonesome. Here the aspect was friendly, livable, almost home-like. We seemed to have come out, after a long journey, to a place where one might be content to stay for some time—to a far but fair country, on top of the world, as it were. Not that the elevation is great—only about 3000 feet above the sea—nor the horizon illimitable, as on the great plains ; its spaciousness is brought within human sympathy by guardian hills and distant mountain ranges.

A more sweet, smiling picture than the Sun River Valley the traveller may go far to see. With an average breadth of not over two and a half to five miles, level, richly grassed, flanked by elevations that swell up to plateaus, through the valley the Sun River, clear, full to the grassy banks, comes down like a ribbon of silver, perhaps 800 feet broad before its junction. Across the far end of it, seventy-five miles distant, but seemingly not more than twenty, run the silver serrated peaks of the Rocky Mountains, snow-clad and sparkling in the sun. At distances of twelve and fifty miles up the valley have been for years prosperous settlements, with school-houses and churches, hitherto cut off from the world.

The whole rolling, arable, though treeless country in view is beautiful, and the far prospects are magnificent. I suppose that something of the homelikeness of the region is due to the presence of the great Missouri River (a connection with the world we know), which is here a rapid, clear stream, in permanent rock-laid banks. At the town a dam has been thrown across it, and the width above the dam, where we crossed it, is about 1800 feet. The day was fair and not cold, but a gale of wind from the south-west blew with such violence that the ferry-boat was unmanageable, and we went over in little skiffs, much tossed about by the white-capped waves.

In June, 1886, there was not a house within twelve miles of this place. The country is now taken up and dotted with claim shanties, and Great Falls is a town of over 1000 inhabitants, regularly laid out, with streets indeed extending far on to the prairie, a handsome and commodious hotel, several brick buildings, and new houses going up in all directions. Central lots, fifty feet by two hundred and fifty, are said to sell for $5000, and I was offered a corner lot on Tenth Street, away out on the prairie, for $1500, including the corner stake.

It is difficult to write of this country without seeming exaggeration, and the habitual frontier boastfulness makes the acquisition of bottom facts difficult. It is plain to be seen that it is a good grazing country, and the experimental fields of wheat near the town show that it is equally well adapted to wheat-raising. The vegetables grown there are enormous and solid, especially potatoes and turnips; I have the outline of a turnip which measured seventeen inches

across, seven inches deep, and weighed twenty-four
pounds. The region is underlaid by bituminous coal,
good coking quality, and extensive mines are opening
in the neighborhood. I have no doubt from what I
saw and heard that iron of good quality (hematite) is
abundant. It goes without saying that the Montana
mountains are full of other minerals. The present
advantage of Great Falls is in the possession of unlimited water-power in the Missouri River.

As to rainfall and climate? The grass shows no
lack of rain, and the wheat was raised in 1887 without
irrigation. But irrigation from the Missouri and
Sun rivers is easy, if needed. The thermometer
shows a more temperate and less rigorous climate
than Minnesota and north Dakota. Unless everybody
fibs, the winters are less severe, and stock ranges and
fattens all winter. Less snow falls here than farther
east and south, and that which falls does not usually
remain long. The truth seems to be that the mercury
occasionally goes very low, but that every few days a
warm Pacific wind from the south-west, the "Chinook,"
blows a gale, which instantly raises the temperature,
and sweeps off the snow in twenty-four hours. I was
told that ice rarely gets more than ten inches thick,
and that ploughing can be done as late as the 20th of
December, and recommenced from the 1st to the 15th
of March. I did not stay long enough to verify these
statements. There had been a slight fall of snow in
October, which speedily disappeared. November 20th
was pleasant, with a strong Chinook wind. November
21st there was a driving snow-storm.

The region is attractive to the sight-seer. I can
speak of only two things, the Springs and the Falls.

There is a series of rapids and falls, for twelve miles below the town; and the river drops down rapidly into a cañon which is in some places nearly 200 feet deep. The first fall is twenty-six feet high. The most beautiful is the Rainbow Fall, six miles from town. This cataract, in a wild, deep gorge, has a width of 1400 feet, nearly as straight across as an artificial dam, with a perpendicular plunge of fifty feet. What makes it impressive is the immense volume of water. Dashed upon the rocks below, it sends up clouds of spray, which the sun tinges with prismatic colors the whole breadth of the magnificent fall. Standing half-way down the precipice another considerable and regular fall is seen above, while below are rapids and falls again at the bend, and beyond, great reaches of tumultuous river in the cañon. It is altogether a wild and splendid spectacle. Six miles below, the river takes a continuous though not perpendicular plunge of ninety-six feet.

One of the most exquisitely beautiful natural objects I know is the Spring, a mile above Rainbow Fall. Out of a rocky ledge, sloping up some ten feet above the river, burst several springs of absolutely crystal water, powerfully bubbling up like small geysers, and together forming instantly a splendid stream, which falls into the Missouri. So perfectly transparent is the water that the springs seem to have a depth of only fifteen inches; they are fifteen feet deep. In them grow flat-leaved plants of vivid green, shades from lightest to deepest emerald, and when the sunlight strikes into their depths the effect is exquisitely beautiful. Mingled with the emerald are maroon colors that heighten the effect. The vigor of the outburst, the volume of water, the transparency, the play of sunlight on the lovely colors, give one a positively new sensation.

I have left no room to speak of the road of ninety-eight miles through the cañon of the Missouri and the cañon of the Prickly-Pear to Helena—about 1400 feet higher than Great Falls. It is a marvellously pict-uresque road, following the mighty river, winding through crags and precipices of trap-rock set on end in fantastic array, and wild mountain scenery. On the route are many pleasant places, openings of fine valleys, thriving ranches, considerable stock and oats, much land ploughed and cultivated. The valley broad-ens out before we reach Helena and enter Last Chance Gulch, now the main street of the city, out of which millions of gold have been taken.

At Helena we reach familiar ground. The 21st was a jubilee day for the city and the whole Terri-tory. Cannon, bells, whistles, welcomed the train and the man, and fifteen thousand people hurrahed; the town was gayly decorated; there was a long proces-sion, speeches and music in the Opera-house in the af-ternoon, and fireworks, illumination, and banquet in the evening. The reason of the boundless enthusiasm of Helena was in the fact that the day gave it a new competing line to the East, and opened up the coal, iron, and wheat fields of north Montana.

VIII.

ECONOMIC AND SOCIAL TOPICS. MINNE-
SOTA AND WISCONSIN.

A VISITOR at a club in Chicago was pointed out a
table at which usually lunched a hundred and fifty
millions of dollars! This impressive statement was
as significant in its way as the list of the men, in the
days of Emerson, Agassiz, and Longfellow, who dined
together as the Saturday Club in Boston. We cannot, however, generalize from this that the only thing
considered in the North-west is money, and that the
only thing held in esteem in Boston is intellect.

The chief concerns in the North-west are material,
and the making of money, sometimes termed the "development of resources," is of the first importance.
In Minneapolis and St. Paul, social position is more
determined by money than it is in most Eastern cities,
and this makes social life more democratic, so far as
traditions and family are concerned. I desire not to
overstate this, for money is potent everywhere; but I
should say that a person not devoted to business, or
not succeeding in it, but interested rather in intellectual pursuits—study, research, art (not decorative),
education, and the like—would find less sympathy
there than in Eastern cities of the same size and less
consideration. Indeed, I was told, more than once,
that the spirit of plutocracy is so strong in these cities

as to make a very disagreeable atmosphere for people who value the higher things in life more than money and what money only will procure, and display which is always more or less vulgar. But it is necessary to get closer to the facts than this statement.

The materialistic spirit is very strong in the West; of necessity it is, in the struggle for existence and position going on there, and in the unprecedented opportunities for making fortunes. And hence arises a prevailing notion that any education is of little value that does not bear directly upon material success. I should say that the professions, including divinity and the work of the scholar and the man of letters, do not have the weight there that they do in some other places. The professional man, either in the college or the pulpit, is expected to look alive and keep up with the procession. Tradition is weak; it is no objection to a thing that it is new, and in the general strain "sensations" are welcome. The general motto is, "Be alive ; be practical." Naturally, also, wealth recently come by desires to assert itself a little in display, in ostentatious houses, luxurious living, dress, jewellery, even to the frank delight in the diamond shirt-stud.

But we are writing of Americans, and the Americans are the quickest people in the world to adapt themselves to new situations. The Western people travel much, at home and abroad, and they do not require a very long experience to know what is in bad taste. They are as quick as anybody—I believe they gave us the phrase—to "catch on" to quietness and a low tone. Indeed, I don't know but they would boast that if it is a question of subdued style, they can beat

the world. The revolution which has gone all over
the country since the Exposition of 1876 in house-fur-
nishing and decoration is quite as apparent in the West
as in the East. The West has not suffered more than
the East from eccentricities of architecture in the past
twenty years. Violations of good taste are pretty well
distributed, but of new houses the proportion of handsome, solid, good structures is as large in the West as
in the East, and in the cities I think the West has the
advantage in variety. It must be frankly said that if
the Easterner is surprised at the size, cost, and palatial
character of many of their residences, he is not less
surprised by the refinement and good taste of their interiors. There are cases where money is too evident,
where the splendor has been ordered, but there are
plenty of other cases where individual taste is apparent, and love of harmony and beauty. What I am
trying to say is that the East undervalues the real refinement of living going along with the admitted cost
and luxury in the West. The art of dining is said to
be a test of civilization—on a certain plane. Well,
dining, in good houses (I believe that is the phrase),
is much the same East and West as to appointments,
service, cuisine, and talk, with a trifle more freedom
and sense of newness in the West. No doubt there is
a difference in tone, appreciable but not easy to define.
It relates less to the things than the way the things
are considered. Where a family has had "things" for
two or three generations they are less an object than
an unregarded matter of course ; where things and a
manner of living are newly acquired, they have more
importance in themselves. An old community, if it is
really civilized (I mean a state in which intellectual

concerns are paramount), values less and less, as an end, merely material refinement. The tendency all over the United States is for wealth to run into vulgarity.

In St. Paul and Minneapolis one thing notable is the cordial hospitality, another is the public spirit, and another is the intense devotion to business, the forecast and alertness in new enterprises. Where society is fluid and on the move, it seems comparatively easy to interest the citizens in any scheme for the public good. The public spirit of those cities is admirable. One notices also an uncommon power of organization, of devices for saving time. An illustration of this is the immense railway transfer ground here. Midway between the cities is a mile square of land where all the great railway lines meet, and by means of communicating tracks easily and cheaply exchange freight cars, immensely increasing the facility and lessening the cost of transportation. Another illustration of system is the State office of Public Examiner, an office peculiar to Minnesota, an office supervising banks, public institutions, and county treasuries, by means of which a uniform system of accounting is enforced for all public funds, and safety is insured.

There is a large furniture and furnishing store in Minneapolis, well sustained by the public, which gives one a new idea of the taste of the North-west. A community that buys furniture so elegant and chaste in design, and stuffs and decorations so æsthetically good, as this shop offers it, is certainly not deficient either in material refinement or the means to gratify the love of it.

What is there besides this tremendous energy, very material prosperity, and undeniable refinement in living? I do not know that the excellently managed public-school system offers anything peculiar for comment. But the High-school in St. Paul is worth a visit. So far as I could judge, the method of teaching is admirable, and produces good results. It has no rules, nor any espionage. Scholars are put upon their honor. One object of education being character, it is well to have good behavior consist, not in conformity to artificial laws existing only in school, but to principles of good conduct that should prevail everywhere. There is system here, but the conduct expected is that of well-bred boys and girls anywhere. The plan works well, and there are very few cases of discipline. A manual training school is attached—a notion growing in favor in the West, and practised in a scientific and truly educational spirit. Attendance is not compulsory, but a considerable proportion of the pupils, boys and girls, spend a certain number of hours each week in the workshops, learning the use of tools, and making simple objects to an accurate scale from drawings on the blackboard. The design is not at all to teach a trade. The object is strictly educational, not simply to give manual facility and knowledge in the use of tools, but to teach accuracy, the mental training that there is in working out a definite, specific purpose.

The State University is still in a formative condition, and has attached to it a preparatory school. Its first class graduated only in 1872. It sends out on an average about twenty graduates a year in the various departments, science, literature, mechanic arts, and agriculture. The bane of a State university is politics, and in the West the hand of the Granger is on the college, endeavoring to make it "practical." Probably this modern idea of education will have to run its course, and so long as it is running its course the Eastern colleges which adhere to the idea of intellectual discipline will attract the young men who value a liberal rather than a material education. The State University of Minnesota is thriving in the enlargement of its facilities. About one-third of its scholars are women, but I notice that in the last catalogue, in the Senior Class of twenty-six there is only one woman. There are two independent institutions also that should be mentioned, both within the limits of St. Paul, the Hamline University, under Methodist auspices, and the McAllister College, under Presbyterian. I did not visit the former, but the latter, at least, though just beginning, has the idea of a classical education foremost, and does not adopt co-education. Its library is well begun by the gift of a miscellaneous collection, containing many rare and old books, by the Rev. E. D. Neill, the well-known antiquarian, who has done so much to illuminate the colonial history of Virginia and Maryland. In the State Historical Society, which has rooms in the Capitol in St. Paul, a vigorous and well-managed society, is a valuable collection of books illustrating the history of the North-west. The visitor will notice in St. Paul quite as much taste for reading among business men as exists elsewhere, a growing fancy for rare books, and find some private collections of interest. Though music and art cannot be said to be generally cultivated, there are in private circles musical enthusiasm and musical ability, and many of the best examples of modern painting are to be found in private houses. Indeed, there is one gallery in which is a collection of pictures by foreign artists that would be notable in any city. These things are mentioned as indications of a liberalizing use of wealth.

Wisconsin is not only one of the most progressive, but one of the most enlightened, States in the Union. Physically it is an agreeable and beautiful State, agriculturally it is rich, in the southern and central portions at least, and it is overlaid with a perfect network of railways. All this is well known. I wish to speak of certain other things which give it distinction. I mean the prevailing spirit in education and in social-economic problems. In some respects it leads all the other States.

There seem to be two elements in the State contending for the mastery, one the New England, but emancipated from tradition, the other the foreign, with ideas of liberty not of New England origin. Neither is afraid of new ideas nor of trying social experiments. Co-education seems to be everywhere accepted without question, as if it were already demonstrated that the mingling of the sexes in the higher education will produce the sort of men and women most desirable in the highest civilization. The success of women in the higher schools, the capacity shown by women in the management of public institutions and in reforms and charities, have perhaps something to do with the favor to woman suffrage. It may be that, if women vote there in general elections as well as school matters, on the ground that every public office "relates to education," Prohibition will be agitated as it is in most other States, but at present the lager-bier interest is too strong to give Prohibition much chance. The capital invested in the manufacture of beer makes this interest a political element of great importance.

Milwaukee and Madison may be taken to represent fairly the civilization of Wisconsin. Milwaukee, having a population of about 175,000, is a beautiful city, with some characteristics peculiar to itself, having the settled air of being much older than it is, a place accustomed to money and considerable elegance of living. The situation on the lake is fine, the high curving bluffs offering most attractive sites for residences, and the rolling country about having a quiet beauty. Grand Avenue, an extension of the main business thoroughfare of the city, runs out into the country some two miles, broad, with a solid road, a stately avenue, lined with fine dwellings, many of them palaces in size and elegant in design. Fashion seems to hesitate between the east side and the west side, but the east or lake side seems to have the advantage in situation, certainly in views, and contains a greater proportion of the American population than the other. Indeed, it is not easy to recall a quarter of any busy city which combines more comfort, evidences of wealth and taste and refinement, and a certain domestic character, than this portion of the town on the bluffs, Prospect Avenue and the adjacent streets. With the many costly and elegant houses there is here and there one rather fantastic, but the whole effect is pleasing, and the traveller feels no hesitation in deciding that this would be an agreeable place to live. From the avenue the lake prospect is wonderfully attractive—the beauty of Lake Michigan in changing color and variety of lights in sun and storm cannot be too much insisted on—and this is especially true of the noble Esplanade, where stands the bronze statue (a gift of two citizens) of Solomon Juneau, the first settler of Milwaukee in 1818. It is a very satisfactory figure, and placed where it is, it gives a sort of foreign distinction to the open place which the city has wisely left for public use. In this part of the town is the house of the Milwaukee Club, a good building, one of the most tasteful internally, and one of the best appointed, best arranged, and comfortable club-houses in the country. Near this is the new Art Museum (also the gift of a private citizen), a building greatly to be commended for its excellent proportions, simplicity, and chasteness of style, and adaptability to its purpose. It is a style that will last, to please the eye, and be more and more appreciated as the taste of the community becomes more and more refined.

In this quarter are many of the churches, of the average sort, but none calling for special mention except St. Paul's, which is noble in proportions and rich in color, and contains several notable windows of stained glass, one of them occupying the entire end of one transept, the largest, I believe, in the country. It is a copy of Doré's painting of Christ on the way to the Crucifixion, an illuminated street scene, with superb architecture of marble and porphyry, and crowded with hundreds of figures in colors of Oriental splendor. The colors are rich and harmonious, but it is very brilliant, flashing in the sunlight with magnificent effect, and I am not sure but it would attract the humble sinners of Milwaukee from a contemplation of their little faults which they go to church to confess.

The city does not neglect education, as the many thriving public schools testify. It has a public circulating library of 42,000 volumes, sustained at an expense of $22,000 a year by a tax; is free, and well patronized. There are good private collections of books also, one that I saw large and worthy to be called a library, especially strong in classic English literature.

Perhaps the greatest industry of the city, certainly the most conspicuous, is brewing. I do not say that the city is in the hands of the brewers, but with their vast establishments they wield great power. One of them, about the largest in the country, and said to equal in its capacity any in Europe, has in one group seven enormous buildings, and is impressive by its extent and orderly management, as well as by the rivers of amber fluid which it pours out for this thirsty country. Milwaukee, with its large German element—two-thirds of the population, most of whom are freethinkers—has no Sunday except in a holiday sense; the theatres are all open, and the pleasure-gardens, which are extensive, are crowded with merrymakers in the season. It is, in short, the Continental fashion, and while the churches and church-goers are like churches and church-goers everywhere, there is an air of general Continental freedom.

The general impression of Milwaukee is that it is a city of much wealth and a great deal of comfort, with a settled, almost conservative feeling, like an Eastern city, and charming, cultivated social life, with the grace and beauty that are common in American society any-

where. I think the men generally would be called
well-looking, robust, of the quiet, assured manner of
an old community. The women seen on the street
and in the shops are of good physique and good col-
or and average good looks, without anything startling
in the way of beauty or elegance. I speak of the general aspect of the town, and I mention the well-to-do
physical condition because it contradicts the English
prophecy of a physical decadence in the West, owing
to the stimulating climate and the restless pursuit of
wealth. On the train to Madison (the line runs through
a beautiful country) one might have fancied that he
was on a local New England train: the same plain,
good sort of people, and in abundance the well-looking, domestic sort of young women.

Madison is a great contrast to Milwaukee. Although
it is the political and educational centre, has the Capitol and the State University, and a population of about
15,000, it is like a large village, with the village habits
and friendliness. On elevated, hilly ground, between
two charming lakes, it has an almost unrivalled situation, and is likely to possess, in the progress of years
and the accumulation of wealth, the picturesqueness
and beauty that travellers ascribe to Stockholm. With
the hills of the town, the gracefully curving shores of
the lakes and their pointed bays, the gentle elevations
beyond the lakes, and the capacity of these two bodies
of water as pleasure resorts, with elegant music pavil-
ions and fleets of boats for the sail and the oar—why
do we not take a hint from the painted Venetian sail?
—there is no limit to what may be expected in the way
of refined beauty of Madison in the summer, if it remains a city of education and of laws, and does not

11

get up a "boom," and set up factories, and blacken all the landscape with coal smoke!

The centre of the town is a big square, pleasantly tree-planted, so large that the facing rows of shops and houses have a remote and dwarfed appearance, and in the middle of it is the great pillared State-house, American style. The town itself is one of unpretentious, comfortable houses, some of them with elegant interiors, having plenty of books and the spoils of foreign travel. In one of them, the old-fashioned but entirely charming mansion of Governor Fairchild, I cannot refrain from saying, is a collection which, so far as I know, is unique in the world—a collection to which the helmet of Don Quixote gives a certain flavor; it is of barbers' basins, of all ages and countries.

Wisconsin is working out its educational ideas on an intelligent system, and one that may be expected to demonstrate the full value of the popular method —I mean a more intimate connection of the university with the life of the people than exists elsewhere. What effect this will have upon the higher education in the ultimate civilization of the State is a question of serious and curious interest. Unless the experience of the ages is misleading, the tendency of the "practical" in all education is a downward and material one, and the highest civilization must continue to depend upon a pure scholarship, and upon what are called abstract ideas. Even so practical a man as Socrates found the natural sciences inadequate to the inner needs of the soul. "I thought," he says, "as I have failed in the contemplation of true existence (by means of the sciences), I ought to be careful that I did not lose the eye of the soul, as people may injure

their bodily eye by gazing on the sun during an eclipse.
... That occurred to me, and I was afraid that my soul
might be blinded altogether if I looked at things with
my eyes, or tried by the help of the senses to appre-
hend them. And I thought I had better have re-
course to ideas, and seek in them the truth of existence." The intimate union of the university with the
life of the people is a most desirable object, if the university does not descend and lose its high character in
the process.

The graded school system of the State is vigorous,
all working up to the University. This is a State institution, and the State is fairly liberal to it, so far as
practical education is concerned. It has a magnificent
new Science building, and will have excellent shops
and machinery for the sciences (especially the applied)
and the mechanic arts. The system is elective. A
small per cent. of the students take Greek, a larger
number Latin, French, and German, but the University is largely devoted to science. In all the departments, including law, there are about six hundred students, of whom above one hundred are girls. There
seems to be no doubt about co-education as a practical matter in the conduct of the college, and as a
desirable thing for women. The girls are good students, and usually take more than half the highest
honors on the marking scale. Notwithstanding the
testimony of the marks, however, the boys say that
the girls don't "know" as much as they do about
things generally, and they (the boys) have no doubt
of their ability to pass the girls either in scholarship
or practical affairs in the struggle of life. The idea
seems to be that the girls are serious in education

only up to a certain point, and that marriage will practically end the rivalry.

The distinguishing thing, however, about the State University is its vital connection with the farmers and the agricultural interests. I do not refer to the agricultural department, which it has in common with many colleges, nor to the special short agricultural course of three months in the winter, intended to give farmers' boys, who enter it without examination or other connection with the University, the most available agricultural information in the briefest time, the intention being not to educate boys away from a taste for farming but to make them better farmers. The students must be not less than sixteen years old, and have a common-school education. During the term of twelve weeks they have lectures by the professors and recitations on practical and theoretical agriculture, on elementary and agricultural chemistry, on elemental botany, with laboratory practice, and on the anatomy of our domestic animals and the treatment of their common diseases. But what I wish to call special attention to is the connection of the University with the farmers' institutes.

A special Act of the Legislature, drawn by a lawyer, Mr. C. E. Estabrook, authorized the farmers' institutes, and placed them under the control of the regents of the University, who have the power to select a State superintendent to control them. A committee of three of the regents has special charge of the institutes. Thus the farmers are brought into direct relation with the University, and while, as a prospectus says, they are not actually non-resident students of the University, they receive information and instruction directly from it. The State appropriates twelve thousand dollars a year to this work, which pays the salaries of Mr. W. H. Morrison, the superintendent, to whose tact and energy the success of the institutes is largely due, and his assistants, and enables him to pay the expenses of specialists and agriculturists who can instruct the farmers and wisely direct the discussions at the meetings. By reason of this complete organization, which penetrates every part of the State, subjects of most advantage are considered, and time is not wasted in merely amateur debates.

I know of no other State where a like system of popular instruction on a vital and universal interest of the State, directed by the highest educational authority, is so perfectly organized and carried on with such unity of purpose and detail of administration ; no other in which the farmer is brought systematically into such direct relations to the university. In the current year there have been held eighty-two farmers' institutes in forty-five counties. The list of practical topics discussed is 279, and in this service have been engaged one hundred and seven workers, thirty-one of whom are specialists from other States. This is an "agricultural college," on a grand scale, brought to the homes of the people. The meetings are managed by local committees in such a way as to evoke local pride, interest, and talent. I will mention some of the topics that were thoroughly discussed at one of the institutes : clover as a fertilizer ; recuperative agriculture ; bee-keeping ; taking care of the little things about the house and farm ; the education for farmers' daughters ; the whole economy of sheep husbandry; egg production ; poultry ; the value of

thought and application in farming; horses to breed
for the farm and market; breeding and management
of swine; mixed farming; grain-raising; assessment
and collection of taxes; does knowledge pay? (with
illustrations of money made by knowledge of the
market); breeding and care of cattle, with expert
testimony as to the best sorts of cows; points in
corn culture; full discussion of small-fruit culture;
butter-making as a fine art; the dairy; our country
roads; agricultural education. So, during the winter,
every topic that concerns the well-being of the home,
the profit of the farm, the moral welfare of the people and their prosperity, was intelligently discussed,
with audiences fully awake to the value of this practical and applied education. Some of the best of
these discussions are printed and widely distributed.
Most of them are full of wise details in the way of
thrift and money-making, but I am glad to see that
the meetings also consider the truth that as much
care should be given to the rearing of boys and girls
as of calves and colts, and that brains are as necessary
in farming as in any other occupation.

As these farmers' institutes are conducted, I do not
know any influence comparable to them in waking up
the farmers to think, to inquire into new and improved methods, and to see in what real prosperity
consists. With prosperity, as a rule, the farmer and
his family are conservative, law-keeping, church-going,
good citizens. The little appropriation of twelve
thousand dollars has already returned to the State a
hundred-fold financially and a thousand-fold in general
intelligence.

I have spoken of the habit in Minnesota and Wisconsin of depending mostly upon one crop—that of spring wheat—and the disasters from this single reliance in bad years. Hard lessons are beginning to teach the advantage of mixed farming and stock-raising. In this change the farmers' institutes of Wisconsin have been potent. As one observer says, "They have produced a revolution in the mode of farming, raising crops, and caring for stock." The farmers have been enabled to protect themselves against the effects of drought and other evils. Taking the advice of the institute in 1886, the farmers planted 50,000 acres of ensilage corn, which took the place of the short hay crop caused by the drought. This provision saved thousands of dollars' worth of stock in several counties. From all over the State comes the testimony of farmers as to the good results of the institute work, like this : "Several thousand dollars' worth of improved stock have been brought in. Creameries and cheese-factories have been established and well supported. Farmers are no longer raising grain exclusively as heretofore. Our hill-sides are covered with clover. Our farmers are encouraged to labor anew. A new era of prosperity in our State dates from the farmers' institutes."

There is abundant evidence that a revolution is going on in the farming of Wisconsin, greatly assisted, if not inaugurated, by this systematic popular instruction from the University as a centre. It may not greatly interest the reader that the result of this will be greater agricultural wealth in Wisconsin, but it does concern him that putting intelligence into farming must inevitably raise the level of the home life and the general civilization of Wisconsin. I have

spoken of this centralized, systematic effort in some
detail because it seems more efficient than the work
of agricultural societies and sporadic institutes in
other States.

In another matter Wisconsin has taken a step in
advance of other States ; that is, in the care of the
insane.   The State has about 2600 insane, increasing
at the rate of about 167 a year.   The provisions in
the State for these are the State Hospital (capacity of
500), Northern Hospital (capacity of 600), the Milwaukee Asylum (capacity of 255), and fifteen county
asylums for the chronic insane, including two nearly
ready (capacity 1220).   The improvement in the care
of the insane consists in several particulars—the doing away of restraints, either by mechanical appliances or by narcotics, reasonable separation of the
chronic cases from the others, increased liberty, and
the substitution of wholesome labor for idleness.
Many of these changes have been brought about by
the establishment of county asylums, the feature of
which I wish specially to speak.   The State asylums
were crowded beyond their proper capacity, classification was difficult in them, and a large number of
the insane were miserably housed in county jails and
poor-houses.   The evils of great establishments were
more and more apparent, and it was determined to
try the experiment of county asylums.   These have
now been in operation for six years, and a word about
their constitution and perfectly successful operation
may be of public service.

These asylums, which are only for the chronic insane, are managed by local authorities, but under constant and close State supervision; this last provision

is absolutely essential, and no doubt accounts for the
success of the undertaking. It is not necessary here
to enter into details as to the construction of these
buildings. They are of brick, solid, plain, comfortable, and of a size to accommodate not less than fifty
nor more than one hundred inmates : an institution
with less than fifty is not economical; one with a
larger number than one hundred is unwieldy, and beyond the personal supervision of the superintendent.
A farm is needed for economy in maintenance and to
furnish occupation for the men; about four acres for
each inmate is a fair allowance. The land should be
fertile, and adapted to a variety of crops as well as to
cattle, and it should have woodland to give occupation
in the winter. The fact is recognized that idleness is
no better for an insane than for a sane person. The
house-work is all done by the women; the farm, garden, and general out-door work by the men. Experience shows that three-fourths of the chronic insane
can be furnished occupation of some sort, and greatly
to their physical and moral well-being. The nervous-
ness incident always to restraint and idleness disappears with liberty and occupation. Hence greater
happiness and comfort to the insane, and occasionally
a complete or partial cure.

About one attendant to twenty insane persons is
sufficient, but it is necessary that these should have
intelligence and tact; the men capable of leading in
farm-work, the women to instruct in house-work and
dress-making, and it is well if they can play some
musical instrument and direct in amusements. One
of the most encouraging features of this experiment
in small asylums has been the discovery of so many

efficient superintendents and matrons among the intelligent farmers and business men of the rural districts, who have the practical sagacity and financial ability to carry on these institutions successfully.

These asylums are as open as a school; no locked doors (instead of window-bars, the glass-frames are of iron painted white), no pens made by high fences. The inmates are free to go and come at their work, with no other restraint than the watch of the attendants. The asylum is a home and not a prison. The great thing is to provide occupation. The insane, it is found, can be trained to regular industry, and it is remarkable how little restraint is needed if an earnest effort is made to do without it. In the county asylums of Wisconsin about one person in a thousand is in restraint or seclusion each day. The whole theory seems to be to treat the insane like persons in some way diseased, who need occupation, amusement, kindness. The practice of this theory in the Wisconsin county asylums is so successful that it must ultimately affect the treatment of the insane all over the country.

And the beauty of it is that it is as economical as it is enlightened and humane. The secret of providing occupation for this class is to buy as little material and hire as little labor as possible ; let the women make the clothes, and the men do the farm-work without the aid of machinery. The surprising result of this is that some of these asylums approach the point of being self-supporting, and all of them save money to the counties, compared with the old method. The State has not lost by these asylums, and the counties have gained ; nor has the economy been purchased at the expense of humanity to the insane; the insane in the county asylums have been as well clothed, lodged, and fed as in the State institutions, and have had more freedom, and consequently more personal comfort and a better chance of abating their mania. This is the result arrived at by an exhaustive report on these county asylums in the report of the State Board of Charities and Reforms, of which Mr. Albert O. Wright is secretary. The average cost per week per capita of patients in the asylums by the latest report was, in the State Hospital, $4.39; in the Northern Hospital, $4.33; in the county asylums, $1.89.

The new system considers the education of the chronic insane an important part of their treatment; not specially book-learning (though that may be included), but training of the mental, moral, and physical faculties in habits of order, propriety, and labor. By these means wonders have been worked for the insane. The danger, of course, is that the local asylums may fall into unproductive routine, and that politics will interfere with the intelligent State supervision. If Wisconsin is able to keep her State institutions out of the clutches of men with whom politics is a business simply for what they can make out of it (as it is with those who oppose a civil service not based upon partisan dexterity and subserviency), she will carry her enlightened ideas into the making of a model State. The working out of such a noble reform as this in the treatment of the insane can only be intrusted to men specially qualified by knowledge, sympathy, and enthusiasm, and would be impossible in the hands of changing political workers. The systematized enlightenment of the farmers in the farmers'

institutes by means of their vital connection with the
University needs the steady direction of those who are
devoted to it, and not to any party success. As to
education generally, it may be said that while for the
present the popular favor to the State University depends upon its being "practical" in this and other
ways, the time will come when it will be seen that the
highest service it can render the State is by upholding
pure scholarship, without the least material object.

Another institution of which Winconsin has reason
to be proud is the State Historical Society—a corporation (dating from 1853) with perpetual succession,
supported by an annual appropriation of five thousand
dollars, with provisions for printing the reports of the
society and the catalogues of the library. It is housed
in the Capitol. The society has accumulated interesting historical portraits, cabinets of antiquities, natural history, and curiosities, a collection of copper,
and some valuable MSS. for the library. The library
is one of the best historical collections in the country.
The excellence of it is largely due to Lyman C. Dra-
per, LL.D., who was its secretary for thirty - three
years, but who began as early as 1834 to gather facts
and materials for border history and biography, and
who had in 1852 accumulated thousands of manuscripts and historical statements, the nucleus of the
present splendid library, which embraces rare and valuable works relating to the history of nearly every
State. This material is arranged by States, and readily accessible to the student. Indeed, there are few
historical libraries in the country where historical research in American subjects can be better prosecuted
than in this. The library began in January, 1854,

with fifty volumes. In January, 1887, it had 57,935 volumes and 60,731 pamphlets and documents, making a total of 118,666 titles.

There is a large law library in the State-house, the University has a fair special library for the students, and in the city is a good public circulating library, free, supported by a tax, and much used. For a young city, it is therefore very well off for books.

Madison is not only an educational centre, but an intelligent city; the people read and no doubt buy books, but they do not support book - stores. The shops where books are sold are variety - shops, deal-ing in stationery, artists' materials, cheap pictures, bric-à-brac. Books are of minor importance, and but few are "kept in stock." Indeed, bookselling is not a profitable part of the business; it does not pay to "handle" books, or to keep the run of new publica-tions, or to keep a supply of standard works. In this the shops of Madison are not peculiar. It is true all over the West, except in two or three large cities, and true, perhaps, not quite so generally in the East; the book-shops are not the literary and intellectual centres they used to be.

There are several reasons given for this discour-aging state of the book-trade. Perhaps it is true that people accustomed to newspapers full of "selections," to the flimsy publications found on the cheap count-ers, and to the magazines, do not buy "books that are books," except for "furnishing;" that they depend more and more upon the circulating libraries for any-thing that costs more than an imported cigar or half a pound of candy. The local dealers say that the system of the great publishing houses is unsatisfacto-

ry as to prices and discounts. Private persons can
get the same discounts as the dealers, and can very
likely, by ordering a list, buy more cheaply than of
the local bookseller, and therefore, as a matter of business, he says that it does not pay to keep books ; he
gives up trying to sell them, and turns his attention
to "varieties." Another reason for the decline in the
trade may be in the fact that comparatively few booksellers are men of taste in letters, men who read, or
keep the run of new publications. If a retail grocer
knew no more of his business than many booksellers
know of theirs, he would certainly fail. It is a pity
on all accounts that the book-trade is in this condition.
A bookseller in any community, if he is a man of literary culture, and has a love of books and knowledge
of them, can do a great deal for the cultivation of the
public taste. His shop becomes a sort of intellectual
centre of the town. If the public find there an atmosphere of books, and are likely to have their wants
met for publications new or rare, they will generally
sustain the shop; at least this is my observation. Still,
I should not like to attempt to say whether the falling
off in the retail book-trade is due to want of skill in
the sellers, to the publishing machinery, or to public
indifference. The subject is worthy the attention of
experts. It is undeniably important to maintain everywhere these little depots of intellectual supply. In
a town new to him the visitor is apt to estimate the
taste, the culture, the refinement, as well as the wealth
of the town, by its shops. The stock in the dry goods
and fancy stores tells one thing, that in the art-stores
another thing, that in the book-stores another thing,
about the inhabitants. The West, even on the remote

frontiers, is full of magnificent stores of goods, telling of taste as well as luxury; the book-shops are the poorest of all.

The impression of the North-west, thus far seen, is that of tremendous energy, material refinement, much open-mindedness, considerable self-appreciation, uncommon sagacity in meeting new problems, generous hospitality, the Old Testament notion of possessing this world, rather more recognition of the pecuniary as the only success than exists in the East and South, intense national enthusiasm, and unblushing and most welcome "Americanism."

In these sketchy observations on the North-west nothing has seemed to me more interesting and important than the agricultural changes going on in eastern Dakota, Minnesota, and Wisconsin. In the vast wheat farms, as well as in the vast cattle ranges, there is an element of speculation, if not of gambling, of the chance of immense profits or of considerable loss, that is neither conducive to the stable prosperity nor to the moral soundness of a State. In the breaking up of the great farms, and in the introduction of varied agriculture and cattle-raising on a small scale, there will not be so many great fortunes made, but each State will be richer as a whole, and less liable to yearly fluctuations in prosperity. But the gain most worth considering will be in the home life and the character of the citizens. The best life of any community depends upon varied industries. No part of the United States has ever prospered, as regards the well-being of the mass of the people, that relied upon the production of a single staple.

IX.

CHICAGO.

CHICAGO is becoming modest. Perhaps the inhabitants may still be able to conceal their modesty, but nevertheless they feel it. The explanation is simple. The city has grown not only beyond the most sanguine expectations of those who indulged in the most inflated hope of its future, but it has grown beyond what they said they expected. This gives the citizens pause—as it might an eagle that laid a roc's egg.

The fact is, Chicago has become an independent organism, growing by a combination of forces and opportunities, beyond the contrivance of any combination of men to help or hinder, beyond the need of flaming circulars and reports of boards of trade, and process pictures. It has passed the danger or the fear of rivalry, and reached the point where the growth of any other portion of the great North-west, or of any city in it (whatever rivalry that city may show in industries or in commerce), is in some way a contribution to the power and wealth of Chicago. To them that have shall be given. Cities, under favoring conditions for local expansion, which reach a certain amount of population and wealth, grow by a kind of natural increment, the law of attraction, very well known in human nature, which draws a person to an active city of two hundred thousand rather than to a stagnant city of one hundred thousand. And it is a fortunate thing for civilization that this attraction is almost as strong to men of letters as it is to men of affairs. Chicago has, it seems to me, only recently turned this point of assured expansion, and, as I intimated, the inhabitants have hardly yet become accustomed to this idea; but I believe that the time is near when they will be as indifferent to what strangers think of Chicago as the New-Yorkers are to what strangers think of New York. New York is to-day the only American city free from this anxious note of provincialism—though in Boston it rather takes the form of pity for the unenlightened man who doubts its superiority; but the impartial student of Chicago to-day can see plenty of signs of the sure growth of this metropolitan indifference. And yet there is still here enough of the old Chicago stamp to make the place interesting.

It is everything in getting a point of view. Last summer a lady of New Orleans who had never before been out of her native French city, and who would look upon the whole North with the impartial eyes of a foreigner—and more than that, with Continental eyes—visited Chicago, and afterwards New York. "Which city did you like best?" I asked, without taking myself seriously in the question. To my surprise, she hesitated. This hesitation was fatal to all my preconceived notions. It mattered not thereafter which she preferred: she had hesitated. She was actually comparing Chicago to New York in her mind, as one might compare Paris and London. The audacity of the comparison I saw was excused by its in-

nocence. I confess that it had never occurred to me
to think of Chicago in that Continental light. " Well,"
she said, not seeing at all the humor of my remark,
" Chicago seems to me to have finer buildings and
residences, to be the more beautiful city ; but of
course there is more in New York ; it is a greater
city ; and I should prefer to live there for what I
want." This naïve observation set me thinking, and
I wondered if there was a point of view, say that of
divine omniscience and fairness, in which Chicago
would appear as one of the great cities of the world,
in fact a metropolis, by-and-by to rival in population
and wealth any city of the seaboard. It has certainly
better commercial advantages, so far as water communication and railways go, than Paris or Pekin or
Berlin, and a territory to supply and receive from in-
finitely vaster, richer, and more promising than either.
This territory will have many big cities, but in the
nature of things only one of surpassing importance.
And taking into account its geographical position—a
thousand miles from the Atlantic seaboard on the
one side, and from the mountains on the other, with
the acknowledged tendency of people and of money
to it as a continental centre—it seems to me that Chicago is to be that one.

The growth of Chicago is one of the marvels of the
world. I do not wonder that it is incomprehensible
even to those who have seen it year by year. As I
remember it in 1860, it was one of the shabbiest and
most unattractive cities of about a hundred thousand
inhabitants anywhere to be found ; but even then it
had more than trebled its size in ten years ; the
streets were mud sloughs, the sidewalks were a series

of stairs and more or less rotten planks, half the town was in process of elevation above the tadpole level, and a considerable part of it was on wheels—the moving house being about the only wheeled vehicle that could get around with any comfort to the passengers. The west side was a straggling shanty - town, the north side was a country village with two or three "aristocratic" houses occupying a square, the south side had not a handsome business building in it, nor a public edifice of any merit except a couple of churches, but there were a few pleasant residences on Michigan Avenue fronting the encroaching lake, and on Wabash Avenue. Yet I am not sure that even then the exceedingly busy and excited traders and speculators did not feel that the town was more important than New York. For it had a great business. Aside from its real estate operations, its trade that year was set down at $97,000,000, embracing its dealing in produce, its wholesale supply business, and its manufacturing.

No one then, however, would have dared to predict that the value of trade in 1887 would be, as it was, $1,103,000,000. Nor could any one have believed that the population of 100,000 would reach in 1887 nearly 800,000 (estimated 782,644), likely to reach in 1888, with the annexation of contiguous villages that have become physically a part of the city, the amount of 900,000. Growing at its usual rate for several years past, the city is certain in a couple of years to count its million of people. And there is not probably anywhere congregated a more active and aggressive million, with so great a proportion of young, ambitious blood. Other figures keep pace with those

of trade and population. I will mention only one or
two of them here. The national banks, in 1887, had
a capital of $15,800,000, in which the deposits were
$80,473,746, the loans and discounts $63,113,821, the
surplus and profits $6,320,559. The First National is,
I believe, the second or third largest banking house in
the country, having a deposit account of over twenty-
two millions. The figures given only include the national banks; add to these the private banks, and the
deposits of Chicago in 1887 were $105,367,000. The
aggregate bank clearings of the city were $2,969,216,-
210.60, an increase of 14 per cent. over 1886. It should
be noted that there were only twenty-one banks in the
clearing house (with an aggregate capital and surplus
of $28,514,000), and that the fewer the banks the small-
er the total clearings will be. The aggregate Board of
Trade clearings for 1887 were $78,179,869. In the year
1886 Chicago imported merchandise entered for consumption to the value of $11,574,449, and paid $4,349,-
237 duties on it. I did not intend to go into statistics,
but these and a few other figures will give some idea
of the volume of business in this new city. I found
on inquiry that—owing to legislation that need not
be gone into—there are few savings-banks, and the
visible savings of labor cut a small figure in this way.
The explanation is that there are several important
loan and building associations. Money is received on
deposit in small amounts, and loaned at a good rate
of interest to those wishing to build or buy houses,
the latter paying in small instalments. The result is
that these loan institutions have been very profitable
to those who have put money in them, and that the
laborers who have borrowed to build have also been

benefited by putting all their savings into houses. I believe there is no other large city, except Philadelphia perhaps, where so large a proportion of the inhabitants own the houses they live in. There is no better prevention of the spread of anarchical notions and communist foolishness than this.

It is an item of interest that the wholesale dry-goods jobbing establishments increased their business in 1887 12½ per cent. over 1886. Five houses have a capital of $9,000,000, and the sales in 1887 were nearly $74,000,000. And it is worth special mention that one man in Chicago, Marshall Field, is the largest wholesale and retail dry-goods merchant in the world. In his retail shop and wholesale store there are 3000 employés on the pay-roll. As to being first in his specialty, the same may be said of Philip D. Armour, who not only distances all rivals in the world as a packer, but no doubt also as a merchant of such products as the hog contributes to the support of life. His sales in one year have been over $51,000,000. The city has also the distinction of having among its citizens Henry W. King, the largest dealer, in establishments here and elsewhere, in clothing in the world.

In nothing has the growth of Chicago been more marked in the past five years than in manufactures. I cannot go into the details of all the products, but the totals of manufacture for 1887 were, in 2396 firms, $113,960,000 capital employed, 134,615 workers, $74,-567,000 paid in wages, and the value of the product was $403,109,500—an increase of product over 1886 of about 15½ per cent. A surprising item in this is the book and publishing business. The increase of sales of books in 1887 over 1886 was 20 per cent. The wholesale sales for 1887 are estimated at $10,000,000. It is now claimed that as a book-publishing centre Chicago ranks second only to New York, and that in the issue of subscription-books it does more business than New York, Boston, and Philadelphia combined. In regard to musical instruments the statement is not less surprising. In 1887 the sales of pianos amounted to about $2,600,000—a gain of $300,000 over 1886. My authority for this, and for some, but not all, of the other figures given, is the *Tribune*, which says that Chicago is not only the largest reed-organ market in the world, but that more organs are manufactured here than in any other city in Europe or America. The sales for 1887 were $2,000,000—an increase over 1886 of $500,000. There were $1,000,000 worth of small musical instruments sold, and of sheet music and music-books a total of $450,000. This speaks well for the cultivation of musical taste in the West, especially as there was a marked improvement in the class of the music bought.

The product of the iron manufactures in 1887, including rolling-mills ($23,952,000) and founderies ($10,-000,000), was $61,187,000 against $46,790,000 in 1886, and the wages paid in iron and steel work was $14,-899,000. In 1887 there were erected 4833 buildings, at a reported cost of $19,778,100—a few more buildings, but yet at nearly two millions less cost, than in 1886. A couple of items interested me: that Chicago made in 1887 $900,000 worth of toys and $500,000 worth of perfumes. The soap-makers waged a gallant but entirely unsuccessful war against the soot and smoke of the town in producing $6,250,000 worth of soap and candles. I do not see it mentioned, but I should think the laundry business in Chicago would be the most profitable one at present.

Without attempting at all to set forth the business of Chicago in detail, a few more figures will help to indicate its volume. At the beginning of 1887 the storage capacity for grain in 29 elevators was 27,025,-000 bushels. The total receipts of flour and grain in 1882, '3, '4, '5, and '6, in bushels, were respectively, 126,155,483, 164,924,732, 159,561,474, 156,408,228, 151,932,995. In 1887 the receipts in bushels were: flour, 6,873,544; wheat, 21,848,251; corn, 51,578,410; oats, 45,750,842; rye, 852,726; barley, 12,476,547—total, 139,380,320. It is useless to go into details of the meat products, but interesting to know that in 1886 Chicago shipped 310,039,600 pounds of lard and 573,496,012 pounds of dressed beef.

I was surprised at the amount of the lake commerce, the railway traffic (nearly 50,000 miles tributary to the city) making so much more show. In 1882 the tonnage of vessels clearing this port was 4,904,999; in 1886 it was 3,950,762. The report of the Board of Trade for 1886 says the arrivals and clearances, foreign and coastwise, for this port for the year ending June 30th were 22,096, which was 869 more than at the ports of Baltimore, Boston, New Orleans, Philadelphia, Portland and Falmouth, and San Francisco combined; 315 more than at New York, New Orleans, Portland and Falmouth, and San Francisco; and 100 more than at New York, Baltimore, and Portland and Falmouth. It will not be overlooked that this lake commerce is training a race of hardy sailors, who would come to the front in case of a naval war, though they might have to go out on rafts.

In 1888 Chicago is a magnificent city. Although
it has been incorporated fifty years, during which period its accession of population has been rapid and
steady—hardly checked by the devastating fires of
1871 and 1874—its metropolitan character and appearance is the work of less than fifteen years. There is
in history no parallel to this product of a freely act-
ing democracy: not St. Petersburg rising out of the
marshes at an imperial edict, nor Berlin, the magic
creation of a consolidated empire and a Cæsar's power. The north-side village has become a city of broad
streets, running northward to the parks, lined with
handsome residences interspersed with stately mansions of most varied and agreeable architecture, mar-
red by very little that is bizarre and pretentious—a
region of churches and club-houses and public buildings of importance. The west side, the largest section, and containing more population than the other
two divisions combined, stretching out over the prairie to a horizon fringed with villages, expanding in
three directions, is more mediocre in buildings, but impressive in its vastness; and the stranger driving out
the stately avenue of Washington some four miles to
Garfield Park will be astonished by the evidences of
wealth and the vigor of the city expansion.

But it is the business portion of the south side that
is the miracle of the time, the solid creation of energy and capital since the fire—the square mile containing the Post-office and City Hall, the giant hotels, the
opera-houses and theatres, the Board of Trade building, the many-storied offices, the great shops, the club-
houses, the vast retail and wholesale warehouses. This
area has the advantage of some other great business

centres in having broad streets at right angles, but with all this openness for movement, the throng of passengers and traffic, the intersecting street and cable railways, the loads of freight and the crush of carriages, the life and hurry and excitement are sufficient to satisfy the most eager lover of metropolitan pandemonium. Unfortunately for a clear comprehension of it, the manufactories vomit dense clouds of bituminous coal smoke, which settle in a black mass in this part of the town, so that one can scarcely see across the streets in a damp day, and the huge buildings loom up in the black sky in ghostly dimness. The climate of Chicago, though some ten degrees warmer than the average of its immediately tributary territory, is a harsh one, and in the short winter days the centre of the city is not only black, but damp and chilly. In some of the November and December days I could without any stretch of the imagination fancy myself in London. On a Sunday, when business gives place to amusement and religion, the stately city is seen in all its fine proportions. No other city in the Union can show business warehouses and offices of more architectural nobility. The mind inevitably goes to Florence for comparison with the structures of the Medicean merchant princes. One might name the Pullman Building for offices as an example, and the wholesale warehouse of Marshall Field, the work of that truly original American architect, Richardson, which in massiveness, simplicity of lines, and admirable blending of artistic beauty with adaptability to its purpose, seems to me unrivalled in this country. A few of these buildings are exceptions to the general style of architecture, which is only good of its utilitarian American kind, but they give distinction to the town, and I am sure are prophetic of the concrete form the wealth of the city will take. The visitor is likely to be surprised at the number and size of the structures devoted to offices, and to think, as he sees some of them unfilled, that the business is overdone. At any given moment it may be, but the demand for "offices" is always surprising to those who pay most attention to this subject, and I am told that if the erection of office buildings should cease for a year, the demand would pass beyond the means of satisfying it.

Leaving the business portion of the south side, the city runs in apparently limitless broad avenues southward into suburban villages and a region thickly populated to the Indiana line. The continuous slightly curving lake front of the city is about seven miles, pretty solidly occupied with houses. The Michigan Avenue of 1860, with its wooden fronts and cheap boarding-houses, has taken on quite another appearance, and extends its broad way in unbroken lines of fine residences five miles, which will be six miles next summer, when its opening is completed to the entrance of Washington Park. I do not know such another street in the world. In the evening the converging lines of gas lamps offer a prospective of unequalled beauty of its kind. The south parks are reached now by turning either into the Drexel Boulevard or the Grand Boulevard, a magnificent avenue a mile in length, tree-planted, gay with flower-beds in the season, and crowded in the sleighing-time with fast teams and fancy turnouts.

This leads me to speak of another feature of Chicago, which has no rival in this country: I mean the facility for pleasure driving and riding. Michigan Avenue from the mouth of the river, the centre of town, is macadamized. It and the other avenues immediately connected with the park system are not included in the city street department, but are under the care of the Commissioners of Parks. No traffic is permitted on them, and consequently they are in superb condition for driving, summer and winter. The whole length of Michigan Avenue you will never see a loaded team. These roads—that is, Michigan Avenue and the others of the park system, and the park drives—are superb for driving or riding, perfectly made for drainage and permanency, with a top-dressing of pulverized granite. The cost of the Michigan Avenue drive was two hundred thousand dollars a mile. The cost of the parks and boulevards in each of the three divisions is met by a tax on the property in that division. The tax is considerable, but the wise liberality of the citizens has done for the town what only royalty usually accomplishes — given it magnificent roads; and if good roads are a criterion of civilization, Chicago must stand very high. But it needed a community with a great deal of daring and confidence in the future to create this park system.

One in the heart of the city has not to drive three or four miles over cobble-stones and ruts to get to good driving-ground. When he has entered Michigan Avenue he need not pull rein for twenty to thirty miles. This is almost literally true as to extent, without counting the miles of fine drives in the parks; for the city proper is circled by great parks, already laid out as pleasure-grounds, tree-planted and beautified to a high degree, although they are nothing to what cultivation will make them in ten years more. On the lake shore, at the south, is Jackson Park; next is Washington Park, twice as large as Central Park, New York; then, farther to the west, and north, Douglas Park and Garfield Park; then Humboldt Park, until we come round to Lincoln Park, on the lake shore on the north side. These parks are all connected by broad boulevards, some of which are not yet fully developed, thus forming a continuous park drive, with enough of nature and enough of varied architecture for variety, unsurpassed, I should say, in the world within any city limits. Washington Park, with a slightly rolling surface and beautiful landscape-gardening, has not only fine drive-ways, but a splendid road set apart for horsemen. This is a dirt road, always well sprinkled, and the equestrian has a chance besides of a gallop over springy turf. Water is now so abundantly provided that this park is kept green in the driest season. From anywhere in the south side one may mount his horse or enter his carriage for a turn of fifteen or twenty miles on what is equivalent to a country road—that is to say, an English country road. Of the effect of this facility on social life I shall have occasion to speak. On the lake side of Washington Park are the grounds of the Washington Park Racing Club, with a splendid track, and stables and other facilities which, I am told, exceed anything of the kind in the country. The club-house itself is very handsome and commodious, is open to the members and their families summer and winter, and makes a favorite rendezvous for that part of society which shares its privileges. Besides its large dining and dancing halls, it has elegant apartments set apart for ladies. In winter its hospitable rooms and big wood fires are very attractive after a zero drive.

Almost equal facility for driving and riding is had on the north side by taking the lake-shore drive to Lincoln Park. Too much cannot be said of the beauty of this drive along the curving shore of an inland sea, ever attractive in the play of changing lights and colors, and beginning to be fronted by palatial houses —a foretaste of the coming Venetian variety and splendor. The park itself, dignified by the Lincoln statue, is an exquisite piece of restful landscape, looked over by a thickening assemblage of stately residences. It is a quarter of spacious elegance.

One hardly knows how to speak justly of either the physical aspect or the social life of Chicago, the present performance suggesting such promise and immediate change. The excited admiration waits a little upon expectation. I should like to see it in five years —in ten years; it is a formative period, but one of such excellence of execution that the imagination takes a very high flight in anticipating the result of another quarter of a century. What other city has begun so nobly or has planned so liberally for metropolitan solidity, elegance, and recreation? What other has such magnificent avenues and boulevards, and such a system of parks? The boy is born here who will see the town expanded far beyond these splendid pleasure-grounds, and what is now the circumference of the city will be to Chicago what the vernal gardens from St. James to Hampton are to London. This anticipation hardly seems strange when one remembers what Chicago was fifteen years ago.

Architecturally, Chicago is more interesting than

many older cities. Its wealth and opportunity for
fine building coming when our national taste is beginning to be individual, it has escaped the monotony
and mediocrity in which New York for so many years
put its money, and out of the sameness of which it is
escaping in spots. Having also plenty of room, Chicago has been able to avoid the block system in its
residences, and to give play to variety and creative
genius. It is impossible to do much with the interior
of a house in a block, however much you may load the
front with ornament. Confined to a long parallelogram, and limited as to light and air, neither comfort
nor individual taste can be consulted or satisfied.
Chicago is a city of detached houses, in the humbler
quarters as well as in the magnificent avenues, and
the effect is home-like and beautiful at the same time.
There is great variety—stone, brick, and wood intermingled, plain and ornamental; but drive where you
will in the favorite residence parts of the vast city,
you will be continually surprised with the sight of
noble and artistic houses and homes displaying taste
as well as luxury. In addition to the business and
public buildings of which I spoke, there are several,
like the Art Museum, the Studebaker Building, and
the new Auditorium, which would be conspicuous and
admired in any city in the world. The city is rich in
a few specimens of private houses by Mr. Richardson
(whose loss to the country is still apparently irreparable), houses worth a long journey to see, so simple, so
noble, so full of comfort, sentiment, unique, having
what may be called a charming personality. As to
interiors, there has been plenty of money spent in
Chicago in mere show; but, after all, I know of no

other city that has more character and individuality
in its interiors, more evidences of personal refinement
and taste. There is, of course—Boston knows that—
a grace and richness in a dwelling in which generations have accumulated the best fruits of wealth and
cultivation; but any tasteful stranger here, I am sure,
will be surprised to find in a city so new so many
homes pervaded by the atmosphere of books and art
and refined sensibility, due, I imagine, mainly to the
taste of the women, for while there are plenty of men
here who have taste, there are very few who have leisure to indulge it; and I doubt if there was ever anywhere a livable house—a man can build a palace, but
he cannot make a home—that was not the creation of
a refined woman. I do not mean to say that Chicago
is not still very much the victim of the upholsterer,
and that the eye is not offended by a good deal that
is gaudy and pretentious, but there is so much here
that is in exquisite taste that one has a hopeful heart
about its future. Everybody is not yet educated up
to the "Richardson houses," but nothing is more certain than that they will powerfully influence all the
future architecture of the town.

Perhaps there never was before such an opportunity
to study the growth of an enormous city, physically
and socially, as is offered now in Chicago, where the
development of half a century is condensed into a dec-
ade. In one respect it differs from all other cities of
anything like its size. It is not only surrounded by a
complete net-work of railways, but it is permeated by
them. The converging lines of twenty-one (I think
it is) railways paralleling each other or criss-crossing
in the suburbs concentrate upon fewer tracks as they

enter the dense part of the city, but they literally surround it, and actually pierce its heart. So complete is this environment and interlacing that you cannot enter the city from any direction without encountering a net-work of tracks. None of the water-front, except a strip on the north side, is free from them. The finest residence part of the south side, including the boulevards and parks, is surrounded and cut by them. There are a few viaducts, but for the most part the tracks occupy streets, and the crossings are at grade. Along the Michigan Avenue water-front and down the lake shore to Hyde Park, on the Illinois Central and the Michigan Central and their connections, the foreign and local trains pass incessantly (I believe over sixty a day), and the Illinois crosses above Sixteenth Street, cutting all the great southward avenues; and farther down, the tracks run between Jackson Park and Washington Park, crossing at grade the 500-feet-wide boulevard which connects these great parks and makes them one. These tracks and grade crossings, from which so few parts of the city are free, are a serious evil and danger, and the annoyance is increased by the multiplicity of street railways, and by the swiftly running cable-cars, which are a constant source of alarm to the timid. The railways present a difficult problem. The town covers such a vast area (always extending in a ratio that cannot be calculated) that to place all the passenger stations outside would be a great inconvenience, to unite the lines in a single station probably impracticable. In time, however, the roads must come in on elevated viaducts, or concentrate in three or four stations which communicate with the central parts of the town by elevated roads.

This state of things arose from the fact that the railways antedated, and we may say made, the town, which has grown up along their lines. To a town of pure business, transportation was the first requisite, and the newer roads have been encouraged to penetrate as far into the city as they could. Now that it is necessary to make it a city to live in safely and agreeably, the railways are regarded from another point of view. I suppose a sociologist would make some reflections on the effect of such a thorough permeation of tracks, trains, engines, and traffic upon the temperament of a town, the action of these exciting and irritating causes upon its nervous centres. Living in a big railway-station must have an effect on the nerves. At present this seems a legitimate part of the excited activity of the city; but if it continues, with the rapid increase of wealth and the growth of a leisure class, the inhabitants who can afford to get away will live here only the few months necessary to do their business and take a short season of social gayety, and then go to quieter places early in the spring and for the summer months.

It is at this point of view that the value of the park system appears, not only as a relief, as easily accessible recreation - grounds for the inhabitants in every part of the city, but as an element in society life. These parks, which I have already named, contain 1742 acres. The two south parks, connected so as to be substantially one, have 957 acres. Their great connecting boulevards are interfered with somewhat by railway-tracks, and none of them, except Lincoln, can be reached without crossing tracks on which locomotives run, yet, as has been said, the most important of

them are led to by good driving-roads from the heart
of the city. They have excellent roads set apart for
equestrians as well as for driving. These facilities
induce the keeping of horses, the setting up of fine
equipages, and a display for which no other city has
better opportunity. This cannot but have an appreciable effect upon the growth of luxury and display
in this direction. Indeed, it is already true that the
city keeps more private carriages—for the pleasure
not only of the rich, but of the well-to-do—in proportion to its population, than any other large city I
know. These broad thoroughfares, kept free from
traffic, furnish excellent sleighing when it does not
exist in the city streets generally, and in the summer
unequalled avenues for the show of wealth and beauty
and style. In a few years the turnouts on the Grand
Boulevard and the Lincoln Park drive will be worth
going far to see for those who admire—and who does
not? for, the world over, wealth has no spectacle more
attractive to all classes—fine horses and the splendor
of moving equipages. And here is no cramped mile
or two for parade, like most of the fashionable drives
of the world, but space inviting healthful exercise as
well as display. These broad avenues and park out-
looks, with ample ground-room, stimulate architectural rivalry, and this opportunity for driving and riding
and being on view cannot but affect very strongly the
social tone. The foresight of the busy men who
planned this park system is already vindicated. The
public appreciate their privileges. On fair days the
driving avenues are thronged. One Sunday afternoon
in January, when the sleighing was good, some one
estimated that there were as many as ten thousand

teams flying up and down Michigan Avenue and the
Grand Boulevard. This was, of course, an over-estimate, but the throng made a ten-thousand impression
on the mind. Perhaps it was a note of Western independence that a woman was here and there seen
"speeding" a fast horse, in a cutter, alone.

I suppose that most of these people had been to
church in the morning, for Chicago, which does everything it puts its hand to with tremendous energy, is
a church-going city, and I believe presents some contrast to Cincinnati in this respect. Religious, mission,
and Sunday-school work is very active, churches are
many, whatever the liberality of the creeds of a majority of them, and there are several congregations of
over two thousand people. One vast music-hall and
one theatre are thronged Sunday after Sunday with
organized, vigorous, worshipful congregations. Besides these are the Sunday meetings for ethical culture and Christian science. It is true that many of
the theatres are open as on week-days, and there is a
vast foreign population that takes its day of rest in
idleness or base-ball and garden amusements, but the
prevailing aspect of the city is that of Sunday observ-
ance. There is a good deal of wholesome New England in its tone. And it welcomes any form of activity—orthodoxy, liberalism, revivals, ethical culture.

A special interest in Chicago at the moment is because it is forming—full of contrasts and of promise,
palaces and shanties side by side. Its forces are gathered and accumulating, but not assimilated. What a
mass of crude, undigested material it has! In one
region on the west side are twenty thousand Bohemians and Poles ; the street signs are all foreign and

of unpronounceable names—a physically strong, but mentally and morally brutal, people for the most part ; the adults generally do not speak English, and clanning as they do, they probably never will. There is no hope that this generation will be intelligent American citizens, or be otherwise than the political prey of demagogues. But their children are in the excellent public schools, and will take in American ideas and take on American ways. Still, the mill has about as much grist as it can grind at present.

Social life is, speaking generally, as unformed, unselected, as the city—that is, more fluid and undetermined than in Eastern large cities. That is merely to say, however, that while it is American, it is young. When you come to individuals, the people in society are largely from the East, or have Eastern connections that determine their conduct. For twenty years the great universities, Harvard, Yale, Amherst, Princeton, and the rest, have been pouring in their young men here. There is no better element in the world, and it is felt in every pulse of the town. Young couples marry and come here from every sort of Eastern circle. But the town has grown so fast, and so many new people have come into the ability suddenly to spend money in fine houses and equipages, that the people do not know each other. You may drive past miles of good houses, with a man who has grown up with the town, who cannot tell you who any of the occupants of the houses are. Men know each other on change, in the courts, in business, and are beginning to know each other in clubs, but society has not got itself sorted out and arranged, or discovered its elements. This is a metropolitan trait, it is true, but the condition is socially very different from what it is in New York or Boston; the small village associations survive a little yet, struggling against the territorial distances, but the social mass is still unorganized, although "society" is a prominent feature in the newspapers. Of course it is understood that there are people "in society," and dinners, and all that, in nowise different from the same people and events the world over.

A striking feature of the town is "youth," visible in social life as well as in business. An Eastern man is surprised to see so many young men in responsible positions, at the head, or taking the managing oar, in great moneyed institutions, in railway corporations, and in societies of charity and culture. A young man, graduate of the city high-school, is at the same time president of a prominent bank, president of the Board of Trade, and president of the Art Institute. This youthful spirit must be contagious, for apparently the more elderly men do not permit themselves to become old, either in the business or the pleasures of life. Everything goes on with youthful vim and spirit.

Next to the youth, and perhaps more noticeable, the characteristic feature of Chicago is money-making, and the money power is as obtrusive socially as on change. When we come to speak of educational and intellectual tendencies, it will be seen how this spirit is being at once utilized and mitigated; but for the moment money is the recognized power. How could it be otherwise? Youth and energy did not flock here for pleasure or for society, but simply for fortune. And success in money-getting was about the only one considered. And it is still that by which Chicago is chiefly known abroad, by that and by a certain consciousness of it which is noticed. And as women reflect social conditions most vividly, it cannot be denied that there is a type known in Europe and in the East as the Chicago young woman, capable rather than timid, dashing rather than retiring, quite able to take care of herself. But this is not by any means an exhaustive account of the Chicago woman of to-day.

While it must be said that the men, as a rule, are too much absorbed in business to give heed to anything else, yet even this statement will need more qualification than would appear at first, when we come to consider the educational, industrial, and reformatory projects. And indeed a veritable exception is the Literary Club, of nearly two hundred members, a mingling of business and professional men, who have fine rooms in the Art Building, and meet weekly for papers and discussions. It is not in every city that an equal number of busy men will give the time to this sort of intellectual recreation. The energy here is superabundant; in whatever direction it is exerted it is very effective; and it may be said, in the language of the street, that if the men of Chicago seriously take hold of culture, they will make it hum.

Still it remains true here, as elsewhere in the United States, that women are in advance in the intellectual revival. One cannot yet predict what will be the result of this continental furor for literary, scientific, and study clubs—in some places in the East the literary wave has already risen to the height of the scientific study of whist—but for the time being Chica-

go women **are in the full swing of literary life. Mr.**
Browning says **that more** of his books **are sold in**
Chicago **than in any** other American **city. Granting**
some affectation, some passing fashion, **in the Brown-**
ing, Dante, and **Shakespeare clubs, I think it** is true
that the **Chicago woman, who is imbued with** the en-
ergy of the place, is more serious in her work than
are women in **many** other places; **at least she is more**
enthusiastic. **Her spirit is open, more that of** frank
admiration than of criticism **of both literature and of**
authors. **This carries her not only further into the**
heart of literature itself, but into a genuine enjoy-
ment **of it—wanting almost to some circles at the**
East, who are too cultivated to admire with warmth
or to surrender themselves to the delights of learn-
ing, **but find their avocation rather in what may be**
called **literary detraction,** the spirit being that of dis-
section **of authors and books, much** as social gossips
pick to pieces the characters **of those of their own**
set. And **one occupation is as** good as **the other.**
Chicago has **some reputation for** beauty, for **having**
pretty, dashing, and attractive women; **it is as much**
entitled to be considered for its intelligent women **who**
are intellectually agreeable. Comparisons are very un-
safe, **but it is my** impression that there **is more love**
for books **in Chicago** than in New York society, and
less of the critical, *nil admirari* spirit than in Boston.
It might be **an indication of** no value **(only of the**
taste of **individuals) that books should be the** principal "favors" **at a fashionable german,** but there is a
book-store **in** the city whose evidence cannot be set
aside by reference **to any** freak of fashion. McClurg's
book - store **is a very extensive** establishment in all

departments — publishing, manufacturing, retailing, wholesaling, and importing. In some respects it has not its equal in this country. The book-lover, whether he comes from London or New York, will find there a stock, constantly sold and constantly replenished, of books rare, curious, interesting, that will surprise him. The general intelligence that sustains a retail shop of this variety and magnitude must be considerable, and speaks of a taste for books with which the city has not been credited; but the cultivation, the special love of books for themselves, which makes possible this rich corner of rare and imported books at McClurg's, would be noticeable in any city, and women as well as men in Chicago are buyers and appreciators of first editions, autograph and presentation copies, and books valued because they are scarce and rare.

Chicago has a physical peculiarity that radically affects its social condition, and prevents its becoming homogeneous. It has one business centre and three distinct residence parts, divided by the branching river. Communication between the residence sections has to be made through the business city, and is further hindered by the bridge crossings, which cause irritating delays the greater part of the year. The result is that three villages grew up, now become cities in size, and each with a peculiar character. The north side was originally the more aristocratic, and having fewer railways and a less-occupied-with-business lake front, was the more agreeable as a place of residence, always having the drawback of the bridge crossings to the business part. After the great fire, building lots were cheaper there than on the south side within reasonable distance of the active city. It has grown amazingly, and is beautified by stately houses and fine architecture, and would probably still be called the more desirable place of residence. But the south side has two great advantages—easy access to the business centre and to the great southern parks and pleasure-grounds. This latter would decide many to live there. The vast west side, with its lumber-yards and factories, its foreign settlements, and its population outnumbering the two other sections combined, is practically an unknown region socially to the north side and south side. The causes which produced three villages surrounding a common business centre will continue to operate. The west side will continue to expand with cheap houses, or even elegant residences on the park avenues—it is the glory of Chicago that such a large proportion of its houses are owned by their occupants, and that there are few tenement rookeries, and even few gigantic apartment houses—over a limitless prairie; the north side will grow in increasing beauty about Lincoln Park; and the south side will more and more gravitate with imposing houses about the attractive south parks. Thus the two fashionable parts of the city, separated by five, eight, and ten miles, will develop a social life of their own, about as distinct as New York and Brooklyn. It remains to be seen which will call the other "Brooklyn." At present these divisions account for much of the disorganization of social life, and prevent that concentration which seems essential to the highest social development.

In this situation Chicago is original, as she is in many other ways, and it makes one of the interesting phases in the guesses at her future.

X.

CHICAGO.

[Second Paper.]

THE country gets its impression of Chicago largely from the Chicago newspapers. In my observation, the impression is wrong. The press is able, vigorous, voluminous, full of enterprise, alert, spirited; its news columns are marvellous in quantity, if not in quality; nowhere are important events, public meetings, and demonstrations more fully, graphically, and satisfactorily reported; it has keen and competent writers in several departments of criticism—theatrical, musical, and occasionally literary; independence, with less of personal bias than in some other cities; the editorial pages of most of the newspapers are bright, sparkling, witty, not seldom spiced with knowing drollery, and strong, vivid, well-informed and well-written, in the discussion of public questions, with an allowance always to be made for the "personal equation" in dealing with particular men and measures—as little provincial in this respect as any press in the country.

But it lacks tone, elevation of purpose; it represents to the world the inferior elements of a great city rather than the better, under a mistaken notion in the press and the public, not confined to Chicago, as to what is "news." It cannot escape the charge of being highly sensational; that is, the elevation into notorie-

ty of mean persons and mean events by every rhetorical and pictorial device. Day after day the leading
news, the most displayed and most conspicuous, will
be of vulgar men and women, and all the more expanded if it have in it a spice of scandal. This sort
of reading creates a diseased appetite, which requires
a stronger dose daily to satisfy; and people who read
it lose their relish for the higher, more decent, if less
piquant, news of the world. Of course the Chicago
newspapers are not by any means alone in this course;
it is a disease of the time. Even New York has recently imitated successfully this feature of what is
called Western journalism.

But it is largely from the Chicago newspapers that
the impression has gone abroad that the city is pre-
eminent in divorces, pre-eminent in scandals, that its
society is fast, that it is vulgar and pretentious, that
its tone is "shoddy," and its culture a sham. The
laws of Illinois in regard to divorces are not more lax
than in some Eastern States, and divorces are not
more numerous there of residents (according to population) than in some Eastern towns ; but while the
press of the latter give merely an official line to the
court separations, the Chicago papers parade all the
details, and illustrate them with pictures. Many people go there to get divorces, because they avoid scandal at their homes, and because the Chicago courts
offer unusual facilities in being open every month in
the year. Chicago has a young, mobile population, an
immense foreign brutal element. I watched for some
weeks the daily reports of divorces and scandals. Almost without exception they related to the lower, not
to say the more vulgar, portions of social life. In

several years the city has had, I believe, only two *causes célèbres* in what is called good society—a remarkable record for a city of its size. Of course a city of this magnitude and mobility is not free from vice and immorality and fast living; but I am compelled to record the deliberate opinion, formed on a good deal of observation and inquiry, that the moral tone in Chicago society, in all the well-to-do industrious classes which give the town its distinctive character, is purer and higher than in any other city of its size with which I am acquainted, and purer than in many much smaller. The tone is not so fast, public opinion is more restrictive, and women take, and are disposed to take, less latitude in conduct. This was not my impression from the newspapers. But it is true not only that social life holds itself to great propriety, but that the moral atmosphere is uncommonly pure and wholesome. At the same time, the city does not lack gayety of movement, and it would not be called prudish, nor in some respects conventional.

It is curious, also, that the newspapers, or some of them, take pleasure in mocking at the culture of the town. Outside papers catch this spirit, and the "culture" of Chicago is the butt of the paragraphers. It is a singular attitude for newspapers to take regarding their own city. Not long ago Mr. McClurg published a very neat volume, in vellum, of the fragments of Sappho, with translations. If the volume had appeared in Boston it would have been welcomed and most respectfully received in Chicago. But instead of regarding it as an evidence of the growing literary taste of the new town, the humorists saw occasion in it for exquisite mockery in the juxtaposition of Sappho

with the modern ability to kill seven pigs a minute,
and in the cleverest and most humorous manner set
all the country in a roar over the incongruity. It
goes without saying that the business men of Chicago
were not sitting up nights to study the Greek poets
in the original; but the fact was that there was
enough literary taste in the city to make the volume
a profitable venture, and that its appearance was an
evidence of intellectual activity and scholarly inclination that would be creditable to any city in the land.
It was not at all my intention to intrude my impressions of a newspaper press so very able and with such
magnificent opportunities as that of Chicago, but it
was unavoidable to mention one of the causes of the
misapprehension of the social and moral condition of
the city.

The business statistics of Chicago, and the story of
its growth, and the social movement, which have
been touched on in a previous paper, give only a half-
picture of the life of the town. The prophecy for its
great and more hopeful future is in other exhibitions
of its incessant activity. My limits permit only a
reference to its churches, extensive charities (which
alone would make a remarkable and most creditable
chapter), hospitals, medical schools, and conservato-
ries of music. Club life is attaining metropolitan proportions. There is on the south side the Chicago, the
Union League, the University, the Calumet, and on
the north side the Union—all vigorous, and most of
them housed in superb buildings of their own. The
Women's Exchange is a most useful organization,
and the Ladies' Fortnightly ranks with the best intellectual associations in the country. The Commercial

Club, composed of sixty representative business men in all departments, is a most vital element in the prosperity of the city. I cannot dwell upon these. But at least a word must be said about the charities, and some space must be given to the schools.

The number of solicitors for far West churches and colleges who pass by Chicago and come to New York and New England for money have created the impression that Chicago is not a good place to go for this purpose. Whatever may be the truth of this, the city does give royally for private charities, and liberally for mission work beyond her borders. It is estimated by those familiar with the subject that Chicago contributes for charitable and religious purposes, exclusive of the public charities of the city and county, not less than five millions of dollars annually. I have not room to give even the partial list of the benevolent societies that lies before me, but beginning with the Chicago Relief and Aid, and the Armour Mission, and going down to lesser organizations, the sum annually given by them is considerably over half a million dollars. The amount raised by the churches of various denominations for religious purposes is not less than four millions yearly. These figures prove the liberality, and I am able to add that the charities are most sympathetically and intelligently administered.

Inviting, by its opportunities for labor and its facilities for business, comers from all the world, a large proportion of whom are aliens to the language and institutions of America, Chicago is making a noble fight to assimilate this material into good citizenship. The popular schools are liberally sustained, intelligently directed, practise the most advanced and inspiring methods, and exhibit excellent results. I have not the statistics of 1887; but in 1886, when the population was only 703,000, there were 129,000 between the ages of six and sixteen, of whom 83,000 were enrolled as pupils, and the average daily attendance in schools was over 65,000. Besides these there were about 43,000 in private schools. The census of 1886 reports only 34 children between the ages of six and twenty-one who could neither read nor write. There were 91 school buildings owned by the city, and two rented. Of these, three are high-schools, one in each division, the newest, on the west side, having 1000 students. The school attendance increases by a large per cent. each year. The principals of the high-schools were men; of the grammar and primary schools, 35 men and 42 women. The total of teachers was 1440, of whom 56 were men. By the census of 1886 there were 106,929 children in the city under six years of age. No kindergartens are attached to the public schools, but the question of attaching them is agitated. In the lower grades, however, the instruction is by object lessons, drawing, writing, modelling, and exercises that train the eye to observe, the tongue to describe, and that awaken attention without weariness. The alertness of the scholars and the enthusiasm of the teachers were marked. It should be added that German is extensively taught in the grammar schools, and that the number enrolled in the German classes in 1886 was over 28,000. There is some public sentiment for throwing out German from the public schools, and generally for restricting studies in the higher branches.

The argument against this is that very few of the children, and the majority of those girls, enter the high-schools ; the boys are taken out early for business, and get no education afterwards. In 1885 were organized public elementary evening schools (which had, in 1886, 6709 pupils), and an evening high-school, in which book-keeping, stenography, mechanical drawing, and advanced mathematics were taught. The School Committee also have in charge day schools for the education of deaf and dumb children.

The total expenditure for 1886 was $2,060,803 ; this includes $1,023,394 paid to superintendents and teachers, and large sums for new buildings, apparatus, and repairs. The total cash receipts for school purposes were $2,091,951. Of this was from the school tax fund $1,758,053 (the total city tax for all purposes was $5,368,409), and the rest from State dividend and school fund bonds and miscellaneous sources. These figures show that education is not neglected.

Of the quality and efficacy of this education there cannot be two opinions, as seen in the schools which I visited. The high-school on the west side is a model of its kind ; but perhaps as interesting an example of popular education as any is the Franklin grammar and primary school on the north side, in a district of laboring people. Here were 1700 pupils, all children of working people, mostly Swedes and Germans, from the age of six years upwards. Here were found some of the children of the late anarchists, and nowhere else can one see a more interesting attempt to manufacture intelligent American citizens. The instruction rises through the several grades from object lessons, drawing, writing and reading (and writing and reading well), to elementary physiology, political and constitutional history, and physical geography. Here is taught to young children what they cannot learn at home, and might never clearly comprehend otherwise; not only something of the geography and history of the country, but the distinctive principles of our government, its constitutional ideas, the growth, creeds, and relations of political parties, and the personality of the great men who have represented them. That the pupils comprehend these subjects fairly well I had evidence in recitations that were as pleasing as surprising. In this way Chicago is teaching its alien population American ideas, and it is fair to presume that the rising generation will have some notion of the nature and value of our institutions that will save them from the inclination to destroy them.

The public mind is agitated a good deal on the question of the introduction of manual training into the public schools. The idea of some people is that manual training should only be used as an aid to mental training, in order to give definiteness and accuracy to thought; others would like actual trades taught; and others think that it is outside the function of the State to teach anything but elementary mental studies. The subject would require an essay by itself, and I only allude to it to say that Chicago is quite alive to the problems and the most advanced educational ideas. If one would like to study the philosophy and the practical working of what may be called physico-mental training, I know no better place in the country to do so than the Cook County Normal School, near Englewood, under the charge of Colonel F. W. Parker, the originator of what is known as the

14

Quincy (Massachusetts) System. This is a training school for about 100 teachers, in a building where they have practice on about 500 children in all stages of education, from the kindergarten up to the eighth grade. This may be called a thorough manual training school, but not to teach trades, work being done in drawing, modelling in clay, making raised maps, and wood - carving. The Quincy System, which is sometimes described as the development of character by developing mind and body, has a literature to itself. This remarkable school, which draws teachers for training from all over the country, is a notable instance of the hospitality of the West to new and advanced ideas. It does not neglect the literary side in education. Here and in some of the grammar schools of Chicago the experiment is successfully tried of interesting young children in the best literature by reading to them from the works of the best authors, ancient and modern, and giving them a taste for what is excellent, instead of the trash that is likely to fall into their hands—the cultivation of sustained and consecutive interest in narratives, essays, and descriptions in good literature, in place of the scrappy selections and reading-books written down to the childish level. The written comments and criticisms of the children on what they acquire in this way are a perfect vindication of the experiment. It is to be said also that this sort of education, coupled with the manual training, and the inculcated love for order and neatness, is beginning to tell on the homes of these children. The parents are actually being educated and civilized through the public schools.

An opportunity for superior technical education is

given in the Chicago Manual Training School, founded
and sustained by the Commercial Club. It has a
handsome and commodious building on the corner of
Michigan Avenue and Twelfth Street, which accom-
modates over two hundred pupils, under the direction
of Dr. Henry H. Belfield, assisted by an able corps of
teachers and practical mechanics. It has only been
in operation since 1884, but has fully demonstrated its
usefulness in the training of young men for places of
responsibility and profit. Some of the pupils are
from the city schools, but it is open to all boys of
good character and promise. The course is three years,
in which the tuition is $80, $100, and $120 a year;
but the club provides for the payment of the tuition
of a limited number of deserving boys whose parents
lack the means to give them this sort of education.
The course includes the higher mathematics, English,
and French or Latin, physics, chemistry—in short, a
high-school course—with drawing, and all sorts of
technical training in work in wood and iron, the use
and making of tools, and the building of machinery,
up to the construction of steam-engines, stationary
and locomotive. Throughout the course one hour each
day is given to drawing, two hours to shop-work, and
the remainder of the school day to study and recitation. The shops—the wood-work rooms, the foundery,
the forge-room, the machine-shop — are exceedingly
well equipped and well managed. The visitor cannot
but be pleased by the tone of the school and the intelligent enthusiasm of the pupils. It is an institution
likely to grow, and perhaps become the nucleus of a
great technical school, which the West much needs.
It is worthy of notice also as an illustration of the

public spirit, sagacity, and liberality of the Chicago business men. They probably see that if the city is greatly to increase its importance as a manufacturing centre, it must train a considerable proportion of its population to the highest skilled labor, and that splendidly equipped and ably taught technical schools would do for Chicago what similar institutions in Zurich have done for Switzerland. Chicago is ready for a really comprehensive technical and industrial college, and probably no other investment would now add more to the solid prosperity and wealth of the town.

Such an institution would not hinder, but rather help, the higher education, without which the best technical education tends to materialize life. Chicago must before long recognize the value of the intellectual side by beginning the foundation of a college of pure learning. For in nothing is the Western society of to-day more in danger than in the superficial half-education which is called "practical," and in the lack of logic and philosophy. The tendency to the literary side—awakening a love for good books—in the public schools is very hopeful. The existence of some well-chosen private libraries shows the same tendency. In art and archæology there is also much promise. The Art Institute is a very fine building, with a vigorous school in drawing and painting, and its occasional loan exhibitions show that the city contains a good many fine pictures, though scarcely proportioned to its wealth. The Historical Society, which has had the irreparable misfortune twice to lose its entire collections by fire, is beginning anew with vigor, and will shortly erect a building from its own funds. Among the private collections which have a historical value is that relating to the Indian history of the West made by Mr. Edward Ayer, and a large library of rare and scarce books, mostly of the English Shakespeare period, by the Rev. Frank M. Bristoll. These, together with the remarkable collection of Mr. C. F. Gunther (of which further mention will be made), are prophecies of a great literary and archæological museum.

The city has reason to be proud of its Free Public Library, organized under the general library law of Illinois, which permits the support of a free library in every incorporated city, town, and township by taxation. This library is sustained by a tax of one half-mill on the assessed value of all the city property. This brings it in now about $80,000 a year, which makes its income for 1888, together with its fund and fines, about $90,000. It is at present housed in the City Hall, but will soon have a building of its own (on Dearborn Park), towards the erection of which it has a considerable fund. It has about 130,000 volumes, including a fair reference library and many expensive art books. The institution has been well managed hitherto, notwithstanding its connection with politics in the appointment of the trustees by the mayor, and its dependence upon the city councils. The reading-rooms are thronged daily; the average daily circulation has increased yearly; it was 2263 in 1887—a gain of eleven per cent. over the preceding year. This is stimulated by the establishment of eight delivering stations in different parts of the city. The cosmopolitan character of the users of the library is indicated by the uncommon number of German,

French, Dutch, Bohemian, Polish, and Scandinavian books. Of the books issued at the delivery stations in 1887 twelve per cent. were in the Bohemian language. The encouraging thing about this free library is that it is not only freely used, but that it is as freely sustained by the voting population.

Another institution, which promises to have still more influence on the city, and indeed on the whole North-west, is the Newberry Library, now organizing under an able board of trustees, who have chosen Mr. W. F. Poole as librarian. The munificent fund of the donor is now reckoned at about $2,500,000, but the value of the property will be very much more than this in a few years. A temporary building for the library, which is slowly forming, will be erected at once, but the library, which is to occupy a square on the north side, will not be erected until the plans are fully matured. It is to be a library of reference and study solely, and it is in contemplation to have the books distributed in separate rooms for each department, with ample facilities for reading and study in each room. If the library is built and the collections are made in accordance with the ample means at command, and in the spirit of its projectors, it will powerfully tend to make Chicago not only the money but the intellectual centre of the North-west, and attract to it hosts of students from all quarters. One can hardly over-estimate the influence that such a library as this may be will have upon the character and the attractiveness of the city.

I hope that it will have ample space for, and that it will receive, certain literary collections, such as are the glory and the attraction, both to students and sight-seers, of the great libraries of the world. And this leads me to speak of the treasures of Mr. Gunther, the most remarkable private collection I have ever seen, and already worthy to rank with some of the most famous on public exhibition. Mr. Gunther is a candy manufacturer, who has an archæological and "curio" taste, and for many years has devoted an amount of money to the purchase of historical relics that if known would probably astonish the public. Only specimens of what he has can be displayed in the large apartment set apart for the purpose over his shop. The collection is miscellaneous, forming a varied and most interesting museum. It contains relics—many of them unique, and most of them having a historical value—from many lands and all periods since the Middle Ages, and is strong in relics and documents relating to our own history, from the colonial period down to the close of our civil war. But the distinction of the collection is in its original letters and manuscripts of famous people, and its missals, illuminated manuscripts, and rare books. It is hardly possible to mention a name famous since America was discovered that is not here represented by an autograph letter or some personal relics. We may pass by such mementos as the Appomattox table, a sampler worked by Queen Elizabeth, a prayer-book of Mary, Queen of Scots, personal belongings of Washington, Lincoln, and hundreds of other historical characters, but we must give a little space to the books and manuscripts, in order that it may be seen that all the wealth of Chicago is not in grain and meat.

It is only possible here to name a few of the original letters, manuscripts, and historical papers in this

wonderful collection of over seventeen thousand. Most
of the great names in the literature of our era are represented. There is an autograph letter of Molière, the
only one known outside of France, except one in the
British Museum; there are letters of Voltaire, Victor
Hugo, Madame Roland, and other French writers. It
is understood that this is not a collection of mere
autographs, but of letters or original manuscripts of
those named. In Germany, nearly all the great poets
and writers—Goethe, Schiller, Uhland, Lessing, etc.;
in England, Milton, Pope, Shelley, Keats, Wordsworth,
Coleridge, Cowper, Hunt, Gray, etc.; the manuscript
of Byron's "Prometheus," the "Auld Lang Syne" of
Burns, and his "Journal in the Highlands;" "Sweet
Home" in the author's hand; a poem by Thackeray;
manuscript stories of Scott and Dickens. Among the
Italians, Tasso. In America, the known authors, almost without exception. There are letters from nearly all the prominent reformers—Calvin, Melanchthon,
Zwingle, Erasmus, Savonarola; a letter of Luther in
regard to the Pope's bull; letters of prominent leaders—William the Silent, John the Steadfast, Gustavus
Adolphus, Wallenstein. There is a curious collection
of letters of the saints—St. Francis de Sales, St. Vin-
cent de Paul, St. Borromeo; letters of the Popes for
three centuries and a half, and of many of the great
cardinals.

I must set down a few more of the noted names,
and that without much order. There is a manuscript
of Charlotte Corday (probably the only one in this
country), John Bunyan, Izaak Walton, John Cotton,
Michael Angelo, Galileo, Lorenzo the Magnificent; letters of Queen Elizabeth, Mary, Queen of Scots, Mary

of England, Anne, several of Victoria (one at the age
of twelve), Catherine de' Medici, Marie Antoinette,
Josephine, Marie Louise; letters of all the Napoleons,
of Frederick the Great, Marat, Robespierre, St. Just;
a letter of Hernando Cortez to Charles the Fifth; a
letter of Alverez; letters of kings of all European nations, and statesmen and generals without number.

The collection is rich in colonial and Revolutionary
material; original letters from Plymouth Colony, 1621,
1622, 1623—I believe the only ones known; manuscript
sermons of the early American ministers; letters of the
first bishops, White and Seabury; letters of John An-
dré, Nathan Hale, Kosciusko, Pulaski, De Kalb, Steu-
ben, and of great numbers of the general and subor-
dinate officers of the French and Revolutionary wars;
William Tudor's manuscript account of the battle of
Bunker Hill; a letter of Aide-de-camp Robert Orhm
to the Governor of Pennsylvania relating Braddock's
defeat; the original of Washington's first Thanksgiv-
ing proclamation; the report of the committee of the
Continental Congress on its visit to Valley Forge on
the distress of the army; the original proceedings of
the Commissioners of the Colonies at Cambridge for
the organization of the Continental army; original returns of the Hessians captured at Princeton; orderly
books of the Continental army; manuscripts and surveys of the early explorers; letters of Lafitte, the pi-
rate, Paul Jones, Captain Lawrence, Bainbridge, and
so on. Documents relating to the Washington family are very remarkable: the original will of Lawrence
Washington bequeathing Mount Vernon to George;
will of John Custis to his family; letters of Martha,
of Mary, the mother of George, of Betty Lewis, his

sister, of all his step and grand children of the Custis family.

In music there are the original manuscript compositions of all the leading musicians in our modern world, and there is a large collection of the choral books from ancient monasteries and churches. There are exquisite illuminated missals on parchment of all periods from the eighth century. Of the large array of Bibles and other early printed books it is impossible to speak, except in a general way. There is a copy of the first English Bible, Coverdale's, also of the very rare second Matthews, and of most of the other editions of the English Bible; the first Scotch, Irish, French, Welsh, and German Luther Bibles; the first Eliot's Indian Bible, of 1662, and the second, of 1685; the first American Bibles; the first American primers, almanacs, newspapers, and the first patent, issued in 1794; the first book printed in Boston; the first printed accounts of New York, Pennsylvania, New Jersey, Virginia, South Carolina, Georgia; the first picture of New York City, an original plan of the city in 1700, and one of it in 1765; early surveys of Boston, Philadelphia, and New York; the earliest maps of America, including the first, second, and third map of the world in which America appears.

Returning to England, there are the Shakespeare folio editions of 1632 and 1685; the first of his printed "Poems" and the "Rape of Lucrece;" an early quarto of "Othello;" the first edition of Ben Jonson, 1616, in which Shakespeare's name appears in the cast for a play; and letters from the Earl of Southampton, Shakespeare's friend, and Sir Walter Raleigh, Francis Bacon, and Essex. There is also a letter written by

Oliver Cromwell while he was engaged in the conquest of Ireland.

The relics, documents, and letters illustrating our civil war are constantly being added to. There are many old engravings, caricatures, and broadsides. Of oil-portraits there are three originals of Washington, one by Stuart, one by Peale, one by Polk, and I think I remember one or two miniatures. There is also a portrait in oil of Shakespeare which may become important. The original canvas has been remounted, and there are indubitable signs of its age, although the picture can be traced back only about one hundred and fifty years. The owner hopes to be able to prove that it is a contemporary work. The interesting fact about it is that while it is not remarkable as a work of art, it is recognizable at once as a likeness of what we suppose from other portraits and the busts to be the face and head of Shakespeare, and yet it is different from all other pictures we know, so that it does not suggest itself as a copy.

The most important of Mr. Gunther's collection is an autograph of Shakespeare; if it prove to be genuine, it will be one of the four in the world, and a great possession for America. This autograph is pasted on the fly-leaf of a folio of 1632, which was the property of one John Ward. In 1839 there was published in London, from manuscripts in possession of the Medical Society, extracts from the diary of John Ward (1648–1679), who was vicar and doctor at Stratford-on-Avon. It is to this diary that we owe certain facts theretofore unknown about Shakespeare. The editor, Mr. Stevens, had this volume in his hands while he was compiling his book, and refers to it in his pref ace. He supposed it to have belonged to the John Ward, vicar, who kept the diary. It turns out, however, to have been the property of John Ward the actor, who was in Stratford in 1740, was an enthusiast in the revival of Shakespeare, and played Hamlet there in order to raise money to repair the bust of the poet in the church. This folio has the appearance of being much used. On the fly-leaf is writing by Ward and his signature; there are marginal notes and directions in his hand, and several of the pages from which parts were torn off have been repaired by manuscript text neatly joined.

The Shakespeare signature is pasted on the leaf above Ward's name. The paper on which it is written is unlike that of the book in texture. The slip was pasted on when the leaf was not as brown as it is now, as can be seen at one end where it is lifted. The signature is written out fairly and in full, *William Shakspeare*, like the one to the will, and differs from the two others, which are hasty scrawls, as if the writer were cramped for room, or finished off the last syllable with a flourish, indifferent to the formation of the letters. I had the opportunity to compare it with a careful tracing of the signature to the will sent over by Mr. Hallowell-Phillips. At first sight the two signatures appear to be identical; but on examination they are not; there is just that difference in the strokes, spaces, and formation of the letters that always appears in two signatures by the same hand. One is not a copy of the other, and the one in the folio had to me the unmistakable stamp of genuineness. The experts in handwriting and the microscopists in this country who have examined ink and paper as to antiquity, I understand, regard it as genuine.

There seems to be all along the line no reason to suspect forgery. What more natural than that John Ward, the owner of the book, and a Shakespeare enthusiast, should have enriched his beloved volume with an autograph which he found somewhere in Stratford? And in 1740 there was no craze or controversy about Shakespeare to make the forgery of his autograph an object. And there is no suspicion that the book has been doctored for a market. It never was sold for a price. It was found in Utah, whither it had drifted from England in the possession of an emigrant, and he readily gave it in exchange for a new and fresh edition of Shakespeare's works.

I have dwelt upon this collection at some length, first because of its intrinsic value, second because of its importance to Chicago as a nucleus for what (I hope in connection with the Newberry Library) will become one of the most interesting museums in the country, and lastly as an illustration of what a Western business man may do with his money.

New York is the first and Chicago the second base of operations on this continent—the second in point of departure, I will not say for another civilization, but for a great civilizing and conquering movement, at once a reservoir and distributing point of energy, power, and money. And precisely here is to be fought out and settled some of the most important problems concerning labor, supply, and transportation. Striking as are the operations of merchants, manufacturers, and traders, nothing in the city makes a greater appeal to the imagination than the railways that centre there, whether we consider their fifty thousand miles of track, the enormous investment in them, or their competition for the carrying trade of the vast regions they pierce, and apparently compel to be tributary to the central city. The story of their building would read like a romance, and a simple statement of their organization, management, and business rivals the affairs of an empire. The present development of a belt road round the city, to serve as a track of freight exchange for all the lines, like the transfer grounds between St. Paul and Minneapolis, is found to be an affair of great magnitude, as must needs be to accommodate lines of traffic that represent an investment in stock and bonds of $1,305,000,000.

As it is not my purpose to describe the railway systems of the West, but only to speak of some of the problems involved in them, it will suffice to mention two of the leading corporations. Passing by the great eastern lines, and those like the Illinois Central, and the Chicago, Alton, and St. Louis, and the Atchison, Topeka, and Santa Fé, which are operating mainly to the south and south-west, and the Chicago, Milwaukee, and St. Paul, one of the greatest corporations, with a mileage which had reached 4921 December 1, 1885, and has increased since, we may name the Chicago and North-western, and the Chicago, Burlington, and Quincy. Each of these great systems, which has grown by accretion and extension and consolidations of small roads, operates over four thousand miles of road, leaving out from the North-western's mileage that of the Omaha system, which it controls. Looked at on the map, each of these systems completely occupies a vast territory, the one mainly to the north of the other, but they interlace to some extent and parallel each other in very important competitions.

The North-western system, which includes, besides the lines that have its name, the St. Paul, Minneapolis, and Omaha, the Fremont, Elkhorn, and Missouri Valley, and several minor roads, occupies northern Illinois and southern Wisconsin, sends a line along Lake Michigan to Lake Superior, with branches, a line to St. Paul, with branches tapping Lake Superior again at Bayfield and Duluth, sends another trunk line, with branches, into the far fields of Dakota, drops down a tangle of lines through Iowa and into Nebraska, sends another great line through northern Nebraska into Wyoming, with a divergence into the Black Hills, and runs all these feeders into Chicago by another trunk line from Omaha. By the report of 1887 the gross earnings of this system (in round numbers) were over twenty-six millions, expenses over twenty millions, leaving a net income of over six million dollars. In these items the receipts for freight were over nineteen millions, and from passengers less than six millions. Not to enter into confusing details, the magnitude of the system is shown in the general balance-sheet for May, 1887, when the cost of road (4101 miles), the sinking funds, the general assets, and the operating assets foot up $176,048,000. Over 3500 miles of this road are laid with steel rails; the equipment required 735 engines and over 23,000 cars of all sorts. It is worthy of note that a table makes the net earnings of 4000 miles of road, 1887, only a little more than those of 3000 miles of road in 1882—a greater gain evidently to the public than to the railroad.

In speaking of this system territorially, I have included the Chicago, St. Paul, Minneapolis, and Omaha, but not in the above figures. The two systems have the same president, but different general managers and other officials, and the reports are separate. To the over 4000 miles of the other North-western lines, therefore, are to be added the 1360 miles of the Omaha system (report of December, 1886, since considerably increased). The balance-sheet of the Omaha system (December, 1886) shows a cost of over fifty-seven millions. Its total net earnings over operating expenses and taxes were about $2,304,000. It then required an equipment of 194 locomotives and about 6000 cars. These figures are not, of course, given for specific railroad information, but merely to give a general idea of the magnitude of operations. This may be illustrated by another item. During the year for which the above figures have been given the entire North-western system ran on the average 415 passenger and 732 freight trains each day through the year. It may also be an interesting comparison to say that all the railways in Connecticut, including those that run into other States, have 416 locomotives, 668 passenger cars, and 11,502 other cars, and that their total mileage in the State is 1405 miles.

The Chicago, Burlington, and Quincy (report of December, 1886) was operating 4036 miles of road. Its only eccentric development was the recent Burlington and Northern, up the Mississippi River to St. Paul. Its main stem from Chicago branches out over northern and western Illinois, runs down to St. Louis, from thence to Kansas City by way of Hannibal, has a trunk line to Omaha, criss-crosses northern Missouri

and southern Iowa, skirts and pierces Kansas, and
fairly occupies three-quarters of Nebraska with a net-
work of tracks, sending out lines north of the Platte,
and one to Cheyenne and one to Denver. The whole
amount of stock and bonds, December, 1886, was reported at $155,920,000. The gross earnings for 1886
were over twenty-six millions (over nineteen of which
was for freight and over five for passengers), operating expenses over fourteen millions, leaving over twelve
millions net earnings. The system that year paid eight
per cent. dividends (as it had done for a long series of
years), leaving over fixed charges and dividends about
a million and a half to be carried to surplus or construction outlays. The equipment for the year required 619 engines and over 24,000 cars. These figures do not give the exact present condition of the
road, but only indicate the magnitude of its affairs.

Both these great systems have been well managed,
and both have been, and continue to be, great agents
in developing the West. Both have been profitable to
investors. The comparatively small cost of building
roads in the West and the profit hitherto have invited capital, and stimulated the construction of roads
not absolutely needed. There are too many miles of
road for capitalists. Are there too many for the accommodation of the public? What locality would be
willing to surrender its road?

It is difficult to understand the attitude of the
Western Granger and the Western Legislatures towards the railways, or it would be if we didn't understand pretty well the nature of demagogues the world
over. The people are everywhere crazy for roads, for
more and more roads. The whole West we are con-

15

sidering is made by railways. Without them the larger
part of it would be uninhabitable, the lands of small
value, produce useless for want of a market. No railways, no civilization. Year by year settlements have
increased in all regions touched by railways, land has
risen in price, and freight charges have diminished.
And yet no sooner do the people get the railways
near them than they become hostile to the companies; hostility to railway corporations seems to be
the dominant sentiment in the Western mind, and
the one most naturally invoked by any political dem-
agogue who wants to climb up higher in elective office. The roads are denounced as "monopolies"—a
word getting to be applied to any private persons
who are successful in business—and their consolidation is regarded as a standing menace to society.

Of course it goes without saying that great corporations with exceptional privileges are apt to be arro-
gant, unjust, and grasping, and especially when, as in
the case of railways, they unite private interests and
public functions, they need the restraint of law and
careful limitations of powers. But the Western situation is nevertheless a very curious one. Naturally
when capital takes great risks it is entitled to propor-
tionate profits; but profits always encourage competition, and the great Western lines are already in a war
for existence that does not need much unfriendly legislation to make fatal. In fact, the lowering of rates
in railway wars has gone on so rapidly of late years
that the most active Granger Legislature cannot frame
hostile bills fast enough to keep pace with it. Consolidation is objected to. Yet this consideration must
not be lost sight of: the West is cut up by local roads

that could not be maintained; they would not pay running expenses if they had not been made parts of a great system. Whatever may be the danger of the consolidation system, the country has doubtless benefited by it.

The present tendency of legislation, pushed to its logical conclusion, is towards a practical confiscation of railway property; that is, its tendency is to so interfere with management, so restrict freedom of arrangement, so reduce rates, that the companies will with difficulty continue operations. The first effect of this will be, necessarily, poorer service and deteriorated equipments and tracks. Roads that do not prosper cannot keep up safe lines. Experienced travellers usually shun those that are in the hands of a receiver. The Western roads of which I speak have been noted for their excellent service and the liberality towards the public in accommodations, especially in fine cars and matters pertaining to the comfort of passengers. Some dining cars on the Omaha system were maintained last year at a cost to the company of ten thousand dollars over receipts. The Western Legislatures assume that because a railway which is thickly strung with cities can carry passengers for two cents a mile, a railway running over an almost unsettled plain can carry for the same price. They assume also that because railway companies in a foolish fight for business cut rates, the lowest rate they touch is a living one for them. The same logic that induces Legislatures to fix rates of transportation, directly or by means of a commission, would lead it to set a price on meat, wheat, and groceries. Legislative restriction is one thing; legislative destruction is another. There is a craze of prohibition and interference. Iowa has an attack of it. In Nebraska, not only the Legislature but the courts have been so hostile to railway enterprise that one hundred and fifty miles of new road graded last year, which was to receive its rails this spring, will not be railed, because it is not safe for the company to make further investments in that State. Between the Grangers on the one side and the labor unions on the other, the railways are in a tight place. Whatever restrictions great corporations may need, the sort of attack now made on them in the West is altogether irrational. Is it always made from public motives? The legislators of one Western State had been accustomed to receive from the various lines that centred at the capital trip passes, in addition to their personal annual passes. Trip passes are passes that the members can send to their relations, friends, and political allies who want to visit the capital. One year the several roads agreed that they would not issue trip passes. When the members asked the agent for them they were told that they were not ready. As days passed and no trip passes were ready, hostile and annoying bills began to be introduced into the Legislature. In six weeks there was a shower of them. The roads yielded, and began to give out the passes. After that, nothing more was heard of the bills.

What the public have a right to complain of is the manipulation of railways in Wall Street gambling. But this does not account for the hostility to the corporations which are developing the West by an extraordinary outlay of money, and cutting their own throats by a war of rates. The vast in-

terests at stake, and the ignorance of the relation of
legislation to the laws of business, make the railway
problem to a spectator in Chicago one of absorbing
interest.

In a thorough discussion of all interests it must
be admitted that the railways have brought many of
their troubles upon themselves by their greedy wars
with each other, and perhaps in some cases by teaching Legislatures that have bettered their instructions,
and that tyrannies in management and unjust dis-
criminations (such as the Inter-State Commerce Law
was meant to stop) have much to do in provoking
hostility that survives many of its causes.

I cannot leave Chicago without a word concerning
the town of Pullman, although it has already been
fully studied in the pages of HARPER'S MONTHLY.
It is one of the most interesting experiments in the
world. As it is only a little over seven years old,
it would be idle to prophesy about it, and I can only
say that thus far many of the predictions as to the
effect of "paternalism" have not come true. If it
shall turn out that its only valuable result is an "object lesson" in decent and orderly living, the experiment will not have been in vain. It is to be remembered that it is not a philanthropic scheme, but a
purely business operation, conducted on the idea that
comfort, cleanliness, and agreeable surroundings conduce more to the prosperity of labor and of capital
than the opposites.

Pullman is the only city in existence built from the
foundation on scientific and sanitary principles, and
not more or less the result of accident and variety of
purpose and incapacity. Before anything else was

done on the flat prairie, perfect drainage, sewerage, and water supply were provided. The shops, the houses, the public buildings, the parks, the streets, the recreation grounds, then followed in intelligent creation. Its public buildings are fine, and the grouping of them about the open flower-planted spaces is very effective. It is a handsome city, with the single drawback of monotony in the well-built houses. Pullman is within the limits of the village of Hyde Park, but it is not included in the annexation of the latter to Chicago.

It is certainly a pleasing industrial city. The workshops are spacious, light, and well ventilated, perfectly systematized; for instance, timber goes into one end of the long car-shop and, without turning back, comes out a freight car at the other, the capacity of the shop being one freight car every fifteen minutes of the working hours. There are a variety of industries, which employ about 4500 workmen. Of these about 500 live outside the city, and there are about 1000 workmen who live in the city and work elsewhere. The company keeps in order the streets, parks, lawns, and shade trees, but nothing else except the schools is free. The schools are excellent, and there are over 1300 children enrolled in them. The company has a well-selected library of over 6000 volumes, containing many scientific and art books, which is open to all residents on payment of an annual subscription of three dollars. Its use increases yearly, and study classes are formed in connection with it. The company rents shops to dealers, but it carries on none of its own. Wages are paid to employés without deduction, except as to rent, and the women appreciate

a provision that secures them a home beyond perad-
venture. The competition among dealers brings prices
to the Chicago rates, or lower, and then the great city
is easily accessible for shopping. House rent is a little higher for ordinary workmen than in Chicago, but
not higher in proportion to accommodations, and living is reckoned a little cheaper. The reports show
that the earnings of operatives exceed those of other
working communities, averaging per capita (exclusive
of the higher pay of the general management) $590
a year. I noticed that piece-wages were generally
paid, and always when possible. The town is a hive
of busy workers; employment is furnished to all classes except the school-children, and the fine moral and
physical appearance of the young women in the up-
holstery and other work rooms would please a philanthropist.

Both the health and the *morale* of the town are
exceptional; and the moral tone of the workmen has
constantly improved under the agreeable surroundings. Those who prefer the kind of independence
that gives them filthy homes and demoralizing associations seem to like to live elsewhere. Pullman has
a population of 10,000. I do not know another city
of 10,000 that has not a place where liquor is sold,
nor a house nor a professional woman of ill repute.
With the restrictions as to decent living, the community is free in its political action, its church and
other societies, and in all healthful social activity.
It has several ministers; it seems to require the services of only one or two policemen; it supports four
doctors and one lawyer.

I know that any control, any interference with in-

dividual responsibility, is un-American. Our theory
is that every person knows what is best for himself.
It is not true, but it may be safer, in working out all
the social problems, than any lessening of responsibility either in the home or in civil affairs. When I
contrast the dirty tenements, with contiguous seduc-
tions to vice and idleness, in some parts of Chicago,
with the homes of Pullman, I am glad that this experiment has been made. It may be worth some sacrifice to teach people that it is better for them, morally
and pecuniarily, to live cleanly and under educational
influences that increase their self-respect. No doubt
it is best that people should own their homes, and that
they should assume all the responsibilities of citizenship. But let us wait the full evolution of the Pullman idea. The town could not have been built as an
object lesson in any other way than it was built. The
hope is that laboring people will voluntarily do here-
after what they have here been induced to accept.
The model city stands there as a lesson, the wonderful
creation of less than eight years. The company is
now preparing to sell lots on the west side of the rail-
way-tracks, and we shall see what influence this nucleus of order, cleanliness, and system will have upon
the larger community rapidly gathering about it. Of
course people should be free to go up or go down.
Will they be injured by the opportunity of seeing
how much pleasanter it is to go up than to go down?

XI.

THREE CAPITALS—SPRINGFIELD, INDIAN-APOLIS, COLUMBUS.

To one travelling over this vast country, especially the northern and western portions, the superficial impression made is that of uniformity, and even monotony: towns are alike, cities have a general resemblance, State lines are not recognized, and the idea of conformity and centralization is easily entertained. Similar institutions, facility of communication, a disposition to stronger nationality, we say, are rapidly fusing us into one federal mass.

But when we study a State at its centre, its political action, its organization, its spirit, the management of its institutions of learning and of charity, the tendencies, restrictive or liberal, of its legislation, even the tone of social life and the code of manners, we discover distinctions, individualities, almost as many differences as resemblances. And we see—the saving truth in our national life—that each State is a well-nigh indestructible entity, an empire in itself, proud and conscious of its peculiarities, and jealous of its rights. We see that State boundaries are not imaginary lines, made by the geographers, which could be easily altered by the central power. Nothing, indeed, in our whole national development, considering the common influences that have made us, is so remarkable as the difference of the several States. Even on the lines of a common settlement, say from New England and New York, note the differences between northern Ohio, northern Indiana, northern Illinois, Wisconsin, and Minnesota. Or take another line, and see the differences between southern Ohio, southern Indiana, southern Illinois, and northern Missouri. But each State, with its diverse population, has a certain homogeneity and character of its own. We can understand this where there are great differences of climate, or when one is mountainous and the other flat. But why should Indiana be so totally unlike the two States that flank it, in so many of the developments of civilized life or in retarded action ; and why should Iowa, in its entire temper and spirit, be so unlike Illinois? One State copies the institutions of another, but there is always something in its life that it does not copy from any other. And the perpetuity of the Union rests upon the separateness and integrity of this State life. I confess that I am not so much impressed by the magnitude of our country as I am by the wonderful system of our complex government in unity, which permits the freest development of human nature, and the most perfect adaptability to local conditions. I can conceive of no greater enemy to the Union than he who would by any attempt at further centralization weaken the self-dependence, pride, and dignity of a single State. It seems to me that one travels in vain over the United States if he does not learn that lesson.

The State of Illinois is geographically much favored both for agriculture and commerce. With access to the Gulf by two great rivers that bound it on two

sides, and communicating with the Atlantic by Lake
Michigan, enterprise has aided these commercial advantages by covering it with railways. Stretching
from Galena to Cairo, it has a great variety of climate ; it is well watered by many noble streams, and
contains in its great area scarcely any waste land. It
has its contrasts of civilization. In the northern half
are the thriving cities ; the extreme southern portion,
owing in part to a more debilitating, less wholesome
climate, and in part to a less virile, ambitious population, still keeps its "Egyptian" reputation. But the
railways have already made a great change in southern
Illinois, and education is transforming it. The establishment of a normal school at Carbondale in 1874–75
has changed the aspect of a great region. I am told
by the State Superintendent of Education that the
contrast in dress, manners, cultivation, of the country
crowd which came to witness the dedication of the first
building, and those who came to see the inauguration
of the new school, twelve years later, was something
astonishing.

Passing through the central portion of the State to
Springfield, after an interval of many years, let us say
a generation, I was impressed with the transformation
the country had undergone by tree-planting and the
growth of considerable patches of forest. The State
is generally prosperous. The farmers have money,
some surplus to spend in luxuries, in the education of
their children, in musical instruments, in the adornment of their homes. This is the universal report of
the commercial travellers, those modern couriers of
business and information, who run in swarms to and
fro over the whole land. To them it is significant—

their opinion can go for what it is worth—that Illinois
has not tried the restrictive and prohibitory legislation
of its western neighbor, Iowa, which, with its rolling
prairies and park-like timber, loved in the season of
birds and flowers, is one of the most fertile and lovely
States in the West.

Springfield, which spreads its 30,000 people extensively over a plain on the Sangamon River, is prosperous, and in the season when any place can be agreeable, a beautiful city. The elm grows well in the rich
soil, and its many broad, well-shaded streets, with
pretty detached houses and lawns, make it very attractive, a delightful rural capital. The large Illinois
towns are slowly lifting themselves out of the slough
of rich streets, better adapted to crops than to trade;
though good material for pavement is nowhere abundant. Springfield has recently improved its condition
by paving, mostly with cedar blocks, twenty-five
miles of streets. I notice that in some of the Western
towns tile pavement is being tried. Manufacturing
is increasing—there is a prosperous rolling-mill and a
successful watch factory—but the overwhelming interest of the city is that it is the centre of the political and educational institutions—of the life emanating
from the State-house.

The State-house is, I believe, famous. It is a big
building, a great deal has been spent on it in the way
of ornamentation, and it enjoys the distinction of the
highest State-house dome in the country—350 feet.
It has the merit also of being well placed on an elevation, and its rooms are spacious and very well planned.
It is an incongruous pile externally, mixing many
styles of architecture, placing Corinthian capitals on

Doric columns, and generally losing the impression of a dignified mass in details. Within, it is especially rich in wall-casings of beautiful and variegated marbles, each panel exquisite, but all together tending to dissipate any idea of unity of design or simplicity. Nothing whatever can be said for many of the scenes in relief, or the mural paintings (except that they illustrate the history of the State), nor for most of the statues in the corridors, but the decoration of the chief rooms, in mingling of colors and material, is frankly barbarous.

Illinois has the reputation of being slow in matters of education and reform. A day in the State offices, however, will give the visitor an impression of intelligence and vigor in these directions. The office of the State Board of Pharmacy in the Capitol shows a strict enforcement of the law in the supervision of drugs and druggists. Prison management has also most intelligent consideration. The two great penitentiaries, the Southern, at Chester (with about 800 convicts), and the Northern, at Joliet (with about 1600 convicts), call for no special comment. The one at Joliet is a model of its kind, with a large library, and such schooling as is practicable in the system, and is well administered ; and I am glad to see that Mr. Mc-Claughry, the warden, believes that incorrigibles should be permanently held, and that grading, the discipline of labor and education, with a parole system, can make law-abiding citizens of many convicts.

In school education the State is certainly not supine in efforts. Out of a State population of about 3,500,000, there were, in 1887, 1,627,841 under twenty-one years, and 1,096,464 between the ages of six and

twenty-one. The school age for free attendance is
from six to twenty-one ; for compulsory attendance,
from eight to fourteen. There were 749,994 children
enrolled, and 506,197 in daily attendance. Those enrolled in private schools numbered 87,725. There were
2258 teachers in private schools, and 22,925 in public
schools ; of this latter, 7462 were men and 15,463
women. The average monthly salary of men was
\$51.48, and of women \$42.17. The sum available for
school purposes in 1887 was \$12,896,515, in an assessed
value of taxable property of \$797,752,888. These
figures are from Dr. N. W. Edwards, Superintendent
of Public Instruction, whose energy is felt in every
part of the State.

The State prides itself on its institutions of charity.
I saw some of them at Jacksonville, an hour's ride
west of Springfield. Jacksonville is a very pretty
city of some 15,000, with elm-shaded avenues that
suggest but do not rival New Haven—one of those
intellectual centres that are a continual surprise to
our English friends in their bewildered exploration of
our monotonous land. In being the Western centre
of Platonic philosophy, it is more like Concord than
like New Haven. It is the home of a large number of
people who have travelled, who give intelligent attention to art, to literary study in small societies and
clubs—its Monday Evening Club of men long antedated most of the similar institutions at the East—
and to social problems. I certainly did not expect to
find, as I did, water-colors by Turner in Jacksonville,
besides many other evidences of a culture that must
modify many Eastern ideas of what the West is and
is getting to be.

The Illinois College is at Jacksonville. It is one of twenty-five small colleges in the State, and I believe the only one that adheres to the old curriculum, and does not adopt co-education. It has about sixty students in the college proper, and about one hundred and thirty in the preparatory academy. Most of the Illinois colleges have preparatory departments, and so long as they do, and the various sects scatter their energies among so many institutions, the youth of the State who wish a higher education will be obliged to go East. The school perhaps the most vigorous just now is the University of Illinois, at Urbana, a school of agriculture and applied science mainly. The Central Hospital for the Insane (one of three in the State), under the superintendence of Dr. Henry F. Carriel, is a fine establishment, a model of neatness and good management, with over nine hundred patients, about a third of whom do some light work on the farm or in the house. A large conservatory of plants and flowers is rightly regarded as a remedial agency in the treatment of the patients. Here also is a fine school for the education of the blind.

The Institution for the Education of Deaf-Mutes, Dr. Philip H. Gillette, superintendent, is, I believe, the largest in the world, and certainly one of the most thoroughly equipped and successful in its purposes. It has between five hundred and six hundred pupils. All the departments found in many other institutions are united here. The school has a manual training department; articulation is taught; the art school exhibits surprising results in aptitude for both drawing and painting; and industries are taught to the extent of giving every pupil a trade or some means of support

—shoemaking, cabinet-making, printing, sewing, gardening, and baking.

Such an institution as this raises many interesting questions. It is at once evident that the loss of the sense of hearing has an effect on character, moral and intellectual. Whatever may be the education of the deaf-mute, he will remain, in some essential and not easily to be characterized respects, different from other people. It is exceedingly hard to cultivate in them a spirit of self-dependence, or eradicate the notion that society owes them perpetual care and support. The education of deaf-mutes, and the teaching them trades, so that they become intelligent and productive members of society, of course induce marriages among them. Is not this calculated to increase the number of deaf-mutes? Dr. Gillette thinks not. The vital statistics show that consanguineous marriages are a large factor in deaf-muteism; about ten per cent., it is estimated, of the deaf-mutes are the offspring of parents related by blood. Ancestral defects are not always perpetuated in kind; they may descend in physical deformity, in deafness, in imbecility. Deafness is more apt to descend in collateral branches than in a straight line. It is a striking fact in a table of relationships prepared by Dr. Gillette that, while the 450 deaf-mutes enumerated had 770 relationships to other deaf-mutes, making a total of 1220, only twelve of them had deaf-mute parents, and only two of them one deaf-mute parent, the mother of these having been able to hear, and that in no case was the mother alone a deaf-mute. Of the pupils who have left this institution, 251 have married deaf-mutes, and 19 hearing persons. These marriages have been as fruitful as the average, and among them

all only sixteen have deaf-mute children; in some of
the families having a deaf child there are other children who hear. These facts, says the report, clearly indicate that the probability of deaf offspring from deaf
parentage is remote, while other facts may clearly indicate that a deaf person probably has or will have a
deaf relation other than a child.

Springfield is old enough to have a historic flavor
and social traditions; perhaps it might be called a
Kentucky flavor, so largely did settlers from Kentucky
determine it. There was a leisurely element in it, and
it produced a large number of men prominent in politics and in the law, and women celebrated for beauty
and spirit. It was a hospitable society, with a certain
tone of "family" that distinguished it from other frontier places, a great liking for the telling of racy stories,
and a hearty enjoyment of life. The State has provided a Gubernatorial residence which is at once spacious and pleasant, and is a mansion, with its present
occupants, typical in a way of the old *régime* and of
modern culture.

To the country at large Springfield is distinguished
as the home of Abraham Lincoln to an extent perhaps
not fully realized by the residents of the growing capital, with its ever new interests. And I was perhaps
unreasonably disappointed in not finding that sense of
his personality that I expected. It is, indeed, emphasized by statues in the Capitol and by the great mau-
soleum in the cemetery—an imposing structure, with
an excellent statue in bronze, and four groups, relating
to the civil war, of uncommon merit. But this great
monumental show does not satisfy the personal longing of which I speak. Nor is the Lincoln residence

16

much more satisfactory in this respect. The plain two-story wooden house has been presented to the State by his son Robert, and is in charge of a custodian. And although the parlor is made a show-room and full of memorials, there is no atmosphere of the man about it. On Lincoln's departure for Washington the furniture was sold and the house rented, never to be again occupied by him. There is here nothing of that personal presence that clings to the Hermitage, to Marshfield, to Mount Vernon, to Monticello. Lincoln was given to the nation, and—a frequent occurrence in our uprooting business life—the home disappeared. Lincoln was honored and beloved in Springfield as a man, but perhaps some of the feeling towards him as a party leader still lingers, although it has disappeared almost everywhere else in the country. Nowhere else was the personal partisanship hotter than in this city, and it is hardly to be expected that political foes in this generation should quite comprehend the elevation of Lincoln, in the consenting opinion of the world, among the greatest characters of all ages. It has happened to Lincoln that every year and a more intimate knowledge of his character have added to his fame and to the appreciation of his moral grandeur. There is a natural desire to go to some spot pre-eminently sacred to his personality. This may be his birthplace. At any rate, it is likely that before many years Kentucky will be proud to distinguish in some way the spot where the life began of the most illustrious man born in its borders.

When we come to the capital of Indiana we have, in official language, to report progress. One reason assigned for the passing of emigrants through Indiana to Illinois was that the latter was a prairie country, more easily subdued than the more wooded region of Indiana. But it is also true that the sluggish, illiterate character of its early occupants turned aside the stream of Western emigration from its borders. There has been a great deal of philosophic speculation upon the acknowledged backwardness of civilization in Indiana, its slow development in institutions of education, and its slow change in rural life, compared with its sister States. But this concerns us less now than the awakening which is visible at the capital and in some of the northern towns. The forests of hard timber which were an early disadvantage are now an important element in the State industry and wealth. Recent developments of coal-fields and the discovery of natural gas have given an impetus to manufacturing, which will powerfully stimulate agriculture and traffic, and open a new career to the State.

Indianapolis, which stood still for some years in a reaction from real-estate speculation, is now a rapidly improving city, with a population of about 125,000. It is on the natural highway of the old National Turnpike, and its central location in the State, in the midst of a rich agricultural district, has made it the centre of fifteen railway lines, and of active freight and passenger traffic. These lines are all connected for freight purposes by a belt road, over which pass about 5000 freight cars daily. This belt road also does an enormous business for the stock-yards, and its convenient line is rapidly filling up with manufacturing establishments. As a consequence of these facilities the trade of the city in both wholesale and retail houses is good

and increasing. With this increase of business there
has been an accession of banking capital. The four
national and two private banks have an aggregate
capital of about three millions, and the Clearing-house
report of 1887 showed a business of about one hundred
millions, an increase of nearly fifty per cent. over the
preceding year. But the individual prosperity is largely due to the building and loan associations, of which
there are nearly one hundred, with an aggregate capital of seven millions, the loans of which exceed those
of the banks. These take the place of savings-banks,
encourage the purchase of homesteads, and are pre-
ventives of strikes and labor troubles in the factories.

The people of Indianapolis call their town a Park
City. Occupying a level plain, its streets (the principal
ones with a noble width of ninety feet) intersect each
other at right angles; but in the centre of the city is a
Circle Park of several acres, from which radiate to the
four quarters of the town avenues ninety feet broad
that relieve the monotony of the right lines. These
streets are for the most part well shaded, and getting
to be well paved, lined with pleasant but not ambitious
residences, so that the whole aspect of the city is open
and agreeable. The best residences are within a few
squares of the most active business streets, and if the
city has not the distinction of palaces, it has fewer
poor and shabby quarters than most other towns of its
size. In the Circle Park, where now stands a statue
of Governor Morton, is to be erected immediately the
Soldiers' Monument, at a cost of $250,000.

The city is fortunate in its public buildings. The
County Court-house (which cost $1,600,000) and City
Hall are both fine buildings; in the latter are the city

markets, and above, a noble auditorium with seats for 4000 people. But the State Capitol, just finished within the appropriation of $2,000,000, is pre-eminent among State Capitols in many respects. It is built of the Bedford limestone, one of the best materials both for color and endurance found in the country. It follows the American plan of two wings and a dome; but it is finely proportioned; and the exterior, with rows of graceful Corinthian columns above the basement story, is altogether pleasing. The interior is spacious and impressive, the Chambers fine, the furnishing solid and in good taste, with nowhere any over-ornamentation or petty details to mar the general noble effect. The State Library contains, besides the law-books, about 20,000 miscellaneous volumes.

When Matthew Arnold first came to New York the place in the West about which he expressed the most curiosity was Indianapolis; that he said he must see, if no other city. He had no knowledge of the place, and could give no reason for his preference except that the name had always had a fascination for him. He found there, however, a very extensive book-store, where his own works were sold in numbers that pleased and surprised him. The shop has a large miscellaneous stock, and does a large jobbing and retail business, but the miscellaneous books dealt in are mostly cheap reprints of English works, with very few American copyright books. This is a significant comment on the languishing state of the market for works of American authors in the absence of an international copyright law.

The city is not behind any other in educational efforts. In its five free public libraries are over 70,000 volumes. The city has a hundred churches and a vigorous Young Men's Christian Association, which cost $75,000. Its private schools have an excellent reputation. There are 20,000 children registered of school age, and 11,000 in daily attendance in twenty-eight free-school houses. In methods of efficacy these are equal to any in the Union, as is shown by the fact that there are reported in the city only 325 persons between the ages of six and twenty-one unable to read and write. The average cost of instruction for each pupil is $19.64 a year. In regard to advanced methods and manual training, Indianapolis schools claim to be pioneers.

The latest reports show educational activity in the State as well as in the capital. In 1886 the revenues expended in public schools were about $5,000,000. The State supports the Indiana University at Bloomington, with about 300 students, the Agricultural College at Lafayette, with over 300, and a normal school at Terre Haute, with an attendance of about 500. There are, besides, seventeen private colleges and several other normal schools. In 1886 the number of school-children enrolled in the State was 506,000, of whom 346,000 were in daily attendance. To those familiar with Indiana these figures show a greatly increased interest in education.

Several of the State benevolent institutions are in Indianapolis: a hospital for the insane, which cost $1,200,000, and accommodates 1600 patients; an asylum for the blind, which has 132 pupils; and a school for deaf-mutes which cost $500,000, and has about 400 scholars. The novel institution, however, that I saw at Indianapolis is a reformatory for women and girls, controlled entirely by women. The board of trustees are women, the superintendent, physician, and keepers are women. In one building, but in separate departments, were the female convicts, 42 in number, several of them respectable - looking elderly women who had killed their husbands, and about 150 young girls. The convicts and the girls—who are committed for restraint and reform—never meet except in chapel, but it is more than doubtful if it is wise for the State to subject girls to even this sort of contiguity with convicts, and to the degradation of penitentiary suggestions. The establishment is very neat and well ordered and well administered. The work of the prison is done by the convicts, who are besides kept employed at sewing and in the laundry. The girls in the reformatory work half a day, and are in school the other half.

This experiment of the control of a State-prison by women is regarded as doubtful by some critics, who say that women will obey a man when they will not obey a woman. Female convicts, because they have fallen lower than men, or by reason of their more nervous organization, are commonly not so easily controlled as male convicts, and it is insisted that they indulge in less "tantrums" under male than under female authority. This is denied by the superintendent of this prison, though she has incorrigible cases who can only be controlled by solitary confinement. She has daily religious exercises, Bible reading and exposition, and a Sunday-school; and she doubts if she could control the convicts without this religious influence. It not only has a daily quieting effect, but has resulted in several cases in "conversion." There are in the institution several girls and women of color, and I asked the superintendent if the white inmates exhibited any prejudice against them on account of their color. To my surprise, the answer was that the contrary is the case. The whites look up to the colored girls, and seem either to have a respect for them or to be fascinated by them. This surprising statement was supplemented by another, that the influence of the colored girls on the whites is not good; the white girl who seeks the company of the colored girl deteriorates, and the colored girl does not change.

Indianapolis, which is attractive by reason of a climate that avoids extremes, bases its manufacturing and its business prosperity upon the large coal-beds lying to the west and south of it, the splendid and very extensive quarries of Bedford limestone contiguous to the coal-fields, the abundant supply of various sorts of hard-wood for the making of furniture, and the recent discovery of natural gas. The gas-field region, which is said to be very much larger than any other in the country, lies to the north-west, and comes within eight miles of the city. Pipes are already laid to the city limits, and the whole heating and manufacturing of the city will soon be done by the gas. I saw this fuel in use in a large and successful pottery, where are made superior glazed and encaustic tiles, and nothing could be better for the purpose. The heat in the kilns is intense; it can be perfectly regulated; as fuel the gas is free from smoke and smut, and its cost is merely nominal. The excitement over this new agent is at present extraordinary. The field where it has been found is so extensive as to make the supply seem inexhaustible. It was first discovered in Indiana at Eaton, in Delaware County, in 1886. From January 1, 1887,

to February, 1838, it is reported that 1000 wells were
opened in the gas territory, and that 245 companies
were organized for various manufactures, with an
aggregate capital of $25,000,000. Whatever the fig-
ures may be, there are the highest expectations of
immense increase of manufactures in Indianapolis and
in all the gas region. Of some effects of this revolution in fuel we may speak when we come to the gas
wells of Ohio.

I had conceived of Columbus as a rural capital,
pleasant and slow, rather a village than a city. I was
surprised to find a city of 80,000 people, growing with
a rapidity astonishing even for a Western town, with
miles of prosperous business blocks (High Street is
four miles long), and wide avenues of residences extending to suburban parks. Broad Street, with its
four rows of trees and fine houses and beautiful lawns,
is one of the handsomest avenues in the country, and
it is only one of many that are attractive. The Capitol Square, with several good buildings about it, makes
an agreeable centre of the city. Of the Capitol building not much is to be said. The exterior is not wholly
bad, but it is surmounted by a truncated something
that is neither a dome nor a revolving turret, and the
interior is badly arranged for room, light, and ventila-
tion. Space is wasted, and many of the rooms, among
them the relic-room and the flag-room, are inconvenient and almost inaccessible. The best is the
room of the Supreme Court, which has attached a
large law library. The general State Library contains about 54,000 volumes, with a fair but not large
proportion of Western history.

Columbus is a city of churches, of very fine public
schools, of many clubs, literary and social, in which
the intellectual element predominates, and of an intelligent, refined, and most hospitable society.   Here
one may study the educational and charitable institutions of the State, many of the more important of
which are in the city, and also the politics.   It was
Ohio's hard fate to be for many years an "October
State," and the battle-field and corruption-field of
many outside influences.   This no doubt demoralized
the politics of the State, and lowered the tone of public morality.   With the removal of the cause of this
decline, I believe the tone is being raised.   Recent
trials for election frauds, and the rehabilitation of
the Cincinnati police, show that a better spirit prevails.

Ohio is growing in wealth as it is in population,
and is in many directions an ambitious and progressive State.   Judged by its institutions of benevolence
and of economics, it is a leading State.   No other
State provides more liberally for its unfortunates, in
asylums for the insane, the blind, the deaf-mutes, the
idiotic, the young waifs and strays, nor shows a more
intelligent comprehension of the legitimate functions
of a great commonwealth, in the creation of boards
of education and of charities and of health, in a State
inspection of workshops and factories, in establishing
bureaus of meteorology and of forestry, a fish commission, and an agricultural experiment station.   The State
has thirty-four colleges and universities, a public-school
system which has abolished distinctions of color, and
which by the reports is as efficient as any in the Union.
Cincinnati, the moral tone of which, the Ohio people say,

is not fairly represented by its newspapers, is famous
the world over for its cultivation in music and its progress in the fine and industrial arts. It would be possible for a State to have and be all this and yet rise in
the general scale of civilization only to a splendid mediocrity, without the higher institutions of pure learning, and without a very high standard of public morality. Ohio is in no less danger of materialism, with all
its diffused intelligence, than other States. There is a
recognizable limit to what a diffused level of education, say in thirty-four colleges, can do for the higher
life of a State. I heard an address in the Capitol by
ex-President Hayes on the expediency of adding a
manual-training school to the Ohio State University
at Columbus. The comment of some of the legislators on it was that we have altogether too much
book-learning; what we need is workshops in our
schools and colleges. It seems to a stranger that
whatever first-class industrial and technical schools
Ohio needs, it needs more the higher education, and
the teaching of philosophy, logic, and ethics. In
1886 Governor Foraker sent a special message to
the Legislature pointing out the fact that notwithstanding the increase of wealth in the State, the revenue was inadequate to the expenditure, principally
by reason of the undervaluation of taxable property
(there being a yearly decline in the reported value of
personal property), and a fraudulent evasion of taxes.
There must have been a wide insensibility to the
wrong of cheating the State to have produced this
state of things, and one cannot but think that it went
along with the low political tone before mentioned.
Of course Ohio is not a solitary sinner among States

in this evasion of duty, but she helps to point the moral that the higher life of a State needs a great deal of education that is neither commercial nor industrial nor simply philanthropic.

It is impossible and unnecessary for the purposes of this paper to speak of many of the public institutions of the State, even of those in the city. But educators everywhere may study with profit the management of the public schools under the City Board of Education, of which Mr. R. W. Stevenson is superintendent. The High-school, of over 600 pupils, is especially to be commended. Manual training is not introduced into the schools, and the present better sentiment is against it; but its foundation, drawing, is thoroughly taught from the primaries up to the High-school, and the exhibits of the work of the schools of all grades in modelling, drawing, and form and color studies, which were made last year in New York and Chicago, gave these Columbus schools a very high rank in the country. Any visitor to them must be impressed with the intelligence of the methods employed, the apprehension of modern notions, and also the conservative spirit of common-sense.

The Ohio State University has an endowment from the State of over half a million dollars, and a source of ultimate wealth in its great farm and grounds, which must increase in value as the city extends. It is a very well equipped institution for the study of the natural sciences and agriculture, and might easily be built up into a university in all departments, worthy of the State. At present it has 335 students, of whom 150 are in the academic department, 41 in special practical courses, and 143 in the preparatory school. All the students are organized in companies, under an officer of the United States, for military discipline; the uniform, the drill, the lessons of order and obedience, are invaluable in the transforming of carriage and manners. The University has a museum of geology which ranks among the important ones of the country. It is a pity that a consolidation of other State institutions with this cannot be brought about.

The Ohio Penitentiary at Columbus is an old building, not in keeping with the modern notions of prison construction. In 1887 it had about 1300 convicts, some 100 less than in the preceding year. The management is subject to political changes, and its officers have to be taken from various parts of the State at the dictation of political workers. Under this system the best management is liable to be upset by an election. The special interest in the prison at this time was in the observation of the working of the Parole Law. Since the passage of the Act in May, 1885, 283 prisoners have been paroled, and while several of the convicts have been returned for a violation of parole, nearly the whole number are reported as law-abiding citizens. The managers are exceedingly pleased with the working of the law; it promotes good conduct in the prison, and reduces the number in confinement. The reduction of the number of convicts in 1887 from the former year was ascribed partially to the passage of the General Sentence Law in 1884, and the Habitual Crimes Act in 1885. The criminals dread these laws, the first because it gives no fixed time to build their hopes upon, but all depends upon their previous record and good conduct in prison, while the latter affects the incorrigible, who are careful to shun the State after being convicted twice, and avoid imprisonment for life. The success of these laws and the condition of the State finances delay the work on the Intermediate Prison, or Reformatory, begun at Mansfield. This Reformatory is intended for first offenders, and has the distinct purpose of prevention of further deterioration, and of reformation by means of the discipline of education and labor. The success of the tentative laws in this direction, as applied to the general prisons, is, in fact, a strong argument for the carrying out of the Mansfield scheme.

There cannot be a more interesting study of the "misfits" of humanity than that offered in the Institution for Feeble-minded Youth, under the superintendence of Dr. G. A. Doren. Here are 715 imbeciles in all stages of development from absolute mental and physical incapacity. There is scarcely a problem that exists in education, in the relation of the body and mind, in the inheritance of mental and physical traits, in regard to the responsibility for crime, in psychology or physiology, that is not here illustrated. It is the intention of the school to teach the idiot child some trade or occupation that will make him to some degree useful, and to carry him no further than the common branches in learning. The first impression, I think, made upon a visitor is the almost invariable physical deformity that attends imbecility—ill-proportioned, distorted bodies, dwarfed, misshapen gelatinoids, with bones that have no stiffness. The next impression is the preponderance of the animal nature, the persistence of the lower passions, and the absence of moral qualities in the general immaturity. And perhaps the next impression is of the extraordi-

nary effect that physical training has in awakening the
mind, and how soon the discipline of the institution
creates the power of self-control. From almost blank
imbecility and utter lack of self-restraint the majority of these children, as we saw them in their school-
rooms and workshops, exhibited a sense of order, of
entire decency, and very considerable intelligence. It
was demonstrated that most imbeciles are capable of
acquiring the rudiments of an education and of learning some useful occupation. Some of the boys work
on the farm, others learn trades. The boys in the
shoe-shop were making shoes of excellent finish. The
girls do plain sewing and house-work apparently almost as well as girls of their age outside. Two or
three things that we saw may be mentioned to show
the scope of the very able management and the capacities of the pupils. There was a drill of half a hundred boys and girls in the dumb-bell exercise, to music, under the leadership of a pupil, which in time,
grace, and exact execution of complicated movements
would have done credit to any school. The institution has two bands, one of brass and one of strings,
which perform very well. The string band played
for dancing in the large amusement hall. Several
hundred children were on the floor dancing cotillons,
and they went through the variety of changes not
only in perfect time and decorum, but without any
leader to call the figures. It would have been a remarkable performance for any children. There were
many individual cases of great and deplorable interest. Cretins, it was formerly supposed, were only
born in mountainous regions. There are three here
born in Ohio. There were five imbeciles of what I

should call the ape type, all of one Ohio family. Two
of them were the boys exhibited some years ago by
Barnum as the Aztec children—the last of an extinct
race. He exhibited them as a boy and a girl. When
they had grown a little too large to show as children,
or the public curiosity was satisfied about the extinct
race, he exhibited them as wild Australians.

The humanity of so training these imbeciles that
they can have some enjoyment of life, and be occasionally of some use to their relations, is undeniable.
But since the State makes this effort in the survival
of the unfittest, it must go further and provide a permanent home for them. The girls who have learned
to read and write and sew and do house-work, and are
of decent appearance, as many of them are, are apt to
marry when they leave the institution. Their offspring
are invariably idiots. I saw in this school the children
of mothers who had been trained here. It is no more
the intention of the State to increase the number of
imbeciles than it is the number of criminals. Many
of our charitable and penal institutions at present do
both.

I should like to approach the subject of Natural
Gas in a proper spirit, but I have neither the imagination nor the rhetoric to do justice to the expectations formed of it. In the restrained language of one
of the inhabitants of Findlay, its people "have caught
the divine afflatus which came with the discovery of
natural gas." If Findlay had only natural gas, "she
would be the peer, if not the superior, of any municipality on earth;" but she has much more, "and in
all things has no equal or superior between the oceans

and the lakes and the gulf, and is marching on to the grandest destiny ever prepared for any people, in any land, or in any period, since the morning stars first sang together, and the flowers in the garden of Eden budded and blossomed for man." In fact, "this she has been doing in the past two years in the grandest and most satisfactory way, and that she will continue to progress is as certain as the stars that hold their midnight revel around the throne of Omnipotence."

Notwithstanding this guarded announcement, it is evident that the discovery of natural gas has begun a revolution in fuel, which will have permanent and far-reaching economic and social consequences, whether the supply of gas is limited or inexhaustible.

Those who have once used fuel in this form are not likely to return to the crude and wasteful heating by coal. All the cities and large towns west of the Alleghanies are made disagreeable by bituminous coal smoke. The extent of this annoyance and its detraction from the pleasure of daily living cannot be exaggerated. The atmosphere is more or less vitiated, and the sky obscured, houses, furniture, clothing, are dirty, and clean linen and clean hands and face are not expected. All this is changed where gas is used for fuel. The city becomes cheerful, and the people can see each other. But this is not all. One of the great burdens of our Northern life, fire building and replenishing, disappears, house-keeping is simplified, the expense of servants reduced, cleanliness restored. Add to this that in the gas regions the cost of fuel is merely nominal, and in towns distant some thirty or forty miles it is not half that of coal. It is easy to see that this revolution in fuel will make as great a change in so-

17

cial life as in manufacturing, and that all the change may not be agreeable. This natural gas is a very subtle fluid, somewhat difficult to control, though I have no doubt that invention will make it as safe in our houses as illuminating gas is. So far as I have seen its use, the heat from it is intense and withering. In a closed stove it is intolerable; in an open grate, with a simulated pile of hard coal or logs, it is better, but much less agreeable than soft coal or wood. It does not, as at present used, promote a good air in the room, and its intense dryness ruins the furniture. But its cheapness, convenience, and neatness will no doubt prevail; and we are entering upon a gas age, in which, for the sake of progress, we shall doubtless surrender something that will cause us to look back to the more primitive time with regret. If the gas-wells fail, artificial gas for fuel will doubtless be manufactured.

I went up to the gas-fields of northern Ohio in company with Prof. Edward Orton, the State Geologist, who has made a study of the subject, and pretty well defined the fields of Indiana and Ohio. The gas is found at a depth of between 1100 and 1200 feet, after passing through a great body of shale and encountering salt-water, in a porous Trenton limestone. The drilling and tubing enter this limestone several feet to get a good holding. This porous limestone holds the gas like a sponge, and it rushes forth with tremendous force when released. It is now well settled that these are reservoirs of gas that are tapped, and not sources of perpetual supply by constant manufacture. How large the supply may be in any case cannot be told, but there is a limit to it. It can be exhausted, like a vein of coal. But the fields are so large, both in Indi-

ana and Ohio, that it seems probable that by sinking
new wells the supply will be continued for a long time.
The evidence that it is not inexhaustible in any one
well is that in all in which the flow of gas has been
tested at intervals the force of pressure is found to
diminish. For months after the discovery the wells
were allowed to run to waste, and billions of feet of
gas were lost. A better economy now prevails, and
this wastefulness is stopped. The wells are all under
control, and large groups of them are connected by
common service-pipes. The region about Fostoria is
organized under the North-western Gas Company, and
controls a large territory. It supplies the city of To-
ledo, which uses no other fuel, through pipes thirty
miles long, Fremont, and other towns. The loss per
mile in transit through the pipes is now known, so
that the distance can be calculated at which it will
pay to send it. I believe that this is about fifty to
sixty miles. The gas when it comes from the well is
about the temperature of 32° Fahr., and the common
pressure is 400 pounds to the square inch. The veloc-
ity with which it rushes, unchecked, from the pipe at
the mouth of the well may be said to be about that of
a minie-ball from an ordinary rifle. The Ohio area
of gas is between 2000 and 3000 square miles. The
claim for the Indiana area is that it is 20,000 square
miles, but the geologists make it much less.

The speculation in real estate caused by this discovery has been perhaps without parallel in the history of
the State, and, as is usual in such cases, it is now in a
lull, waiting for the promised developments. But these
have been almost as marvellous as the speculation.
Findlay was a sleepy little village in the black swamp

district, one of the most backward regions of Ohio.
For many years there had been surface indications of
gas, and there is now a house standing in the city
which used gas for fuel forty years ago. When the
first gas-well was opened, ten years ago, the village
had about 4500 inhabitants. It has now probably 15,-
000, it is a city, and its limits have been extended to
cover an area six miles long by four miles wide. This
is dotted over with hastily built houses, and is rapidly
being occupied by manufacturing establishments. The
city owns all the gas-wells, and supplies fuel to factories and private houses at the simple cost of maintaining the service-pipes. So rapid has been the growth
and the demand for gas that there has not been time
to put all the pipes underground, and they are encountered on the surface all over the region. The town is
pervaded by the odor of the gas, which is like that of
petroleum, and the traveller is notified of his nearness
to the town by the smell before he can see the houses.
The surface pipes, hastily laid, occasionally leak, and
at these weak places the gas is generally ignited in
order to prevent its tainting the atmosphere. This
immediate neighborhood has an oil-field contiguous
to the gas, plenty of limestone (the kilns are burned
by gas), good building stone, clay fit for making bricks
and tiles, and superior hard-wood forests. The cheap
fuel has already attracted here manufacturing industries of all sorts, and new plants are continually made.
I have a list of over thirty different mills and factories
which are either in full operation or getting under way.
Among the most interesting of these are the works for
making window-glass and table glass. The superiority
of this fuel for the glass-furnaces seems to be admitted.

Although the wells about Findlay are under control, the tubing is anchored, and the awful force is held under by gates and levers of steel, it is impossible to escape a feeling of awe in this region at the subterranean energies which seem adequate to blow the whole country heavenward. Some of the wells were opened for us. Opening a well is unscrewing the service-pipe and letting the full force of the gas issue from the pipe at the mouth of the well. When one of these wells is thus opened the whole town is aware of it by the roaring and the quaking of the air. The first one exhibited was in a field a mile and a half from the city. At the first freedom from the screws and clamps the gas rushed out in such density that it was visible. Although we stood several rods from it, the roar was so great that one could not make himself heard shouting in the ear of his neighbor. The geologist stuffed cotton in his ears and tied a shawl about his head, and, assisted by the chemist, stood close to the pipe to measure the flow. The chemist, who had not taken the precaution to protect himself, was quite deaf for some time after the experiment. A four-inch pipe, about sixty feet in length, was then screwed on, and the gas ignited as it issued from the end on the ground. The roaring was as before. For several feet from the end of the tube there was no flame, but beyond was a sea of fire sweeping the ground and rioting high in the air—billows of red and yellow and blue flame, fierce and hot enough to consume everything within reach. It was an awful display of power.

We had a like though only a momentary display at the famous Karg well, an eight-million-feet well. This could only be turned on for a few seconds at a time, for it is in connection with the general system. If the gas is turned off, the fires in houses and factories would go out, and if it were turned on again without notice, the rooms would be full of gas, and an explosion follow an attempt to relight it. This danger is now being removed by the invention of an automatic valve in the pipe supplying each fire, which will close and lock when the flow of gas ceases, and admit no more gas until it is opened. The ordinary pressure for house service is about two pounds to the square inch. The Karg well is on the bank of the creek, and the discharge-pipe through which the gas (though not in its full force) was turned for our astonishment extends over the water. The roar was like that of Niagara; all the town shakes when the Karg is loose. When lighted, billows of flame rolled over the water, brilliant in color and fantastic in form, with a fury and rage of conflagration enough to strike the spectator with terror. I have never seen any other display of natural force so impressive as this. When this flame issues from an upright pipe, the great mass of fire rises eighty feet into the air, leaping and twisting in fiendish fury. For six weeks after this well was first opened its constant roaring shook the nerves of the town, and by night its flaming torch lit up the heaven and banished darkness. With the aid of this new agent anything seems possible.

The feverishness of speculation will abate; many anticipations will not be realized. It will be discovered that there is a limit to manufacturing, even with fuel that costs next to nothing. The supply of natural gas no doubt has its defined limits. But nothing seems more certain to me than that gas, manufactured if not natural, is to be the fuel of the future in the West, and that the importance of this economic change in social life is greater than we can at present calculate.

XII.

CINCINNATI AND LOUISVILLE.

CINCINNATI is a city that has a past. As Daniel
Webster said, that at least is secure. Among the
many places that have been and are the Athens of
America, this was perhaps the first. As long ago as
the first visit of Charles Dickens to this country it
was distinguished as a town of refinement as well as
cultivation; and the novelist, who saw little to admire,
though much to interest him in our raw country, was
captivated by this little village on the Ohio. It was
already the centre of an independent intellectual life,
and produced scholars, artists, writers, who subsequently went east instead of west. According to tradition,
there seems to have been early a tendency to free
thought, and a response to the movement which, for
lack of a better name, was known in Massachusetts as
transcendentalism.

The evolution of Cincinnati seems to have been a
little peculiar in American life. It is a rich city,
priding itself on the solidity of its individual fortunes
and business, and the freedom of its real property
from foreign mortgages. Usually in our development
the pursuit of wealth comes first, and then all other
things are added thereto, as we read the promise. In
Cincinnati there seems to have been a very considerable cultivation first in time, and we have the spectacle
of what wealth will do in the way of the sophistication

and materialization of society. Ordinarily we have the process of an uncultivated community gradually working itself out into a more or less ornamented and artistic condition as it gets money. The reverse process we might see if the philosophic town of Concord, Massachusetts, should become the home of rich men engaged in commerce and manufacturing. I may be all wrong in my notion of Cincinnati, but there is a sort of tradition, a remaining flavor of old-time culture before the town became commercially so important as it was before the war.

It is difficult to think of Cincinnati as in Ohio. I cannot find their similarity of traits. Indeed, I think that generally in the State there is a feeling that it is an alien city; the general characteristics of the State do not flow into and culminate in Cincinnati as its metropolis. It has had somehow an independent life. If you look on a geologic map of the State, you see that the glacial drift, I believe it is called, which flowed over three-fourths of the State and took out its wrinkles did not advance into the south-west. And Cincinnati lies in the portion that was not smoothed into a kind of monotony. When a settlement was made here it was a good landing-place for trade up and down the river, and was probably not so much thought of as a distributing and receiving point for the interior north of it. Indeed, up to the time of the war, it looked to the South for its trade, and naturally, even when the line of war was drawn, a good deal of its sympathies lay in the direction of its trade. It had become a great city, and grown rich both in trade and manu-factures, but in the decline of steamboating and in the era of railways there were physical difficulties in the way of adapting itself easily to the new conditions. It was not easy to bring the railways down the irregular hills and to find room for them on the landing. The city itself had to contend with great natural obstacles to get adequate foothold, and its radiation over, around, and among the hills produced some novel features in business and in social life.

What Cincinnati would have been, with its early culture and its increasing wealth, if it had not become so largely German in its population, we can only conjecture. The German element was at once conservative as to improvements and liberalizing, as the phrase is, in theology and in life. Bituminous coal and the Germans combined to make a novel American city. When Dickens saw the place it was a compact, smiling little city, with a few country places on the hills. It is now a scattered city of country places, with a little nucleus of beclouded business streets. The traveller does not go there to see the city, but to visit the suburbs, climbing into them, out of the smoke and grime, by steam "inclines" and grip railways. The city is indeed difficult to see. When you are in it, by the river, you can see nothing; when you are outside of it you are in any one of half a dozen villages, in regions of parks and elegant residences, altogether charming and geographically confusing; and if from some commanding point you try to recover the city idea, you look down upon black roofs half hid in black smoke, through which the fires of factories gleam, and where the colored Ohio rolls majestically along under a dark canopy. Looked at in one way, the real Cincinnati is a German city, and you can only study its true character "Over the Rhine," and see it success-

fully through the bottom of an upturned beer glass.
Looked at another way, it is mainly an affair of elegant
suburbs, beautifully wooded hills, pleasure - grounds,
and isolated institutions of art or charity. I am thank-
ful that there is no obligation on me to depict it.

It would probably be described as a city of art
rather than of theology, and one of rural homes rather
than metropolitan society. Perhaps the German element has had something to do in giving it its musical
character, and the early culture may have determined
its set more towards art than religion. As the cloud
of smoke became thicker and thicker in the old city
those who disliked this gloom escaped out upon the
hills in various directions. Many, of course, still cling
to the solid ancestral houses in the city, but the country movement was so general that church-going became an affair of some difficulty, and I can imagine
that the church-going habit was a little broken up
while the new neighborhoods were forming on the
hills and in the winding valleys, and before the new
churches in the suburbs were erected. Congregations
were scattered, and society itself was more or less dis-
integrated. Each suburb is fairly accessible from the
centre of the city, either by a winding valley or by a
bold climb up a precipice, but owing to the configura-
tion of the ground, it is difficult to get from one
suburb to another without returning to the centre
and taking a fresh start. This geographical hinderance must necessarily interfere with social life, and
tend to isolation of families, or to merely neighborhood association.

Although much yet remains to be done in the way
of good roads, nature and art have combined to make

the suburbs of the city wonderfully beautiful. The surface is most picturesquely broken, the forests are fine, from this point and that there are views pleasing, poetic, distant, perfectly satisfying in form and variety, and in advantageous situations taste has guided wealth in the construction of stately houses, having ample space in the midst of manorial parks. You are not out of sight of these fine places in any of the suburbs, and there are besides, in every direction, miles of streets of pleasing homes. I scarcely know whether to prefer Clifton, with its wide sweeping avenues rounding the hills, or the perhaps more commanding heights of Walnut, nearer the river, and overlooking Kentucky. On the East Walnut Hills is a private house worth going far to see for its color. It is built of broken limestone, the chance find of a quarry, making the richest walls I have anywhere seen, comparable to nothing else than the exquisite colors in the rocks of the Yellowstone Falls, as I recall them in Mr. Moran's original studies.

If the city itself could substitute gas fuel for its smutty coal, I fancy that, with its many solid homes and stately buildings, backed by the picturesque hills, it would be a city at once curious and attractive to the view. The visitor who ascends from the river as far as Fourth Street is surprised to find room for fair avenues, and many streets and buildings of mark. The Probasco fountain in another atmosphere would be a thing of beauty, for one may go far to find so many groups in bronze so good. The Post-office building is one of the best of the Mullet-headed era of our national architecture—so good generally that one wonders that the architect thought it expedient to destroy the effect of the monolith columns by cutting them to resemble superimposed blocks. A very remarkable building also is the new Chamber of Commerce structure, from Richardson's design, massive, mediæval, challenging attention, and compelling criticism to give way to genuine admiration. There are other buildings, public and private, that indicate a city of solid growth; and the activity of its strong Chamber of Commerce is a guarantee that its growth will be maintained with the enterprise common to American cities. The effort is to make manufacturing take the place in certain lines of business that, as in the item of pork-packing, has been diverted by various causes. Money and effort have been freely given to regain the Southern trade interrupted by the war, and I am forced to believe that the success in this respect would have been greater if some of the city newspapers had not thought it all-important to manufacture political capital by keeping alive old antagonisms and prejudices. Whatever people may say, sentiment does play a considerable part in business, and it is within the knowledge of the writer that prominent merchants in at least one Southern city have refused trade contracts that would have been advantageous to Cincinnati, on account of this exhibition of partisan spirit, as if the war were not over. Nothing would be more contemptible than to see a community selling its principles for trade; but it is true that men will trade, other things being equal, where they are met with friendly cordiality and toleration, and where there is a spirit of helpfulness instead of suspicion. Professional politicians, North and South, may be able to demonstrate to their satisfaction that they should have a chance to make a living, but they ask too much when this shall be at the expense of free-flowing trade, which is in itself the best solvent of any remaining alienation, and the surest disintegrator of the objectionable political solidity, and to the hinderance of that entire social and business good feeling which is of all things desirable and necessary in a restored and compacted Union. And it is as bad political as it is bad economic policy. As a matter of fact, the politicians of Kentucky are grateful to one or two Republican journals for aid in keeping their State "solid." It is a pity that the situation has its serious as well as its ridiculous aspect.

Cincinnati in many respects is more an Eastern than a Western town; it is developing its own life, and so far as I could see, without much infusion of young fortune-hunting blood from the East. It has attained its population of about 275,000 by a slower growth than some other Western cities, and I notice in its statistical reports a pause rather than excitement since 1878–79–80. The valuation of real and personal property has kept about the same for nearly ten years (1886, real estate about $129,000,000, personal about $42,000,000), with a falling off in the personalty, and a noticeable decrease in the revenue from taxation. At the same time manufacturing has increased considerably. In 1880 there was a capital of $60,523,350, employing 74,798 laborers, with a product of $148,957,280. In 1886 the capital was $76,248,200, laborers 93,103, product $190,722,153. The business at the Post-office was a little less in 1886 than in 1883. In the seven years ending with 1886 there was a considerable increase in banking capital, which reached in the city proper over ten millions, and there was an increase in clearings from 1881 to 1886.

It would teach us nothing to follow in detail the fluctuations of the various businesses in Cincinnati, either in appreciation or decline, but it may be noted that it has more than held its own in one of the great staples — leaf tobacco — and still maintains a leading position. Yet I must refer to one of the industries for the sake of an important experiment made in connection with it. This is the experiment of profit-sharing at Ivorydale, the establishment of Messrs. Procter and Gamble, now, I believe, the largest soap factory in the world. The soap and candle industry has always been a large one in Cincinnati, and it has increased about seventy-five per cent. within the past two years. The proprietors at Ivorydale disclaim any intention of philanthropy in their new scheme—that is, the philanthropy that means giving something for nothing, as a charity: it is strictly a business operation. It is an experiment that I need not say will be watched with a good deal of interest as a means of lessening the friction between the interests of capital and labor. The plan is this: Three trustees are named who are to declare the net profits of the concern every six months; for this purpose they are to have free access to the books and papers at all times, and they are to permit the employés to designate a book-keeper to make an examination for them also. In determining the net profits, interest on all capital invested is calculated as an expense at the rate of six per cent., and a reasonable salary is allowed to each member of the firm who gives his entire time to the business. In order to share in the profits, the employé must have been at work for three consecutive months, and must be at work when the semi-annual account is made up. All the men share whose wages have exceeded $5 a week, and all the women whose wages have exceeded $4.25 a week. The proportion divided to each employé is determined by the amount of wages earned; that is, the employés shall share as between themselves in the profits exactly as they have shared in the entire fund paid as wages to the whole body, excluding the first three months' wages. In order to determine the profits for distribution, the total amount of wages paid to all employés (except travelling salesmen, who do not share) is ascertained. The amount of all expenses, including interest and salaries, is ascertained, and the total net profits shall be divided between the firm and the employés sharing in the fund. The amount of the net profit to be distributed will be that proportion of the whole net profit which will correspond to the proportion of the wages paid as compared with the entire cost of production and the expense of the business. To illustrate: If the wages paid to all employés shall equal twenty per cent. of the entire expenditure in the business, including interest and salaries of members of the firm, then twenty per cent. of the net profit will be distributed to employés.

It will be noted that this plan promotes steadiness in work, stimulates to industry, and adds a most valuable element of hopefulness to labor. As a business enterprise for the owners it is sound, for it makes every workman an interested party in increasing the profits of the firm—interested not only in production, but in the marketableness of the thing produced. There have been two divisions under this plan. At the declaration of the first the workmen had no confidence in it; many of them would have sold their chances for a glass of beer. They expected that "expenses" would make such a large figure that nothing would be left to divide. When they received, as the good workmen did, considerable sums of money, life took on another aspect to them, and we may suppose that their confidence in fair dealing was raised. The experiment of a year has been entirely satisfactory; it has not only improved the class of employés, but has introduced into the establishment a spirit of industrial cheerfulness. Of course it is still an experiment. So long as business is good, all will go well; but if there is a bad six months, and no profits, it is impossible that suspicion should not arise. And there is another consideration: the publishing to the world that the business of six months was without profit might impair credit. But, on the other hand, this openness in legitimate business may be contagious, and in the end promotive of a wider and more stable business confidence. Ivorydale is one of the best and most solidly built industrial establishments anywhere to be found, and doubly interesting for the intelligent attempt to solve the most difficult problem in modern society. The first semi-annual dividend amounted to about an eighth increase of wages. A girl who was earning five dollars a week would receive as dividend about thirty dollars a year. I think it was not in my imagination that the laborers in this establishment worked with more than usual alacrity, and seemed contented. If this plan shall prevent strikes, that alone will be as great a benefit to the workmen as to those who risk capital in employing them.

Probably to a stranger the chief interest of Cincinnati is not in its business enterprises, great as they are, but in another life just as real and important, but which is not always considered in taking account of the prosperity of a community—the development of education and of the fine arts. For a long time the city has had an independent life in art and in music. Whether a people can be saved by art I do not know. The pendulum is always swinging backward and forward, and we seem never to be able to be enthusiastic in one direction without losing something in another. The art of Cincinnati has a good deal the air of being indigenous, and the outcome in the arts of carving and design and in music has exhibited native vigor. The city has made itself a reputation for wood-carving and for decorative pottery. The Rockwood pottery, the private enterprise of Mrs. Bellamy Storer, is the only pottery in this country in which the instinct of beauty is paramount to the desire of profit. Here for a series of years experiments have been going on with clays and glazing, in regard to form and color, and in decoration purely for effect, which have resulted in pieces of marvellous interest and beauty. The effort has always been to satisfy a refined sense rather than to cater to a vicious taste, or one for startling effects already formed. I mean that the effort has not been to suit the taste of the market, but to raise that taste. The result is some of the most exquisite work in texture and color anywhere to be found, and I was glad to learn that it is gaining an appreciation which will not in this case leave virtue to be its own reward,

18

The various private attempts at art expression have been consolidated in a public Museum and an Art School, which are among the best planned and equipped in the country. The Museum Building in Eden Park, of which the centre pavilion and west wing are completed (having a total length of 214 feet from east to west), is in Romanesque style, solid and pleasing, with exceedingly well-planned exhibition-rooms and picture-galleries, and its collections are already choice and interesting. The fund was raised by the subscriptions of 455 persons, and amounts to $316,501, of which Mr. Charles R. West led off with the contribution of $150,000, invested as a permanent fund. Near this is the Art School, also a noble building, the gift of Mr. David Sinton, who in 1855 gave the Museum Association $75,000 for this purpose. It should be said that the original and liberal endowment of the Art School was made by Mr. Nicholas Longworth, in accordance with the wish of his father, and that the association also received a legacy of $40,000 from Mr. R. R. Springer. Altogether the association has received considerably over a million of dollars, and has in addition, by gift and purchase, property valued at nearly $200,000. The Museum is the fortunate possessor of one of the three Russian Reproductions, the other two being in the South Kensington Museum of London and the Metropolitan of New York. Thus, by private enterprise, in the true American way, the city is graced and honored by art buildings which give it distinction, and has a school of art so well equipped and conducted that it attracts students from far and near, filling its departments of drawing, painting, sculpture, and wood-carving with eager learners. It has over 400 scholars in the various departments. The ample endowment fund makes the school really free, there being only a nominal charge of about $5 a year.

In the collection of paintings, which has several of merit, is one with a history, which has a unique importance. This is B. R. Haydon's "Public Entry of Christ into Jerusalem." This picture of heroic size, and in the grand style which had a great vogue in its day, was finished in 1820, sold for £170 in 1831, and brought to Philadelphia, where it was exhibited. The exhibition did not pay expenses, and the picture was placed in the Academy as a companion piece to Benjamin West's "Death on the Pale Horse." In the fire of 1845 both canvases were rescued by being cut from the frames and dragged out like old blankets. It was finally given to the Cathedral in Cincinnati, where its existence was forgotten until it was discovered lately and loaned to the Museum. The interest in the picture now is mainly an accidental one, although it is a fine illustration of the large academic method, and in certain details is painted with the greatest care. Haydon's studio was the resort of English authors of his day, and the portraits of several of them are introduced into this picture. The face of William Hazlitt does duty as St. Peter; Wordsworth and Sir Isaac Newton and Voltaire appear as spectators of the pageant—the cynical expression of Voltaire is the worldly contrast to the believing faith of the disciples—and the inspired face of the youthful St. John is that of John Keats. This being the only portrait of Keats in life, gives this picture extraordinary interest.

The spirit of Cincinnati, that is, its concern for interests not altogether material, is also illustrated by its College of Music. This institution was opened in 1878. It was endowed by private subscription, the largest being $100,000 by Mr. R. R. Springer. It is financially very prosperous; its possessions in real estate, buildings—including a beautiful concert hall—and invested endowments amount to over $300,000. Its average attendance is about 550, and during the year 1887 it had about 650 different scholars. From tuition alone about $45,000 were received, and although the expenditures were liberal, the college had at the beginning of 1888 a handsome cash balance. The object of the college is the development of native talent, and to evoke this the best foreign teachers obtainable have been secured. In the departments of the voice, the piano, and the violin, American youth are said to show special proficiency, and the result of the experiment thus far is to strengthen the belief that out of our mixed nationality is to come most artistic development in music. Free admission is liberally given to pupils who have talent but not the means to cultivate it. Recognizing the value of broad culture in musical education, the managers have provided courses of instruction in English literature, lectures upon American authors, and for the critical study of Italian. The college proper has forty teachers, and as many rooms for instruction. Near it, and connected by a covered way, is the great Music Hall, with a seating capacity of 5400, and the room to pack in nearly 7000 people. In this superb hall the great annual musical festivals are held. It has a plain interior, sealed entirely in wood,

and with almost no ornamentation to impair its reso-
nance. The courage of the projectors who dared to
build this hall for a purely musical purpose and not
for display is already vindicated. It is no doubt the
best auditorium in the country. As age darkens the
wood, the interior grows rich, and it is discovered
that the effect of the seasoning of the wood or of
the musical vibrations steadily improves the acoustic
properties, having the same effect upon the sonorous-
ness of the wood that long use has upon a good violin. The whole interior is a magnificent sounding-
board, if that is the proper expression, and for fifty
years, if the hall stands, it will constantly improve,
and have a resonant quality unparalleled in any other
auditorium.

The city has a number of clubs, well housed, such
as are common to other cities, and some that are peculiar. The Cuvier Club, for the preservation of
game, has a very large museum of birds, animals, and
fishes, beautifully prepared and arranged. The Historical and Philosophical Society has also good quarters, a library of about 10,000 books and 44,000 pamphlets, and is becoming an important depository of
historical manuscripts. The Literary Society, composed of 100 members, who meet weekly, in commodious apartments, to hear an essay, discuss general topics, and pass an hour socially about small tables, with
something to eat and drink, has been vigorously
maintained since 1848.

An institution of more general importance is the
Free Public Library, which has about 150,000 books
and 18,000 pamphlets. This is supported in part by
an accumulated fund, but mainly by a city tax, which

is appropriated through the Board of Education.
The expenditures for it in 1887 were about $50,000.
It has a notably fine art department. The Library is
excellently managed by Mr. A. W. Whelpley, the librarian, who has increased its circulation and usefulness by recognizing the new idea that a librarian
is not a mere custodian of books, but should be a
stimulator and director of the reading of a community. This office becomes more and more important
now that the good library has to compete for the attention of the young with the "cheap and nasty"
publications of the day. It is probably due somewhat to direction in reading that books of fiction
taken from the Library last year were only fifty-one
per cent. of the whole.

An institution established in many cities as a help-
ing hand to women is the Women's Exchange. The
Exchange in Cincinnati is popular as a restaurant.
Many worthy women support themselves by preparing food which is sold here over the counter, or
served at the tables. The city has for many years
sustained a very good Zoological Garden, which is
much frequented except in the winter. Interest in it
is not, however, as lively as it was formerly. It
seems very difficult to keep a "zoo" up to the mark
in America.

I do not know that the public schools of Cincinnati
call for special mention. They seem to be conservative schools, not differing from the best elsewhere,
and they appear to be trying no new experiments.
One of the high-schools which I saw with 600 pupils
is well conducted, and gives good preparation for college. The city enumeration is over 87,000 children

between the ages of six and twenty-one, and of these about 36,000 are reported not in school. Of the 2300 colored children in the city, about half were in school. When the Ohio Legislature repealed the law establishing separate schools for colored people, practically creating mixed schools, a majority of the colored parents in the city petitioned and obtained branch schools of their own, with colored teachers in charge. The colored people everywhere seem to prefer to be served by teachers and preachers of their own race.

The schools of Cincinnati have not adopted manual training, but a Technical School has been in existence about a year, with promise of success. The Cincinnati University under the presidency of Governor Cox shows new vitality. It is supported in part by taxation, and is open free to all resident youth, so that while it is not a part of the public-school system, it supplements it.

Cincinnati has had a great many discouragements of late, turbulent politics and dishonorable financial failures. But, for all that, it impresses one as a solid city, with remarkable development in the higher civilization.

In its physical aspect Louisville is in every respect a contrast to Cincinnati. Lying on a plain, sloping gently up from the river, it spreads widely in rectangular uniformity of streets—a city of broad avenues, getting to be well paved and well shaded, with ample spaces in lawns, houses detached, somewhat uniform in style, but with an air of comfort, occasionally of elegance and solid good taste. The city has an exceedingly open, friendly, cheerful appearance. In May, with its abundant foliage and flowery lawns, it is a beautiful city : a beautiful, healthful city in a temperate climate, surrounded by a fertile country, is Louisville. Beyond the city the land rises into a rolling country of Blue-Grass farms, and eastward along the river are fine bluffs broken into most advantageous sites for suburban residences. Looking northward across the Ohio are seen the Indiana "Knobs." In high-water the river is a majestic stream, covering almost entirely the rocks which form the "Falls," and the beds of "cement" which are so profitably worked. The canal, which makes navigation round the rapids, has its mouth at Shipping-port Island. About this spot clusters much of the early romance of Louisville. Here are some of the old houses and the old mill built by the Frenchman Tarascon in the early part of the century. Here in a weather-beaten wooden tenement, still standing, Tarascon offered border hospitality to many distinguished guests; Aaron Burr and Blennerhasset were among his visitors, and General Wilkinson, the projector of the canal, then in command of the armies of the United States; and it was probably here that the famous "Spanish conspiracy" was concocted. Corn Island, below the rapids, upon which the first settlement of Louisville was made in 1778, disappeared some years ago, gradually washed away by the swift river.

Opposite this point, in Indiana, is the village of Clarksville, which has a unique history. About 1785 Virginia granted to Gen. George Rogers Clark, the most considerable historic figure of this region, a large tract of land in recognition of his services in the war. When Virginia ceded this territory to Indiana the township of Clarksville was excepted from the grant. It had been organized with a governing board of trustees, self-perpetuating, and this organization still continues. Clarksville has therefore never been ceded to the United States, and if it is not an independent community, the eminent domain must still rest in the State of Virginia.

Some philosophers say that the character of a people is determined by climate and soil. There is a notion in this region that the underlying limestone and the consequent succulent Blue-Grass produce a race of large men, frank in manner, brave in war, inclined to oratory and ornamental conversation, women of uncommon beauty, and the finest horses in the Union. Of course a fertile soil and good living conduce to beauty of form and in a way to the free graces of life. But the contrast of Cincinnati and Louisville in social life and in the manner of doing business cannot all be accounted for by Blue-Grass. It would be very interesting, if one had the knowledge, to study the causes of this contrast in two cities not very far apart. In late years Louisville has awakened to a new commercial life, as one finds in it a strong infusion of Western business energy and ambition. It is jubilant in its growth and prosperity. It was always a commercial town, but with a dash of Blue-Grass leisure and hospitality, and a hereditary flavor of manners and fine living. Family and pedigree have always been held in as high esteem as beauty. The Kentuckian of society is a great contrast to the Virginian, but it may be only the development of the tide-water gentleman in the freer, wider opportunities of the Blue-Grass region. The pioneers of Kentucky were

backwoodsmen, but many of the early settlers, whose
descendants are now leaders in society and in the professions, came with the full-blown tastes and habits of
Virginia civilization, as their spacious colonial houses,
erected in the latter part of the last century and the
early part of this, still attest. They brought and
planted in the wilderness a highly developed social
state, which was modified into a certain freedom by
circumstances. One can fancy in the abundance of a
temperate latitude a certain gayety and joyousness in
material existence, which is contented with that, and
has not sought the art and musical development which
one finds in Cincinnati. All over the South, Louisville is noted for the beauty of its women, but the other ladies of the South say that they can always tell
one from Louisville by her dress, something in it quite
aware of the advanced fashion, something in the "cut"
—a mystery known only to the feminine eye.

I did not intend, however, to enter upon a disquisition
of the different types of civilization in Cincinnati and
in Louisville. One observes them as evidences of what
has heretofore been mentioned, the great variety in
American life, when one looks below the surface.
The traveller enjoys both types, and is rejoiced to
find such variety, culture, taking in one city the form
of the worship of beauty and the enjoyment of life,
and in the other greater tendency to the fine arts.
Louisville is a city of churches, of very considerable
religious activity, and of pretty stanch orthodoxy. I
do not mean to say that what are called modern ideas
do not leaven its society. In one of its best literary
clubs I heard the Spencerian philosophy expounded
and advocated with the enthusiasm and keenness of

an emancipated Eastern town. But it is as true of
Louisville as it is of other Southern cities that traditional faith is less disturbed by doubts and isms than
in many Eastern towns. One notes here also, as all
over the South, the marked growth of the temperance
movement. The Kentuckians believe that they produce the best fluid from rye and corn in the Union,
and that they are the best judges of it. Neither proposition will be disputed, nor will one trifle with a legitimate pride in a home production ; but there is a
new spirit abroad, and both Bourbon and the game
that depends quite as much upon the knowledge of
human nature as upon the turn of the cards are silent-
ly going to the rear. Always Kentuckians have been
distinguished in politics, in oratory, in the professions
of law and of medicine ; nor has the city ever wanted
scholars in historical lore, men who have not only kept
alive the traditions of learning and local research, like
Col. John Mason Brown, but have exhibited the true
antiquarian spirit of Col. H. T. Durrett, whose historical library is worth going far to see and study. It
will be a great pity if his exceedingly valuable collection is not preserved to the State to become the nucleus of a Historical Society worthy of the State's history. When I spoke of art it was in a public sense ;
there are many individuals who have good pictures
and especially interesting portraits, and in the early
days Kentucky produced at least one artist, wholly
self-taught, who was a rare genius. Matthew H.
Jouett was born in Mercer County in 1780, and died
in Louisville in 1820. In the course of his life he
painted as many as three hundred and fifty portraits,
which are scattered all over the Union. In his ma-

ture years he was for a time with Stuart in Boston. Some specimens of his work in Louisville are wonderfully fine, recalling the style and traditions of the best masters, some of them equal if not superior to the best by Stuart, and suggesting in color and solidity the vigor and grace of Vandyck. He was the product of no school but nature and his own genius. Louisville has always had a scholarly and aggressive press, and its traditions are not weakened in Mr. Henry Watterson. On the social side the good-fellowship of the city is well represented in the Pendennis Club, which is thoroughly home-like and agreeable. The town has at least one book-store of the first class, but it sells very few American copyright books. The city has no free or considerable public library. The Polytechnic Society, which has a room for lectures, keeps for circulation among subscribers about 38,000 books. It has also a geological and mineral collection, and a room devoted to pictures, which contains an allegorical statue by Canova.

In its public schools and institutions of charity the city has a great deal to show that is interesting. In medicine it has always been famous. It has four medical colleges, a college of dentistry, a college of pharmacy, and a school of pharmacy for women. In nothing, however, is the spirit of the town better exhibited than in its public-school system. With a population of less than 180,000, the school enrolment, which has advanced year by year, was in 1887 21,601, with an aggregate belonging of 17,392. The amount expended on schools, which was in 1880 $197,699, had increased to $323,943 in 1887—a cost of $18.62 per pupil. Equal provision is made for colored schools as for white, but the number of colored pupils is less than 3000, and the colored high-school is small, as only a few are yet fitted to go so far in education. The negroes all prefer colored teachers, and so far as I could learn, they are quite content with the present management of the School Board. Co-education is not in the Kentucky idea, nor in its social scheme. There are therefore two high-schools—one for girls and one for boys—both of the highest class and efficiency, in excellent buildings, and under most intelligent management. Among the teachers in the schools are ladies of position, and the schools doubtless owe their good character largely to the fact that they are in the fashion: as a rule, all the children of the city are educated in them. Manual training is not introduced, but all the advanced methods in the best modern schools, object-lessons, word-building, moulding, and drawing, are practised. During the fall and winter months there are night schools, which are very well attended. In one of the intermediate schools I saw an exercise which illustrates the intelligent spirit of the schools. This was an account of the early settlement, growth, and prosperity of Louisville, told in a series of very short papers—so many that a large number of the pupils had a share in constructing the history. Each one took up connectively a brief period or the chief events in chronological order, with illustrations of manners and customs, fashions of dress and mode of life. Of course this mosaic was not original, but made up of extracts from various local histories and statistical reports. This had the merit of being a good exercise as well as inculcating an intelligent pride in the city.

Nearly every religious denomination is represented

in the 142 churches of Louisville. Of these 9 are Northern Presbyterian and 7 Southern Presbyterian, 11 of the M.E. Church South and 6 of the M.E. Church North, 18 Catholic, 7 Christian, 1 Unitarian, and 31 colored. There are seven convents and monasteries, and a Young Men's Christian Association. In proportion to its population, the city is pre-eminent for public and private charities: there are no less than thirty-eight of these institutions, providing for the infirm and unfortunate of all ages and conditions. Unique among these in the United States is a very fine building for the maintenance of the widows and orphans of deceased Freemasons of the State of Kentucky, supported mainly by contributions of the Masonic lodges. One of the best equipped and managed industrial schools of reform for boys and girls is on the outskirts of the city. Mr. P. Caldwell is its superintendent, and it owes its success, as all similar schools do, to the peculiar fitness of the manager for this sort of work. The institution has three departments. There were 125 white boys and 79 colored boys, occupying separate buildings in the same enclosure, and 41 white girls in their own house in another enclosure. The establishment has a farm, a garden, a greenhouse, a library building, a little chapel, ample and pleasant play-yards. There is as little as possible the air of a prison about the place, and as much as possible that of a home and school. The boys have organized a very fair brass band. The girls make all the clothes for the establishment; the boys make shoes, and last year earned $8000 in bottoming chairs. The school is mainly sustained by taxation and city appropriations; the yearly cost is about $26,000. Children are

indentured out when good homes can be found for
them.

The School for the Education of the Blind is a
State institution, and admits none from outside the
State. The fine building occupies a commanding
situation on hills not far from the river, and is admirably built, the rooms spacious and airy, and the whole
establishment is well ordered. There are only 79
scholars, and the few colored are accommodated by
themselves in a separate building, in accordance with
an Act of the Legislature in 1884 for the education of
colored blind children. The distinction of this institution is that it has on its premises the United States
printing-office for furnishing publications for the blind
asylums of the country. Printing is done here both
in letters and in points, by very ingenious processes,
and the library is already considerable. The space
required to store a library of books for the blind may
be reckoned from the statement that the novel of "Ivanhoe" occupies three volumes, each larger than Webster's
Unabridged Dictionary. The weekly *Sunday-school
Times* is printed here. The point writing consists
entirely of dots in certain combinations to represent
letters, and it is noticed that about half the children
prefer this to the alphabet. The preference is not explained by saying that it is merely a matter of feeling.

The city has as yet no public parks, but the very
broad streets—from sixty to one hundred and twenty
feet in width—the wide spacing of the houses in the residence parts, and the abundant shade make them less a
necessity than elsewhere. The city spreads very freely and openly over the plain, and short drives take
one into lovely Blue-Grass country. A few miles out

on Churchill Downs is the famous Jockey Club Park, a perfect racing track and establishment, where world-wide reputations are made at the semi-annual meetings. The limestone region, a beautifully rolling country, almost rivals the Lexington plantations in the raising of fine horses. Driving out to one of these farms one day, we passed, not far from the river, the old Taylor mansion and the tomb of Zachary Taylor. It is in the reserved family burying-ground, where lie also the remains of Richard Taylor, of Revolutionary memory. The great tomb and the graves are overrun thickly with myrtle, and the secluded irregular ground is shaded by forest-trees. The soft wind of spring was blowing sweetly over the fresh green fields, and there was about the place an air of repose and dignity most refreshing to the spirit. Near the tomb stands the fine commemorative shaft bearing on its summit a good portrait statue of the hero of Buena Vista. I liked to linger there, the country was so sweet; the great river flowing in sight lent a certain grandeur to the resting-place, and I thought how dignified and fit it was for a President to be buried at his home.

The city of Louisville in 1888 has the unmistakable air of confidence and buoyant prosperity. This feeling of confidence is strengthened by the general awakening of Kentucky in increased immigration of agriculturists, and in the development of extraordinary mines of coal and iron, and in the railway extension. But locally the Board of Trade (an active body of 700 members) has in its latest report most encouraging figures to present. In almost every branch of business there was an increase in 1887 over 1886; in both manufactures and trade the volume of business increased from twenty to fifty per cent. For instance, stoves and castings increased from 16,574,547 pounds to 19,386,808; manufactured tobacco, from 12,729,421 pounds to 17,059,006; gas and water pipes, from 56,-083,380 pounds to 63,745,216; grass and clover seed, from 4,240,908 bushels to 6,601,451. A conclusive item as to manufactures is that there were received in 1887 951,767 tons of bituminous coal, against 204,221 tons in 1886. Louisville makes the claim of being the largest tobacco market in the world in bulk and variety. It leads largely the nine principal leaf-tobacco markets in the West. The figures for 1887 are—receipts, 123,569 hogsheads; sales, 135,192 hogsheads; stock in hand, 36,431 hogsheads, against the corresponding figures of 62,074, 65,924, 13,972 of its great rival, Cincinnati. These large figures are a great increase over 1886, when the value of tobacco handled here was estimated at nearly $20,000,000. Another great interest always associated with Louisville, whiskey, shows a like increase, there being shipped in 1887 119,637 barrels, against 101,943 barrels in 1886. In the Louisville collection district there were registered one hundred grain distilleries, with a capacity of 80,000 gallons a day. For the five years ending June 30, 1887, the revenue taxes on this product amounted to nearly $30,000,000. I am not attempting a conspectus of the business of Louisville, only selecting some figures illustrating its growth. Its manufacture of agricultural implements has attained great proportions. The reputation of Louisville for tobacco and whiskey is widely advertised, but it is not generally known that it has the largest plough factory in the world. This is one of four which altogether employ about

19

2000 hands, and make a product valued at $2,275,000. In 1880 Louisville made 80,000 ploughs; in 1886, 190,000. The capacity of manufacture in 1887 was increased by the enlargement of the chief factory to a number not given, but there were shipped that year 11,005,151 pounds of ploughs. There is a steadily increasing manufacture of woollen goods, and the production of the mixed fabric known as Kentucky jeans is another industry in which Louisville leads the world, making annually 7,500,000 yards of cloth, and its four mills increased their capacity twenty per cent. in 1887. The opening of the hard-wood lumber districts in eastern Kentucky has made Louisville one of the important lumber markets: about 125,000,000 feet of lumber, logs, etc., were sold here in 1887. But it is unnecessary to particularize. The Board of Trade think that the advantages of Louisville as a manufacturing centre are sufficiently emphasized from the fact that during the year 1887 seventy - three new manufacturing establishments, mainly from the North and East, were set up, using a capital of $1,290,500, and employing 1621 laborers. The city has twenty-two banks, which had, July 1, 1887, $8,200,200 capital, and $19,927,138 deposits. The clearings for 1887 were $281,110,402—an increase of nearly $50,000,000 over 1886.

Another item which helps to explain the buoyant feeling of Louisville is that its population increased over 10,000 from 1886 to 1887, reaching, according to the best estimate, 177,000 people. I should have said also that no city in the Union is better served by street railways, which are so multiplied and arranged as to "correspondences" that for one fare nearly every inhabitant can ride within at least two blocks of his residence. In these cars, as in the railway cars of the State, there is the same absence of discrimination against color that prevails in Louisiana and in Arkansas. And it is an observation hopeful, at least to the writer, of the good time at hand when all party lines shall be drawn upon the broadest national issues, that there seems to be in Kentucky no social distinction between Democrats and Republicans.

XIII.

MEMPHIS AND LITTLE ROCK.

THE State of Tennessee gets its diversity of climate and productions from the irregularity of its surface, not from its range over degrees of latitude, like Illinois; for it is a narrow State, with an average breadth of only a hundred and ten miles, while it is about four hundred miles in length, from the mountains in the east—the highest land east of the Rocky Mountains —to the alluvial bottom of the Mississippi in the west. In this range is every variety of mineral and agricultural wealth, with some of the noblest scenery and the fairest farming-land in the Union, and all the good varieties of a temperate climate.

In the extreme south-west corner lies Memphis, differing as entirely in character from Knoxville and Nashville as the bottom-lands of the Mississippi differ from the valleys of the Great Smoky Mountains. It is the natural centre of the finest cotton-producing district in the world, the county of Shelby, of which it is legally known as the Taxing District, yielding more cotton than any other county in the Union except that of Washington in Mississippi. It is almost as much aloof politically from east and middle Tennessee as it is geographically. A homogeneous State might be constructed by taking west Tennessee, all of Mississippi above Vicksburg and Jackson, and a slice off Arkansas, with Memphis for its capital. But the redistricting would be a good thing neither for the States named nor for Memphis, for the more variety within convenient limits a State can have, the better, and Memphis could not wish a better or more distinguished destiny than to become the commercial metropolis of a State of such great possibilities and varied industries as Tennessee. Her political influence might be more decisive in the homogeneous State outlined, but it will be abundant for all reasonable ambition in its inevitable commercial importance. And besides, the western part of the State needs the moral tonic of the more elevated regions.

The city has a frontage of about four miles on the Mississippi River, but is high above it on the Chickasaw Bluffs, with an uneven surface and a rolling country back of it, the whole capable of perfect drainage. Its site is the best on the river for a great city from St. Louis to the Gulf; this advantage is emphasized by the concentration of railways at this point, and the great bridge, which is now on the eve of construction, to the Arkansas shore, no doubt fixes its destiny as the inland metropolis of the South-west. Memphis was the child of the Mississippi, and this powerful, wayward stream is still its fostering mother, notwithstanding the decay of river commerce brought about by the railways; for the river still asserts its power as a regulator of rates of transportation. I do not mean to say that the freighting on it in towed barges is not still enormous, but if it did not carry a pound to the markets of the world it is still the friend of all the inner continental regions, which says to the railroads, beyond a certain rate of charges you shall not go. With this advantage of situation, the natural receiver of the products of an inexhaustible agricultural region (one has only to take a trip by rail through the Yazoo Valley to be convinced of that), and an equally good point for distribution of supplies, it is inevitable that Memphis should grow with an accelerating impulse.

The city has had a singular and instructive history, and that she has survived so many vicissitudes and calamities, and entered upon an extraordinary career of prosperity, is sufficient evidence of the territorial necessity of a large city just at this point on the river. The student of social science will find in its history a striking illustration of the relation of sound sanitary and business conditions to order and morality. Before the war, and for some time after it, Memphis was a place for trade in one staple, where fortunes were quickly made and lost, where no attention was paid to sanitary laws. The cloud of impending pestilence always hung over it, the yellow-fever was always a possibility, and a devastating epidemic of it must inevitably be reckoned with every few years. It seems to be a law of social life that an epidemic, or the probability of it, engenders a recklessness of life and a low condition of morals and public order. Memphis existed, so to speak, on the edge of a volcano, and it cannot be denied that it had a reputation for violence and disorder. While little or nothing was done to make the city clean and habitable, or to beautify it, law was weak in its mobile, excitable population, and differences of opinion were settled by the revolver. In spite of these disadvantages, the profits of trade were so great there that its population of twenty thousand at the close of the war had doubled by 1878. In that year the yellow-fever came as an epidemic, and so increased in 1879 as nearly to depopulate the city; its population was reduced from nearly forty thousand to about fourteen thousand, two-thirds of which were negroes; its commerce was absolutely cut off, its manufactures were suspended, it was bankrupt. There is nothing more unfortunate for a State or a city than loss of financial credit. Memphis struggled in vain with its enormous debt, unable to pay it, unable to compromise it.

Under these circumstances the city resorted to a novel expedient. It surrendered its charter to the State, and ceased to exist as a municipality. The leaders of this movement gave two reasons for it, the wish not to repudiate the city debt, but to gain breathing-time, and that municipal government in this country is a failure. The Legislature erected the former Memphis into The Taxing District of Shelby County, and provided a government for it. This government consists of a Legislative Council of eight members, made up of the Board of Fire and Police Commissioners, consisting of three, and the Board of Public Works, consisting of five. These are all elected by popular vote to serve a term of four years, but the elections are held every two years, so that the council always contains members who have had experience. The Board of Fire and Police Commissioners elects a President, who is the executive officer of the Taxing District, and has the power and duties of a mayor; he has a salary of $2000, inclusive of his fees as police magistrate, and the other members of his board have salaries of $500. The members of the Board of Public Works serve without compensation. No man can be eligible to either board who has not been a resi-

dent of the district for five years. In addition there
is a Board of Health, appointed by the council. This
government has the ordinary powers of a city government, defined carefully in the Act, but it cannot run
the city in debt, and it cannot appropriate the taxes
collected except for the specific purpose named by
the State Legislature, which specific appropriations
are voted annually by the Legislature on the recom-
mendation of the council. Thus the government of
the city is committed to eight men, and the execution
of its laws to one man, the President of the Taxing
District, who has extraordinary power. The final success of this scheme will be watched with a great deal
of interest by other cities. On the surface it can be
seen that it depends upon securing a non-partisan council, and an honest, conscientious President of the Taxing District—that is to say, upon the choice by popular vote of the best eight men to rule the city. Up to
this time, with only slight hitches, it has worked exceedingly well, as will appear in a consideration of the
condition of the city. The slight hitch mentioned was
that the President was accused of using temporarily
the sum appropriated for one city purpose for another.

The Supreme Court of the United States decided
that Memphis had not evaded its obligations by a
change of name and form of government. The result was a settlement with the creditors at fifty cents
on the dollar; and then the city gathered itself together for a courageous effort and a new era of prosperity.
The turning-point in its career was the adoption of a
system of drainage and sewerage which transformed
it immediately into a fairly healthful city. With its

uneven surface and abundance of water at hand, it was
well adapted to the Waring system, which works to
the satisfaction of all concerned, and since its introduction the inhabitants are relieved from apprehension
of the return of a yellow-fever epidemic. Population
and business returned with this sense of security, and
there has been a change in the social atmosphere as
well. In 1880 it had a population of less than 34,000;
it can now truthfully claim between 75,000 and 80,000;
and the business activity, the building both of fine business blocks and handsome private residences, are proportioned to the increase in inhabitants. In 1879–80
the receipt of cotton was 409,809 bales, valued at $23,-
752,529; in 1886–87, 663,277 bales, valued at $30,099,-
510. The estimate of the Board of Trade for 1888,
judging from the first months of the year, is 700,000
bales. I notice in the comparative statement of leading articles of commerce and consumption an exceedingly large increase in 1887 over 1886. The banking
capital in 1887 was $3,360,000—an increase of $1,560,-
000 over 1886. The clearings were $101,177,377 in
1877, against $82,642,192 in 1886.

The traveller, however, does not need figures to con-
vince him of the business activity of the town; the
piles of cotton beyond the capacity of storage, the
street traffic, the extension of streets and residences
far beyond the city limits, all speak of growth. There
is in process of construction a union station to accommodate the six railways now meeting there and others
projected. On the west of the river it has lines to
Kansas City and Little Rock and to St. Louis; on the
east, to Louisville and to the Atlantic seaboard direct,
and two to New Orleans. With the building of the

bridge, which is expected to be constructed in a couple of years, Memphis will be admirably supplied with transportation facilities.

As to its external appearance, it must be said that the city has grown so fast that city improvements do not keep pace with its assessable value. The inability of the city to go into debt is a wholesome provision, but under this limitation the city offices are shabby, the city police quarters and court would disgrace an indigent country village, and most of the streets are in bad condition for want of pavement. There are fine streets, many attractive new residences, and some fine old places, with great trees, and the gravelled pikes running into the country are in fine condition, and are favorite drives. There is a beautiful country round about, with some hills and pleasant woods. Looked at from an elevation, the town is seen to cover a large territory, and presents in the early green of spring a charming appearance. Some five miles out is the Montgomery race-track, park, and club-house—a handsome establishment, prettily laid out and planted, already attractive, and sure to be notable when the trees are grown.

The city has a public-school system, a Board of Education elected by popular vote, and divides its fund fairly between schools for white and colored children. But it needs good school-houses as much as it needs good pavements. In 1887 the tax of one and a half mills produced $54,000 for carrying on the schools, and $19,000 for the building fund. It was not enough — at least $75,000 were needed. The schools were in debt. There is a plan adopted for a fine High-school building, but the city needs altogether more money and more energy for the public schools. According to some reports the public schools have suffered from politics, and are not as good as they were years ago, but they are undoubtedly gaining in public favor, notwithstanding some remaining Bourbon prejudice against them. The citizens are making money fast enough to begin to be liberal in matters educational, which are only second to sanitary measures in the well-being of the city. The new free Public Library, which will be built and opened in a couple of years, will do much for the city in this direction. It is the noble gift of the late F. H. Cossitt, of New York, formerly a citizen of Memphis, who left $75,000 for that purpose.

Perhaps the public schools of Memphis would be better (though not so without liberal endowment) if the city had not two exceptionally good private schools for young ladies. These are the Clara Conway Institute and the Higby School for Young Ladies, taking their names from their principals and founders. Each of these schools has about 350 pupils, from the age of six to the mature age of graduation, boys being admitted until they are twelve years old. Each has pleasant grounds and fine buildings, large, airy, well planned, with ample room for all the departments—literature, science, art, music—of the most advanced education. One finds in them the best methods of the best schools, and a most admirable spirit. It is not too much to say that these schools give distinction to Memphis, and that the discipline and intellectual training the young ladies receive there will have a marked effect upon the social life of the city. If one who spent some delightful hours in the company of

these graceful and enthusiastic scholars, and who
would like heartily to acknowledge their cordiality,
and his appreciation of their admirable progress in
general study, might make a suggestion, it would be
that what the frank, impulsive Southern girl, with her
inborn talent for being agreeable and her vivid apprehension of life, needs least of all is the cultivation of the emotional, the rhetorical, the sentimental side. However cleverly they are done, the
recitation of poems of sentiment, of passion, of love-
making and marriage, above all, of those doubtful
dialect verses in which a touch of pseudo-feeling is
supposed to excuse the slang of the street and the
vulgarity of the farm, is not an exercise elevating to
the taste. I happen to speak of it here, but I confess
that it is only a text from which a little sermon might
be preached about "recitations" and declamations
generally, in these days of overdone dialect and innu-
endoes about the hypocrisy of old-fashioned morality.

The city has a prosperous college of the Christian
Brothers, another excellent school for girls in the St.
Agnes Academy, and a colored industrial school, the
Lemoyne, where the girls are taught cooking and the
art of house-keeping, and the boys learn carpentering.
This does not belong to the public-school system.

Whatever may be the opinion about the propriety
of attaching industrial training to public schools generally, there is no doubt that this sort of training is in-
dispensable to the colored people of the South, whose
children do not at present receive the needed domestic
training at home, and whose education must contribute
to their ability to earn a living. Those educated in
the schools, high and low, cannot all be teachers or

preachers, and they are not in the way of either social elevation or thrifty lives if they have neither a trade nor the taste to make neat and agreeable homes. The colored race cannot have it too often impressed upon them that their way to all the rights and privileges under a free government lies in industry, thrift, and morality. Whatever reason they have to complain of remaining discrimination and prejudice, there is only one way to overcome both, and that is by the acquisition of property and intelligence. In the history of the world a people were never elevated otherwise. No amount of legislation can do it. In Memphis—in Southern cities generally—the public schools are impartially administered as to the use of money for both races. In the country districts they are as generally inadequate, both in quality and in the length of the school year. In the country, where farming and domestic service must be the occupations of the mass of the people, industrial schools are certainly not called for; but in the cities they are a necessity of the present development.

Ever since Memphis took itself in hand with a new kind of municipal government, and made itself a healthful city, good-fortune of one kind and another seems to have attended it. Abundant water it could get from the river for sewerage purposes, but for other uses either extensive filters were needed or cisterns were resorted to. The city was supplied with water, which the stranger would hesitate to drink or bathe in, from Wolf River, a small stream emptying into the Mississippi above the city. But within the year a most important discovery has been made for the health and prosperity of the town. This was the

striking, in the depression of the Gayoso Bayou, at a
depth of 450 feet, perfectly pure water, at a temperature of about 62°, in abundance, with a head sufficient
to bring it in fountains some feet about the level of
the ground. Ten wells had been sunk, and the water
flowing was estimated at ten millions of gallons daily,
or half enough to supply the city. It was expected
that with more wells the supply would be sufficient
for all purposes, and then Memphis will have drinking
water not excelled in purity by that of any city in the
land. It is not to be wondered at that this incalculable good-fortune should add buoyancy to the business, and even to the advance in the price, of real
estate. The city has widely outgrown its corporate
limits, there is activity in building and improvements
in all the pleasant suburbs, and with the new pavements which are in progress, the city will be as attractive as it is prosperous.

Climate is much a matter of taste. The whole area
of the alluvial land of the Mississippi has the three
requisites for malaria—heat, moisture, and vegetable
decomposition. The tendency to this is overcome, in
a measure, as the land is thoroughly drained and cultivated. Memphis has a mild winter, long summer, and
a considerable portion of the year when the temperature is just about right for enjoyment. In the table
of temperature for 1887 I find that the mean was 61.9°,
the mean of the highest by months was 84.9°, and the
mean lowest was 37.4°. The coldest month was January, when the range of the thermometer was from
72.2° to 4.3°, and the hottest was July, when the range
was from 99° to 67.3°. There is a preponderance of
fair, sunny weather. The record for 1887 was: 157

days of clear, 132 fair, 65 cloudy, 91 days of frost. From this it appears that Memphis has a pretty agreeable climate for those who do not insist upon a good deal of "bracing," and it has a most genial and hospitable society.

Early on the morning of the 12th of April we crossed the river to the lower landing of the Memphis and Little Rock Railway, the upper landing being inaccessible on account of the high water. It was a delicious spring morning, the foliage, half unfolded, was in its first flush of green, and as we steamed down the stream the town, on bluffs forty feet high, was seen to have a noble situation. All the opposite country for forty miles from the river was afloat, and presented the appearance of a vast swamp, not altogether unpleasing in its fresh dress of green. For forty miles, to Madison, the road ran upon an embankment just above the flood; at intervals were poor shanties and little cultivated patches, but shanties, corn patches, and trees all stood in the water. The inhabitants, the majority colored, seemed of the sort to be content with half-amphibious lives. Before we reached Madison and crossed St. Francis River we ran through a streak of gravel. Forest City, at the crossing of the Iron Mountain Railway, turned out to be not exactly a city, in the Eastern meaning of the word, but a considerable collection of houses, with a large hotel. It seemed, so far in the wilderness, an irresponsible sort of place, and the crowd at the station were in a festive, hilarious mood. This was heightened by the playing of a travelling band which we carried with us in the

second - class car, and which good - naturedly unlim-
bered at the stations. It consisted of a colored bass-
viol, violin, and guitar, and a white cornet. On the
way the negro population were in the majority, all
the residences were shabby shanties, and the moving
public on the trains and about the stations had not
profited by the example of the commercial travellers,
who are the only smartly dressed people one sees in
these regions. A young girl who got into the car
here told me that she came from Marianna, a town to
the south, on the Languille River, and she seemed to
regard it as a central place. At Brinkley we crossed
the St. Louis, Arkansas, and Texas road, ran through
more swamps to the Cache River, after which there
was prairie and bottom-land, and at De Valle's Bluff
we came to the White River. There is no doubt that
this country is well watered. After White River fine
reaches of prairie-land were encountered—in fact, a
good deal of prairie and oak timber. Much of this
prairie had once been cultivated to cotton, but was
now turned to grazing, and dotted with cattle. A
place named Prairie Centre had been abandoned ; indeed, we passed a good many abandoned houses before
we reached Carlisle and the Galloway. Lonoke is one of
the villages of rather mean appearance, but important
enough to be talked about and visited by the five
aspirants for the gubernatorial nomination, who were
travelling about together, each one trying to con-
vince the people that the other four were unworthy
the office. This is lowland Arkansas, supporting a
few rude villages, inhabited by negroes and unam-
bitious whites, and not a fairly representative portion
of a great State.

At Argenta, a sort of railway and factory suburb of the city, we crossed the muddy, strong-flowing Arkansas River on a fine bridge, elevated so as to strike high up on the bluff on which Little Rock is built. The rock of the bluff, which the railway pierces, is a very shaly slate. The town lying along the bluff has a very picturesque appearance, in spite of its newness and the poor color of its brick. The situation is a noble one, commanding a fine prospect of river and plain, and mountains to the west rising from the bluff on a series of gentle hills, with conspicuous heights farther out for public institutions and country houses. The city, which has nearly thirty thousand inhabitants, can boast a number of handsome business streets with good shops and an air of prosperous trade, with well-shaded residence streets of comfortable houses; but all the thoroughfares are bad for want of paving, Little Rock being forbidden by the organic law (as Memphis is) to run in debt for city improvements. A city which has doubled its population within eight years, and been restrained from using its credit, must expect to suffer from bad streets, but its caution about debt is reassuring to intending settlers. The needed street improvements, it is understood, however, will soon be under way, and the citizens have the satisfaction of knowing that when they are made, Little Rock will be a beautiful city.

Below the second of the iron bridges which span the river is a bowlder which gave the name of Little Rock to the town. The general impression is that it is the first rock on the river above its confluence with the Mississippi; this is not literally true, but this rock is the first conspicuous one, and has become historic. On the opposite side of the river, a mile above, is a bluff several hundred feet high, called Big Rock. On the summit is a beautiful park, a vineyard, a summer hotel, and pleasure-grounds — a delightful resort in the hot weather. From the top one gains a fair idea of Arkansas — the rich delta of the river, the mighty stream itself, the fertile rolling land and forests, the mountains on the border of the Indian Territory, the fair city, the sightly prominences about it dotted with buildings — altogether a magnificent and most charming view.

There is a United States arsenal at Little Rock; the Government Post-office is a handsome building, and among the twenty-seven churches there are some of pleasing architecture. The State-house, which stands upon the bluff overlooking the river, is a relic of old times, suggesting the easy-going plantation style. It is an indescribable building, or group of buildings, with classic pillars of course, and rambling galleries that lead to old-fashioned, domestic-looking State offices. It is shabby in appearance, but has a certain interior air of comfort. The room of the Assembly—plain, with windows on three sides, open to the sun and air, and not so large that conversational speaking cannot be heard in it—is not at all the modern notion of a legislative chamber, which ought to be lofty, magnificently decorated, lighted from above, and shut in as much as possible from the air and the outside world. Arkansas, which is rapidly growing in population and wealth, will no doubt very soon want a new State-house. Heaven send it an architect who will think first of the comfort-

able, cheerful rooms, and second of imposing outside display! He might spend a couple of millions
on a building which would astonish the natives, and
not give them as agreeable a working room for the
Legislature as this old chamber. The fashion is to
put up an edifice whose dimensions shall somehow
represent the dignity of the State, a vast structure of
hall-ways and staircases, with half-lighted and ill-
ventilated rooms. It seems to me that the American
genius ought to be able to devise a capitol of a different sort, certainly one better adapted to the Southern
climate. A group of connected buildings for the
various departments might be better than one solid
parallelogram, and I have a fancy that legislators
would be clearer-headed, and would profit more by
discussion, if they sat in a cheerful chamber, not too
large to be easily heard in, and open as much as possible to the sun and air and the sight of tranquil
nature. The present Capitol has an air of lazy neglect, and the law library which is stored in it could
not well be in a worse condition; but there is something rather pleasing about the old, easy-going establishment that one would pretty certainly miss in a
smart new building. Arkansas has an opportunity to
distinguish itself by a new departure in State-houses.

In the city are several of the State institutions,
most of them occupying ample grounds with fine sites
in the suburbs. Conspicuous on high ground in the
city is the Blind Asylum, a very commodious, and
well-conducted institution, with about 80 inmates.
The School for Deaf-mutes, with 125 pupils, is under
very able management. But I confess that the State
Lunatic Asylum gave me a genuine surprise, and if

the civilization of Arkansas were to be judged by it,
it would take high rank among the States. It is a
very fine building, well constructed and admirably
planned, on a site commanding a noble view, with
eighty acres of forest and garden. More land is
needed to carry out the superintendent's idea of labor,
and to furnish supplies for the patients, of whom
there are 450, the men and women, colored and white,
in separate wings. The builders seem to have taken
advantage of all the Eastern experience and shunned
the Eastern mistakes, and the result is an establishment
with all the modern improvements and conveniences,
conducted in the most enlightened spirit. I do not
know a better large State asylum in the United
States. Of the State penitentiary nothing good can
be said. Arkansas is still struggling with the wretched lease system, the frightful abuses of which she is
beginning to appreciate. The penitentiary is a sort
of depot for convicts, who are distributed about the
State by the contractors. At the time of my visit a
considerable number were there, more or less crippled
and sick, who had been rescued from barbarous treatment in one of the mines. A gang were breaking
stones in the yard, a few were making cigars, and the
dozen women in the women's ward were doing laun-
dry-work. But nothing appeared to be done to improve the condition of the inmates. In Southern
prisons I notice comparatively few of the "professional" class which so largely make the population of
Northern penitentiaries, and I always fancy that in
the rather easy-going management, wanting the cast-
iron discipline, the lot of the prisoners is not so
hard. Thus far among the colored people not much

odium attaches to one of their race who has been in prison.

The public-school system of the State is slowly improving, hampered by want of Constitutional power to raise money for the schools. By the Constitution, State taxes are limited to one per cent.; county taxes to one-half of one per cent., with an addition of one-half of one per cent. to pay debts existing when the Constitution was adopted in 1874; city taxes the same as county; in addition, for the support of common schools, the Assembly may lay a tax not to exceed two mills on the dollar on the taxable property of the State, and an annual *per capita* tax of one dollar on every male inhabitant over the age of twenty-one years; and it may also authorize each school district to raise for itself, by vote of its electors, a tax for school purposes not to exceed five mills on the dollar. The towns generally vote this additional tax, but in most of the country districts schools are not maintained for more than three months in the year. The population of the State is about 1,000,000, in an area of 53,045 square miles. The scholastic population enrolled has increased steadily for several years, and in 1886 was 164,757, of which 122,296 were white and 42,461 were colored. The total population of school age (including the enrolled) was 358,006, of which 266,188 were white and 91,818 colored. The school fund available for that year was $1,327,710. The increased revenue and enrolment are encouraging, but it is admitted that the schools of the State (sparsely settled as it is) cannot be what they should be without more money to build decent school-houses, employ competent teachers, and have longer sessions.

Little Rock has fourteen school-houses, only one or two of which are commendable. The High-school, with 50 pupils and 2 teachers, is held in a district building. The colored people have their fair proportion of schools, with teachers of their own race. Little Rock is abundantly able to tax itself for better schools, as it is for better pavements. In all the schools most attention seems to be paid to mathematics, and it is noticeable how proficient colored children under twelve are in figures.

The most important school in the State, which I did not see, is the Industrial University at Fayetteville, which received the Congressional land grant and is a State beneficiary; its property, including endowments and the University farm, is reckoned at $300,000. The general intention is to give a practical industrial education. The collegiate department, a course of three years, has 77 pupils; in the preparatory department are about 200; but the catalogue, including special students in art and music, the medical department at Little Rock of 60, and the Normal School at Pine Bluff of 215, foots up about 600 students. The University is situated in a part of the State most attractive in its scenery and most healthful, and offers a chance for every sort of mental and manual training.

The most widely famous place in the State is the Hot Springs. I should like to have seen it when it was in a state of nature; I should like to see it when it gets the civilization of a European bath-place. It has been a popular and even crowded resort for several years, and the medical treatment which can be given there in connection with the use of the waters is so nearly a specific for certain serious diseases, and going there is so much a necessity for many invalids, that access to it ought by this time to be easy. But it is not. It is fifty-five miles south-west of Little Rock, but to reach it the traveller must leave the Iron Mountain road at Malvern for a ride over a branch line of some twenty miles. Unfortunately this is a narrow-gauge road, and however ill a person may be, a change of cars must be made at Malvern. This is a serious annoyance, and it is a wonder that the main railways and the hotel and bath keepers have not united to rid themselves of the monopoly of the narrow-gauge road.

The valley of the Springs is over seven hundred feet above the sea; the country is rough and broken; the hills, clad with small pines and hard-wood, which rise on either side of the valley to the height of two or three hundred feet, make an agreeable impression of greenness; and the place is capable, by reason of its irregularity, of becoming beautiful as well as picturesque. It is still in the cheap cottage and raw brick stage. The situation suggests Carlsbad, which is also jammed into a narrow valley. The Hot Springs Mountain—that is, the mountain from the side of which all the hot springs (about seventy) flow—is a Government reservation. Nothing is permitted to be built on it except the Government hospital for soldiers and sailors, the public bath-houses along the foot, and one hotel, which holds over on the reserved land. The Government has enclosed and piped the springs, built a couple of cement reservoirs, and lets the bath privileges to private parties at thirty dollars a tub, the number of tubs being limited. The rent money the Government is supposed to devote to the improvement of the mountain. This has now a private lookout tower on the summit, from which a most extensive view is had over the well-wooded State, and it can be made a lovely park. There is a good deal of criticism about favoritism in letting the bath privileges, and the words "ring" and "syndicate" are constantly heard. Before improvements were made, the hot water discharged into a creek at the base of the hill. This creek is now arched over and become a street, with the bath-houses on one side and shops and shanties on the other. Difficulty about obtaining a good title to land has until recently stood in the way of permanent improvements. All claims have now been adjudicated upon, the Government is prepared to give a perfect title to all its own land, except the mountain, forever reserved, and purchasers can be sure of peaceful occupation.

Opposite the Hot Springs Mountain rises the long sharp ridge of West Mountain, from which the Government does not permit the foliage to be stripped. The city runs around and back of this mountain, follows the winding valley to the north, climbs up all the irregular ridges in the neighborhood, and spreads itself over the valley on the south, near the Ouachita River. It is estimated that there are 10,000 residents in this rapidly growing town. Houses stick on the sides of the hills, perch on terraces, nestle in the ravines. Nothing is regular, nothing is as might have been expected, but it is all interesting, and promising of something pleasing and picturesque in the future. All the springs, except one, on Hot Springs Mountain are hot, with a temperature ranging from 93° to 157°

Fahrenheit; there are plenty of springs in and among the other hills, but they are all cold. It is estimated that the present quantity of hot water, much of which runs to waste, would supply about 19,000 persons daily with 25 gallons each. The water is perfectly clear, has no odor, and is very agreeable for bathing. That remarkable cures are performed here the evidence does not permit one to doubt, nor can one question the wonderfully rejuvenating effect upon the system of a course of its waters.

It is necessary to suggest, however, that the value of the springs to invalids and to all visitors would be greatly enhanced by such regulations as those that govern Carlsbad and Marienbad in Bohemia. The success of those great "cures" depends largely upon the regimen enforced there, the impossibility of indulging in an improper diet, and the prevailing regularity of habits as to diet, sleep, and exercise. There is need at Hot Springs for more hotel accommodation of the sort that will make comfortable invalids accustomed to luxury at home, and at least one new and very large hotel is promised soon to supply this demand; but what Hot Springs needs is the comforts of life, and not means of indulgence at table or otherwise. Perhaps it is impossible for the American public, even the sick part of it, to submit itself to discipline, but we never will have the full benefit of our many curative springs until it consents to do so. Patients, no doubt, try to follow the varying regimen imposed by different doctors, but it is difficult to do so amid all the temptations of a go-as-you-please bath-place. A general regimen of diet applicable to all visitors is the only safe rule. Under such enlightened rules as prevail at Marienbad, and with the opportunity for mild entertainment in pretty shops, agreeable walks and drives, with music and the hundred devices to make the time pass pleasantly, Hot Springs would become one of the most important sanitary resorts in the world. It is now in a very crude state; but it has the water, the climate, the hills and woods; good saddle-horses are to be had, and it is an interesting country to ride over; those who frequent the place are attached to it; and time and taste and money will, no doubt, transform it into a place of beauty.

Arkansas surprised the world by the exhibition it made of itself at New Orleans, not only for its natural resources, but for the range and variety of its productions. That it is second to no other State in its adaptability to cotton-raising was known; that it had magnificent forests and large coal-fields and valuable minerals in its mountains was known; but that it raised fruit superior to any other in the South-west, and quite equal to any in the North, was a revelation. The mountainous part of the State, where some of the hills rise to the altitude of 2500 feet, gives as good apples, pears, and peaches as are raised in any portion of the Union; indeed, this fruit has taken the first prize in exhibitions from Massachusetts to Texas. It is as remarkable for flavor and firmness as it is for size and beauty. This region is also a good vineyard country. The State boasts more miles of navigable waters than any other, it has variety of soil and of surface to fit it for every crop in the temperate latitudes, and it has a very good climate. The range of northern mountains protects it from "northers," and its elevated portions have cold enough for a tonic. Of course the low and swampy lands are subject to malaria. The State has just begun to appreciate itself, and has organized efforts to promote immigration. It has employed a competent State geologist, who is doing excellent service. The United States has still a large quantity of valuable land in the State open to settlement under the homestead and pre-emption laws. The State itself has over 2,000,000 acres of land, forfeited and granted to it in various ways ; of this, the land forfeited for taxes will be given to actual settlers in tracts of 160 acres to each person, and the rest can be purchased at a low price. I cannot go into all the details, but the reader may be assured that the immigration committee make an exceedingly good showing for settlers who wish to engage in farming, fruit-raising, mining, or lumbering. The Constitution of the State is very democratic, the statute laws are stringent in morality, the limitations upon town and city indebtedness are severe, the rate of taxation is very low, and the State debt is small. The State, in short, is in a good condition for a vigorous development of its resources.

There is a popular notion that Arkansas is a "bowie-knife" State, a lawless and an ignorant State. I shared this before I went there. I cannot disprove the ignorance of the country districts. As I said, more money is needed to make the public-school system effective. But in its general aspect the State is as orderly and moral as any. The laws against carrying concealed weapons are strict, and are enforced. It is a fairly temperate State. Under the high license and local option laws, prohibition prevails in two-

thirds of the State, and the popular vote is strictly
enforced.   In forty-eight of the seventy-five counties
no license is granted, in other counties only a single
town votes license, and in many of the remaining
counties many towns refuse it.   In five counties only
is liquor perfectly free.   A special law prohibits
liquor-selling within five miles of a college ; within
three miles of a church or school, a majority of the
adult inhabitants can prohibit it.   With regard to
liquor-selling, woman suffrage practically exists.   The
law says that on petition of a majority of the adult
population in any district the county judge must refuse license.   The women, therefore, without going
into politics, sign the petitions and create prohibition.

The street-cars and railways make no discrimination
as to color of passengers.   Everywhere I went I noticed that the intercourse between the two races was
friendly.   There is much good land on the railway between Little Rock and Arkansas City, heavily tim-
bered, especially with the clean-boled, stately gum-
trees.   At Pine Bluff, which has a population of 5000,
there is a good colored Normal School, and the town
has many prosperous negroes, who support a race-
track of their own, and keep up a county fair.   I was
told that the most enterprising man in the place, the
largest street-railway owner, is black as a coal.   Farther down the road the country is not so good, the
houses are mostly poor shanties, and the population,
largely colored, appears to be of a shiftless character.
Arkansas City itself, low-lying on the Mississippi, has
a bad reputation.

Little Rock, already a railway centre of importance,
is prosperous and rapidly improving.   It has the set-

tled, temperate, orderly society of an Eastern town,
but democratic in its habits, and with a cordial hospitality which is more provincial than fashionable. I
heard there a good chamber concert of stringed instruments, one of a series which had been kept up by
subscription all winter, and would continue the coming
winter. The performers were young Bohemians. The
gentleman at whose pleasant, old-fashioned house I
was entertained, a leading lawyer and jurist in the
South-west, was a good linguist, had travelled in most
parts of the civilized globe, had on his table the current literature of France, England, Germany, and
America, a daily Paris newspaper, one New York
journal (to give its name might impugn his good taste
in the judgment of every other New York journal),
and a very large and well-selected library, two-thirds
of which was French, and nearly half of the remainder
German. This was one of the many things I found in
Arkansas which I did not expect to find.

XIV.

ST. LOUIS AND KANSAS CITY.

St. Louis is eighty years old. It was incorporated as a town in 1808, thirteen years before the admission of Missouri into the Union as a State. In 1764 a company of thirty Frenchmen made a settlement on its site and gave it its distinguished name. For nearly half a century, under French and Spanish jurisdiction alternately, it was little more than a trading post, and at the beginning of this century it contained only about a thousand inhabitants. This period, however, gave it a romantic historic background, and as late as 1853, when its population was a hundred thousand, it preserved French characteristics and a French appearance—small brick houses and narrow streets crowded down by the river. To the stranger it was the Planters' Hotel and a shoal of big steamboats moored along an extensive levee roaring with river traffic. Crowded, ill-paved, dirty streets, a few country houses on elevated sites, a population forced into a certain activity by trade, but hindered in municipal improvement by French conservatism, and touched with the rust of slavery—that was the St. Louis of thirty-five years ago.

Now everything is changed as by some magic touch. The growth of the city has always been solid, unspeculative, conservative in its business methods, with some persistence of the old French influence, only gradually parting from its ancient traditions, preserving always something of the aristocratic flavor of "old families," accounted "slow" in the impatience of youth. But it has burst its old bounds, and grown with a rapidity that would be marvellous in any other country. The levee is comparatively deserted, although the trade on the lower river is actually very large. The traveller who enters the city from the east passes over the St. Louis Bridge, a magnificent structure and one of the engineering wonders of the modern world, plunges into a tunnel under the business portion of the old city, and emerges into a valley covered with a net-work of rail-way-tracks, and occupied by apparently interminable lines of passenger coaches and freight cars, out of the confusion of which he makes his way with difficulty to a carriage, impressed at once by the enormous railway traffic of the city. This is the site of the proposed Union Depot, which waits upon the halting action of the Missouri Pacific system. The eastern outlet for all this growing traffic is over the two tracks of the bridge; these are entirely inadequate, and during a portion of the year there is a serious blockade of freight. A second bridge over the Mississippi is already a necessity to the commerce of the city, and is certain to be built within a few years.

St. Louis, since the war, has spread westward over the gentle ridges which parallel the river, and become a city vast in territory and most attractive in appearance. While the business portion has expanded into noble avenues with stately business and public edifices, the residence parts have a beauty, in handsome streets and varied architecture, that is a continual surprise to one who has not seen the city for twenty years. I had set down the length of the city along the river-front as thirteen miles, with a depth of about six miles; but the official statistics are : length of river-front, 19.15 miles; length of western limits, 21.27; extent north and south in an air line, 17; and length east and west on an air line, 6.62. This gives an area of 61.37 square miles, or 39,276 acres. This includes the public parks (containing 2095 acres), and is sufficient room for the population of 450,000, which the city doubtless has in 1888. By the United States census of 1870 the population was reported much larger than it was, the figures having no doubt been manipulated for political purposes. Estimating the natural increase from this false report, the city was led to claim a population far beyond the actual number, and unjustly suffered a little ridicule for a mistake for which it was not responsible. The United States census of 1880 gave it 350,522. During the eight years from 1880 there were erected 18,574 new dwelling-houses, at a cost of over fifty millions of dollars.

The great territorial extension of the city in 1876 was for a time a disadvantage, for it threw upon the city the care of enormous street extensions, made a sporadic movement of population beyond Grand Avenue, which left hiatuses in improvement, and created a sort of furor of fashion for getting away from what to me is still the most attractive residence portion of the town, namely, the elevated ridges west of Fourteenth Street, crossed by Lucas Place and adjoining avenues. In this quarter, and east of Grand Avenue, are fine high streets, with detached houses and grounds, many of them both elegant and comfortable, and this is the region of the Washington University, some of the finest club-houses, and handsomest churches. The movements of city populations, however, are not to be accounted for. One of the finest parts of the town, and one of the oldest of the better residence parts, that south of the railways, containing broad, well-planted avenues, and very stately old homes, and the exquisite Lafayette Park, is almost wholly occupied now by Germans, who make up so large a proportion of the population.

One would have predicted at an early day that the sightly bluffs below the city would be the resort of fashion, and be occupied with fine country houses. But the movement has been almost altogether westward and away from the river. And this rolling, wooded region is most inviting, elevated, open, cheerful. No other city in the West has fairer suburbs for expansion and adornment, and its noble avenues, dotted with conspicuously fine residences, give promise of great beauty and elegance. In its late architectural development, St. Louis, like Chicago, is just in time to escape a very mediocre and merely imitative period in American building. Beyond Grand Avenue the stranger will be shown Vandeventer Place, a semi-private oblong park, surrounded by many pretty and some notably fine residences. Two of them are by Richardson, and the city has other specimens of his work. I cannot refrain from again speaking of the effect that this original genius has had upon American architecture, especially in the West, when money and enterprise afforded him free scope. It is not too much to say that he created a new era, and the influence of his ideas is seen everywhere in the work of architects who have caught his spirit.

The city has addressed itself to the occupation and

21

adornment of its great territory and the improvement of its most travelled thoroughfares with admirable public spirit. The rolling nature of the ground has been taken advantage of to give it a nearly perfect system of drainage and sewerage. The old pavements of soft limestone, which were dust in dry weather and liquid mud in wet weather, are being replaced by granite in the business parts and asphalt and wood blocks (laid on a concrete base) in the residence portions. Up to the beginning of 1888 this new pavement had cost nearly three and a half million dollars, and over thirty-three miles of it were granite blocks. Street railways have also been pushed all over the territory. The total of street lines is already over one hundred and fifty-four miles, and over thirty miles of these give rapid transit by cable. These facilities make the whole of the wide territory available for business and residence, and give the poorest inhabitants the means of reaching the parks.

The park system is on the most liberal scale, both public and private; the parks are already famous for extent and beauty, but when the projected connecting boulevards are made they will attain world - wide notoriety. The most extensive of the private parks is that of the combined Agricultural Fair Grounds and Zoological Gardens. Here is held annually the St. Louis Fair, which is said to be the largest in the United States. The enclosure is finely laid out and planted, and contains an extensive park, exhibition buildings, cottages, a race-track, an amphitheatre, which suggests in size and construction some of the largest Spanish bull-rings, and picturesque houses for wild animals. The zoological exhibition is a very good one. There are eighteen public parks. One of the smaller (thirty acres) of these, and one of the oldest, is Lafayette Park, on the south side. Its beauty surprised me more than almost anything I saw in the city. It is a gem; just that artificial control of nature which most pleases—forest-trees, a pretty lake, fountains, flowers, walks planned to give everywhere exquisite vistas. It contains a statue of Thomas H. Benton, which may be a likeness, but utterly fails to give the character of the man. The largest is Forest Park, on the west side, a tract of 1372 acres, mostly forest, improved by excellent drives, and left as much as possible in a natural condition. It has ten miles of good driving-roads. This park cost the city about $850,000, and nearly as much more has been expended on it since its purchase. The surface has great variety of slopes, glens, elevations, lakes, and meadows. During the summer music is furnished in a handsome pagoda, and the place is much resorted to. Fronting the boulevard are statues of Governor Edward Bates and Frank P. Blair, the latter very characteristic.

Next in importance is Tower Grove Park, an oblong of 276 acres. This and Shaw's Garden, adjoining, have been given to the city by Mr. Henry Shaw, an Englishman who made his fortune in the city, and they remain under his control as to care and adornment during his life. Those who have never seen foreign parks and pleasure-gardens can obtain a very good idea of their formal elegance and impressiveness by visiting Tower Grove Park and the Botanical Gardens. They will see the perfection of lawns, avenues ornamented by statuary, flower-beds, and tasteful walks. The entrances, with stone towers and lodges, suggest

similar effects in France and in England. About the
music-stand are white marble busts of six chief musical
composers. The drives are adorned with three statues
in bronze, thirty feet high, designed and cast in Munich
by Frederick Müller. They are figures of Shakespeare, Humboldt, and Columbus, and so nobly conceived and executed that the patriotic American must
wish they had been done in this country. Of Shaw's
Botanical Garden I need to say little, for its fame as
a comprehensive and classified collection of trees,
plants, and flowers is world-wide. It has no equal in
this country. As a place for botanical study no one
appreciated it more highly than the late Professor Asa
Gray. Sometimes a peculiar classification is followed;
one locality is devoted to economic plants—camphor,
quinine, cotton, tea, coffee, etc.; another to " Plants of
the Bible." The space of fifty-four acres, enclosed by
high stone walls, contains, besides the open garden and
allées and glass houses, the summer residence and the
tomb of Mr. Shaw. This old gentleman, still vigorous in his eighty-eighth year, is planning new adornments in the way of statuary and busts of statesmen,
poets, and scientists. His plans are all liberal and
cosmopolitan. For over thirty years his botanical
knowledge, his taste, and abundant wealth and leisure
have been devoted to the creation of this wonderful
garden and park, which all bear the stamp of his
strong individuality, and of a certain pleasing foreign
formality. What a source of unfailing delight it
must have been to him! As we sat talking with him
I thought how other millionaires, if they knew how,
might envy a matured life, after the struggle for a
competency is over, devoted to this most rational en-

joyment, in an occupation as elevating to the taste as
to the character, and having in mind always the public
good. Over the entrance gate is the inscription,
"Missouri Botanical Gardens." When the city has
full control of the garden the word "Missouri" should
be replaced by "Shaw."

The money expended for public parks gives some
idea of the liberal and far-sighted provision for the
health and pleasure of a great city. The parks originally cost the city $1,309,944, and three millions
more have been spent upon their improvement and
maintenance. This indicates an enlightened spirit,
which we shall see characterizes the city in other
things, and is evidence of a high degree of culture.

Of the commerce and manufactures of the town I
can give no adequate statement without going into
details, which my space forbids. The importance of
the Mississippi River is much emphasized, not only
as an actual highway of traffic, but as a regulator of
railway rates. The town has by the official reports
been discriminated against, and even the Inter-State
Act has not afforded all the relief expected. In 1887
the city shipped to foreign markets by way of the
Mississippi and the jetties 3,973,000 bushels of wheat
and 7,365,000 bushels of corn—a larger exportation
than ever before except in the years 1880 and 1881.
An outlet like this is of course a check on railway
charges. The trade of the place employs a banking
capital of fifteen millions. The deposits in 1887 were
thirty-seven millions; the clearings over $894,527,731
—the largest ever reached, and over ten per cent. in
excess of the clearings of 1886. To whatever departments I turn in the report of the Merchants' Ex-

change for 1887 I find a vigorous growth—as in building—and in most articles of commerce a great increase. It appears by the tonnage statements that, taking receipts and shipments together, 12,060,995 tons of freight were handled in and out during 1886, against 14,359,059 tons in 1887—a gain of nineteen and a half per cent. The buildings in 1886 cost $7,030,819; in 1887, $8,162,914. There were $44,740 more stamps sold at the post-office in 1887 than in 1886. The custom-house collections were less than in 1886, but reached the figures of $1,414,747. The assessed value of real and personal property in 1887 was $217,142,320, on which the rate of taxation in the old city limits was $2.50.

It is never my intention in these papers to mention individual enterprises for their own sake, but I do not hesitate to do so when it is necessary in order to illustrate some peculiar development. It is a curious matter of observation that so many Western cities have one or more specialties in which they excel—houses of trade or manufacture larger and more important than can be found elsewhere. St. Louis finds itself in this category in regard to several establishments. One of these is a wooden-ware company, the largest of the sort in the country, a house which gathers its peculiar goods from all over the United States, and distributes them almost as widely—a business of gigantic proportions and bewildering detail. Its annual sales amount to as much as the sales of all the houses in its line in New York, Chicago, and Cincinnati together. Another is a hardware company, wholesale and retail, also the largest of its kind in the country, with sales annually amounting to six mill-

ions of dollars, a **very large amount when we con-**
sider that **it is made up of an infinite number of**
small and **cheap articles in iron, from a fish-hook up—**
indeed, **over** fifty thousand separate articles. **I spent**
half a day in this establishment, **walking through its**
departments, **noting the unequalled system of com-**
pact display, **classification, and methods of sale and**
shipment. Merely as a method of system in busi-
ness I have never seen anything more interesting.
Another establishment, important on account of its
central position in the continent and its relation to
the Louisiana sugar-fields, is the St. Louis Sugar Re-
finery.

The refinery proper is the largest building in the
Western country used for manufacturing purposes,
and, **together with its adjuncts of cooper-shops and**
warehouses, covers five **entire blocks and employs 500**
men. It has a capacity of working up 400 tons of
raw sugar a day, but runs only to the extent of about
200 tons a day, making the **value of its present prod-**
uct $7,500,000 a year.

During the winter and spring it uses Louisiana
sugars; the remainder **of the** year, **sugars of Cuba**
and the Sandwich Islands. Like all **other refineries**
of which I have inquired, this reckons the advent
of the Louisiana crop as an important regulator of
prices. **This establishment, in common with other**
industries of **the city, has had to complain of busi-**
ness somewhat **hampered by discrimination in railway**
rates. St. Louis also **has what I suppose, from the**
figures accessible, **to be the largest lager-beer brew-**
ing establishment **in the world; its solid, gigantic,**
and architecturally **imposing buildings lift** themselves

up like a fortress over the thirty acres of ground they
cover. Its manufacture and sales in 1887 were 456,-
511 barrels of beer—an increase of nearly 100,000
since 1885-86. It exports largely to Mexico, South
America, the West Indies, and Australia. The establishment is a marvel of system and ingenious devices. It employs 1200 laborers, to whom it pays
$500,000 a year. Some of the details are of interest.
In the bottling department we saw workmen filling,
corking, labelling, and packing at the rate of 100,000
bottles a day. In a year 25,000,000 bottles are used,
packed in 400,000 barrels and boxes. The consumption of barley is 1,100,000 bushels yearly, and of
hops over 700,000 pounds, and the amount of water
used for all purposes is 250,000,000 gallons—nearly
enough to float our navy. The charges for freight
received and shipped by rail amount to nearly a million dollars a year. There are several other large brew-
eries in the city. The total product manufactured
in 1887 was 1,383,361 barrels, equal to 43,575,872
gallons—more than three times the amount of 1877.
The barley used in the city and vicinity was 2,932,-
192 bushels, of which 340,335 bushels came from
Canada. The direct export of beer during 1887 to
foreign countries was equal to 1,924,108 quart bottles.
The greater part of the barley used comes from Iowa,
Minnesota, and Wisconsin.

It is useless to enumerate the many railways which
touch and affect St. Louis. The most considerable is
the agglomeration known as the Missouri Pacific, or
South-western System, which operated 6994 miles of
road on January 1, 1888. This great aggregate is
likely to be much diminished by the surrender of

lines, but the railway facilities of the city are constantly extending.

There are figures enough to show that St. Louis is a prosperous city, constantly developing new enterprises with fresh energy ; to walk its handsome streets and drive about its great avenues and parks is to obtain an impression of a cheerful town on the way to be most attractive ; but its chief distinction lies in its social and intellectual life, and in the spirit that has made it a pioneer in so many educational movements. It seems to me a very good place to study the influence of speculative thought in economic and practical affairs. The question I am oftenest asked is, whether the little knot of speculative philosophers accidentally gathered there a few years ago, and who gave a sort of fame to the city, have had any permanent influence. For years they discussed abstractions ; they sustained for some time a very remarkable periodical of speculative philosophy, and in a limited sphere they maintained an elevated tone of thought and life quite in contrast with our general materialism. The circle is broken, the members are scattered. Probably the town never understood them, perhaps they did not altogether understand each other, and maybe the tremendous conflict of Kant and Hegel settled nothing. But if there is anything that can be demonstrated in this world it is the influence of abstract thought upon practical affairs in the long-run. And although one may not be able to point to any definite thing created or established by this metaphysical movement, I think I can see that it was a leaven that had a marked effect in the social, and especially in the educational, life of the town, and liberalized minds, and opened the way for the trial of theories in education. One of the disciples declares that the State Constitution of Missouri and the charter of St. Louis are distinctly Hegelian. However this may be, both these organic laws are uncommonly wise in their provisions. A study of the evolution of the city government is one of the most interesting that the student can make. Many of the provisions of the charter are admirable, such as those securing honest elections, furnishing financial checks, and guarding against public debt. The mayor is elected for four years, and the important offices filled by his appointment are not vacant until the beginning of the third year of his appointment, so that hope of reward for political work is too dim to affect the merits of an election. The composition and election of the school board is also worthy of notice. Of the twenty-one members, seven are elected on a general ticket, and the remaining fourteen by districts, made by consolidating the twenty-eight city wards, members to serve four years, divided into two classes. This arrangement secures immunity from the ward politician.

St. Louis is famous for its public schools, and especially for the enlightened methods, and the willingness to experiment in improving them. The school expenditures for the year ending June 30, 1887, were $1,095,773; the school property in lots, buildings, and furniture in 1885 was estimated at $3,445,254. The total number of pupils enrolled was 56,936. These required about 1200 teachers, of whom over a thousand were women. The actual average of pupils to each teacher was about 42. There were 106 school buildings, with a seating capacity for about 50,000 scholars. Of the district schools 13 were colored, in which were employed 78 colored teachers. The salaries of teachers are progressive, according to length of service. As for instance, the principal of the High-school has $2400 the first year, $2500 the second, $2600 the third, $2750 the fourth ; a head assistant in a district school, $650 the first year, $700 the second, $750 the third, $800 the fourth, $850 the fifth.

The few schools that I saw fully sustained their public reputation as to methods, discipline, and attainments. The Normal School, of something over 100 pupils, nearly all the girls being graduates of the High-school, was admirable in drill, in literary training, in calisthenic exercises. The High-school is also admirable, a school with a thoroughly elevated tone and an able principal. Of the 600 pupils at least two-thirds were girls. From appearances I should judge that it is attended by children of the most intelligent families, for certainly the girls of the junior and senior classes, in manner, looks, dress, and attainments, compared favorably with those of one of the best girls' schools I have seen anywhere, the Mary Institute, which is a department of the Washington University. This fact is most important, for the excellence of our public schools (for the product of good men and women) depends largely upon their popularity with the well-to-do classes. One of the most interesting schools I saw was the Jefferson, presided over by a woman, having fine fire-proof buildings and 1100 pupils, nearly all whom are of foreign parentage—German, Russian, and Italian, with many

Hebrews also—a finely ordered, wide-awake school of
eight grades. The kindergarten here was the best I
saw; good teachers, bright and happy little children,
with natural manners, throwing themselves gracefully
into their games with enjoyment and without self-
consciousness, and exhibiting exceedingly pretty fancy and kindergarten work. In St. Louis the kindergarten is a part of the public-school system, and the
experiment is one of general interest. The question
cannot be called settled. In the first place the experiment is hampered in St. Louis by a decision of
the Supreme Court that the public money cannot be
used for children out of the school age, that is, under
six and over twenty. This prevents teaching English
to adult foreigners in the evening schools, and, rigidly
applied, it shuts out pupils from the kindergarten under six. One advantage from the kindergarten was
expected to be an extension of the school period; and
there is no doubt that the kindergarten instruction
ought to begin before the age of six, especially for
the mass of children who miss home training and
home care. As a matter of fact, many of the children I saw in the kindergartens were only construct-
ively six years old. It cannot be said, also, that the
Froebel system is fully understood or accepted. In
my observation, the success of the kindergarten depends entirely upon the teacher; where she is competent, fully believes in and understands the Froebel
system, and is enthusiastic, the pupils are interested
and alert; otherwise they are listless, and fail to get
the benefit of it. The Froebel system is the developing the concrete idea in education, and in the opinion
of his disciples this is as important for children of the

intelligent and well-to-do as for those of the poor and
ignorant. They resist, therefore, the attempt which
is constantly made, to introduce the primary work
into the kindergarten. But for the six years' limit
the kindergarten in St. Louis would have a better
chance in its connection with the public schools. As
the majority of children leave school for work at the
age of twelve or fourteen, there is little time enough
given for book education; many educators think time
is wasted in the kindergarten, and they advocate the
introduction of what they call kindergarten features
in the primary classes. This is called by the disciples of Froebel an entire abandonment of his system.
I should like to see the kindergarten in connection
with the public school tried long enough to demonstrate all that is claimed for it in its influence on
mental development, character, and manners, but it
seems unlikely to be done in St. Louis, unless the
public-school year begins at least as early as five, or,
better still, is specially unlimited for kindergarten
pupils.

Except in the primary work in drawing and modelling, there is no manual training feature in the St.
Louis public schools. The teaching of German is recently dropped from all the district schools (though
retained in the High), in accordance with the well-
founded idea of Americanizing our foreign population as rapidly as possible.

One of the most important institutions in the Mississippi Valley, and one that exercises a decided influence
upon the intellectual and social life of St. Louis, and is
a fair measure of its culture and the value of the higher education, is the Washington University, which was

incorporated in 1853, and was presided over until his death, in 1887, by the late Chancellor William Greenleaf Eliot, of revered memory. It covers the whole range of university studies, except theology, and allows no instruction either sectarian in religion or partisan in politics, nor the application of any sectarian or party test in the election of professors, teachers, or officers. Its real estate and buildings in use for educational purposes cost $625,000; its libraries, scientific apparatus, casts, and machinery cost over $160,000, and it has investments for revenue amounting to over $650,-000. The University comprehends an undergraduate department, including the college (a thorough classical, literary, and philosophical course, with about sixty students), open to women, and the polytechnic, an admirably equipped school of science; the St. Louis Law School, of excellent reputation; the Manual Training School, the most celebrated school of this sort, and one that has furnished more manual training teachers than any other; the Henry Shaw School of Botany; the St. Louis School of Fine Arts; the Smith Academy, for boys; and the Mary Institute, one of the roomiest and most cheerful school buildings I know, where 400 girls, whose collective appearance need not fear comparison with any in the country, enjoy the best educational advantages. Mary Institute is justly the pride of the city.

The School of Botany, which is endowed and has its own laboratory, workshop, and working library, was, of course, the outgrowth of the Shaw Botanical Garden; it has usually from twenty to thirty special students.

The School of Fine Arts, which was reorganized

under the University in 1879, has enrolled over 200 students, and gives a wide and careful training in all the departments of drawing, painting, and modelling, with instructions in anatomy, perspective, and composition, and has life classes for both sexes, in drawing from draped and nude figures. Its lecture, working rooms, and galleries of paintings and casts are in its Crow Art Museum—a beautiful building, well planned and justly distinguished for architectural excellence. It ranks among the best Art buildings in the country.

The Manual Training School has been in operation since 1880. It may be called the most fully developed pioneer institution of the sort. I spent some time in its workshops and schools, thinking of the very interesting question at the bottom of the experiment, namely, the mental development involved in the training of the hand and the eye, and the reflex help to manual skill in the purely intellectual training of study. It is, it may be said again, not the purpose of the modern manual training to teach a trade, but to teach the use of tools as an aid in the symmetrical development of the human being. The students here certainly do beautiful work in wood-turning and simple carving, in iron-work and forging. They enjoy the work; they are alert and interested in it. I am certain that they are the more interested in it in seeing how they can work out and apply what they have learned in books, and I doubt not they take hold of literary study more freshly for this manual training in exactness. The school exacts close and thoughtful study with tools as well as in books, and I can believe that it gives dignity in the opinion of the working student to hand labor. The school is large, its graduates have been generally successful in practical pursuits and in teaching, and it has demonstrated in itself the correctness of the theory of its authors, that intellectual drill and manual training are mutually advantageous together. Whether manual training shall be a part of all district school education is a question involving many considerations that do not enter into the practicability of this school, but I have no doubt that manual training schools of this sort would be immensely useful in every city. There are many boys in every community who cannot in any other way be awakened to any real study. This training school deserves a chapter by itself, and as I have no space for details, I take the liberty of referring those interested to a volume on its aims and methods by Dr. C. M. Woodward, its director.

Notwithstanding the excellence of the public-school system of St. Louis, there is no other city in the country, except New Orleans, where so large a proportion of the youths are being educated outside the public schools. A very considerable portion of the population is Catholic. There are forty-four parochial schools, attended by nineteen thousand pupils, and over a dozen different Sisterhoods are engaged in teaching in them. Generally each parochial school has two departments—one for boys and one for girls. They are sustained entirely by the parishes. In these schools, as in the two Catholic universities, the prominence of ethical and religious training is to be noted. Seven-eighths of the schools are in charge of thoroughly trained religious teachers. Many of the boys' schools are taught by Christian Brothers. The girls are almost invariably taught by members of religious Sisterhoods. In most of the German schools the

girls and smaller boys are taught by Sisters, the
larger boys by lay teachers. Some reports of school
attendance are given in the Catholic Directory : SS.
Peter and Paul's (German), 1300 pupils ; St. Joseph's
(German), 957; St. Bridget's, 950; St. Malachy's, 756;
St. John's, 700 ; St. Patrick's, 700. There is a school
for colored children of 150 pupils taught by colored
Sisters.

In addition to these parochial schools there are a
dozen academies and convents of higher education for
young ladies, all under charge of Catholic Sisterhoods, commonly with a mixed attendance of boarders and day scholars, and some of them with a reputation for learning that attracts pupils from other
States, notably the Academy of the Sacred Heart, St.
Joseph's Academy, and the Academy of the Visita-
tion, in charge of cloistered nuns of that order. Besides these, in connection with various reformatory
and charitable institutions, such as the House of the
Good Shepherd and St. Mary's Orphan Asylum, there
are industrial schools in charge of the Sisterhoods,
where girls receive, in addition to their education,
training in some industry to maintain themselves re-
spectably when they leave their temporary homes.
Statistics are wanting, but it will be readily inferred
from these statements that there are in the city a
great number of single women devoted for life, and
by special religious and intellectual training, to the
office of teaching.

For the higher education of Catholic young men
the city is distinguished by two remarkable institutions. The one is the old St. Louis University, and
the other is the Christian Brothers' College. The

22

latter, which a few years ago outgrew its old buildings in the city, has a fine pile of buildings at Côte
Brillante, on a commanding site about five miles out,
with ample grounds, and in the neighborhood of the
great parks and the Botanical Garden. The character of the school is indicated by the motto on the
façade of the building — *Religio, Mores, Cultura.*
The institution is designed to accommodate a thousand boarding students. The present attendance is
450, about half of whom are boarders, and represent
twenty States. There is a corps of thirty - five professors, and three courses of study are maintained—
the classical, the scientific, and the commercial. As
several of the best parochial schools are in charge of
Christian Brothers, these schools are feeders of the
college, and the pupils have the advantage of an unbroken system with a consistent purpose from the
day they enter into the primary department till they
graduate at the college. The order has, at Glencoe, a
large Normal School for the training of teachers.
The fame and success of the Christian Brothers as educators in elementary and the higher education, in Europe and the United States, is largely due to the fact
that they labor as a unit in a system that never varies
in its methods of imparting instruction, in which the
exponents of it have all undergone the same peda-
gogic training, in which there is no room for the personal fancy of the teacher in correction, discipline, or
scholarship, for everything is judiciously governed by
prescribed modes of procedure, founded on long experience, and exemplified in the co-operative plan of
the Brothers. In vindication of the exceptional skill
acquired by its teachers in the thorough drill of the

order, the Brotherhood points to the success of its
graduates in competitive examinations for public employment in this country and in Europe, and to the
commendation its educational exhibits received at
London and New Orleans.

The St. Louis University, founded in 1829 by members of the Society of Jesus, and chartered in 1834, is
officered and controlled by the Jesuit Fathers. It is
an unendowed institution, depending upon fees paid
for tuition. Before the war its students were largely the children of Southern planters, and its graduates
are found all over the South and South-west ; and
up to 1881 the pupils boarded and lodged within the
precincts of the old buildings on the corner of Ninth
Street and Washington, where for over half a century the school has vigorously flourished. The place,
which is now sold and about to be used for business
purposes, has a certain flavor of antique scholarship,
and the quaint buildings keep in mind the plain but
rather pleasing architecture of the French period.
The University is in process of removal to the new
buildings on Grand Avenue, which are a conspicuous
ornament to one of the most attractive parts of the
city. Soon nothing will be left of the institution on
Ninth Street except the old college church, which is
still a favorite place of worship for the Catholics of
the city. The new buildings, in the early decorated
English Gothic style, are ample and imposing ; they
have a front of 270 feet, and the northern wing extends 325 feet westward from the avenue. The library, probably the finest room of the kind in the
West, is sixty-seven feet high, amply lighted, and provided with three balconies. The library, which was

packed for removal, has over 25,000 volumes, is said to contain many rare and interesting books, and to fairly represent science and literature. Besides this, there are special libraries, open to students, of over 6000 volumes. The museum of the new building is a noble hall, one hundred feet by sixty feet, and fifty-two feet high, without columns, and lighted from above and from the side. The University has a valuable collection of ores and minerals, and other objects of nature and art that will be deposited in this hall, which will also serve as a picture-gallery for the many paintings of historical interest. Philosophical apparatus, a chemical laboratory, and an astronomical observatory are the equipments on the scientific side.

The University has now no dormitories and no boarders. There are twenty-five professors and instructors. The entire course, including the preparatory, is seven years. A glance at the catalogue shows that in the curriculum the institution keeps pace with the demands of the age. Besides the preparatory course (89 pupils), it has a classical course (143 pupils), an English course (82 pupils), and 85 post-graduate students, making a total of 399. Its students form societies for various purposes; one, the Sodality of the Blessed Virgin Mary, with distinct organizations in the senior and junior classes, is for the promotion of piety and the practice of devotion towards the Blessed Virgin; another is for training in public speaking and philosophic and literary disputation; there is also a scientific academy, to foster a taste for scientific culture; and there is a student's library of 4000 volumes, independent of the religious books of the Sodality societies.

In a conversation with the president I learned that the prevailing idea in the courses of study is the gradual and healthy development of the mind. The classes are carefully graded. The classics are favorite branches, but mental philosophy, chemistry, physics, astronomy, are taught with a view to practical application. Much stress is laid upon mathematics. During the whole course of seven years, one hour each day is devoted to this branch. In short, I was impressed with the fact that this is an institution for mental training. Still more was I struck with the prominence in the whole course of ethical and religious culture. On assembling every morning, all the Catholic students hear mass. In every class in every year Christian doctrine has as prominent a place as any branch of study; beginning in the elementary class with the small catechism and practical instructions in the manner of reciting the ordinary prayers, it goes on through the whole range of doctrine—creed, evidences, ritual, ceremonial, mysteries—in the minutest details of theory and practice ; ingraining, so far as repeated instruction can, the Catholic faith and pure moral conduct in the character, involving instructions as to what occasions and what amusements are dangerous to a good life, on the reading of good books and the avoiding bad books and bad company.

In the post-graduate course, lectures are given and examinations made in ethics, psychology, anthropology, biology, and physics ; and in the published abstracts of lectures for the past two years I find that none of the subjects of modern doubt and speculation are ignored—spiritism, psychical research, the cell theory, the idea of God, socialism, agnosticism, the Noach-

ian deluge, theories of government, fundamental notions of physical science, unity of the human species,
potency of matter, and so on. During the past fifty
years this faculty has contained many men famous as
pulpit orators and missionaries, and this course of
lectures on philosophic and scientific subjects has
brought it prominently before the cultivated inhabitants of the town.

Another educational institution of note in St. Louis
is the Concordia Seminar of the Old Lutheran, or the
Evangelical Lutheran Church. This denomination,
which originated in Saxony, and has a large membership in our Western States, adheres strictly to the
Augsburg Confession, and is distinguished from the
general Lutheran Church by greater strictness of doctrine and practice, or, as may be said, by a return to
primitive Lutheranism; that is to say, it grounds
itself upon the literal inspiration of the Scriptures,
upon salvation by faith alone, and upon individual
liberty. This Seminar is one of several related institutions in the Synod of Missouri, Ohio, and other
States: there is a college at Fort Wayne, Indiana, a
Progymnasium at Milwaukee, a Seminar of practical
theology at Springfield, Illinois, and this Seminar at
St. Louis, which is wholly devoted to theoretical theology. This Church numbers, I believe, about 200,000
members.

The Concordia Seminar is housed in a large, commodious building, effectively set upon high ground in
the southern part of the city. It was erected and the
institution is sustained by the contributions of the
congregations. The interior, roomy, light, and commodious, is plain to barrenness, and has a certain mo-

nastic severity, which is matched by the discipline and
the fare. In visiting it one takes a step backward into
the atmosphere and theology of the sixteenth century. The ministers of the denomination are distinguished for learning and earnest simplicity. The
president, a very able man, only thirty-five years of
age, is at least two centuries old in his opinions, and
wholly undisturbed by any of the doubts which have
agitated the Christian world since the Reformation.
He holds the faith "once for all" delivered to the
saints. The Seminar has a hundred students. It is
requisite to admission, said the president, that they
be perfect Latin, Greek, and Hebrew scholars. A
large proportion of the lectures are given in Latin,
the remainder in German and English, and Latin is
current in the institution, although German is the
familiar speech. The course of study is exacting, the
rules are rigid, and the discipline severe. Social intercourse with the other sex is discouraged. The pursuit of love and learning are considered incompatible
at the same time ; and if a student were inconsiderate
enough to become engaged, he would be expelled.
Each student from abroad may select or be selected
by a family in the communion, at whose house he may
visit once a week, which attends to his washing, and
supplies to a certain extent the place of a home. The
young men are trained in the highest scholarship and
the strictest code of morals. I know of no other denomination which holds its members to such primitive
theology and such strictness of life. Individual liberty and responsibility are stoutly asserted, without any
latitude in belief. It repudiates Prohibition as an in-
fringement of personal liberty, would make the use of

wine or beer depend upon the individual conscience, but no member of the communion would be permitted to sell intoxicating liquors, or to go to a beer-garden or a theatre. In regard to the sacrament of communion, there is no authority for altering the plain directions in the Scripture, and communion without wine, or the substitution of any concoction for wine, would be a sin. No member would be permitted to join any labor union or secret society. The sacrament of communion is a mystery. It is neither transubstantiation nor consubstantiation. The president, whose use of English in subtle distinctions is limited, resorted to Latin and German in explanation of the mystery, but left the question of real and actual presence, of spirit and substance, still a matter of terms ; one can only say that neither the ordinary Protestant nor the Catholic interpretation is accepted. Conversion is not by any act or ability of man ; salvation is by faith alone. As the verbal inspiration of the Scriptures is insisted on in all cases, the world was actually created in six days of twenty-four hours each. When I asked the president what he did with geology, he smiled and simply waved his hand. This communion has thirteen flourishing churches in the city. In a town so largely German, and with so many freethinkers as well as free-livers, I cannot but consider this strict sect, of a simple unquestioning faith and high moral demands, of the highest importance in the future of the city. But one encounters with surprise, in our modern life, this revival of the sixteenth century, which plants itself so squarely against so much that we call " progress."

As to the institutions of charity, I must content my-

self with saying that they are many, and worthy of a
great and enlightened city. There are of all denominations 211 churches ; of these the Catholics lead with
47 ; the Presbyterians come next with 24 ; and the
Baptists have 22 ; the Methodists North, 4 ; and the
Methodists South, 8. The most interesting edifices,
both for associations and architecture, are the old
Cathedral ; the old Christ Church (Episcopalian),
excellent Gothic ; and an exquisite edifice, the Church
of the Messiah (Unitarian), in Locust Street.

The city has two excellent libraries. The Public
Library, an adjunct of the public-school system, in
the Polytechnic Building, has an annual appropriation
of about $14,000 from the School Board, and receives
about $5000 more from membership and other sources.
It contains about 67,000 volumes, and is admirably
managed. The Mercantile Library is in process of
removal into a magnificent six-story building on
Broadway and Locust Street. It is a solid and imposing structure, the first story of red granite, and
the others of brick and terra-cotta. The library and
reading-rooms are on the fifth story, the rest of the
building is rented. This association, which is forty-
two years old, has 3500 members, and had an income
in 1887 of $120,000, nearly all from membership. In
January, 1888, it had 68,732 volumes, and in a circulation of over 168,000 in the year, it had the unparalleled distinction of reducing the fiction given out to
41.95 per cent. Both these libraries have many
treasures interesting to a book - lover, and though
neither is free, the liberal, intelligent management of
each has been such as to make it a most beneficent
institution for the city.

There are many handsome and stately buildings in the city, the recent erections showing growth in wealth and taste. The Chamber of Commerce, which is conspicuous for solid elegance, cost a million and a half dollars. There are 3295 members of the Merchants' Exchange. The Court-house, with its noble dome, is as well proportioned a building as can be found in the country. A good deal may be said for the size and effect of the Exposition Building, which covers what was once a pretty park at the foot of Lucas Place, and cost $750,000. There are clubs many and flourishing. The St. Louis Club (social) has the finest building, an exceedingly tasteful piece of Romanesque architecture on Twenty-ninth Street. The University Club, which is like its namesake in other cities, has a charming old-fashioned house and grounds on Pine Street. The Commercial Club, an organization limited in its membership to sixty, has no club-house, but, like its namesake in Chicago, is a controlling influence in the prosperity of the city. Representing all the leading occupations, it is a body of men who, by character, intellect, and wealth, can carry through any project for the public good, and which is animated by the highest public spirit.

Of the social life of the town one is permitted to speak only in general terms. It has many elements to make it delightful—long use in social civilities, interest in letters and in education, the cultivation of travel, traditions, and the refinement of intellectual pursuits. The town has no academy of music, but there is a good deal of musical feeling and cultivation ; there is a very good orchestra, one of the very best choruses in the country, and Verdi's " Requiem "

was recently given splendidly. I am told by men and
women of rare and special cultivation that the city is
a most satisfactory one to live in, and certainly to the
stranger its society is charming. The city has, however, the Mississippi Valley climate—extreme heat in
the summer, and trying winters.

There is no more interesting industrial establishment in the West than the plate-glass works at Crystal City, thirty miles south on the river. It was built
up after repeated failures and reverses—for the business, like any other, had to be learned. The plant is
very extensive, the buildings are of the best, the machinery is that most approved, and the whole represents a cash investment of $1,500,000. The location
of the works at this point was determined by the existence of a mountain of sand which is quarried out
like rock, and is the finest and cleanest silica known
in the country. The production is confined entirely
to plate-glass, which is cast in great slabs, twelve feet
by twelve and a half in size, each of which weighs,
before it is reduced half in thickness by grinding,
smoothing, and polishing, about 750 pounds. The
product for 1887 was 1,200,000 feet. The coal used
in the furnaces is converted into gas, which is found
to be the most economical and most easily regulated fuel. This industry has drawn together a population of about 1500. I was interested to learn that
labor in the production of this glass is paid twice
as much as similar labor in England, and from three
to four times as much as similar labor in France
and Belgium. As the materials used in making
plate-glass are inexpensive, the main cost, after the
plant, is in labor. Since plate-glass was first made

in this country, eighteen years ago, the price of it in the foreign market has been continually forced down, until now it costs the American consumer only half what it cost him before, and the jobber gets it at an average cost of 75 cents a foot, as against the $1.50 a foot which we paid the foreign manufacturer before the establishment of American factories. And in these eighteen years the Government has had from this source a revenue of over seventeen millions, at an average duty, on all sizes, of less than 59 per cent.

Missouri is one of the greatest of our States in resources and in promise, and it is conspicuous in the West for its variety and capacity of interesting development. The northern portion rivals Iowa in beautiful rolling prairie, with high divides and park-like forests; its water communication is unsurpassed; its mineral resources are immense; it has noble mountains as well as fine uplands and fertile valleys, and it never impresses the traveller as monotonous. So attractive is it in both scenery and resources that it seems unaccountable that so many settlers have passed it by. But, first slavery, and then a rural population disinclined to change, have stayed its development. This state of things, however, is changing, has changed marvellously within a few years in the northern portion, in the iron regions, and especially in larger cities of the west, St. Joseph and Kansas City. The State deserves a study by itself, for it is on the way to be a great empire of most varied interests. I can only mention here one indication of its moral progress. It has adopted a high license and local option law. Under this the saloons are closed in nearly all

the smaller villages and country towns. A shaded
map shows more than three-fourths of the area of the
State, including three-fifths of the population, free
from liquor-selling. The county court may grant a
license to sell liquor to a person of good moral character on the signed petition of a majority of the tax-
paying citizens of a township or of a city block; it
must grant it on the petition of two-thirds of the citizens. Thus positive action is required to establish a
saloon. On the map there are 76 white counties free
of saloons, 14 counties in which there are from one to
three saloons only, and 24 shaded counties which have
altogether 2263 saloons, of which 1450 are in St. Louis
and 520 in Kansas City. The revenue from the
saloons in St. Louis is about $800,000, in Kansas City
about $375,000, annually. The heavily shaded portions
of the map are on the great rivers.

Of all the wonderful towns in the West, none has
attracted more attention in the East than Kansas City.
I think I am not wrong in saying that it is largely
the product of Eastern energy and capital, and that its
closest relations have been with Boston. I doubt if
ever a new town was from the start built up so solidly or has grown more substantially. The situation, at
the point where the Missouri River makes a sharp
bend to the east, and the Kansas River enters it, was
long ago pointed out as the natural centre of a great
trade. Long before it started on its present career
it was the great receiving and distributing point of
South-western commerce, which left the Missouri River at this point for Santa Fé and other trading marts
in the South-west. Aside from this river advantage,
if one studies the course of streams and the incline of

the land in a wide circle to the westward, he is impressed with the fact that the natural business drainage of a vast area is Kansas City. The city was therefore not fortuitously located, and when the railways centred there, they obeyed an inevitable law. Here nature intended, in the development of the country, a great city. Where the next one will be in the South-west is not likely to be determined until the Indian Territory is open to settlement. To the north, Omaha, with reference to Nebraska and the West, possesses many similar advantages, and is likewise growing with great vigor and solidity. Its situation on a slope rising from the river is commanding and beautiful, and its splendid business houses, handsome private residences, and fine public schools give ample evidence of the intelligent enterprise that is directing its rapid growth.

It is difficult to analyze the impression Kansas City first makes upon the Eastern stranger. It is usually that of immense movement, much of it crude, all of it full of purpose. At the Union Station, at the time of the arrival and departure of trains, the whole world seems afloat; one is in the midst of a continental movement of most varied populations. I remember that the first time I saw it in passing, the detail that most impressed me was the racks and rows of baggage checks; it did not seem to me that the whole travelling world could need so many. At that time a drive through the city revealed a chaos of enterprise—deep cuts for streets, cable roads in process of construction over the sharp ridges, new buildings, hills shaved down, houses perched high up on slashed knolls, streets swarming with traffic and roaring with speculation. A little more than a year later the change towards order was marvellous : the cable roads were running in all directions ; gigantic buildings rising upon enormous blocks of stone gave distinction to the principal streets ; the great residence avenues have been beautified, and showed all over the hills stately and picturesque houses. And it is worthy of remark that while the "boom" of speculation in lots had subsided, there was no slacking in building, and the reports showed a steady increase in legitimate business. I was confirmed in my theory that a city is likely to be most attractive when it has had to struggle heroically against natural obstacles in the building.

I am not going to describe the city. The reader knows that it lies south of the river Missouri, at the bend, and that the notable portion of it is built upon a series of sharp hills. The hill portion is already a beautiful city ; the flat part, which contains the railway depot and yards, a considerable portion of the manufactories and wholesale houses, and much refuse and squatting population (white and black), is unattractive in a high degree. The Kaw, or Kansas, River would seem to be the natural western boundary, but it is not the boundary ; the city and State line runs at some distance east of Kansas River, leaving a considerable portion of low ground in Kansas City, Kansas, which contains the larger number of the great packing-houses and the great stock-yards. This identity of names is confusing. Kansas City (Kansas), Wyandotte, Armourdale, Armstrong, and Riverview (all in the State of Kansas) have been recently consolidated under the name of Kansas City, Kansas. It is to be regretted that this thriving town of Kansas, which already claims a population of 40,000, did not take the name of Wyandotte. In its boundaries are the second largest stock-yards in the country, which received last year 670,000 cattle, nearly 2,500,000 hogs, and 210,000 sheep, estimated worth $51,000,000. There also are half a dozen large packing-houses, one of them ranking with the biggest in the country, which last year slaughtered 195,933 cattle, and 1,907,- 164 hogs. The great elevated railway, a wonderful structure, which connects Kansas City, Missouri, with Wyandotte, is owned and managed by men of Kansas City, Kansas. The city in Kansas has a great area of level ground for the accommodation of manufacturing enterprises, and I noticed a good deal of speculative feeling in regard to this territory. The Kansas side has fine elevated situations for residences, but Wyandotte itself does not compare in attractiveness with the Missouri city, and I fancy that the controlling impetus and capital will long remain with the city that has so much the start.

Looking about for the specialty which I have learned to expect in every great Western city, I was struck by the number of warehouses for the sale of agricultural implements on the flats, and I was told that Kansas City excels all others in the amount of sales of farming implements. The sale is put down at $15,- 000,000 for the year 1887—a fourth of the entire reported product manufactured in the United States. Looking for the explanation of this, one largely accounts for the growth of Kansas City, namely, the vast rich agricultural regions to the west and southwest, the development of Missouri itself, and the facilities of distribution. It is a general belief that

settlement is gradually pushing the rainy belt farther
and farther westward over the prairies and plains,
that the breaking up of the sod by the plough and
the tilling have increased evaporation and consequently rainfall. I find this questioned by competent ob-
servers, who say that the observation of ten years is
not enough to settle the fact of a change of climate,
and that, as not a tenth part of the area under consideration has been broken by the plough, there is not
cause enough for the alleged effect, and that we do
not yet know the cycle of years of drought and years
of rain. However this may be, there is no doubt of
the vast agricultural yield of these new States and
Territories, nor of the quantities of improved machinery they use. As to facility of distribution, the railways are in evidence. I need not name them, but I
believe I counted fifteen lines and systems centring
there. In 1887, 4565 miles of railway were added to
the facilities of Kansas City, stretching out in every
direction. The development of one is notable as peculiar and far-sighted, the Fort Scott and Gulf, which
is grasping the East as well as the South-west; turning eastward from Fort Scott, it already reaches the
iron industries of Birmingham, pushes on to Atlanta,
and seeks the seaboard. I do not think I over-estimate
the importance of this quite direct connection of Kansas City with the Atlantic.

The population of Kansas City, according to the
statistics of the Board of Trade, increased from 41,-
786 in 1877 to 165,924 in 1887, the assessed valuation
from $9,370,287 in 1877 to $53,017,290 in 1887, and
the rate of taxation was reduced in the same period
from about 22 mills to 14. I notice also that the

23

banking capital increased in a year—1886 to 1887—
from $3,873,000 to $6,950,000, and the Clearing-house
transactions in the same year from $251,963,441 to
$353,895,458. This, with other figures which might
be given, sustains the assertion that while real-estate
speculation has decreased in the current year, there
was a substantial increase of business. During the
year ending June 30, 1886, there were built 4054 new
houses, costing $10,393,207; during the year ending
June 30, 1887, 5889, costing $12,839,868. An impor-
tant feature of the business of Kansas City is in the
investment and loan and trust companies, which are
many, and aggregate a capital of $7,773,000. Loans
are made on farms in Kansas, Missouri, Nebraska,
and Iowa, and also for city improvements.

Details of business might be multiplied, but enough
have been given to illustrate the material prosperity
of the city. I might add a note of the enterprise
which last year paved (mainly with cedar blocks on
concrete) thirteen miles of the city; the very handsome churches in process of erection, and one or two
(of the many) already built, admirable in plan and
appearance; the really magnificent building of the
Board of Trade—a palace, in fact; and other handsome, costly structures on every hand. There are
thirty-five miles of cable road. I am not sure but
these cable roads are the most interesting—certainly
the most exciting—feature of the city to a stranger.
They climb such steeps, they plunge down such grades,
they penetrate and whiz through such crowded, lively
thoroughfares, their trains go so rapidly, that the
rider is in a perpetual exhilaration. I know no other
locomotion more exciting and agreeable. Life seems

a sort of holiday when one whizzes through the crowded city, up and down and around amid the tall buildings, and then launches off in any direction into the suburbs, which are alive with new buildings. Independence Avenue is shown as one of the finest avenues, and very handsome it and that part of the town are, but I fancied I could detect a movement of fashion and preference to the hills southward.

In the midst of such a material expansion one has learned to expect fine houses, but I was surprised to find three very good book-stores (as I remember, St. Louis has not one so good), and a very good start for a public library, consisting of about 16,000 well-arranged and classified books. Members pay $2 a year, and the library receives only about $2500 a year from the city. The citizens could make no better-paying investment than to raise this library to the first rank. There is also the beginning of an art school in some pretty rooms, furnished with casts and auto-types, where pupils practise drawing under direction of local artists. There are two social clubs—the University, which occupies pleasant apartments, and the Kansas City Club, which has just erected a handsome club-house. In these respects, and in a hundred refinements of living, the town, which has so largely drawn its young, enterprising population from the extreme East, has little the appearance of a frontier place; it is the push, the public spirit, the mixture of fashion and slouching negligence in street attire, the mingling of Eastern smartness with border emancipation in manner, and the general restlessness of movement, that proclaim the newness. It seems to me that the incessant stir, and especially the clatter, whir,

and rapidity of the cable cars, must have a decided
effect on the nerves of the whole population. The
appearance is certainly that of an entire population
incessantly in motion.

I have spoken of the public spirit. Besides the
Board of Trade there is a Merchants' and Manufacturers' Bureau, which works vigorously to bring to the
city and establish mercantile and manufacturing enterprises. The same spirit is shown in the public
schools. The expenditures in 1887 were, for school
purposes, $226,923; for interest on bonds, $18,408; for
grounds and buildings, $110,087 ; in all, $355,418.
The total of children of school age was, white, 31,-
667; colored, 4204. Of these in attendance at school
were, white, 12,933 ; colored, 1975. There were 25
school-houses and 212 teachers. The schools which I
saw—one large grammar-school, a colored school, and
the High-school of over 600 pupils—were good all
through, full of intelligent emulation, the teachers
alert and well equipped, and the attention to literature, to the science of government, to what, in short,
goes to make intelligent citizens, highly commendable. I find the annual reports, under Prof. J. M.
Greenwood, most interesting reading. Topics are
taken up and investigations made of great public interest. These topics relate to the even physical and
mental development of the young in distinction from
the effort merely to stuff them with information.
There is a most intelligent attempt to remedy defect-
ive eyesight. Twenty per cent. of school children
have some anomaly of refraction or accommodation
which should be recognized and corrected early; girls
have a larger per cent. of anomalies than boys. Irish,

Swedish, and German children have the highest percentage of affections of the eyes; English, French, Scotch, and Americans the lowest. Scientific observations of the eyes are made in the Kansas City schools, with a view to remedy defects. Another curious topic is the investigation of the Contents of Children's Minds—that is, what very small children know about common things. Prof. Stanley Hall published recently the result of examinations made of very little folks in Boston schools. Professor Greenwood made similar investigations among the lowest grade of pupils in the Kansas City schools, and a table of comparisons is printed. The per cent. of children ignorant of common things is astonishingly less in Kansas City schools than in the Boston; even the colored children of the Western city made a much better showing. Another subject of investigation is the alleged physical deterioration in this country. Examinations were made of hundreds of school children from the age of ten to fifteen, and comparisons taken with the tables in Mulhall's "Dictionary of Statistics," London, 1884. It turns out that the Kansas City children are taller, taking sex into account, than the average English child at the age of either ten or fifteen, weigh a fraction less at ten, but upwards of four pounds more at fifteen, while the average Belgian boy and girl compare favorably with American children two years younger. The tabulated statistics show two facts, that the average Kansas child stands fully as tall as the tallest, and that in weight he tips the beam against an older child on the other side of the Atlantic. With this showing, we trust that our American experiment will be permitted to go on.

In reaching the necessary limit of a paper too short for its subject, I can only express my admiration of the indomitable energy and spirit of that portion of the West which Kansas City represents, and congratulate it upon so many indications of attention to the higher civilization, without which its material prosperity will be wonderful but not attractive.

XV.

KENTUCKY.

ALL Kentucky, like Gaul, is divided into three parts. This division, which may not be sustained by the geologists or the geographers, perhaps not even by the ethnologists, is, in my mind, one of character: the east and south-east mountainous part, the central blue-grass region, and the great western portion, thrifty in both agriculture and manufactures. It is a great self-sustaining empire, lying midway in the Union, and between the North and the South (never having yet exactly made up its mind whether it is North or South), extending over more than seven degrees of longitude. Its greatest length east and west is 410 miles; its greatest breadth, 178 miles. Its area by latest surveys, and larger than formerly estimated, is 42,283 square miles. Within this area prodigal nature has brought together nearly everything that a highly civilized society needs: the most fertile soil, capable of producing almost every variety of product for food or for textile fabrics; mountains of coals and iron ores and limestone; streams and springs everywhere; almost all sorts of hard-wood timber in abundance. Nearly half the State is still virgin forest of the noblest trees, oaks, sugar-maple, ash, poplar, black-walnut, linn, elm, hickory, beech, chestnut, red cedar. The climate may honestly be called temperate: its inhabitants do not need to live in cellars in the summer, nor burn up their fences and furniture in the winter.

Kentucky is loved of its rivers. It can be seen by their excessively zigzag courses how reluctant they are to leave the State, and if they do leave it they are certain to return. The Kentucky and the Green wander about in the most uncertain way before they go to the Ohio, and the Licking and Big Sandy exhibit only a little less reluctance. The Cumberland, after a wide detour in Tennessee, returns; and Powell's River, joining the Clinch and entering the Tennessee, finally persuades that river, after it has looked about the State of Tennessee and gladdened northern Alabama, to return to Kentucky.

Kentucky is an old State, with an old civilization. It was the pioneer in the great western movement of population after the Revolution. Although it was first explored in 1770, and the Boone trail through the wilderness of Cumberland Gap was not marked till 1775, a settlement had been made in Frankfort in 1774, and in 1790 the Territory had a population of 73,677. This was a marvellous growth, considering the isolation by hundreds of miles of wilderness from Eastern communities, and the savage opposition of the Indians, who slew fifteen hundred white settlers from 1783 to 1790. Kentucky was the home of no Indian tribe, but it was the favorite hunting and fighting ground of those north of the Ohio and south of the Cumberland, and they united to resent white interference. When the State came into the Union in 1792 —the second admitted—it was the equal in population and agricultural wealth of some of the original States that had been settled a hundred and fifty years, and in 1800 could **boast 220,759 inhabitants, and in 1810, 406,511.**

At the time of the settlement, New York west of the Hudson, western Pennsylvania, and western Virginia were almost unoccupied except by hostile Indians; there was only chance and dangerous navigation down the Ohio from Pittsburg, and it was nearly eight hundred miles of a wilderness road, which was nothing but a bridle-path, from Philadelphia by way of the Cumberland Gap to central Kentucky. The majority of emigrants came this toilsome way, which was, after all, preferable to the river route, and all passengers and produce went that way eastward, for the steamboat had not yet made the ascent of the Ohio feasible. In 1779 Virginia resolved to construct a wagon-road through the wilderness, but no road was made for many years afterwards, and indeed no vehicle of any sort passed over it till a road was built by action of the Kentucky Legislature in 1796. I hope it was better then than the portion of it I travelled from Pineville to the Gap in 1888.

Civilization made a great leap over nearly a thousand miles into the open garden-spot of central Kentucky, and the exploit is a unique chapter in our frontier development. Either no other land ever lent itself so easily to civilization as the blue-grass region, or it was exceptionally fortunate in its occupants. They formed almost immediately a society distinguished for its amenities, for its political influence, prosperous beyond precedent in farming, venturesome and active in trade, developing large manufactures, especially from hemp, of such articles as could be transported by river, and sending annually through

the wilderness road to the East and South immense
droves of cattle, horses, and swine. In the first necessity, and the best indication of superior civilization,
good roads for transportation, Kentucky was conspicuous in comparison with the rest of the country. As
early as 1825 macadam roads were projected, the turnpike from Lexington to Maysville on the Ohio was
built in 1829, and the work went on by State and
county co-operation until the central region had a
system of splendid roads, unexcelled in any part of
the Union. In 1830 one of the earliest railways in the
United States, that from Lexington to Frankfort, was
begun; two years later seven miles were constructed,
and in 1835 the first locomotive and train of cars ran
on it to Frankfort, twenty-seven miles, in two hours
and twenty-nine minutes. The structure was composed of stone sills, in which grooves were cut to
receive the iron bars. These stone blocks can still be
seen along the line of the road, now a part of the
Louisville and Nashville system. In all internal improvements the State was very energetic. The canal
around the Falls of the Ohio at Louisville was opened
in 1831, with some aid from the General Government.
The State expended a great deal in improving the
navigation of the Kentucky, the Green, and other
rivers in its borders by an expensive system of locks
and dams; in 1837 it paid $19,500 to engineers engaged
in turnpike and river improvement, and in 1839 $31,-
675 for the same purpose.

The story of early Kentucky reads like a romance.
By 1820 it counted a population of over 516,000, and
still it had scarcely wagon-road communication with
the East. Here was a singular phenomenon, a pros-

perous community, as one might say a garden in the
wilderness, separated by natural barriers from the
great life of the East, which pushed out north of it a
connected, continuous development; a community almost self-sustaining, having for his centre the loveli-
est agricultural region in the Union, and evolving a
unique social state so gracious and attractive that it
was thought necessary to call in the effect of the blue-
grass to explain it, unaided human nature being inadequate, it was thought, to such a result. Almost
from the beginning fine houses attested the taste and
prosperity of the settlers ; by 1792 the blue-grass region was dotted with neat and commodious dwellings,
fruit orchards and gardens, sugar groves, and clusters
of villages; while, a little later, rose, in the midst of
broad plantations and park-like forests, lands luxuriant
with wheat and clover and corn and hemp and tobacco,
the manorial dwellings of the colonial period, like the
stately homes planted by the Holland Land Company
along the Hudson and the Mohawk and in the fair
Genesee, like the pillared structures on the James and
the Staunton, and like the solid square mansions of
old New England. A type of some of them stands in
Frankfort now, a house which was planned by Thomas
Jefferson and built in 1796, spacious, permanent, elegant in the low relief of its chaste ornamentation.
For comfort, for the purposes of hospitality, for the
quiet and rest of the mind, there is still nothing so
good as the colonial house, with the slight modifications required by our changed conditions.

From 1820 onward the State grew by a natural increment of population, but without much aid from
native or foreign emigration. In 1860 its population

was only about 919,000 whites, with some 225,000 slaves and over 10,000 free colored persons. It had no city of the first class, nor any villages specially thriving. Louisville numbered only about 68,000, Lexington less than 15,000, and Frankfort, the capital, a little over 5000. It retained the lead in hemp and a leading position in tobacco ; but it had fallen away behind its much younger rivals in manufactures and the building of railways, and only feeble efforts had been made in the development of its extraordinary mineral resources.

How is this arrest of development accounted for? I know that a short way of accounting for it has been the presence of slavery. I would not underestimate this. Free labor would not go where it had to compete with slave labor; white labor now does not like to come into relations with black labor; and capital also was shy of investment in a State where both political economy and social life were disturbed by a color line. But this does not wholly account for the position of Kentucky as to development at the close of the war. So attractive is the State in most respects, in climate, soil, and the possibilities of great wealth by manufactures, that I doubt not the State would have been forced into the line of Western progress and slavery become an unimportant factor long ago, but for certain natural obstacles and artificial influences.

Let the reader look on the map, at the ranges of mountains running from the north-east to the south-west—the Blue Ridge, the Alleghanies, the Cumberland, and Pine mountains, continuous rocky ridges, with scarcely a water gap, and only at long intervals a passable mountain gap—and notice how these would both hinder and deflect the tide of emigration. With such barriers the early development of Kentucky becomes ten times a wonder. But about 1825 an event occurred that placed her at a greater disadvantage in the competition. The Erie Canal was opened. This made New York, and not Virginia, the great commercial highway. The railway development followed. It was easy to build roads north of Kentucky, and the tide of settlement followed the roads, which were mostly aided by land grants; and in order to utilize the land grants the railways stimulated emigration by extensive advertising. Capital and population passed Kentucky by on the north. To the south somewhat similar conditions prevailed. Comparatively cheap roads could be built along the eastern slope of the Alleghanies, following the great valley from Pennsylvania to Alabama ; and these south-westwardly roads were also aided by the General Government. The North and South Railway of Alabama, and the Alabama and Great Southern, which cross at Birmingham, were land-grant roads. The roads which left the Atlantic seaboard passed naturally northward and southward of Kentucky, and left an immense area in the centre of the Union—all of western and southwestern Virginia and eastern Kentucky — without transportation facilities. Until 1880 here was the largest area east of the Mississippi unpenetrated by railways.

The war removed one obstacle to the free movement of men desiring work and seeking agreeable homes, a movement marked in the great increase of the industrial population of Louisville and the awakening to

varied industries and trade in western Kentucky. The
offer of cheap land, which would reward skilful farming in agreeable climatic conditions, has attracted
foreign settlers to the plateau south of the blue-grass
region ; and scientific investigation has made the
mountain district in the south-east the object of the
eager competition of both domestic and foreign capital. Kentucky, therefore, is entering upon a new era
of development. Two phases of it, the Swiss colonies,
and the opening of the coal, iron, and timber resources,
present special points of interest.

This incoming of the commercial spirit will change
Kentucky for the better and for the worse, will change
even the tone of the blue-grass country, and perhaps
take away something of that charm about which so
much has been written. So thoroughly has this region
been set forth by the pen and the pencil and the lens
that I am relieved of the necessity of describing it.
But I must confess that all I had read of it, all the
pictures I had seen, gave me an inadequate idea of its
beauty and richness. So far as I know, there is nothing like it in the world. Comparison of it with England is often made in the use of the words "garden"
and "park." The landscape is as unlike the finer
parts of Old England as it is unlike the most carefully
tended parts of New England. It has neither the intense green, the subdivisions in hedges, the bosky lanes,
the picturesque cottages, the niceness of minute garden-
culture, of England, nor the broken, mixed lawn gardening and neglected pastures and highways, with the
sweet wild hills, of the Berkshire region. It is an
open, elevated, rolling land, giving the traveller often
the most extended views over wheat and clover, hemp

and tobacco fields, forests and blue-grass pastures. One may drive for a hundred miles north and south over the splendid macadam turnpikes, behind blooded roadsters, at an easy ten-mile gait, and see always the same sight—a smiling agricultural paradise, with scarcely a foot, in fence corners, by the road-side, or in low grounds, of uncultivated, uncared-for land. The open country is more pleasing than the small villages, which have not the tidiness of the New England small villages; the houses are for the most part plain; here and there is a negro cabin, or a cluster of them, apt to be unsightly, but always in view somewhere is a plantation-house, more or less pretentious, generally old-fashioned and with the colonial charm. These are frequently off the main thoroughfare, approached by a private road winding through oaks and ash-trees, seated on some gentle knoll or slope, maybe with a small flower-garden, but probably with the old sentimental blooms that smell good and have reminiscences, in the midst of waving fields of grain, blue-grass pastures, and open forest glades watered by a clear stream. There seems to be infinite peace in a house so surrounded. The house may have pillars, probably a colonial porch and door-way with carving in bass-relief, a wide hall, large square rooms, low studded, and a general air of comfort. What is new in it in the way of art, furniture, or bric-à-brac may not be in the best taste, and may "swear" at the old furniture and the delightful old portraits. For almost always will be found some portraits of the post-Revolutionary period, having a traditional and family interest, by Copley or Jouett, perhaps a Stuart, maybe by some artist who evidently did not paint for fame,

which carry the observer back to the colonial society in Virginia, Philadelphia, and New York. In a
country house and in Lexington I saw portraits, life-
size and miniature, of Rebecca Gratz, whose loveliness
of person and character is still a tender recollection of
persons living. She was a great beauty and toast in
her day. It was at her house in Philadelphia, a centre
of wit and gayety, that Washington Irving and Henry
Brevoort and Gulian C. Verplanck often visited. She
shone not less in New York society, and was the most
intimate friend of Matilda Hoffman, who was betrothed
to Irving; indeed, it was in her arms that Matilda died,
fadeless always to us as she was to Irving, in the loveliness of her eighteenth year. The well-founded tradition is that Irving, on his first visit to Abbotsford,
told Scott of his own loss, and made him acquainted
with the beauty and grace of Rebecca Gratz, and that
Scott, wanting at the moment to vindicate a race that
was aspersed, used her as a model for Rebecca in
" Ivanhoe."

One distinction of the blue-grass region is the
forests, largely of gigantic oaks, free of all undergrowth, carpeted with the close-set, luscious, nutritive
blue-grass, which remains green all the season when
it is cropped by feeding. The blue-grass thrives elsewhere, notably in the upper Shenandoah Valley, where
somewhat similar limestone conditions prevail ; but
this is its natural habitat. On all this elevated rolling
plateau the limestone is near the surface. This grass
blooms towards the middle of June in a bluish, almost
a peacock blue, blossom, which gives to the fields an
exquisite hue. By the end of the month the seed
ripens into a yellowish color, and while the grass is

still green and lush underneath, the surface presents much the appearance of a high New England pasture in August. When it is ripe, the top is cut for the seed. The limestone and the blue-grass together determine the agricultural pre-eminence of the region, and account for the fine breeding of the horses, the excellence of the cattle, the stature of the men, and the beauty of the women; but they have social and moral influence also. It could not well be otherwise, considering the relation of the physical condition to disposition and character. We should be surprised if a rich agricultural region, healthful at the same time, where there is abundance of food, and wholesome cooking is the rule, did not affect the tone of social life. And I am almost prepared to go further, and think that blue-grass is a specific for physical beauty and a certain graciousness of life. I have been told that there is a natural relation between Presbyterianism and blue-grass, and am pointed to the Shenandoah and to Kentucky as evidence of it. Perhaps Presbyterians naturally seek a limestone country. But the relation, if it exists, is too subtle and the facts are too few to build a theory on. Still, I have no doubt there is a distinct variety of woman known as the blue-grass girl. A geologist told me that once when he was footing it over the State with a geologist from another State, as they approached the blue-grass region from the southward they were carefully examining the rock formation and studying the surface indications, which are usually marked on the border line, to determine exactly where the peculiar limestone formation began. Indications, however, were wanting. Suddenly my geologist looked up the road and exclaimed:

24

" We are in the blue-grass region now."

" How do you know?" asked the other.

" Why, there is a blue-grass girl."

There was no mistaking the neat dress, the style, the rounded contours, the gracious personage. A few steps farther on the geologists found the outcropping of the blue limestone.

Perhaps the people of this region are trying to live up to the thorough-bred. A pedigree is a necessity. The horse is of the first consideration, and either has or gives a sort of social distinction; first, the running horse, the thorough-bred, and now the trotting horse, which is beginning to have a recognizable descent, and is on the way to be a thorough-bred. Many of the finest plantations are horse farms; one might call them the feature of the country. Horse-raising is here a science, and as we drive from one estate to another, and note the careful tillage, the trim fences, the neat stables, the pretty paddocks, and the houses of the favorites, we see how everything is intended to contribute to the perfection in refinement of fibre, speed, and endurance of the noble animal. Even persons who are usually indifferent to horses cannot but admire these beautiful high-bred creatures, either the famous ones displayed at the stables, or the colts and fillies, which have yet their reputations to make, at play in the blue-grass pastures; and the pleasure one experiences is a refined one in harmony with the landscape. Usually horse-dealing carries with it a lowering of the moral tone, which we quite understand when we say of a man that he is " horsy." I suppose the truth is that man has degraded the idea of the horse by his own evil passions, using him to gamble

and cheat with. Now, the visitor will find little of
these degrading associations in the blue-grass region.
It is an orthodox and a moral region. The best and
most successful horse-breeders have nothing to do
with racing or betting. The yearly product of their
farms is sold at auction, without reserve or favor.
The sole business is the production of the best animals
that science and care can breed. Undeniably where the
horse is of such importance he is much in the thought,
and the use of " horsy " phrases in ordinary conversation shows his effect upon the vocabulary. The re-
cital of pedigree at the stables, as horse after horse is
led out, sounds a little like a chapter from the Book
of Genesis, and naturally this Biblical formula gets
into a conversation about people.

And after the horses there is whiskey. There are
many distilleries in this part of the country, and a
great deal of whiskey is made. I am not defending
whiskey, at least any that is less than thirty years old
and has attained a medicinal quality. But I want to
express my opinion that this is as temperate as any
region in the United States. There is a wide-spread
strict temperance sentiment, and even prohibition prevails to a considerable degree. Whiskey is made and
stored, and mostly shipped away; rightly or wrongly,
it is regarded as a legitimate business, like wheat-
raising, and is conducted by honorable men. I believe
this to be the truth, and that drunkenness does not
prevail in the neighborhood of the distilleries, nor did I
see anywhere in the country evidence of a habit of dram
drinking, of the traditional matter-of-course offering of
whiskey as a hospitality. It is true that mint grows
in Kentucky, and that there are persons who would

win the respect of a tide-water Virginian in the concoction of a julep.   And no doubt in the mind of the
born Kentuckian there is a rooted belief that if a person needed a stimulant, the best he can take is old
hand - made whiskey.   Where the manufacture of
whiskey is the source of so much revenue, and is
carried on with decorum, of course the public sentiment about it differs from that of a community that
makes its money in raising potatoes for starch.   Where
the horse is so beautiful, fleet, and profitable, of course
there is intense interest in him, and the general public
take a lively pleasure in the races; but if the reader has
been accustomed to associate this part of Kentucky
with horse-racing and drinking as prominent characteristics, he must revise his opinion.

Perhaps certain colonial habits lingered longer in
Kentucky than elsewhere.   Travellers have spoken
about the habit of profanity and gambling, especially
the game of poker.   In the West generally profane
swearing is not as bad form as it is in the East.   But
whatever distinction central Kentucky had in profanity or poker, it has evidently lost it.   The duel
lingered long, and prompt revenge for insults, especially to women.   The blue-grass region has "histo-
ries"—beauty has been fought about; women have
had careers; families have run out through dissipation.
One may hear stories of this sort even in the Berkshire Hills, in any place where there have been long
settlement, wealth, and time for the development of
family and personal eccentricities.   And there is still
a flavor left in Kentucky; there is still a subtle difference in its social tone; the intelligent women are attractive in another way from the intelligent New

England women—they have a charm of their own.
May Heaven long postpone the day when, by the
commercial spirit and trade and education, we shall all
be alike in all parts of the Union ! Yet it would be
no disadvantage to anybody if the graciousness, the
simplicity of manner, the refined hospitality, of the
blue-grass region should spread beyond the blue limestone of the Lower Silurian.

In the excellent State Museum at Frankfort, under
the charge of Prof. John R. Procter,* who is State
Geologist and also Director of the Bureau of Immigration, in addition to the admirable exhibit of the natural resources of Kentucky, are photographs, statistics,
and products showing the condition of the Swiss and
other foreign farming colonies recently established in
the State, which were so interesting and offered so
many instructive points that I determined to see some
of the colonies.

This museum and the geological department, the
intelligent management of which has been of immense
service to the commonwealth, is in one of the detached buildings which make up the present Capitol. The
Capitol is altogether antiquated, and not a credit to
the State. The room in which the Lower House
meets is shabby and mean, yet I noticed that it is
fairly well lighted by side windows, and debate can
be heard in it conducted in an ordinary tone of voice.
Kentucky will before many years be accommodated

---

* Whatever value this paper has is so largely due to Professor Procter that I desire to make to him the most explicit
acknowledgments. One of the very best results of the war
was keeping him in the Union.

with new State buildings more suited to her wealth and dignity. But I should like to repeat what was said in relation to the Capitol of Arkansas. Why cannot our architects devise a capitol suited to the wants of those who occupy it? Why must we go on making these huge inconvenient structures, mainly for external display, in which the legislative Chambers are vast air-tight and water-tight compartments, commonly completely surrounded by other rooms and lobbies, and lighted only from the roof, or at best by high windows in one or two sides that permit no outlook—rooms difficult to speak or hear in, impossible to ventilate, needing always artificial light? Why should the Senators of the United States be compelled to occupy a gilded dungeon, unlighted ever by the sun, unvisited ever by the free wind of heaven, in which the air is so foul that the Senators sicken? What sort of legislation ought we to expect from such Chambers? It is perfectly feasible to build a legislative room cheerful and light, open freely to sun and air on three sides. In order to do this it may be necessary to build a group of connected buildings, instead of the parallelogram or square, which is mostly domed, with gigantic halls and stair-ways, and, considering the purpose for which it is intended, is a libel on our ingenuity and a burlesque on our civilization.

Kentucky has gone to work in a very sensible way to induce immigration and to attract settlers of the right sort. The Bureau of Immigration was established in 1880. It began to publish facts about the State, in regard to the geologic formation, the soils, the price of lands, both the uncleared and the lands injured by slovenly culture, the kind and amount of

products that might be expected by thrifty farming,
and the climate ; not exaggerated general proclama-
tions promising sudden wealth with little labor, but
facts such as would attract the attention of men willing
to work in order to obtain for themselves and their
children comfortable homes and modest independence.
Invitations were made for a thorough examination
of lands—of the different sorts of soils in different
counties—before purchase and settlement. The leading idea was to induce industrious farmers who were
poor, or had not money enough to purchase high-
priced improved lands, to settle upon lands that the
majority of Kentuckians considered scarcely worth
cultivating, and the belief was that good farming
would show that these neglected lands were capable
of becoming very productive. Eight years' experience has fully justified all these expectations. Colonies of Swiss, Germans, Austrians, have come, and
Swedes also, and these have attracted many from the
North and North-west. In this period I suppose as
many as ten thousand immigrants of this class, thrifty
cultivators of the soil, have come into the State, many
of whom are scattered about the State, unconnected
with the so-called colonies. These colonies are not
organized communities in any way separated from the
general inhabitants of the State. They have merely
settled together for companionship and social reasons,
where a sufficiently large tract of cheap land was
found to accommodate them. Each family owns its
own farm, and is perfectly independent. An indis-
criminate immigration has not been desired or encouraged, but the better class of laboring agriculturists,
grape-growers, and stock-raisers. There are several

settlements of these, chiefly Swiss, dairy-farmers, cheese-makers, and vine-growers, in Laurel County; others in Lincoln County, composed of Swiss, Germans, and Austrians; a mixed colony in Rock Castle County; a thriving settlement of Austrians in Boyle County; a temperance colony of Scandinavians in Edmonson County; another Scandinavian colony in Grayson County; and scattered settlements of Germans and Scandinavians in Christian County. These settlements have from one hundred to over a thousand inhabitants each. The lands in Laurel and Lincoln counties, which I travelled through, are on a high plateau, with good air and temperate climate, but with a somewhat thin, loamy, and sandy soil, needing manure, and called generally in the State poor land — poor certainly compared with the blue-grass region and other extraordinarily fertile sections. These farms, which had been more or less run over by Kentucky farming, were sold at from one to five dollars an acre. They are farms that a man cannot live on in idleness. But they respond well to thrifty tillage, and it is a sight worth a long journey to see the beautiful farms these Swiss have made out of land that the average Kentuckian thought not worth cultivating. It has not been done without hard work, and as most of the immigrants were poor, many of them have had a hard struggle in building comfortable houses, reducing the neglected land to order, and obtaining stock. A great attraction to the Swiss was that this land is adapted to vine culture, and a reasonable profit was expected from selling grapes and making wine. The vineyards are still young; experiment has not yet settled what kind of grapes flourish

best, but many vine-growers have realized handsome
profits in the sale of fruit, and the trial is sufficient to
show that good wine can be produced. The only interference thus far with the grapes has been the unprecedented late freeze last spring.

At the recent exposition in Louisville the exhibit of
these Swiss colonies—the photographs showing the
appearance of the unkempt land when they bought
it, and the fertile fields of grain and meadow and
vineyards afterwards, and the neat, plain farm cottages, the pretty Swiss chalet with its attendants of
intelligent comely girls in native costumes offering
articles illustrating the taste and the thrift of the colonies, wood-carving, the products of the dairy, and
the fruit of the vine—attracted great attention.

I cannot better convey to the reader the impression
I wish to in regard to this colonization and its lesson
for the country at large than by speaking more in
detail of one of the Swiss settlements in Laurel County.
This is Bernstadt, about six miles from Pittsburg, on
the Louisville and Nashville road, a coal-mining region, and offering a good market for the produce of
the Swiss farmers. We did not need to be told when
we entered the colony lands ; neater houses, thrifty
farming, and better roads proclaimed it. It is not a
garden-spot ; in some respects it is a poor-looking
country ; but it has abundant timber, good water,
good air, a soil of light sandy loam, which is productive under good tillage. There are here, I suppose,
some two hundred and fifty families, scattered about
over a large area, each on its farm. There is no collection of houses ; the church (Lutheran), the school-
house, the store, the post-office, the hotel, are widely

separated ; for the hotel-keeper, the store-keeper, the postmaster, and, I believe, the school-master and the parson, are all farmers to a greater or less extent. It must be understood that it is a primitive settlement, having as yet very little that is picturesque, a community of simple working-people. Only one or two of the houses have any pretension to taste in architecture, but this will come in time—the vine-clad porches, the quaint gables, the home-likeness. The Kentuckian, however, will notice the barns for the stock, and a general thriftiness about the places. And the appearance of the farms is an object-lesson of the highest value.

The chief interest to me, however, was the character of the settlers. Most of them were poor, used to hard work and scant returns for it in Switzerland. What they have accomplished, therefore, is the result of industry, and not of capital. There are among the colonists skilled laborers in other things than vine-growing and cheese-making—watch-makers and wood-carvers and adepts in various trades. The thrifty young farmer at whose pretty house we spent the night, and who has saw-mills at Pittsburg, is of one of the best Swiss families; his father was for many years President of the republic, and he was a graduate of the university at Lucerne. There were others of the best blood and breeding and schooling, and men of scientific attainments. But they are all at work close to the soil. As a rule, however, the colonists were men and women of small means at home. The notable thing is that they bring with them a certain old civilization, a unity of simplicity of life with real refinement, courtesy, politeness, good-humor. The girls

would not be above going out to service, and they
would not lose their self-respect in it. Many of them
would be described as "peasants," but I saw some, not
above the labors of the house and farm, with real
grace and dignity of manner and charm of conversation. Few of them as yet speak any English, but in
most houses are evidences of some German culture.
Uniformly there was courtesy and frank hospitality.
The community amuses itself rationally. It has a
very good brass band, a singing club, and in the even-
ings and holidays it is apt to assemble at the hotel and
take a little wine and sing the songs of father-land.
The hotel is indeed at present without accommodations for lodgers — nothing but a *Wirthshaus*, with a
German garden where dancing may take place now
and then. With all the hard labor, they have an idea
of the simple comforts and enjoyments of life. And
they live very well, though plainly. At a house where
we dined, in the colony Strasburg, near Bernstadt, we
had an excellent dinner, well served, and including
delicious soup. If the colony never did anything else
than teach that part of the State how to make soup,
its existence would be justified. Here, in short, is an
element of homely thrift, civilization on a rational
basis, good-citizenship, very desirable in any State.
May their vineyards flourish! When we departed
early in the morning—it was not yet seven—a dozen
Switzers, fresh from the dewy fields, in their working
dresses, had assembled at the hotel, where the young
landlady also smiled a welcome, to send us off with a
song, which ended, as we drove away, in a good-bye
yodel.

A line drawn from the junction of the Scioto River

with the Ohio south-west to a point in the southern
boundary about thirty miles east of where the Cumberland leaves the State defines the eastern coal-measures of Kentucky. In area it is about a quarter of the
State—a region of plateaus, mountains, narrow valleys, cut in all directions by clear, rapid streams, stuffed, one may say, with coals, streaked with iron,
abounding in limestone, and covered with superb forests. Independent of other States a most remarkable
region, but considered in its relation to the coals and
iron ores of West Virginia, western Virginia, and eastern Tennessee, it becomes one of the most important
and interesting regions in the Union. Looking to the
south-eastern border, I hazard nothing in saying that
the country from the Breaks of Sandy down to Big
Creek Gap (in the Cumberland Mountain), in Tennessee, is on the eve of an astonishing development—one
that will revolutionize eastern Kentucky, and powerfully affect the iron and coal markets of the country.
It is a region that appeals as well to the imagination
of the traveller as to the capitalist. My personal observation of it extends only to the portion from Cumberland Gap to Big Stone Gap, and the head-waters
of the Cumberland between Cumberland Mountain
and Pine Mountain, but I saw enough to comprehend
why eager purchasers are buying the forests and the
mining rights, why great companies, American and
English, are planting themselves there and laying
the foundations of cities, and why the gigantic railway corporations are straining every nerve to penetrate the mineral and forest heart of the region. A
dozen roads, projected and in progress, are pointed
towards this centre. It is a race for the prize. The

Louisville and Nashville, running through soft-coal fields to Jellico and on to Knoxville, branches from Corbin to Barboursville (an old and thriving town) and to Pineville. From Pineville it is under contract, thirteen miles, to Cumberland Gap. This gap is being tunnelled (work going on at both ends) by an independent company, the tunnel to be open to all roads. The Louisville and Nashville may run up the south side of the Cumberland range to Big Stone Gap, or it may ascend the Cumberland River and its Clover Fork, and pass over to Big Stone Gap that way, or it may do both. A road is building from Knoxville to Cumberland Gap, and from Johnson City to Big Stone Gap. A road is running from Bristol to within twenty miles of Big Stone Gap; another road nears the same place—the extension of the Norfolk and Western—from Pocahontas down the Clinch River. From the north-west many roads are projected to pierce the great deposits of coking and cannel coals, and find or bore a way through the mountain ridges into south-western Virginia. One of these, the Kentucky Union, starting from Lexington (which is becoming a great railroad centre), has reached Clay City, and will soon be open to the Three Forks of the Kentucky River, and on to Jackson, in Breathitt County. These valley and transridge roads will bring within short hauling distance of each other as great a variety of iron ores of high and low grade, and of coals, coking and other, as can be found anywhere—according to the official reports, greater than anywhere else within the same radius. As an item it may be mentioned that the rich, pure, magnetic iron ore used in the manufacture of Bessemer steel, found in East

Tennessee and North Carolina, and developed in greatest abundance at Cranberry Forge, is within one hundred miles of the superior Kentucky coking coal. This contiguity (a contiguity of coke, ore, and limestone) in this region points to the manufacture of Bessemer steel here at less cost than it is now elsewhere made.

It is unnecessary that I should go into details as to the ore and coal deposits of this region : the official reports are accessible. It may be said, however, that the reports of the Geological Survey as to both coal and iron have been recently perfectly confirmed by the digging of experts. Aside from the coal-measures below the sandstone, there have been found above the sandstone, north of Pine Mountain, 1650 feet of coal-measures, containing nine beds of coal of workable thickness, and between Pine and Cumberland mountains there is a greater thickness of coal-measures, containing twelve or more workable beds. Some of these are coking coals of great excellence. Cannel-coals are found in sixteen of the counties in the eastern coal-fields. Two of them at least are of unexampled richness and purity. The value of a cannel-coal is determined by its volatile combustible matter. By this test some of the Kentucky cannel-coal excels the most celebrated coals of Great Britain. An analysis of a cannel-coal in Breathitt County gives 66.28 of volatile combustible matter ; the highest in Great Britain is the Boghead, Scotland, 51.60 per cent. This beautiful cannel-coal has been brought out in small quantities *via* the Kentucky River ; it will have a market all over the country when the railways reach it. The first coal identified as coking was named the Elkhorn, from the stream where it was found in Pike County. A thick bed of it has been traced over **an** area of 1600 square miles, covering several counties, **but attaining** its greatest thickness in Letcher, Pike, and Harlan. This **discovery of coking** coal adds greatly **to the** value of the iron ores in north-eastern Kentucky, and in the Red and Kentucky valleys, and also of the great deposits of ore on the south-east boundary, along the western base of the Cumberland, along **the** slope of Powell's Mountain, and also along Wallin's **Ridge,** three parallel lines, convenient to the coking **coal in** Kentucky. **This is the** Clinton **or red fossil ore,** stratified, having from 45 to 54 **per cent. of metallic iron.** Recently has been found **on the north side of** Pine Mountain in **Kentucky, a third deposit of rich** "brown" ore, **averaging 52 per cent. of metallic iron.** This is the **same as the celebrated brown ore used in** the furnaces at Clifton **Forge; it makes a very tough** iron. I saw a vein of **it on Straight Creek, three** miles north of **Pineville, just opened, at least eight** feet thick.

The railway **to** Pineville **follows the old Wilder-** ness road, the trail of Boone and the stage-road, along which are seen the ancient tavern stands where the jolly story-telling travellers of fifty years ago were **entertained** and the droves of horses and cattle were **fed.** The railway has been stopped a mile west of Pineville by a belligerent property owner, who sits there with his Winchester rifle, and **will** not let the work go on until the courts compel **him.** The railway will not cross the Cumberland at Pineville, but higher up, near the great elbow. There was no bridge over **the** stream, and we crossed at a very rough and rocky wagon-ford. Pineville, where there has long been a backwoods settlement on the south bend of the river just after it breaks through Pine Mountain, is now the centre of a good deal of mining excitement and real-estate speculation. It has about five hundred inhabitants, and a temporary addition of land buyers, mineral experts, engineers, furnace projectors, and railway contractors. There is not level ground for a large city, but what there is is plotted out for sale. The abundant iron ore, coal, and timber here predict for it a future of some importance. It has already a smart new hotel, and business buildings, and churches are in process of erection. The society of the town had gathered for the evening at the hotel. A wandering one-eyed fiddler was providentially present who could sing and play " The Arkansas Traveller " and other tunes that lift the heels of the young, and also accompany the scream of the violin with the droning bagpipe notes of the mouth-harmonica. The star of the gay company was a graduate of Annapolis, in full evening dress uniform, a native boy of the valley, and his vis-à-vis was a heavy man in a long linen duster and carpet slippers, with a palm-leaf fan, who crashed through the cotillon with good effect. It was a pleasant party, and long after it had dispersed, the troubadour, sitting on the piazza, wiled away sleep by the break-downs, jigs, and songs of the frontier.

Pineville and its vicinity have many attractions; the streams are clear, rapid, rocky, the foliage abundant, the hills picturesque. Straight Creek, which comes in along the north base of Pine Mountain, is an exceedingly picturesque stream, having along its banks fertile little stretches of level ground, while the gentle bordering hills are excellent for grass, fruit orchards, and vineyards. The walnut-trees have been culled out, but there is abundance of oak, beech, poplar, cucumber, and small pines. And there is no doubt about the mineral wealth.

We drove from Pineville to Cumberland Gap, thirteen miles, over the now neglected Wilderness road, the two mules of the wagon unable to pull us faster than two miles an hour. The road had every variety of badness conceivable—loose stones, ledges of rock, bowlders, sloughs, holes, mud, sand, deep fords. We crossed and followed up Clear Creek (a muddy stream) over Log Mountain (full of coal) to Cañon Creek. Settlements were few—only occasional poor shanties. Climbing over another ridge, we reached the Yellow Creek Valley, through which the Yellow Creek meanders in sand. This whole valley, lying very prettily among the mountains, has a bad name for "difficulties." The hills about, on the sides and tops of which are ragged little farms, and the valley itself, still contain some lawless people. We looked with some interest at the Turner house, where a sheriff was killed a year ago, at a place where a "severe" man fired into a wagon-load of people and shot a woman, and at other places where in recent times differences of opinion had been settled by the revolver. This sort of thing is, however, practically over. This valley, close to Cumberland Gap, is the site of the great city, already plotted, which the English company are to build as soon as the tunnel is completed. It is called Middleborough, and the streets are being graded and preparations made for building furnaces. The north side of Cumberland Mountain, like the south side of Pine, is a conglomerate, covered with superb oak and chestnut trees. We climbed up to the mountain over a winding road of ledges, bowlders, and deep gullies, rising to an extended pleasing prospect of mountains and valleys. The pass has a historic interest, not only as the ancient highway, but as the path of armies in the Civil War. It is narrow, a deep road between overhanging rocks. It is easily defended. A light bridge thrown over the road, leading to rifle-pits and breastworks on the north side, remains to attest the warlike occupation. Above, on the bald highest rocky head on the north, guns were planted to command the pass. Two or three houses, a blacksmith's shop, a drinking tavern, behind which on the rocks four men were playing old sledge, made up the sum of its human attractions as we saw it. Just here in the pass Kentucky, Tennessee, and Virginia touch each other. Virginia inserts a narrow wedge between the other two. On our way down the wild and picturesque road we crossed the State of Virginia and went to the new English hotel in Tennessee. We passed a magnificent spring, which sends a torrent of water into the valley, and turns a great millwheel—a picture in its green setting — saw the opening of the tunnel with its shops and machinery, noted the few houses and company stores of the new settlement, climbed the hill to the pretty hotel, and sat down on the piazza to look at the scene. The view is a striking one. The valley through which the Powell River runs is pleasant, and the bold, bare mountain of rock at the right of the pass is a noble feature in the landscape. With what joy must the early wilderness pilgrims have hailed this landmark, this gate-way to the

Paradise beyond the mountains! Some miles **north** in the range are the White Rocks, gleaming in the sun and conspicuous from afar, the first signal to the weary travellers from **the east of the** region they sought. Cumberland Gap is full of expectation, and only awaits the completion of the tunnel to enter upon its development. Here railways from the north, south, and west are expected to meet, and in the Yellow Creek Valley beyond, the English are to build a great manufacturing city. The valleys and sides of these mountain ranges (which have a uniform **elevation** of not much more than 2000 to 2500 feet) enjoy a delightful climate, moderate in the winter and temperate in the summer. This whole region, when **it is** accessible by rail, will be attractive to **tourists.**

We pursued our journey up the Powell River Valley, along **the base of** the Cumberland, on horseback —one day in a wagon in this country ought to satisfy anybody. The roads, however, are better on this side of the mountain; all through Lee County, in Virginia, in spots very good. This is a very fine valley, with good water, cold and clear, growing in abundance oats and corn, a constant succession of pretty views. **We** dined excellently at a neat farm-house on the river, and slept at the house of a very prosperous farmer near Boon's Path post-office. Here we are abreast the White Rocks, the highest point of the Cumberland (3451 feet), that used to be the beacon of immigration. The valley grows more and more beautiful as we go up, full fields of wheat, corn, oats, friendly to fruit of all sorts, with abundance of walnut, oak, and chestnut timber—a fertile, agreeable valley, settled with well-to-do farmers. The next morning, beauti-

fully clear and sparkling, we were off at seven o'clock
through a lovely broken country, following the line of
Cumberland (here called Stone) Mountain, alternately
little hills and meadows, cultivated hill-sides, stretches
of rich valley, exquisite views—a land picturesque and
thriving. Continuing for nine miles up Powell Valley, we turned to the left through a break in the hills
into Poor Valley, a narrow, wild, sweet ravine among
the hills, with a swift crystal stream overhung by
masses of rhododendrons in bloom, and shaded by
magnificent forest-trees. We dined at a farm-house
by Pennington's Gap, and had a swim in the north
fork of Powell River, which here, with many a leap,
breaks through the bold scenery in the gap. Farther
on, the valley was broader and more fertile, and along
the wide reaches of the river grew enormous beech-
trees, the russet foliage of which took on an exquisite
color towards evening. Indeed, the ride all day was
excitingly interesting, with the great trees, the narrow
rich valleys, the frequent sparkling streams, and lovely
mountain views. At sunset we came to the house of
an important farmer who has wide possessions, about
thirteen miles from Big Stone Gap. We have nothing
whatever against him except that he routed us out at
five o'clock of a foggy Sunday morning, which promised to be warm—July 1st—to send us on our way to
"the city." All along we had heard of "the city."
In a radius of a hundred miles Big Stone Gap is called
nothing but "the city," and our anticipations were
raised.

That morning's ride I shall not forget. We crossed
and followed Powell River. All along the banks are
set the most remarkable beech-trees I have ever seen

—great, wide-spreading, clean-boled trees, overshading the stream, and giving under their boughs, nearly all the way, ravishingly lovely views. This was the paradisiacal way to Big Stone Gap, which we found to be a round broken valley, shut in by wooded mountains, covered more or less with fine trees, the meeting-place of the Powell River, which comes through the gap, and its south fork. In the round elevation between them is the inviting place of the future city. There are two Big Stone Gaps—the one open fields and forests, a settlement of some thirty to forty houses, most of them new and many in process of building, a hotel, and some tents ; the other, the city on the map. The latter is selling in small lots, has wide avenues, parks, one of the finest hotels in the South, banks, warehouses, and all that can attract the business man or the summer lounger.

The heavy investments in Big Stone Gap and the region I should say were fully justified by the natural advantages. It is a country of great beauty, noble mountain ranges, with the valleys diversified by small hills, fertile intervales, fine streams, and a splendid forest growth. If the anticipations of an important city at the gap are half realized, the slopes of the hills and natural terraces will be dotted with beautiful residences, agreeable in both summer and winter. It was the warmest time of the year when we were there, but the air was fresh and full of vitality. The Big Stone Gap Improvement Company has the city and its site in charge; it is a consolidation of the various interests of railway companies and heavy capitalists, who have purchased the land. The money and the character of the men behind the enterprise insure a

vigorous prosecution of it. On the west side of the
river are the depot and switching-grounds which the
several railways have reserved for their use, and here
also are to be the furnaces and shops. When the city
outgrows its present site it can extend up valleys in
several directions. We rode through fine forests up
the lovely Powell Valley to Powell Mountain, where
a broad and beautiful meadow offers a site for a suburban village. The city is already planning for suburbs. A few miles south of the city a powerful
stream of clear water falls over precipices and rocks
seven hundred feet in continuous rapids. This is not
only a charming addition to the scenic attractions of
the region, but the stream will supply the town with
excellent water and unlimited " power." Beyond, ten
miles to the north-east, rises High Knob, a very sightly
point, where one gets the sort of view of four States
that he sees on an atlas. It is indeed a delightful
region ; but however one may be charmed by its natural beauty, he cannot spend a day at Big Stone Gap
without being infected with the great enterprises
brooding there.

We forded Powell River and ascended through the
gap on its right bank. Before entering the gorge we
galloped over a beautiful level plateau, the counterpart of that where the city is laid out, reserved for
railways and furnaces. From this point the valley is
seen to be wider than we suspected, and to have ample
room for the manufacturing and traffic expected. As
we turned to see what we shall never see again—the
virgin beauty of nature in this site—the whole attractiveness of this marvellously picturesque region burst
upon us—the great forests, the clear swift streams,

the fertile meadows, the wooded mountains that have so long secluded this beauty and guarded the treasures of the hills.

The pass itself, which shows from a distance only a dent in the green foliage, surprised us by its wild beauty. The stony road, rising little by little above the river, runs through a magnificent forest, gigantic trees growing in the midst of enormous bowlders, and towering among rocks that take the form of walls and buttresses, square structures like the Titanic ruins of castles ; below, the river, full and strong, rages over rocks and dashes down, filling the forest with its roar, which is echoed by the towering cliffs on either side. The woods were fresh and glistening from recent rains, but what made the final charm of the way was the bloom of the rhododendron, which blazed along the road and illuminated the cool recesses of the forest. The time for the blooming of the azalea and the kalmia (mountain-laurel) was past, but the pink and white rhododendron was in full glory, masses of bloom, not small stalks lurking like underbrush, but on bushes attaining the dignity of trees, and at least twenty-five feet high. The splendor of the forest did not lessen as we turned to the left and followed up Pigeon Creek to a high farming region, rough but fertile, at the base of Black Mountain. Such a wealth of oak, beech, poplar, chestnut, and ash, and, sprinkled in, the pretty cucumber-magnolia in bloom! By sunset we found our way, off the main road, to a lonely farm-house hidden away at the foot of Morris Pass, secluded behind an orchard of apple and peach trees. A stream of spring-water from the rocks above ran to the house, and to the eastward the ravine broadened into pastures. It seemed impossible to get farther from the world and its active currents. We were still in Virginia.

Our host, an old man over six feet in height, with spare, straight, athletic form, a fine head, and large clear gray eyes, lived here alone with his aged spouse. He had done his duty by his country in raising twelve children (that is the common and orthodox number in this region), who had all left him except one son, who lived in a shanty up the ravine. It was this son's wife who helped about the house and did the milking, taking care also of a growing family of her own, and doing her share of field-work. I had heard that the women in this country were more industrious than the men. I asked this woman, as she was milking that evening, if the women did all the work. No, she said; only their share. Her husband was all the time in the field, and even her boys, one only eight, had to work with him; there was no time to go to school, and indeed the school didn't amount to much anyway—only a little while in the fall. She had all the care of the cows. "Men," she added, "never notice milking;" and the worst of it was that she had to go miles around in the bush night and morning to find them. After supper we had a call from a bachelor who occupied a cabin over the pass, on the Kentucky side, a loquacious philosopher, who squatted on his heels in the door-yard where we were sitting, and interrogated each of us in turn as to our names, occupations, residence, ages, and politics, and then gave us as freely his own history and views of life. His eccentricity in this mountain region was that he had voted for Cleveland and should do it again. Mr. Morris couldn't go

with him in this; and when pressed for his reasons he
said that Cleveland had had the salary long enough,
and got rich enough out of it. The philosopher
brought the news, had heard it talked about on Sunday, that a man over Clover Fork way had killed his
wife and brother. It was claimed to be an accident;
they were having a game of cards and some whiskey,
and he was trying to kill his son-in-law. Was there
much killing round here? Well, not much lately.
Last year John Cone, over on Clover Fork, shot Mat
Harner in a dispute over cards. Well, what became
of John Cone? Oh, he was killed by Jim Blood, a
friend of Harner. And what became of Blood?
Well, he got shot by Elias Travers. And Travers?
Oh, he was killed by a man by the name of Jacobs.
That ended it. None of 'em was of much account.
There was a pleasing naivete in this narrative. And
then the philosopher, whom the milkmaid described to
me next morning as "a simlar sort of man," went on
to give his idea about this killing business. "All this
killing in the mountains is foolish. If you kill a man,
that don't aggravate him; he's dead and don't care,
and it all comes on you."

In the early morning we crossed a narrow pass in
the Black Mountain into "Canetucky," and followed
down the Clover Fork of the Cumberland. All these
mountains are perfectly tree-clad, but they have not
the sombreness of the high regions of the Great Smoky
and the Black Mountains of North Carolina. There
are few black balsams, or any sort of evergreens, and
the great variety of deciduous trees, from the shining
green of the oak to the bronze hue of the beech, makes
everywhere soft gradations of color most pleasing to

the eye. In the autumn, they say, the brilliant maples in combination with the soberer bronzes and yellows of the other forest-trees give an ineffable beauty to these ridges and graceful slopes. The ride down Clover Fork, all day long, was for the most part through a virgin world. The winding valley is at all times narrow, with here and there a tiny meadow, and at long intervals a lateral opening down which another sparkling brook comes from the recesses of this wilderness of mountains. Houses are miles apart, and usually nothing but cabins half concealed in some sheltered nook. There is, however, hidden on the small streams, on mountain terraces, and high up on the slopes, a considerable population, cabin dwellers, cultivators of corn, on the almost perpendicular hills. Many of these cornfields are so steep that it is impossible to plough them, and all the cultivation is done with the hoe. I heard that a man was recently killed in this neighborhood by falling out of his cornfield. The story has as much foundation as the current belief that the only way to keep a mule in the field where you wish him to stay is to put him into the adjoining lot. But it is true that no one would believe that crops could be raised on such nearly perpendicular slopes as these unless he had seen the planted fields.

In my limited experience I can recall no day's ride equal in simple natural beauty— not magnificence — and splendor of color to that down Clover Fork. There was scarcely a moment of the day when the scene did not call forth from us exclamations of surprise and delight. The road follows and often crosses the swift, clear, rocky stream. The variegated forest rises on either hand, but all along the banks vast trees

without underbrush dot the little intervales. Now
and then, in a level reach, where the road wound
through these monarch stems, and the water spread in
silver pools, the perspective was entrancing. But the
color! For always there were the rhododendrons,
either gleaming in masses of white and pink in the
recesses of the forest, or forming for us an *allée*, close
set, and uninterrupted for miles and miles ; shrubs
like trees, from twenty to thirty feet high, solid bou-
quets of blossoms, more abundant than any cultivated
parterre, more brilliant than the finest display in a
horticultural exhibition. There is an avenue of rhododendrons half a mile long at Hampton Court, which
is world-wide famous. It needs a day to ride through
the rhododendron avenue on Clover Fork, and the
wild and free beauty of it transcends all creations of
the gardener.

The inhabitants of the region are primitive and to
a considerable extent illiterate. But still many strong
and distinguished men have come from these mountain towns. Many families send their children away
to school, and there are fair schools at Barbersville,
Harlan Court-house, and in other places. Long isolated from the moving world, they have retained the
habits of the early settlers, and to some extent the
vernacular speech, though the dialect is not specially
marked. They have been until recently a self-sustaining people, raising and manufacturing nearly everything required by their limited knowledge and wants.
Not long ago the women spun and wove from cotton
and hemp and wool the household linen, the bed-
wear, and the clothes of the family. In many houses
the loom is still at work. The colors used for dyeing

were formerly all of home make except, perhaps, the
indigo; now they use what they call the "brought in"
dyes, bought at the stores; and prints and other
fabrics are largely taking the places of the home-made.
During the morning we stopped at one of the best
houses on the fork, a house with a small apple-orchard
in front, having a veranda, two large rooms, and a
porch and kitchen at the back. In the back porch
stood the loom with its web of half-finished cloth.
The farmer was of the age when men sun themselves
on the gallery and talk. His wife, an intelligent,
barefooted old woman, was still engaged in household
duties, but her weaving days were over. Her daughters did the weaving, and in one of the rooms were
the linsey-woolsey dresses hung up, and piles of gorgeous bed coverlets, enough to set up half a dozen
families. These are the treasures and heirlooms handed down from mother to daughter, for these hand-
made fabrics never wear out. Only eight of the
twelve children were at home. The youngest, the
baby, a sickly boy of twelve, was lounging about the
house. He could read a little, for he had been to
school a few weeks. Reading and writing were not
accomplishments in the family generally. The other
girls and boys were in the cornfield, and going to the
back door, I saw a line of them hoeing at the top of
the field. The field was literally so steep that they
might have rolled from the top to the bottom. The
mother called them in, and they lounged leisurely down,
the girls swinging themselves over the garden fence
with athletic ease. The four eldest were girls : one, a
woman of thirty-five, had lost her beauty, if she ever had
any, with her teeth; one, of thirty, recently married,

had a stately dignity and a certain nobility of figure; one, of sixteen, was undeniably pretty—almost the only woman entitled to this epithet that we saw in the whole journey. This household must have been an exception, for the girls usually marry very young. They were all, of course, barefooted. They were all laborers, and evidently took life seriously, and however much their knowledge of the world was limited, the household evidently respected itself. The elder girls were the weavers, and they showed a taste and skill in their fabrics that would be praised in the Orient or in Mexico. The designs and colors of the coverlets were ingenious and striking. There was a very handsome one in crimson, done in wavy lines and bizarre figures, that was called the Kentucky Beauty, or the Ocean Wave, that had a most brilliant effect. A simple, hospitable family this. The traveller may go all through this region with the certainty of kindly treatment, and in perfect security—if, I suppose, he is not a revenue officer, or sent in to survey land on which the inhabitants have squatted.

We came at night to Harlan Court-house, an old shabby hamlet, but growing and improving, having a new court-house and other signs of the awakening of the people to the wealth here in timber and mines. Here in a beautiful valley three streams—Poor, Martin, and Clover forks—unite to form the Cumberland. The place has fourteen "stores" and three taverns, the latter a trial to the traveller. Harlan has been one of the counties most conspicuous for lawlessness. The trouble is not simply individual wickedness, but the want of courage of public opinion, coupled with a general disrespect for authority. Plenty of people lament the state of things, but want the courage to take a public stand. The day before we reached the Court-house the man who killed his wife and his brother had his examination. His friends were able to take the case before a friendly justice instead of the judge. The facts sworn to were that in a drunken dispute over cards he tried to kill his son-in-law, who escaped out of the window, and that his wife and brother opposed him, and he killed them with his pistol. Therefore their deaths were accidental, and he was discharged. Many people said privately that he ought to be hanged, but there was entire public apathy over the affair. If Harlan had three or four resolute men who would take a public stand that this lawlessness must cease, they could carry the community with them. But the difficulty of enforcing law and order in some of these mountain counties is to find proper judges, prosecuting officers, and sheriffs. The officers are as likely as not to be the worst men in the community, and if they are not, they are likely to use their authority for satisfying their private grudges and revenges. Consequently men take the "law" into their own hands. The most personally courageous become bullies and the terror of the community. The worst citizens are not those who have killed most men, in the opinion of the public. It ought to be said that in some of the mountain counties there has been very little lawlessness, and in some it has been repressed by the local authorities, and there is great improvement on the whole. I was sorry not to meet a well-known character in the mountains, who has killed twenty-one men. He is a very agreeable "square" man, and I believe "high-toned," and it is the uni-

versal testimony that he never killed a man who did
not deserve killing, and whose death was a benefit to
the community. He is called, in the language of the
country, a "severe" man. In a little company that
assembled at the Harlan tavern were two elderly men,
who appeared to be on friendly terms enough. Their
sons had had a difficulty, and two boys out of each family had been killed not very long ago. The fathers
were not involved in the vendetta. About the old Harlan court-house a great many men have been killed
during court week in the past few years. The habit of
carrying pistols and knives, and whiskey, are the immediate causes of these deaths, but back of these is
the want of respect for law. At the ford of the Cumberland at Pineville was anchored a little house-boat,
which was nothing but a whiskey-shop. During our
absence a tragedy occurred there. The sheriff with a
posse went out to arrest some criminals in the mountain near. He secured his men, and was bringing
them into Pineville, when it occurred to him that it
would be a good plan to take a drink at the house-
boat. The whole party got into a quarrel over their
liquor, and in it the sheriff was killed and a couple of
men seriously wounded. A resolute surveyor, formerly a general in our army, surveying land in the neighborhood of Pineville, under a decree of the United
States Court, has for years carried on his work at the
personal peril of himself and his party. The squatters
not only pull up his stakes and destroy his work day
after day, but it was reported that they had shot at
his corps from the bushes. He can only go on with
his work by employing a large guard of armed men.

This state of things in eastern Kentucky will not

be radically changed until the railways enter it, and business and enterprise bring in law and order. The State Government cannot find native material for enforcing law, though there has been improvement within the past two years. I think no permanent gain can be expected till a new civilization comes in, though I heard of a bad community in one of the counties that had been quite subdued and changed by the labors of a devout and plain-spoken evangelist. So far as our party was concerned, we received nothing but kind treatment, and saw little evidences of demoralization, except that the young men usually were growing up to be " roughs," and liked to lounge about with shot-guns rather than work. But the report of men who have known the country for years was very unfavorable as to the general character of the people who live on the mountains and in the little valleys—that they were all ignorant; that the men generally were idle, vicious, and cowardly, and threw most of the hard labor in the field and house upon the women; that the killings are mostly done from ambush, and with no show for a fair fight. This is a tremendous indictment, and it is too sweeping to be sustained. The testimony of the gentlemen of our party, who thoroughly know this part of the State, contradicted it. The fact is there are two sorts of people in the mountains, as elsewhere.

The race of American mountaineers occupying the country from western North Carolina to eastern Kentucky is a curious study. Their origin is in doubt. They have developed their peculiarities in isolation. In this freedom stalwart and able men have been from time to time developed, but ignorance and freedom from the restraints of law have had their logical result as to the mass. I am told that this lawlessness has only existed since the war; that before, the people, though ignorant of letters, were peaceful. They had the good points of a simple people, and if they were not literate, they had abundant knowledge of their own region. During the war the mountaineers were carrying on a civil war at home. The opposing parties were not soldiers, but bushwhackers. Some of the best citizens were run out of the country, and never returned. The majority were Unionists, and in all the mountain region of eastern Kentucky I passed through there are few to-day who are politically Democrats. In the war, home-guards were organized, and these were little better than vigilance committees for private revenge. Disorder began with this private and partly patriotic warfare. After the war, when the bushwhackers got back to their cabins, the animosities were kept up, though I fancy that politics has little or nothing to do with them now. The habit of reckless shooting, of taking justice into private hands, is no doubt a relic of the disorganization during the war.

Worthless, good-for-nothing, irreclaimable, were words I often heard applied to people of this and that region. I am not so despondent of their future. Railways, trade, the sight of enterprise and industry, will do much with this material. Schools will do more, though it seems impossible to have efficient schools there at present. The people in their ignorance and their undeveloped country have a hard struggle for life. This region is, according to the census, the most prolific in the United States. The

26

girls marry young, bear many children, work like
galley-slaves, and at the time when women should be
at their best they fade, lose their teeth, become ugly,
and look old. One great cause of this is their lack of
proper nourishment. There is nothing unhealthy in
out-door work in moderation if the body is properly sustained by good food. But healthy, handsome
women are not possible without good fare. In a considerable part of eastern Kentucky (not I hear in
all) good wholesome cooking is unknown, and civilization is not possible without that. We passed a cabin
where a man was very ill with dysentery. No doctor
could be obtained, and perhaps that, considering what
the doctor might have been, was not a misfortune.
But he had no food fit for a sick man, and the women
of the house were utterly ignorant of the diet suitable
to a man in his state. I have no doubt that the abom-
inable cookery of the region has much to do with the
lawlessness, as it visibly has to do with the poor
physical condition.

The road down the Cumberland, in a valley at times
spreading out into fertile meadows, is nearly all the
way through magnificent forests, along hill-sides fit
for the vine, for fruit, and for pasture, while frequent
outcroppings of coal testify to the abundance of the
fuel that has been so long stored for the new civilization. These mountains would be profitable as sheep
pastures did not the inhabitants here, as elsewhere in
the United States, prefer to keep dogs rather than
sheep.

I have thus sketched hastily some of the capacities
of the Cumberland region. It is my belief that this
central and hitherto neglected portion of the United

States will soon become the theatre of vast and controlling industries.

I want space for more than a concluding word about western Kentucky, which deserves, both for its capacity and its recent improvements, a chapter to itself. There is a limestone area of some 10,000 square miles, with a soil hardly less fertile than that of the blue-grass region, a high agricultural development, and a population equal in all respects to that of the famous and historic grass country. Seven of the ten principal tobacco-producing counties in Kentucky and the largest Indian corn and wheat raising counties are in this part of the State. The western coal-field has both river and rail transportation, thick deposits of iron ore, and more level and richer farming lands than the eastern coal-field. Indeed, the agricultural development in this western coal region has attracted great attention.

Much also might be written of the remarkable progress of the towns of western Kentucky within the past few years. The increase in population is not more astonishing than the development of various industries. They show a vigorous, modern activity for which this part of the State has not, so far as I know, been generally credited. The traveller will find abundant evidence of it in Owensborough, Henderson, Hopkinsville, Bowling Green, and other places. As an illustration: Paducah, while doubling its population since 1880, has increased its manufacturing 150 per cent. The town had in 1880 twenty-six factories, with a capital of $600,000, employing 950 men; now it has fifty factories, with a cash capital of $2,000,000, employing 3250 men, engaged in a variety of industries—to which a large iron furnace is now being added. Taking it all together—variety of resources, excellence of climate, vigor of its people—one cannot escape the impression that Kentucky has a great future.

COMMENTS ON CANADA.

I.

THE area of the Dominion of Canada is larger than that of the United States, excluding Alaska. It is fair, however, in the comparison, to add Alaska, for Canada has in its domain enough arctic and practically uninhabitable land to offset Alaska. Excluding the boundary great lakes and rivers, Canada has 3,470,257 square miles of territory, or more than one-third of the entire British Empire; the United States has 3,026,494 square miles, or, adding Alaska (577,390), 3,603,884 square miles. From the eastern limit of the maritime provinces to Vancouver Island the distance is over three thousand five hundred miles. This whole distance is settled, but a considerable portion of it only by a thin skirmish line. I have seen a map, colored according to the maker's idea of fertility, on which Canada appears little more than a green flush along the northern boundary of the United States. With a territory equal to our own, Canada has the population of the single State of New York—about five millions.

Most of Canada lies north of the limit of what was reckoned agreeably habitable before it was discovered that climate depends largely on altitude, and that the isothermal lines and the lines of latitude do not coincide. The division between the two countries is, however, mainly a natural one, on a divide sloping one way to the arctic regions, the other way to the tropics. It would seem better map-making to us if our line fol-

lowed the northern mountains of Maine and included
New Brunswick and the other maritime provinces.
But it would seem a better rectification to Canadians
if their line included Maine with the harbor of Portland, and dipped down in the North-west so as to take
in the Red River of the North, and all the waters
discharging into Hudson's Bay.

The great bulk of Canada is on the arctic slope.
When we pass the highlands of New Hampshire, Vermont, and New York we fall away into a wide cham-
paign country. The only break in this is the Laurentian granite mountains, north of the St. Lawrence,
the oldest land above water, now degraded into hills
of from 1500 to 2000 feet in height. The central
mass of Canada consists of three great basins : that
portion of the St. Lawrence in the Dominion, 460,000
square miles; the Hudson's Bay, 2,000,000 square
miles; the Mackenzie, 550,000 square miles. That is
to say, of the 3,470,257 square miles of the area of
Canada, 3,010,000 have a northern slope.

This decrease in altitude from our northern boundary makes Canada a possible nation. The Rocky
Mountains fall away north into the Mackenzie plain.
The highest altitude attained by the Union Pacific
Railroad is 8240 feet; the highest of the Canadian
Pacific is 5296; and a line of railway still farther
north, from the North Saskatchewan region, can, and
doubtless some time will, reach the Pacific without
any obstruction by the Rockies and the Selkirks. In
estimating, therefore, the capacity of Canada for sustaining a large population we have to remember that
the greater portion of it is but little above the sea-level;
that the climate of the interior is modified by vast

bodies of water; that the maximum summer heat of
Montreal and Quebec exceeds that of New York; and
that there is a vast region east of the Rockies and
north of the Canadian Pacific Railway, not only the
plains drained by the two branches of the Saskatchewan, but those drained by the Peace River still farther
north, which have a fair share of summer weather, and
winters much milder than are enjoyed in our Territories farther south but higher in altitude. The summers of this vast region are by all reports most
agreeable, warm days and refreshing nights, with a
stimulating atmosphere; winters with little snow, and
usually bright and pleasant, occasional falls of the
thermometer for two or three days to arctic temperature, but as certain a recovery to mildness by the
"Chinook" or Pacific winds. It is estimated that the
plains of the Saskatchewan—500,000 square miles—are
capable of sustaining a population of thirty millions.
But nature there must call forth a good deal of human
energy and endurance. There is no doubt that frosts
are liable to come very late in the spring and very
early in the autumn; that persistent winds are hostile
to the growth of trees; and that varieties of hardy
cereals and fruits must be selected for success in agriculture and horticulture. The winters are exceedingly severe on all the prairies east of Winnipeg, and
westward on the Canadian Pacific as far as Medicine
Hat, the crossing of the South Saskatchewan. Heavy
items in the cost of living there must always be fuel,
warm clothing, and solid houses. Fortunately the
region has an abundance of lignite and extensive fields
of easily workable coal.

Canada is really two countries, separated from each

other by the vast rocky wilderness between the lakes
and James Bay. For a thousand miles west of Ottawa, till the Manitoba prairie is reached, the traveller
on the line of the railway sees little but granite rock
and stunted balsams, larches, and poplars—a dreary
region, impossible to attract settlers. Copper and
other minerals there are; and in the region north of
Lake Superior there is no doubt timber, and arable
land is spoken of ; but the country is really unknown.
Portions of this land, like that about Lake Nipigon,
offer attractions to sportsmen. Lake navigation is
impracticable about four months in the year, so that
Canada seems to depend for political and commercial
unity upon a telegraph wire and two steel rails running a thousand miles through a region where local
traffic is at present insignificant.

The present government of Canada is an evolution
on British lines, modified by the example of the republic of the United States. In form the resemblances
are striking to the United States, but underneath, the
differences are radical. There is a supreme federal
government, comprehending a union of provinces,
each having its local government. But the union in
the two countries was brought about in a different
way, and the restrictive powers have a different origin.
In the one, power descends from the Crown; in the
other, it originates with the people. In the Dominion
Government all the powers not delegated to the
provinces are held by the Federal Government. In
the United States, all the powers not delegated to the
Federal Government by the States are held by the
States. In the United States, delegates from the colonies, specially elected for the purpose, met to put in

shape a union already a necessity of the internal and
external situation. And the union expressed in the
Constitution was accepted by the popular vote in each
State. In the provinces of Canada there was a long
and successful struggle for responsible government.
The first union was of the two Canadas, in 1840; that
is, of the provinces of Upper and Lower Canada—
Ontario and Quebec—with Parliaments sitting sometimes in Quebec and sometimes in Toronto, and at
last in Ottawa, a site selected by the Queen. This
Government was carried on with increasing friction.
There is not space here to sketch the politics of
this epoch. Many causes contributed to this friction,
but the leading ones were the antagonism of French
and English ideas, the superior advance in wealth
and population of Ontario over Quebec, and the
resistance of what was called French domination.
At length, in 1863–64, the two parties, the Conservatives and the Liberals (or, in the political nomen-
clature of the day, the "Tories" and the "Grits"
—*i. e.*, those of "clear grit"), were so evenly divided that a dead-lock occurred, neither was able to
carry on the government, and a coalition ministry
was formed. Then the subject of colonial confederation was actively agitated. Nova Scotia and New
Brunswick contemplated a legislative union of the
maritime provinces, and a conference was called at
Charlottetown, Prince Edward Island, in the summer
of 1864. Having in view a more comprehensive union, the Canadian Government sought and obtained
admission to this conference, which was soon swal-
lowed up in a larger scheme, and a conference of all
the colonies was appointed to be held at Quebec in

October. Delegates, thirty-three in number, were present from all the provinces, probably sent by the respective legislatures or governments, for I find no note of a popular election. The result of this conference was the adoption of resolutions as a basis of an act of confederation. The Canadian Parliament adopted this scheme after a protracted debate. But the maritime provinces stood out. Meantime the Civil War in the United States, the Fenian invasion, and the abrogation of the reciprocity treaty fostered a spirit of Canadian nationality, and discouraged whatever feeling existed for annexation to the United States. The colonies, therefore, with more or less willingness, came into the plan, and in 1867 the English Parliament passed the British North American Act, which is the charter of the Dominion. It established the union of the provinces of Canada, Nova Scotia, and New Brunswick, and provided for the admission to the union of the other parts of British North America; that is, Prince Edward Island, the Hudson Bay Territory, British Columbia, and Newfoundland, with its dependency Labrador. Nova Scotia was, however, still dissatisfied with the terms of the union, and was only reconciled on the granting of additional annual subsidies.

In 1868, by Act of the British Parliament, the Hudson's Bay Company surrendered to the Crown its territorial rights over the vast region it controlled, in consideration of £300,000 sterling, grants of land around its trading posts to the extent of fifty thousand acres in all, and one-twentieth of all the fertile land south of the north branch of the Saskatchewan, retaining its privileges of trade, without its exclusive monopoly. The attempt of the Dominion Government to take possession of this north-west territory (Manitoba was created a province July 15, 1870) was met by the rising of the squatters and half-breeds under Louis Riel in 1869–70. Riel formed a provisional government, and proceeded with a high hand to banish persons and confiscate property, and on a drumhead court-martial put to death Thomas Scott, a Canadian militia officer. The murder of Scott provoked intense excitement throughout Canada, especially in Ontario. Colonel Garnet Wolseley's expedition to Fort Garry (now Winnipeg) followed, and the Government authority was restored. Riel and his squatter confederates fled, and he was subsequently pardoned.

In 1871 British Columbia was admitted into the Dominion. In 1873 Prince Edward Island came in. The original Act for establishing the province of Manitoba provided for a Lieutenant-governor, a Legislative Council, and an elected Legislative Assembly. In 1876 Manitoba abolished the Council, and the government took its present form of a Lieutenant-governor and one Assembly. By subsequent legislation of the Dominion the district of Keewatin was created out of the eastern portion of the north-west territory, under the jurisdiction of the Lieutenant-governor of Manitoba, *ex officio*. The Territories of Assiniboin, Alberta, and Saskatchewan have been organized into a Territory called the North-west Territory, with a Lieutenant-governor and Council, and a representative in Parliament, the capital being Regina. Outside of this Territory, to the northward, lies Athabasca, of which the Lieutenant-governor at Regina is *ex*

officio ruler.   Newfoundland still remains independent,
although negotiations for union were revived in 1888.
Some years ago overtures were made for taking in
Jamaica to the union, and a delegation from that
island visited Ottawa; but nothing came of the pro-
posal.   It was said that the Jamaica delegates thought
the Dominion debt too large.

The Dominion of Canada, therefore, has a central
government at Ottawa, and is composed of the provinces of Nova Scotia (including Cape Breton), New
Brunswick, Prince Edward Island, Quebec, Ontario,
Manitoba, British Columbia, and the North-west Territory.

It has been necessary to speak in this brief detail
of the manner of the formation of the union in
order to understand the politics of Canada.   For
there are radicals in the Liberal party who still regard the union as forced and artificial, and say that
the provinces outside of Ontario and Quebec were
brought in only by the promise of local railways and
the payment of large subsidies.   And this idea more
or less influences the opposition to the "strong government" at Ottawa.   I do not say that the Liberals
oppose the formation of a "nation"; but they are
critics of its methods, and array themselves for provincial rights as against federal consolidation.

The Federal Government consists of the Queen, the
Senate, and the House of Commons.   The Queen is
represented by the Governor-general, who is paid by
Canada a salary of fifty thousand dollars a year.   He
has his personal staff, and is aided and advised by
a council, called the Queen's Privy Council of Canada, thirteen members, constituting the ministry, who

must be sustained by a Parliamentary majority. The English model is exactly followed. The Governor has nominally the power of veto, but his use of it is as much in abeyance as is the Queen's prerogative in regard to Acts of Parliament. The premier is in fact the ruler, but his power depends upon possessing a majority in the House of Commons. This responsible government, therefore, more quickly responds to popular action than ours. The Senators are chosen for life, and are in fact appointed by the premier in power. The House of Commons is elected for five years, unless Parliament is sooner dissolved, and according to a ratio of population to correspond with the province of Quebec, which has always the fixed number of sixty-five members. The voter for members of Parliament must have certain property qualifications, as owner or tenant, or, if in a city or town, as earning three hundred dollars a year—qualifications so low as practically to exclude no one who is not an idler and a waif; the Indian may vote (though not in the Territories), but the Mongolian or Chinese is excluded. Members of the House may be returned by any constituency in the Dominion without reference to residence. All bills affecting taxation or revenue must originate in the House, and be recommended by a message from the Governor-general. The Government introduces bills, and takes the responsibility of them. The premier is leader of the House; there is also a recognized leader of the Opposition. In case the Government cannot command a majority it resigns, and the Governor-general forms a new cabinet. In theory, also, if the Crown (represented by the Governor-general) should resort to the extreme exercise of its prerogative in refusing the advice of its ministers, the ministers must submit, or resign and give place to others.

The Federal Government has all powers not granted expressly to the provinces. In practice its jurisdiction extends over the public debt, expenditure, and public loans; treaties; customs and excise duties; trade and commerce ; navigation, shipping, and fisheries ; light-houses and harbors; the postal, naval, and military services; public statistics; monetary institutions, banks, banking, currency, coining (but all coining is done in England); insolvency; criminal law; marriage and divorce; public works, railways, and canals.

The provinces have no militia; that all belongs to the Dominion. Marriage is solemnized according to provincial regulations, but the power of divorce exists in Canada in the Federal Parliament only, except in the province of New Brunswick. This province has a court of divorce and matrimonial causes, with a single judge, a survival of pre-confederation times, which grants divorces *a vinculo* for scriptural causes, and *a mensâ et thoro* for desertion or cruelty, with right of appeal to the Supreme Court of the province and to the Privy Council of the Dominion. Criminal law is one all over the Dominion, but there is no law against adultery or incest. The British Act contains no provision analogous to that in the Constitution of the United States which forbids any State to pass a law impairing the obligation of contracts — a serious defect.

The Federal Government has a Supreme Court, consisting of a chief-justice and five puisne judges, which has original jurisdiction in civil suits involving the validity of Dominion and provincial acts, and appellate in appeals from the provincial courts. The Federal Government appoints and pays the judges of the Superior, District, and County courts of the provinces; but the provinces may constitute, maintain, and organize provincial courts, civil and criminal, including procedure in civil matters in those courts. But as the provinces cannot appoint any judicial officer above the rank of magistrate, it may happen that a constituted court may be inoperative for want of a judge. This is one of the points of friction between the federal and provincial authorities, and in the fall of 1888 it led to the trouble in Quebec, when the Ottawa cabinet disallowed the appointment of two provincial judges made by the Quebec premier.

The Dominion has another power unknown to our Constitution; that is, disallowance or veto of provincial acts. This power is regarded with great jealousy by the provinces. It is claimed by one party that it should only be exercised on the ground of unconstitutionality; by the other, that it may be exercised in the interest of the Dominion generally. As a matter of fact it has been sometimes exercised in cases that the special province felt to be an interference with its rights.

Another cause of friction, aggravated by the power of disallowance, has arisen from conflict in jurisdiction as to railways. Both the Dominion and the provinces may charter and build railways. But the British Act forbids the province to legislate as to lines of steam or other ships, railways, canals, and telegraphs connecting the province with any other province, or extending beyond its limits, or any such

27

work actually within the limits which the Canadian Parliament may declare for the general advantage of Canada; that is, declare it to be a Dominion work. A promoter, therefore, cannot tell with any certainty what a charter is worth, or who will have jurisdiction over it. The trouble in Manitoba in the fall of 1888 between the province and the Canadian Pacific road (which is a Dominion road in the meaning of the Act) could scarcely have arisen if the definition of Dominion and provincial rights had been clearer.

But a more serious cause of weakness to the provinces and embarrassment to the Dominion is in the provincial subsidies. When the present confederation was formed the Dominion took on the provincial debts up to a certain amount. It also agreed to pay annually to each province, in half-yearly payments, a subsidy. By the British Act this annual payment was $80,000 to Ontario, $70,000 to Quebec, $60,000 to Nova Scotia, $50,000 to New Brunswick, with something additional to the last two. In 1886–87 the subsidies paid to all the provinces amounted to $4,169,341. This is as if the United States should undertake to raise a fixed revenue to distribute among the States— a proceeding alien to our ideas of the true function of the General Government, and certain to lead to State demoralization, and tending directly to undermine its self-support and dignity. It is an idea quite foreign to the conception of political economy that it is best for people to earn what they spend, and only spend what they earn. This subsidy under the Act was a grant equal to eighty cents a head of the population. Besides this there is given to each province an annual allowance for government; also an annual allowance of interest on the amount of debt allowed where the province has not reached the limit of the authorized debt. It is the theory of the Federal Government that in taking on these pecuniary burdens of the provinces they will individually feel them less, and that if money is to be raised the Dominion can procure it on more favorable terms than the provinces. The system, nevertheless, seems vicious to our apprehension, for nothing is clearer to us than that neither the State nor the general welfare would be promoted if the States were pensioners of the General Government.

The provinces are miniature copies of the Dominion Government. Each has a Lieutenant-governor, who is appointed by the Ottawa Governor-general and ministry (that is, in fact, by the premier), whose salary is paid by the Dominion Parliament. In theory he represents the Crown, and is above parties. He forms his cabinet out of the party in majority in the elective Assembly. Each province has an elective Assembly, and most of them have two Houses, one of which is a Senate appointed for life. The provincial cabinet has a premier, who is the leader of the House, and the Opposition is represented by a recognized leader. The Government is as responsible as the Federal Government. This organization of recognized and responsible leaders greatly facilitates the despatch of public business. Affairs are brought to a direct issue; and if the Government cannot carry its measures, or a dead-lock occurs, the ministry is changed, or an appeal is had to the people. Canadian statesmen point to the want of responsibility in the conduct of public business in our House, and the dead-lock between the Senate and the House, as a state of things that needs a remedy.

The provinces retain possession of the public lands belonging to them at the time of confederation; Manitoba, which had none when it was created a province out of north-west territory, has since had a gift of swamp lands from the Dominion. Emigration and immigration are subjects of both federal and provincial legislation, but provincial laws must not conflict with federal laws.

The provinces appoint all officers for the adminis-tration of justice except judges, and are charged with the general administration of justice and the mainten-ance of civil and criminal courts; they control jails, prisons, and reformatories, but not the penitentiaries, to which convicts sentenced for over two years must be committed. They control also asylums and chari-table institutions, all strictly municipal institutions, local works, the solemnization of marriage, property and civil rights, and shop, tavern, and other licenses. In regard to the latter, a conflict of jurisdiction arose on the passage in 1878 by the Canadian Parliament of a temperance Act. The result of judicial and Privy Council decisions on this was to sustain the right of the Dominion to legislate on temperance, but to give to the provincial legislatures the right to deal with the subject of licenses for the sale of liquors. In the Territories prohibition prevails under the federal statutes, modified by the right of the Lieutenant-governor to grant special permits. The effect of the general law has been most salutary in excluding liquor from the Indians.

But the most important subject left to the provinces

is education, over which they have exclusive control. What this means we shall see when we come to consider the provinces of Quebec and Ontario as illustrations.

Broadly stated, Canada has representative government by ministers responsible to the people, a federal government charged with the general good of the whole, and provincial governments attending to local interests. It differs widely from the English Government in subjects remitted to the provincial legislatures and in the freedom of the municipalities, so that Canada has self-government comparable to that in the United States. Two striking limitations are that the provinces cannot keep a militia force, and that the provinces have no power of final legislation, every Act being subject to Dominion revision and veto.

The two parties are arranged on general lines that we might expect from the organization of the central and the local governments. The Conservative, which calls itself Liberal-Conservative, inclines to the consolidation and increase of federal power; the Liberal (styled the "Grits") is what we would call a State-rights party. Curiously enough, while the Ottawa Government is Conservative, and the ministry of Sir John A. Macdonald is sustained by a handsome majority, all the provincial governments are at present Liberal. The Conservatives say that this is because the opinion of the country sustains the general Conservative policy for the development of the Dominion, so that the same constituency will elect a Conservative member to the Dominion House and a Liberal member to the provincial House. The Liberals say that this result in some cases is brought about by the manner

in which the central Government has arranged the
voting districts for the central Parliament, which do
not coincide with the provincial districts. There is
no doubt some truth in this, but I believe that at
present the sentiment of nationality is what sustains
the Conservative majority in the Ottawa Government.

The general policy of the Conservative Government
may fairly be described as one for the rapid development of the country. This leads it to desire more
federal power, and there are some leading spirits who,
although content with the present Constitution, would
not oppose a legislative union of all the provinces.
The policy of "development" led the party to adopt
the present moderate protective tariff. It led it to
the building of railways, to the granting of subsidies,
in money and in land, to railways, to the subsidizing
of steamship lines, to the active stimulation of immigration by offering extraordinary inducements to settlers. Having a vast domain, sparsely settled, but
capable of sustaining a population not less dense than
that in the northern parts of Europe, the ambition of
the Conservative statesmen has been to open up the resources of the country and to plant a powerful nation.
The Liberal criticism of this programme I shall speak
of later. At present it is sufficient to say that the
tariff did stimulate and build up manufactories in cotton, leather, iron, including implements of agriculture,
to the extent that they were more than able to supply
the Canadian market. As an item, after the abrogation of the reciprocity treaty, the factories of Ontario
were able successfully to compete with the United
States in the supply of agricultural implements to the
great North-west, and in fact to take the market. I

think it cannot be denied that the protective tariff did
not only build up home industries, but did give an extraordinary stimulus to the general business of the
Dominion.

Under this policy of development and subsidies the
Dominion has been accumulating a debt, which now
reaches something over $260,000,000. Before esti-
mating the comparative size of this debt, the statis-
tician wants to see whether this debt and the provincial debts together equal, per capita, the federal and
State debts together of the United States. It is estimated by one authority that the public lands of the Dominion could pay the debt, and it is noted that it has
mainly been made for railways, canals, and other permanent improvements, and not in offensive or defensive
wars. The statistical record of 1887 estimates that the
provincial debts added to the public debt give a per capita of $48.88. The same year the united debts of States
and general government in the United States gave a
per capita of $32, but, the municipal and county debts
added, the per capita would be $55. If the unreport-
ed municipal debts in Canada were added, I suppose
the per capita would somewhat exceed that in the
United States.

Before glancing at the development and condition
of Canada in confederation we will complete the
official outline by a reference to the civil service and
to the militia. The British Government has withdrawn all the imperial troops from Canada except
a small garrison at Halifax, and a naval establishment
there and at Victoria. The Queen is commander-in-
chief of all the military and naval forces in Canada,
but the control of the same is in the Dominion Parlia-

ment. The general of the military force is a British
officer. There are permanent corps and schools of instruction in various places, amounting in all to about
950 men, exclusive of officers, and the number is limited to 1000. There is a royal military school at Kings-
ton, with about 80 cadets. The active militia, December 31, 1887, in all the provinces, the whole being
under Dominion control, amounted to 38,152. The
military expenditure that year was $1,281,255. The
diminishing military pensions of that year amounted
to $35,100. The reserve militia includes all the male
inhabitants of the age of eighteen and under sixty.
In 1887 the total active cavalry was under 2000.

The members of the civil service are nearly all Canadians. In the Federal Government and in the provinces there is an organized system; the federal system
has been constantly amended, and is not yet free of
recognized defects. The main points of excellence,
more or less perfectly attained, may be stated to be a
decent entrance examination for all, a special, strict,
and particular examination for some who are to un-
dertake technical duties, and a secure tenure of office.
The federal Act of 1886, which has since been amended
in details, was not arrived at without many experiments and the accumulation of testimonies and diverse reports ; and it did not follow exactly the
majority report of 1881, but leaned too much, in the
judgment of many, to the English system, the working
of which has not been satisfactory. The main features of the Act, omitting details, are these: The service
has two divisions—first, deputy heads of departments
and employés in the Ottawa departments ; second,
others than those employed in Ottawa departments,

including customs officials, inland revenue officials, post-office inspectors, railway mail clerks, city postmasters, their assistants, clerks, and carriers, and inspector of penitentiaries. A board of three examiners is appointed by the Governor in council. All appointments shall be "during pleasure," and no persons shall be appointed or promoted to any place below that of deputy head unless he has passed the requisite examination and served the probationary term of six months; he must not be over thirty-five years old for appointment in Ottawa departments (this limit is not fixed for the "outside" appointments), nor under fifteen in a lower grade than third-class clerk, nor under eighteen in other cases. Appointees must be sound in health and of good character. Women are not appointed. A deputy head may be removed "on pleasure," but the reasons for the removal must be laid before both Houses of Parliament. Appointments may be made without reference to age on the report of the deputy head, on account of technical or professional qualifications or the public interest. City postmasters, and such officers as inspectors and collectors, may be appointed without examination or reference to the rules for promotion. Examinations are dispensed with in other special cases. Removals may be made by the Governor in council. Reports of all examinations and of the entire civil service list must be laid before Parliament each session. Amendments have been made to the law in the direction of relieving from examination on their promotion men who have been long in the service, and an amendment of last session omitted some examinations altogether.

It must be stated also that the service is not free from

favoritism, and that influence is used, if not always necessary, to get in and to get on in it. The law has been gone around by means of the plea of "special qualifications," and this evasion has sometimes been considered a political necessity on account of service to a minister or to the party generally. I suppose that the party in power favors its own adherents. The competitive system of England has a mischievous effect in the encouragement of the examinations to direct studies towards a service which nine in ten of the applicants will never reach. This evil, of numbers qualified but not appointed, has grown so great in Canada that it has lately been ordered that there shall be only one examination in each year.

The federal pension system cannot be considered settled. A man may be superannuated at any time, but by custom, not law, he retires at the full age of sixty. While in service he pays a superannuation allowance of two and a half per cent. on his salary for thirty-five years; after that, no more. If he is superannuated after ten years' service, say, he gets one-fiftieth of his salary for each year. If he is not in fault in any way, Government may add ten years more to his service, so as to give him a larger allowance. If a man serves the full term of thirty-five years he gets thirty-five fiftieths of his salary in pension. This pension system, recognized as essential to a good civil service, has this weakness : A man pays two and a half per cent. of his salary for twenty years. If the salary is $3000, his payments would have amounted to $1200, with interest, in that time. If he then dies, his widow gets only two months' salary as a solatium; all the rest is lost to her, and goes to the superannuation fund of the treasury. Or, a man is superannuated after thirty-five years; he has paid perhaps $2100, with interest; he draws, say, one year's superannuative allowance, and then dies. His family get nothing at all, not even the two months' salary they would have had if he had died in service. This is illogical and unjust. If the two and a half per cent. had been put into a life policy, the insurance being undertaken by the Government, a decent sum would have been realized at death.

A civil service is also established in the provinces. That in Quebec is better organized than the federal; the Government adds to the pension fund one-fourth of that retained from the salaries, and half pensions are extended to widows and children.

It will be seen that this pension is an essential part of the civil service system, and the method of it is at once a sort of insurance and a stimulation to faithful service. Good service is a constant inducement to retention, to promotion, and to increase of pension. The Canadians say that the systems work well both in the federal and provincial services, and in this respect, as well as in the matter of responsible government, they think their government superior to ours.

The policy of the Dominion Government, when confederation had given it the form and territory of a great nation, was to develop this into reality and solidity by creating industries, building railways, and filling up the country with settlers. As to the means of carrying out this the two parties differed somewhat. The Conservatives favored active stimulation to the extent of drawing on the future; the Liberals favored what they call a more natural if a slower growth. To illustrate: the Conservatives enacted a tariff, which was protective, to build up industries, and it is now continued, as in their view a necessity for raising the revenue needed for government expenses and for the development of the country. The Liberals favored a low tariff, and in the main the principles of free-trade. It might be impertinence to attempt to say now whether the Canadian affiliations are with the Democratic or the Republican party in the United States, but it is historical to say that for the most part the Unionists had not the sympathy of the Conservatives during our Civil War, and that they had the sympathy of the Liberals generally, and that the sympathy of the Liberals continued with the Republican party down to the Presidential campaign of 1884. It seemed to the Conservatives a necessity for the unity and growth of the Dominion to push railway construction. The Liberals, if I understand their policy, opposed mortgaging the future, and would rather let railways spring from local action and local necessity throughout the Dominion. But whatever the policies of parties may be, the Conservative Government has promoted by subsidies of money and grants of land all the great so-called Dominion railways. The chief of these in national importance, because it crosses the continent, is the Canadian Pacific. In order that I might understand its relation to the development of the country, and have some comprehension of the extent of Canadian territory, I made the journey on this line—3000 miles—from Montreal to Vancouver.

The Canadians have contributed liberally to the promotion of railways. The Hand-book of 1886 says that $187,000,000 have been given by the governments (federal and provincial) and by the municipalities towards the construction of the 13,000 miles of railways within the Dominion. The same authority says that from 1881 to July, 1885, the Federal Government gave $74,500,000 to the Canadian Pacific. The Conservatives like to note that the railway development corresponds with the political life of Sir John A. Macdonald, for upon his entrance upon political life in 1844 there were only fourteen miles of railway in operation.

The Federal Government began surveys for the Canadian Pacific road in 1871, a company was chartered the same year to build it, but no results followed. The Government then began the construction itself, and built several disconnected sections. The present company was chartered in 1880. The Dominion Government granted it a subsidy of $25,000,000 and 25,000,000 acres of land, and transferred to it, free of cost, 713 miles of railway which had been built by the Government, at a cost of about $35,000,000. In November, 1885, considerably inside the time of contract, the road was finished to the Pacific, and in 1886 cars were running regularly its entire length. In point of time, and considering the substantial character of the road, it is a marvellous achievement. Subsequently, in order to obtain a line from Montreal to the maritime ports, a subsidy of $186,000 per annum for a term of twenty years was granted to the Atlantic and North-west Railway Company, which undertook to build or acquire a line from Montreal *via* Sherbrooke, and across the State of Maine to St. John, St. Andrews, and Halifax. This is one of the leased lines of the Canadian Pacific, which finished it last December.

The main line, from Quebec to Montreal and Vancouver, is 3065 miles. The leased lines measure 2412 miles, one under construction 112, making a total mileage of 5589. Adding to this the lines in which the company's influence amounts to a control (including those on American soil to St. Paul and Chicago), the total mileage of the company is over 6500. The branch lines, built or acquired in Quebec, Ontario, and Manitoba, are all necessary feeders to the main line. The cost of the Canadian Pacific, including the line built by the Government and acquired (not leased) lines, is: Cost of road, $170,689,629.51; equipment, $10,570,933.22; amount of deposit with Government to guarantee three per cent. on capital stock until August 17, 1893, $10,310,954.75. Total, $191,571,517.48.

Without going into the financial statement, nor appending the leases and guarantees, any further than to note that the capital stock is $65,000,000 and the first mortgage bonds (five per cent.) are $34,999,633, it is only necessary to say that in the report the capital foots up $112,908,019. The total earnings for 1885 were $8,368,493; for 1886, $10,081,803; for 1887, $11,606,412, while the working expenses for 1887 were $8,102,294. The gross earnings for 1888 are about $14,000,000, and the net earnings about $4,000,000. These figures show the steady growth of business.

Being a Dominion road, and favored, the company had a monopoly in Manitoba for building roads south of its line and roads connecting with foreign lines. This monopoly was surrendered in 1887 upon agreement of the Dominion Government to guarantee 3½ per cent. interest on $15,000,000 of the company's land grant bonds for fifty years. The company has

paid its debt to the Government, partly by surrender
of a portion of its lands, and now absolutely owns its
entire line free of Government obligations. It has,
however, a claim upon the Government of something
like six million dollars, now in litigation, on portions
of the mountain sections of the road built by the
Government, which are not up to the standard guaranteed in the contract with the company.

The road was extended to the Pacific as a necessity
of the national development, and the present Government is convinced that it is worth to the country
all it has cost. The Liberals' criticism is that the Government has spent a vast sum for what it can show
no assets, and that it has enriched a private company instead of owning the road itself. The property
is no doubt a good one, for the road is well built as
to grades and road-bed, excellently equipped, and notwithstanding the heavy Lake Superior and mountain
work, at a less cost than some roads that preceded it.

The full significance of this transcontinental line
to Canada, Great Britain, and the United States will
appear upon emphasizing the value of the line across
the State of Maine to connect with St. John and Halifax; upon the fact that its western terminus is in regular steamer communication with Hong-Kong *via* Yokohama; that the company is building new and swift
steamers for this line, to which the British Government has granted an annual subsidy of £60,000, and
the Dominion one of $15,000; that a line will run
from Vancouver to Australia; and that a part of this
round-the-world route is to be a line of fast steamers
between Halifax and England. The Canadian Pacific
is England's shortest route to her Pacific colonies,

and to Japan and China; and in case of a blockade in the Suez Canal it would become of the first importance for Australia and India. It is noted as significant by an enthusiast of the line that the first loaded train that passed over its entire length carried British naval stores transferred from Quebec to Vancouver, and that the first car of merchandise was a cargo of Jamaica sugar refined at Halifax and sent to British Columbia.

II.

WE left Montreal, attached to the regular train, on the evening of September 22d. The company runs six through trains a week, omitting the despatch of a train on Sunday from each terminus. The time is six days and five nights. We travelled in the private car of Mr. T. G. Shaughnessy, the manager, who was on a tour of inspection, and took it leisurely, stopping at points of interest on the way. The weather was bad, rainy and cold, in eastern Canada, as it was all over New England, and as it continued to be through September and October. During our absence there was snow both in Montreal and Quebec. We passed out of the rain into lovely weather north of Lake Superior; encountered rain again at Winnipeg; but a hundred miles west of there, on the prairie, we were blessed with as delightful weather as the globe can furnish, which continued all through the remainder of the trip until our return to Montreal, October 12th. The climate just east of the Rocky Mountains was a little warmer than was needed for comfort (at the time Ontario and Quebec had snow), but the air was always pure and exhilarating; and all through the mountains

we had the perfection of lovely days. On the Pacific
it was still the dry season, though the autumn rains,
which continue all winter, with scarcely any snow,
were not far off. For mere physical pleasure of living and breathing, I know no atmosphere superior to
that we encountered on the rolling lands east of the
Rockies.

Between Ottawa and Winnipeg (from midnight of
the 22d till the morning of the 25th) there is not
much to interest the tourist, unless he is engaged in
lumbering or mining. What we saw was mainly a
monotonous wilderness of rocks and small poplars,
though the country has agricultural capacities after
leaving Rat Portage (north of Lake of the Woods),
just before coming upon the Manitoba prairies. There
were more new villages and greater crowds of people
at the stations than I expected. From Sudbury the
company runs a line to the Sault Sainte Marie to connect with lines it controls to Duluth and St. Paul.
At Port Arthur and Fort William is evidence of
great transportation activity, and all along the Lake
Superior Division there are signs that the expectations of profitable business in lumber and minerals
will be realized. At Port Arthur we strike the
Western Division. On the Western, Mountain, and
Pacific divisions the company has adopted the 24-
hour system, by which A.M. and P.M. are abolished,
and the hours from noon till midnight are counted
as from 12 to 24 o'clock. For instance, the train
reaches Eagle River at 24.55, Winnipeg at 9.30, and
Brandon at 16.10.

At Winnipeg we come into the real North-west,
and a condition of soil, climate, and political develop-
28

ment as different from eastern Canada as Montana is from New England. This town, at the junction of the Red and Assiniboin rivers, in a valley which is one of the finest wheat-producing sections of the world, is a very important place. Railways, built and projected, radiate from it like spokes from a wheel hub. Its growth has been marvellous. Formerly known as Fort Garry, the chief post of the Hudson's Bay Company, it had in 1871 a population of only one hundred. It is now the capital of the province of Manitoba, contains the chief workshops of the Canadian Pacific between Montreal and Vancouver, and has a population of 25,000. It is laid out on a grand scale, with very broad streets—Main Street is 200 feet wide—has many substantial public and business buildings, street-cars, and electric-lights, and abundant facilities for trade. At present it is in a condition of subsided "boom;" the whole province has not more than 120,-000 people, and the city for that number is out of proportion. Winnipeg must wait a little for the development of the country. It seems to the people that the town would start up again if it had more railroads. Among the projects much discussed is a road northward between Lake Winnipeg and Lake Manitoba, turning eastward to York Factory on Hudson's Bay. The idea is to reach a short water route to Europe. From all the testimony I have read as to ice in Hudson's Bay harbors and in the straits, the short period the straits are open, and the uncertainty from year to year as to the months they will be open, this route seems chimerical. But it does not seem so to its advocates, and there is no doubt that a portion of the line between the lakes first named would develop a good country and pay. A more important line—indeed, of the first importance—is built for 200 miles north-west from Portage la Prairie, destined to go to Prince Albert, on the North Saskatchewan. This is the Manitoba and North-west, and it makes its connection from Portage la Prairie with Winnipeg over the Canadian Pacific. An antagonism has grown up in Manitoba towards the Canadian Pacific. This arose from the monopoly privileges enjoyed by it as a Dominion road. The province could build no road with extra-territorial connections. This monopoly was surrendered in consideration of the guarantee spoken of from the Government. The people of Winnipeg also say that the company discriminated against them in the matter of rates, and that the province must have a competing outlet. The company says that it did not discriminate, but treated Winnipeg like other towns on the line, having an eye to the development of the whole prairie region, and that the trouble was that it refused to discriminate in favor of Winnipeg, so that it might become the distributing-point of the whole North-west. Whatever the truth may be, the province grew increasingly restless, and determined to build another road. The Canadian Pacific has two lines on either side of the Red River, connecting at Emerson and Gretna with the Red River branches of the St. Paul, Minneapolis, and Manitoba. It has also two branches running westward south of its main line, penetrating the fertile wheat-fields of Manitoba. The province graded a third road, paralleling the two to the border, and the river, southward from Winnipeg to the border connecting there with a branch of the Northern Pacific, which was eager to reach the rich

wheat-fields of the North-west. The provincial Red
River Railway also proposed to cross the branches of
the Canadian Pacific, and connect at Portage la Prairie
with the Manitoba and North-west. The Canadian
Pacific, which had offered to sell to the province its
Emerson branch, saying that there was not business
enough for three parallel routes, insisted upon its legal
rights and resisted this crossing. Hence the provincial
and railroad conflict of the fall of 1888. The province
built the new road, but it was alleged that the Northern Pacific was the real party, and that Manitoba has
so far put itself into the hands of that corporation.
There can be no doubt that Manitoba will have its
road and connect the Northern Pacific with the Saskatchewan country, and very likely will parallel the
main line of the Canadian Pacific. But whether it
will get from the Northern Pacific the relief it thought
itself refused by the Canadian, many people in Winnipeg begin to doubt; for however eager rival railways may be for new territory, they are apt to come
to an understanding in order to keep up profitable
rates. They must live.

I went down on the southern branch of the Canadian Pacific, which runs west, not far from our border, as far as Boissevain. It is a magnificent wheat
country, and already very well settled and sprinkled
with villages. The whole prairie was covered with
yellow wheat-stacks, and teams loaded with wheat
were wending their way from all directions to the elevators on the line. There has been quite an emigration of Russian Mennonites to this region, said to be
9000 of them. We passed near two of their villages—
a couple of rows of square unbeautiful houses facing

each other, with a street of mud between, as we see
them in pictures of Russian communes. These people
are a peculiar and somewhat mystical sect, separate
and unassimilated in habits, customs, and faith from
their neighbors, but peaceful, industrious, and thrifty.
I shall have occasion to speak of other peculiar immigration, encouraged by the governments and by private companies.

There can be no doubt of the fertility of all the
prairie region of Manitoba and Assiniboin. Great
heat is developed in the summers, but cereals are
liable, as in Dakota, to be touched, as in 1888, by early
frost. The great drawback from Winnipeg on westward is the intense cold of winter, regarded not as
either agreeable or disagreeable, but as a matter of
economy. The region, by reason of extra expense for
fuel, clothing, and housing, must always be more expensive to live in than, say, Ontario.

The province of Manitoba is an interesting political
and social study. It is very unlike Ontario or British
Columbia. Its development has been, in freedom and
self-help, very like one of our Western Territories, and
it is like them in its free, independent spirit. It has
a spirit to resist any imposed authority. We read of
the conflicts between the Hudson's Bay and the North-
western Fur companies and the Selkirk settlers, who
began to come in in 1812. Gradually the vast territory of the North-west had a large number of "free-
men," independent of any company, and of half-breed
Frenchmen. Other free settlers sifted in. The territory was remote from the Government, and had no
facilities of communication with the East, even after
the union. The rebellion of 1870-71 was repeated in

1885, when Riel was called back from Montana to head
the discontented. The settlers could not get patents
for their lands, and they had many grievances, which
they demanded should be redressed in a "bill of
rights." There were aspects of the insurrection, not
connected with the race question, with which many
well-disposed persons sympathized. But the discontent became a violent rebellion, and had to be suppressed. The execution of Riel, which some of the
Conservatives thought ill-advised, raised a race storm
throughout Canada; the French element was in a tu-
mult, and some of the Liberals made opposition capital out of the event. In the province of Quebec it is
still a deep grievance, for party purposes partly, as
was shown in the recent election of a federal member
of Parliament in Montreal.

Manitoba is Western in its spirit and its sympathies.
Before the building of the Canadian Pacific its communication was with Minnesota. Its interests now
largely lie with its southern neighbors. It has a feeling of irritation with too much federal dictation, and
frets under the still somewhat undefined relations of
power between the federal and the provincial governments, as was seen in the railway conflict. Besides,
the natural exchange of products between south and
north — between the lower Mississippi and the Red
River of the North and the north-west prairies — is
going to increase; the north and south railway lines
will have, with the development of industries and exchange of various sorts, a growing importance compared with the great east and west lines. Nothing
can stop this exchange and the need of it along our
whole border west of Lake Superior. It is already

active and growing, even on the Pacific, between Washington Territory and British Columbia.

For these geographical reasons, and especially on account of similarity of social and political development, I was strongly impressed with the notion that if the Canadian Pacific Railway had not been built when it was, Manitoba would by this time have gravitated to the United States, and it would only have been a question of time when the remaining North-west should have fallen in. The line of the road is very well settled, and yellow with wheat westward to Regina, but the farms are often off from the line, as the railway sections are for the most part still unoccupied; and there are many thriving villages: Portage la Prairie, from which the Manitoba and North-western Railway starts north-west, with a population of 3000; Brandon, a busy grain mart, standing on a rise of ground 1150 feet above the sea, with a population of 4000 and over; Qu'Appelle, in the rich valley of the river of that name, with 700; Regina, the capital of the North-west Territory, on a vast plain, with 800; Moosejay, a market-town towards the western limit of the settled country, with 600. This is all good land, but the winters are severe.

Naturally, on the rail we saw little game, except ducks and geese on the frequent fresh-water ponds, and occasionally coyotes and prairie-dogs. But plenty of large game still can be found farther north. At Stony Mountain, fifteen miles north of Winnipeg, the site of the Manitoba penitentiary, we saw a team of moose, which Colonel Bedson, the superintendent, drives — fleet animals, going easily fifteen miles an hour. They were captured only thirty-five miles north of the prison, where moose are abundant. Colonel Bedson has the only large herd of the practically extinct buffalo. There are about a hundred of these uncouth and picturesque animals, which have a range of twenty or thirty miles over the plains, and are watched by mounted keepers. They were driven in, bulls, cows, and calves, the day before our arrival—it seemed odd that we could order up a herd of buffaloes by telephone, but we did—and we saw the whole troop lumbering over the prairie, exactly as we were familiar with them in pictures. The colonel is trying the experiment of crossing them with common cattle. The result is a half-breed of large size, with heavier hind-quarters and less hump than the buffalo, and said to be good beef. The penitentiary has taken in all the convicts of the North-west Territory, and there were only sixty-five of them. The institution is a model one in its management. We were shown two separate chapels—one for Catholics and another for Protestants.

All along the line settlers are sifting in, and there are everywhere signs of promoted immigration. Not only is Canada making every effort to fill up its lands, but England is interested in relieving itself of troublesome people. The experiment has been tried of bringing out East-Londoners. These barbarians of civilization are about as unfitted for colonists as can be. Small bodies of them have been aided to make settlements, but the trial is not very encouraging ; very few of them take to the new life. The Scotch crofters do better. They are accustomed to labor and thrift, and are not a bad addition to the population. A company under the management of Sir John Lister

Kaye is making a larger experiment. It has received sections from the Government and bought contiguous sections from the railway, so as to have large blocks of land on the road. A dozen settlements are projected. The company brings over laborers and farmers, paying their expenses and wages for a year. A large central house is built on each block, tools and cattle are supplied, and the men are to begin the cultivation of the soil. At the end of a year they may, if they choose, take up adjacent free Government land and begin to make homes for themselves, working meantime on the company land, if they will. By this plan they are guaranteed support for a year at least, and a chance to set up for themselves. The company secures the breaking up of its land and a crop, and the nucleus of a town. The further plan is to encourage farmers, with a capital of a thousand dollars, to follow and settle in the neighborhood. There will then be three ranks—the large company proprietors, the farmers with some capital, and the laborers who are earning their capital. We saw some of these settlements on the line that looked promising. About 150 settlers, mostly men, arrived last fall, and with them were sent out English tools and English cattle. The plan looks to making model communities, on something of the old-world plan of proprietor, farmer, and laborer. It would not work in the United States.

Another important colonization is that of Icelanders. These are settled to the north-east of Winnipeg and in southern Manitoba. About 10,000 have already come over, and the movement has assumed such large proportions that it threatens to depopulate Iceland. This is good and intelligent material. Climate

and soil are so superior to that of Iceland that the
emigrants are well content. They make good farmers,
but they are not so clannish as the Mennonites; many
of them scatter about in the towns as laborers.

Before we reached Medicine Hat, and beyond that
place, we passed through considerable alkaline country
—little dried-up lakes looking like patches of snow.
There was an idea that this land was not fertile. The
Canadian Pacific Company have been making several
experiments on the line of model farms, which prove
the contrary. As soon as the land is broken up and
the crust turned under, the soil becomes very fertile,
and produces excellent crops of wheat and vegetables.

Medicine Hat, on a branch of the South Saskatchewan, is a thriving town. Here are a station and barracks of the Mounted Police, a picturesque body of
civil cavalry in blue pantaloons and red jackets. This
body of picked men, numbering about a thousand, and
similar in functions to the *Guarda Civil* of Spain, are
scattered through the North-west Territory, and are the
Dominion police for keeping in order the Indians, and
settling disputes between the Indians and whites. The
sergeants have powers of police-justices, and the organization is altogether an admirable one for the purpose, and has a fine *esprit de corps*.

Here we saw many Cree Indians, physically a cred-
itable-looking race of men and women, and picturesque
in their gay blankets and red and yellow paint daubed
on the skin without the least attempt at shading or
artistic effect. A fair was going on, an exhibition
of horses, cattle, and vegetable and cereal products of
the region. The vegetables were large and of good
quality. Delicate flowers were still blooming (Sep-

tember 28th) untouched by frost in the gardens. These Crees are not on a reservation. They cultivate the soil a little, but mainly support themselves by gathering and selling buffalo bones, and well set-up and polished horns of cattle, which they swear are buffalo. The women are far from a degraded race in appearance, have good heads, high foreheads, and are well-favored. As to morals, they are reputed not to equal the Blackfeet.

The same day we reached Gleichen, about 2500 feet above the sea. The land is rolling, and all good for grazing and the plough. This region gets the "Chinook" wind. Ploughing is begun in April, sometimes in March; in 1888 they ploughed in January. Flurries of snow may be expected any time after October 1st, but frost is not so early as in eastern Canada. A fine autumn is common, and fine, mild weather may continue up to December. At Dunmore, the station before Medicine Hat, we passed a branch railway running west to the great Lethbridge coal-mines, and Dunmore Station is a large coal depot.

The morning at Gleichen was splendid; cool at sunrise, but no frost. Here we had our first view of the Rockies, a long range of snow-peaks on the horizon, 120 miles distant. There is an immense fascination in this rolling country, the exhilarating air, and the magnificent mountains in the distance. Here is the beginning of a reservation of the Blackfeet, near 3000. They live here on the Bow River, and cultivate the soil to a considerable extent, and have the benefit of a mission and two schools. They are the best-looking race of Indians we have seen, and have most self-respect.

We went over a rolling country to Calgary, at an altitude of 3388 feet, a place of some 3000 inhabitants, and of the most distinction of all between Brandon and Vancouver. On the way we passed two stations where natural gas was used, the boring for which was only about 600 feet. The country is underlaid with coal. Calgary is delightfully situated at the junction of the Bow and Elbow rivers, rapid streams as clear as crystal, with a greenish hue, on a small plateau, surrounded by low hills and overlooked by the still distant snow-peaks. The town has many good shops, several churches, two newspapers, and many fanciful cottages. We drove several miles out on the McCloud trail, up a lovely valley, with good farms, growing wheat and oats, and the splendid mountains in the distance. The day was superb, the thermometer marking 70°. This is, however, a ranch country, wheat being an uncertain crop, owing to summer frosts. But some years, like 1888, are good for all grains and vegetables. A few Sarcee Indians were loafing about here, inferior savages. Much better are the Stony Indians, who are settled and work the soil beyond Calgary, and are very well cared for by a Protestant mission.

Some of the Indian tribes of Canada are self-supporting. This is true of many of the Siwash and other west coast tribes, who live by fishing. At Lytton, on the upper Fraser, I saw a village of the Siwash civilized enough to live in houses, wear our dress, and earn their living by working on the railway, fishing, etc. The Indians have done a good deal of work on the railway, and many of them are still employed on it. The coast Indians are a different race from the plains Indians, and have a marked resemblance to the

Chinese and Japanese. The polished carvings in black slate of the Haida Indians bear a striking resemblance to archaic Mexican work, and strengthen the theory that the coast Indians crossed the straits from Asia, are related to the early occupiers of Arizona and Mexico, and ought not to be classed with the North American Indian. The Dominion has done very well by its Indians, of whom it has probably a hundred thousand. It has tried to civilize them by means of schools, missions, and farm instructors, and it has been pretty successful in keeping ardent spirits away from them. A large proportion of them are still fed and clothed by the Government. It is doubtful if the plains Indians will ever be industrious. The Indian fund from the sale of their lands has accumulated to $3,000,000. There are 140 teachers and 4000 pupils in school. In 1885 the total expenditure on the Indian population, beyond that provided by the Indian fund, was $1,109,604, of which $478,038 was expended for provisions for destitute Indians.

At Cochrane's we were getting well into the hills. Here is a large horse and sheep ranch and a very extensive range. North and south along the foot-hills is fine grazing and ranging country. We enter the mountains by the Bow River Valley, and plunge at once into splendid scenery, bare mountains rising on both sides in sharp, varied, and fantastic peaks, snow-dusted, and in lateral openings assemblages of giant summits of rock and ice. The change from the rolling prairie was magical. At Mountain House the Three Sisters were very impressive. Late in the afternoon we came to Banff.

Banff will have a unique reputation among the resorts of the world. If a judicious plan is formed and adhered to for the development of its extraordinary beauties and grandeur, it will be second to few in attractions. A considerable tract of wilderness about it is reserved as a National Park, and the whole ought to be developed by some master landscape expert. It is in the power of the Government and of the Canadian Pacific Company to so manage its already famous curative hot sulphur springs as to make Banff the resort of invalids as well as pleasure-seekers the year round. This is to be done not simply by established good bathing-places, but by regulations and restrictions such as give to the German baths their virtue.

The Banff Hotel, unsurpassed in situation, amid magnificent mountains, is large, picturesque, many gabled and windowed, and thoroughly comfortable. It looks down upon the meeting of the Bow and the Spray, which spread in a pretty valley closed by a range of snow-peaks. To right and left rise mountains of savage rock ten thousand feet high. The whole scene has all the elements of beauty and grandeur. The place is attractive for its climate, its baths, and excellent hunting and fishing.

For two days, travelling only by day, passing the Rockies, the Selkirks, and the Gold range, we were kept in a state of intense excitement, in a constant exclamation of wonder and delight. I would advise no one to attempt to take it in the time we did. Nobody could sit through Beethoven's nine symphonies played continuously. I have no doubt that when carriage-roads and foot-paths are made into the mountain recesses, as they will be, and little hotels are established in the valleys and in the passes and advantageous sites, as in

Switzerland, this region will rival the Alpine resorts.
I can speak of two or three things only.

The highest point on the line is the station at Mount
Stephen, 5296 feet above the sea. The mountain, a
bald mass of rock in a rounded cone, rises about 8000
feet above this. As we moved away from it the mountain was hidden by a huge wooded intervening mountain. The train was speeding rapidly on the down
grade, carrying us away from the base, and we stood
upon the rear platform watching the apparent reces-
sion of the great mass, when suddenly, and yet de-
liberately, the vast white bulk of Mount Stephen began
to rise over the intervening summit in the blue sky,
lifting itself up by a steady motion while one could
count twenty, until its magnificence stood revealed.
It was like a transformation in a theatre, only the cur-
tain here was lowered instead of raised. The surprise
was almost too much for the nerves; the whole company was awe-stricken. It is too much to say that
the mountain " shot up;" it rose with conscious grandeur and power. The effect, of course, depends much
upon the speed of the train. I have never seen anything to compare with it for awakening the emotion
of surprise and wonder.

The station of Field, just beyond Mount Stephen,
where there is a charming hotel, is in the midst of
wonderful mountain and glacier scenery, and would be
a delightful place for rest. From there the descent
down the cañon of Kickinghorse River, along the edge
of precipices, among the snow-monarchs, is very exciting. At Golden we come to the valley of the Columbia River and in view of the Selkirks. The river
is navigable about a hundred miles above Golden, and

this is the way to the mining district of the Kootenay
Valley. The region abounds in gold and silver. The
broad Columbia runs north here until it breaks through
the Selkirks, and then turns southward on the west
side of that range.

The railway follows down the river, between the
splendid ranges of the Selkirks and the Rockies, to the
mouth of the Beaver, and then ascends its narrow gorge.
I am not sure but that the scenery of the Selkirks is
finer than that of the Rockies. One is bewildered by
the illimitable noble snow-peaks and great glaciers.
At Glacier House is another excellent hotel. In savage grandeur, nobility of mountain-peaks, snow-ranges,
and extent of glacier it rivals anything in Switzerland.
The glacier, only one arm of which is seen from the
road, is, I believe, larger than any in Switzerland.
There are some thirteen miles of flowing ice; but the
monster lies up in the mountains, like a great octopus,
with many giant arms. The branch which we saw,
overlooked by the striking snow-cone of Sir Donald,
some two and a half miles from the hotel, is immense
in thickness and breadth, and seems to pour out of the
sky. Recent measurements show that it is moving at
the rate of twenty inches in twenty-four hours—about
the rate of progress of the Mer de Glace. In the midst
of the main body, higher up, is an isolated mountain
of pure ice three hundred feet high and nearly a quarter of a mile in length. These mountains are the home
of the mountain sheep.

From this amphitheatre of giant peaks, snow, and
glaciers we drop by marvellous loops—wonderful engineering, four apparently different tracks in sight
at one time—down to the valley of the Illicilliweat,

the lower part of which is fertile, and blooming with irrigated farms. We pass a cluster of four lovely lakes, and coast around the great Shuswap Lake, which is fifty miles long. But the traveller is not out of excitement. The ride down the Thompson and Fraser cañons is as amazing almost as anything on the line. At Spence's Bridge we come to the old Government road to the Cariboo gold-mines, three hundred miles above. This region has been for a long time a scene of activity in mining and salmon-fishing. It may be said generally of the Coast or Gold range that its riches have yet to be developed. The villages all along these mountain slopes and valleys are waiting for this development.

The city of Vancouver, only two years old since the beginnings of a town were devoured by fire, is already an interesting place of seven to eight thousand inhabitants, fast building up, and with many substantial granite and brick buildings, and spreading over a large area. It lies upon a high point of land between Burrard Inlet on the north and the north arm of the Fraser River. The inner harbor is deep and spacious. Burrard Inlet entrance is narrow but deep, and opens into English Bay, which opens into Georgia Sound, that separates the island of Vancouver, three hundred miles long, from the main-land. The round headland south of the entrance is set apart for a public park, called now Stanley Park, and is being improved with excellent driving-roads, which give charming views. It is a tangled wilderness of nearly one thousand acres. So dense is the undergrowth, in this moist air, of vines, ferns, and small shrubs, that it looks like a tropical thicket. But in the midst of it are gigantic Douglas

29

firs and a few noble cedars. One veteran cedar, partly decayed at the top, measured fifty-six feet in circumference, and another, in full vigor and of gigantic
height, over thirty-nine feet. The hotel of the Canadian Pacific Company, a beautiful building in modern
style, is, in point of comfort, elegance of appointment,
abundant table, and service, not excelled by any in
Canada, equalled by few anywhere.

Vancouver would be a very busy and promising city
merely as the railway terminus and the shipping-point
for Japan and China and the east generally. But it
has other resources of growth. There is a very good
country back of it, and south of it all the way into
Washington Territory. New Westminster, twelve
miles south, is a place of importance for fish and lumber. The immensely fertile alluvial bottoms of the
Fraser, which now overflows its banks, will some day
be diked, and become exceedingly valuable. Its relations to Washington Territory are already close. The
very thriving city of Seattle, having a disagreement
with the North Pacific and its rival, Tacoma, sends
and receives most of its freight and passengers *via*
Vancouver, and is already pushing forward a railway
to that point. It is also building to Spokane Falls,
expecting some time to be met by an extension of the
St. Paul, Minneapolis, and Manitoba from the Great
Falls of the Missouri. I found that many of the emigrants in the loaded trains that we travelled with or
that passed us were bound to Washington Territory.
It is an acknowledged fact that there is a constant
"leakage" of emigrants, who had apparently promised
to tarry in Canada, into United States territories.
Some of them, disappointed of the easy wealth ex-

pected, no doubt return; but the name of "republic" seems to have an attraction for Old World people when they are once set adrift.

We took steamer one afternoon for a five hours' sail to Victoria. A part of the way is among beautiful wooded islands. Once out in the open, we had a view of our "native land," and prominent in it the dim, cloud-like, gigantic peak of Mount Baker. Before we passed the islands we were entertained by a rare show of right-whales. A school of them a couple of weeks before had come down through Behring Strait, and pursued a shoal of fish into this landlocked bay. There must have been as many as fifty of the monsters in sight, spouting up slender fountains, lifting their huge bulk out of water, and diving, with their bifurcated tails waving in the air. They played about like porpoises, apparently only for our entertainment.

Victoria, so long isolated, is the most English part of Canada. The town itself does not want solidity and wealth, but it is stationary, and, the Canadians elsewhere think, slow. It was the dry and dusty time of the year. The environs are broken with inlets, hilly and picturesque; there are many pretty cottages and country places in the suburbs; and one visits with interest the Eskimalt naval station, and the elevated Park, which has a noble coast view. The very mild climate is favorable for grapes and apples. The summer is delightful; the winter damp, and constantly rainy. And this may be said of all this coast. Of the thirteen thousand population six thousand are Chinese, and they form in the city a dense, insoluble, unassimilating mass. Victoria has one railway, that to the prosperous Nanaimo coal-mines. The island has abundance of coal, some copper, and timber. But Vancouver has taken away from Victoria all its importance as a port. The Government and Parliament buildings are detached, but pleasant and commodious edifices. There is a decorous British air about everything. Throughout British Columbia the judges and the lawyers wear the gown and band and the horse-hair wig. In an evening trial for murder which I attended in a dingy upper chamber of the Kamloops court-house, lighted only by kerosene lamps, the wigs and gowns of judge and attorneys lent, I confess, a dignity to the administration of justice which the kerosene lamps could not have given. In one of the Government buildings is a capital museum of natural history and geology. The educational department is vigorous and effective, and I find in the bulky report evidence of most intelligent management of the schools.

It is only by traversing the long distance to this coast, and seeing the activity here, that one can appreciate the importance to Canada and to the British Empire of the Canadian Pacific Railway as a bond of unity, a developer of resources, and a world's highway. The out-going steamers were crowded with passengers and laden with freight. We met on the way two solid trains, of twenty cars each, full of tea. When the new swift steamers are put on, which are already heavily subsidized by both the English and the Canadian governments, the traffic in passengers and goods must increase. What effect the possession of such a certain line of communication with her Oriental domains will have upon the English willingness to surrender Canada either to complete independence or to a union with the United States, any political prophet can estimate.

It must be added that the Canadian Pacific Company are doing everything to make this highway popular as well as profitable. Construction and management show English regard for comfort and safety and order. It is one of the most agreeable lines to travel over I am acquainted with. Most of it is well built, and defects are being energetically removed. The "Colonist" cars are clean and convenient. The first class carriages are luxurious. The dining-room cars are uniformly well kept, the company hotels are exceptionally excellent; and from the railway servants one meets with civility and attention.

III.

I HAD been told that the Canadians are second-hand Englishmen. No estimate could convey a more erroneous impression. A portion of the people have strong English traditions and loyalties to institutions, but in manner and in expectations the Canadians are scarcely more English than the people of the United States; they have their own colonial development, and one can mark already with tolerable distinctness a Canadian type which is neither English nor American. This is noticeable especially in the women. The Canadian girl resembles the American in escape from a purely conventional restraint and in self-reliance, and she has, like the English, a well-modulated voice and distinct articulation. In the cities, also, she has taste in dress and a certain style which we think belongs to the New World. In features and action a certain modification has gone on, due partly to climate and partly to greater social independence. It is unnecessary to make com-

parisons, and I only note that there is a Canadian type
of woman.

But there is great variety in Canada, and in fact a
remarkable racial diversity.   The man of Nova Scotia
is not at all the man of British Columbia or Manitoba.
The Scotch in old Canada have made a distinct impression in features and speech.   And it may be said
generally in eastern Canada that the Scotch element
is a leading and conspicuous one in the vigor and push
of enterprise and the accumulation of fortune.   The
Canadian men, as one sees them in official life, at the
clubs, in business, are markedly a vigorous, stalwart
race, well made, of good stature, and not seldom handsome.   This physical prosperity needs to be remembered when we consider the rigorous climate and the
long winters; these seem to have at least one advantage—that of breeding virile men.   The Canadians
generally are fond of out-door sports and athletic
games, of fishing and hunting, and they give more
time to such recreations than we do.   They are a little less driven by the business goad.   Abundant animal spirits tend to make men good-natured and little
quarrelsome.   The Canadians would make good soldiers.   There was a time when the drinking habit
pervailed very much in Canada, and there are still
places where they do not put water enough in their
grog, but temperance reform has taken as strong a
hold there as it has in the United States.

The feeling about the English is illustrated by the
statement that there is not more aping of English ways
in Montreal and Toronto clubs and social life than in
New York, and that the English superciliousness, or
condescension as to colonists, the ultra-English mau-

ner, is ridiculed in Canada, and resented with even more
warmth than in the United States. The amusing stories of English presumption upon hospitality are current in Canada as well as on this side. All this is not
inconsistent with pride in the empire, loyalty to its
traditions and institutions, and even a considerable
willingness (for human nature is pretty much alike
everywhere) to accept decorative titles. But the underlying fact is that there is a distinct feeling of nationality, and it is increasing.

There is not anywhere so great a contrast between
neighboring cities as between Quebec, Montreal, and
Toronto. Quebec is mediæval, Toronto is modern,
Montreal is in a conflict between the two conditions.
As the travelling world knows, they are all interesting
cities, and have peculiar attractions. Quebec is French,
more decidedly so than Toronto is English, and in Montreal the French have a large numerical majority and
complete political control. In the Canadian cities generally municipal affairs are pretty much divorced from
general party politics, greatly to the advantage of good
city government.

Montreal has most wealth, and from its splendid
geographical position it is the railway centre, and has
the business and commercial primacy. It has grown
rapidly from a population of 140,000 in 1881 to a population of over 200,000—estimated, with its suburbs,
at 250,000. Were it part of my plan to describe these
cities, I should need much space to devote to the finest public buildings and public institutions of Montreal, the handsome streets in the Protestant quarter,
with their solid, tasteful, and often elegant residences,
the many churches, and the almost unequalled posses-

sion of the Mountain as a park and resort, where one has the most striking and varied prospects in the world. Montreal, being a part of the province of Quebec, is not only under provincial control of the government at Quebec, but it is ruled by the same French party in the city, and there is the complaint always found where the poorer majority taxes the richer and more enterprising minority out of proportion to the benefits the latter receives. Various occasions have produced something like race conflicts in the city, and there are prophesies of more serious ones in the strife for ascendency. The seriousness of this to the minority lies in the fact that the French race is more prolific than any other in the province.

Perhaps nothing will surprise the visitor more than the persistence of the French type in Canada, and naturally its aggressiveness. Guaranteed their religion, laws, and language, the French have not only failed to assimilate, but have had hopes—maybe still have—of making Canada French. The French "national" party means simply a French consolidation, and has no relation to the "nationalism" of Sir John Macdonald. So far as the Church and the French politicians are concerned, the effort is to keep the French solid as a political force, and whether the French are Liberal or Conservative, this is the underlying thought. The province of Quebec is Liberal, but the liberalism is of a different hue from that of Ontario. The French recognize the truth that language is so integral a part of a people's growth that the individuality of a people depends upon maintaining it. The French have escaped absorption in Canada mainly by loyalty to their native tongue, aided by the concession to them of their

civil laws and their religious privileges. They owe this
to William Pitt. I quote from a contributed essay in
the Toronto *Week* about three years ago: "Up to 1791
the small French population of Canada was in a position to be converted into an English colony with traces
of French sentiment and language, which would have
slowly disappeared. But at that date William Pitt
the younger brought into the House of Commons two
Quebec Acts, which constituted two provinces—Lower
Canada, with a full provision of French laws, language,
and institutions; Upper Canada, with a reproduction
of English laws and social system. During the debate Pitt declared on the floor of the House that his
purpose was to create two colonies distinct from and
jealous of each other, so as to guard against a repeti-
tion of the late unhappy rebellion which had separated
the thirteen colonies from the empire."

The French have always been loyal to the English
connection under all temptations, for these guarantees
have been continued, which could scarcely be expected
from any other power, and certainly not in a legislative union of the Canadian provinces. In literature
and sentiment the connection is with France; in religion, with Rome ; in politics England has been the
guarantee of both. There will be no prevailing sentiment in favor of annexation to the United States so
long as the Church retains its authority, nor would it
be favored by the accomplished politicians so long as
they can use the solid French mass as a political force.

The relegation of the subject of education entirely
to the provinces is an element in the persistence of the
French type in the province of Quebec, in the same
way that it strengthens the Protestant cause in On-

tario. In the province of Quebec all the public schools are Roman Catholic, and the separate schools are of other sects. In the council of public instruction the Catholics, of course, have a large majority, but the public schools are managed by a Catholic committee and the others by a Protestant committee. In the academies, model and high schools, subsidized by the Government, those having Protestant teachers are insignificant in number, and there are very few Protestants in Catholic schools, and very few Catholics in Protestant schools; the same is true of the schools of this class not subsidized. The bulky report of the superintendent of public instruction of the province of Quebec (which is translated into English) shows a vigorous and intelligent attention to education. The general statistics give the number of pupils in the province as 219,403 Roman Catholics (the term always used in the report) and 37,484 Protestants. In the elementary schools there are 143,848 Roman Catholics and 30,461 Protestants. Of the ecclesiastical teachers, 868 are Roman Catholics and 8 Protestants; of the certificated lay teachers, 256 are Roman Catholic and 105 Protestant; the proportion of schools is four to one. It must be kept in mind that in the French schools it is French literature that is cultivated. In the Laval University, at Quebec, English literature is as purely an ornamental study as French literature would be in Yale. The Laval University, which has a branch in Montreal, is a strong institution, with departments of divinity, law, medicine, and the arts, 80 professors, and 575 students. The institution has a vast pile of buildings, one of the most conspicuous objects in a view of the city. Besides spacious lecture, assembly rooms, and laboratories, it has extensive collections in geology, mineralogy, botany, ethnology, zoology, coins, a library of 100,000 volumes, in which theology is well represented, but which contains a large collection of works on Canada, including valuable manuscripts, the original MS. of the *Journal des Jésuites,* and the most complete set of the *Relation des Jésuites* existing in America. It has also a gallery of paintings, chiefly valuable for its portraits.

Of the 62,000 population of Quebec City, by the census of 1881, not over 6000 were Protestants. By the same census Montreal had 140,747, of whom 78,684 were French, and 28,995 of Irish origin. The Roman Catholics numbered 103,579. I believe the proportion has not much changed with the considerable growth in seven years.

One is struck, in looking at the religious statistics of Canada, by the fact that the Church of England has not the primacy, and that the so-called independent sects have a position they have not in England. In the total population of 4,324,810, given by the census of 1881, the Protestants were put down at 2,436,-554 and the Roman Catholics at 1,791,982. The larger of the Protestant denominations were, Methodists, 742,981; Presbyterians, 676,165; Church of England, 574,818; Baptists, 296,525. Taking as a specimen of the north-west the province of Manitoba, census of 1886, we get these statistics of the larger sects: Presbyterians, 28,406; Church of England, 23,206; Methodists, 18,648; Roman Catholics, 14,651; Mennonites, 9112; Baptists, 3296; Lutherans, 3131.

Some statistics of general education in the Dominion show the popular interest in the matter. In 1885 the total number of pupils in the Dominion, in public and private schools, was 968,193, and the average attendance was 555,404. The total expenditure of the year, not including school buildings, was $9,310,745, and the value of school lands, buildings, and furniture was $25,000,000. Yet in the province of Quebec, out of the total expenditure of $3,162,416, only $353,677 was granted by the provincial Legislature. And in Ontario, of the total of $3,904,797, only $267,084 was granted by the Legislature.

The McGill University at Montreal, Sir William Dawson principal, is a corporation organized under royal charter, which owes its original endowment of land and money (valued at $120,000) to James McGill. It receives small grants from the provincial and Dominion governments, but mainly depends upon its own funds, which in 1885 stood at $791,000. It has numerous endowed professorships and endowments for scholarships and prizes; among them is the Donalda Endowment for the Higher Education of Women (from Sir Donald A. Smith), by which a special course in separate classes, by University professors, is maintained in the University buildings for women. It has faculties of arts, applied sciences, law, and medicine —the latter with one of the most complete anatomical museums and one of the best selected libraries on the continent. It has several colleges affiliated with it for the purpose of conferring University degrees, a model school, and four theological colleges, a Congregational, a Presbyterian, an Episcopalian, and a Wesleyan, the students in which may supplement their own courses in the University. The professors and students wear the University cap and gown, and morning prayers are read to a voluntary attendance. The Redpath Museum, of geology, mineralogy, zoology, and ethnology, has a distinction among museums not only for the size of the collection, but for splendid arrangement and classification. The well-selected library numbers about 30,000 volumes. The whole University is a vigorous educational centre, and its well-planted grounds and fine buildings are an ornament to the city.

Returning to the French element, its influence is not only felt in the province of Quebec, but in the Dominion. The laws of the Dominion and the proceedings are published in French and English; the debates in the Dominion Parliament are conducted indifferently in both languages, although it is observed that as the five years of any Parliament go on English is more and more used by the members, for the French are more likely to learn English than the English are to learn French. Of course the Quebec Parliament is even more distinctly French. And the power of the Roman Catholic Church is pretty much co-extensive with the language. The system of tithes is legal in provincial law, and tithes can be collected of all Roman Catholics by law. The Church has also what is called the fabrique system; that is, a method of raising contributions from any district for churches, priests' houses, and conventual buildings and schools. The tithes and the fabrique assessments make a heavy burden on the peasants. The traveller down the St. Lawrence sees how the interests of religion are emphasized in the large churches raised in the midst of humble villages, and in the great Church establishments of charity and instruction. It is said that the farmers attempted to escape the tithe on cereals by changing to the cultivation of pease, but the Church then decided that pease were cereals. There is no doubt that the French population are devout, and that they support the Church in proportion to their devotion, and that much which seems to the Protestants extortion on the part of the Church is a voluntary contribution. Still the fact remains that the burden is heavy on land that is too cold for the highest productiveness. The desire to better themselves in wages, and perhaps to escape burdens, sends a great many French to New England. Some of them earn money, and return to settle in the land that is dear by tradition and a thousand associations. Many do not return, and I suppose there are over three-quarters of a million of French Canadians now in New England. They go to better themselves, exactly as New Englanders leave their homes for more productive farms in the West. The Church, of course, does not encourage this emigration, but does encourage the acquisition of lands in Ontario or elsewhere in Canada. And there has been recently a marked increase of French in Ontario—so marked that the French representation in the Ontario Parliament will be increased probably by three members in the next election. There are many people in Canada who are seriously alarmed at this increase of the French and of the Roman Catholic power. Others look upon this fear as idle, and say that immigration is sure to make the Protestant element overwhelming. It is to be noted also that Ontario furnishes Protestant emigrants to the United States in large numbers. It may be that the interchange of ideas caused by the French emigration to New England will be an important make-weight in favor of annexation. Individuals, and even French newspapers, are found to advocate it. But these are at present only surface indications. The political leaders, the Church, and the mass of the people are fairly content with things as they are, and with the provincial autonomy, although they resent federal vetoes, and still make a "cry" of the Riel execution.

The French element in Canada may be considered from other points of view. The contribution of romance and tradition is not an unimportant one in any nation. The French in Canada have never broken with their past, as the French in France have. There is a great charm about Quebec—its language, its social life, the military remains of the last century. It is a Protestant writer who speaks of the volume and wealth of the French Canadian literature as too little known to English-speaking Canada. And it is true that literary men have not realized the richness of the French material, nor the work accomplished by French writers in history, poetry, essays, and romances. Quebec itself is at a commercial stand-still, but its uniquely beautiful situation, its history, and the projection of mediævalism into existing institutions make it one of the most interesting places to the tourist on the continent. The conspicuous, noble, and commodious Parliament building is almost the only one of consequence that speaks of the modern spirit. It was the remark of a high Church dignitary that the object of the French in Canada was the promotion of religion, and the object of the English, commerce. We cannot overlook this attitude against materialism. In the French schools and universities religion is not divorced from education. And even in the highest education, where modern science has a large place, what we may call the literary side is very much emphasized. Indeed, the French students are rather inclined to rhetoric, and in public life the French are distinguished for the graces and charm of oratory. It may be true, as charged, that the public schools of Quebec province, especially in the country, giving special attention to the interest the Church regards as the highest, do little to remove the ignorance of the French peasant. It is our belief that the best Christianity is the most intelligent. Yet there is matter for consideration with all thoughtful men what sort of society we shall ultimately have in States where the common schools have neither religious nor ethical teaching.

Ottawa is a creation of the Federal Government as distinctly as Washington is. The lumber-mills on the Chaudière Falls necessitate a considerable town here, for this industry assumes gigantic proportions, but the beauty and attraction of the city are due to the concentration here of political interest. The situation on the bluffs of the Ottawa River is commanding, and gives fine opportunity for architectural display. The group of Government buildings is surpassingly fine. The Parliament House and the department buildings on three sides of a square are exceedingly effective in color and in the perfection of Gothic details, especially in the noble towers. There are few groups of buildings anywhere so pleasing to the eye, or that appeal more strongly to one's sense of dignity and beauty. The library attached to the Parliament House in the rear, a rotunda in form, has a picturesque exterior, and the interior is exceedingly beautiful and effective. The library, though mainly for Parlia-

mentary uses, is rich in Canadian history, and well up
in polite literature. It contains about 90,000 volumes.
In the Parliament building, which contains the two
fine legislative Chambers, there are residence apartments for the Speakers of the Senate and of the House
of Commons and their families, where entertainments
are given during the session. The opening of Parliament is an imposing and brilliant occasion, graced
by the presence of the Governor-general, who is supposed to visit the Chambers at no other time in the
session. Ottawa is very gay during the session, society
and politics mingling as in London, and the English
habit of night sessions adds a good deal to the excitement and brilliancy of the Parliamentary proceedings.

The growth of the Government business and of
official life has made necessary the addition of a third
department building, and the new one, departing
from the Gothic style, is very solid and tasteful.
There are thirteen members of the Privy Council
with portfolios, and the volume of public business
is attested by the increase of department officials.
I believe there are about 1500 men attached to the
civil service in Ottawa. It will be seen at once
that the Federal Government, which seemed in a
manner superimposed upon the provincial governments, has taken on large proportions, and that there
is in Ottawa and throughout the Dominion in federal
officials and offices a strengthening vested interest in
the continuance of the present form of government.
The capital itself, with its investment in buildings,
is a conservator of the state of things as they are.
The Cabinet has many able men, men who would
take a leading rank as parliamentarians in the Eng-

30

lish Commons, and the Opposition benches in the
House furnish a good quota of the same material.
The power of the premier is a fact as recognizable as
in England. For many years Sir John A. Macdonald
has been virtually the ruler of Canada. He has had
the ability and skill to keep his party in power, while
all the provinces have remained or become Liberal. I
believe his continuance is due to his devotion to the
national idea, to the development of the country, to
bold measures—like the urgency of the Canadian
Pacific Railway construction—for binding the provinces together and promoting commercial activity.
Canada is proud of this, even while it counts its debt.
Sir John is worshipped by his party, especially by the
younger men, to whom he furnishes an ideal, as a
statesman of bold conceptions and courage. He is
disliked as a politician as cordially by the Opposition,
who attribute to him the same policy of adventure
that was attributed to Beaconsfield. Personally he
resembles that remarkable man. Undoubtedly Sir
John adds prudence to his knowledge of men, and his
habit of never crossing a stream till he gets to it has
gained him the sobriquet of " Old To-morrow." He
is a man of the world as well as a man of affairs, with
a wide and liberal literary taste.

The members of Government are well informed
about the United States, and attentive students of its
politics. I am sure that, while they prefer their system of responsible government, they have no sentiment but friendliness to American institutions and
people, nor any expectation that any differences will
not be adjusted in a manner satisfactory and honorable
to both. I happened to be in Canada during the fish-

cry and " retaliation " talk. There was no belief that
the " retaliation " threatened was anything more than
a campaign measure; it may have chilled the *rapport*
for the moment, but there was literally no excitement
over it, and the opinion was general that retaliation as
to transportation would benefit the Canadian railways.
The effect of the moment was that importers made
large foreign orders for goods to be sent by Halifax
that would otherwise have gone to United States
ports. The fishery question is not one that can be
treated in the space at our command. Naturally Canada sees it from its point of view. To a considerable
portion of the maritime provinces fishing means livelihood, and the view is that if the United States shares
in it we ought to open our markets to the Canadian
fishermen. Some, indeed, and these are generally advocates of freer trade, think that our fishermen ought
to have the right of entering the Canadian harbors
for bait and shipment of their catch, and think also
that Canada would derive an equal benefit from this;
but probably the general feeling is that these privileges should be compensated by a United States
market. The defence of the treaty in the United
States Senate debate was not the defence of the Canadian Government in many particulars. For instance, it was said that the " outrages " had been *dis-
owned* as the acts of irresponsible men. The Canadian
defence was that the " outrages "—that is, the most
conspicuous of them which appeared in the debate—
had been *disproved* in the investigation. Several of
them, which excited indignation in the United States,
were declared by a Cabinet minister to have no foundation in fact, and after proof of the falsity of the allega-

tions the complainants were not again heard of. Of course it is known that no arrangement made by England can hold that is not materially beneficial to Canada and the United States; and I believe I state the best judgment of both sides that the whole fishery question, in the hands of sensible representatives of both countries, upon ascertained facts, could be settled between Canada and the United States. Is it not natural that, with England conducting the negotiation, Canada should appear as a somewhat irresponsible litigating party bent on securing all that she can get? But whatever the legal rights are, under treaties or the law of nations, I am sure that the absurdity of making a *casus belli* of them is as much felt in Canada as in the United States. And I believe the Canadians understand that this attitude is consistent with a firm maintenance of treaty or other rights by the United States as it is by Canada.

The province of Ontario is an empire in itself. It is nearly as large as France; it is larger by twenty-five thousand square miles than the combined six New England States, with New York, New Jersey, Pennsylvania, and Maryland. In its varied capacities it is the richest province in Canada, and leaving out the forests and minerals and stony wilderness between the Canadian Pacific and James Bay, it has an area large enough for an empire, which compares favorably in climate and fertility with the most prosperous States of our Union. The climate of the lake region is milder than that of southern New York, and a considerable part of it is easily productive of superior grapes, apples, and other sorts of fruit. The average yield of wheat, per acre, both fall and spring, for five years ending with 1886, was considerably above that of our best grain-producing States, from Pennsylvania to those farthest West. The same is true of oats. The comparison of barley is still more favorable for Ontario, and the barley is of a superior quality. On a carefully cultivated farm in York county, for this period, the average was higher than the general in the province, being, of wheat, 25 bushels to the acre; barley, 47 bushels; oats, 66 bushels; pease, 32 bushels. It has no superior as a wool-producing and cattle-raising country. Its water-power is unexcelled; in minerals it is as rich as it is in timber; every part of it has been made accessible to market by railways and good highways, which have had liberal Government aid; and its manufactures have been stimulated by a protective tariff. Better than all this, it is the home of a very superior people. There are no better anywhere. The original stock was good, the climate has been favorable, the athletic habits have given them vigor and tone and courage, and there prevails a robust, healthful moral condition. In any company, in the clubs, in business houses, in professional circles, the traveller is impressed with the physical development of the men, and even on the streets of the chief towns with the uncommon number of women who have beauty and that attractiveness which generally goes with good taste in dress.

The original settlers of Ontario were 10,000 loyalists, who left New England during and after our Revolutionary War. They went to Canada impoverished, but they carried there moral and intellectual qualities of a high order, the product of the best civilization of their day, the best materials for making a State. I confess that I never could rid myself of the school-boy idea

that the terms "British redcoat" and "enemy" were
synonymous, and that a "Tory" was the worst character Providence had ever permitted to live.   But these
people, who were deported, or went voluntarily away
for an idea, were among the best material we had
in stanch moral traits, intellectual leadership, social
position, and wealth; their crime was superior attachment to England, and utter want of sympathy with
the colonial cause, the cause of "liberty" of the hour.
It is to them, at any rate, that Ontario owes its solid
basis of character, vigor, and prosperity.   I do not
quarrel with the pride of their descendants in the fact
that their ancestors were U. E. (United Empire) loyalists—a designation that still has a vital meaning to
them.   No doubt they inherit the idea that the revolt
was a mistake, that the English connection is better
as a form of government than the republic, and some
of them may still regard the "Yankees" as their Tory
ancestors did.   It does not matter.   In the development of a century in a new world they are more like
us than they are like the English, except in a certain
sentiment and in traditions, and in adherence to English governmental ideas.   I think I am not wrong in
saying that this conservative element in Ontario, or
this aristocratical element which believes that it can
rule a people better than they can rule themselves,
was for a long time an anti-progressive and anti-pop-
ular force.   They did not give up their power readily—
power, however, which they were never accused of
using for personal profit in the way of money.   But
I suppose that the "rule of the best" is only held to-
day as a theory under popular suffrage in a responsible government.

The population of Ontario in 1886 was estimated at 1,819,026. For the seven years from 1872–79 the gain was 250,782. For the seven years from 1879–86 the gain was only 145,459. These figures, which I take from the statistics of Mr. Archibald Blue, secretary of the Ontario Bureau of Industries, become still more significant when we consider that in the second period of seven years the Government had spent more money in developing the railways, in promoting immigration, and raised more money by the protective tariff for the establishing of industries, than in the first. The increase of population in the first period was 17½ per cent.; in the second, only 8⅔ per cent. Mr. Blue also says that but for the accession by immigration in the seven years 1879–86 the population of the province in 1886 would have been 62,640 less than in 1879. The natural increase, added to the immigration reported (208,000), should have given an increase of 442,000. There was an increase of only 145,000. What became of the 297,000? They did not go to Manitoba—the census shows that. "The lamentable truth is that we are growing men for the United States." That is, the province is at the cost of raising thousands of citizens up to a productive age only to lose them by emigration to the United States. Comparisons are also made with Ohio and Michigan, showing in them a proportionally greater increase in population, in acres of land under production, in manufactured products, and in development of mineral wealth. And yet Ontario has as great natural advantages as these neighboring States. The observation is also made that in the six years 1873–79, a period of intense business stringency, the country made decidedly greater progress than in the six years 1879–85, "a period of revival and boom, and vast expenditure of public money." The reader will bear in mind that the repeal (caused mainly by the increase of Canadian duties on American products) of the reciprocity treaty in 1866 (under which an international trade had grown to $70,000,000 annually) discouraged any annexation sentiment that may have existed, aided the scheme of confederation, and seemed greatly to stimulate Canadian manufactures, and the growth of interior and exterior commerce.

We touch here not only political questions active in Canada, but economic problems affecting both Canada and the United States. It is the criticism of the Liberals upon the "development" policy, the protective tariff, the subsidy policy of the Liberal-Conservative party now in power, that a great show of activity is made without any real progress either in wealth or population. To put it in a word, the Liberals want unrestricted trade with the United States, with England, or with the world—preferably with the United States. If this caused separation from England they would accept the consequences with composure, but they vehemently deny that they in any way favor annexation because they desire free-trade. Pointing to the more rapid growth of the States of the Union, their advantage is said to consist in having free exchange of commodities with sixty millions of people, spread over a continent.

As a matter of fact it seems plain that Ontario would benefit and have a better development by sharing in this large circulation and exchange. Would the State of New York be injured by the prosperity of Ontario?

Is it not benefited **by the prosperity of its other neighbor,** Pennsylvania ?

Toronto **represents Ontario. It is its monetary, intellectual, educational centre, and I may add that here,
more than anywhere else in Canada, the visitor is conscious of the complicated energy of a very vigorous
civilization. The city itself has grown rapidly—an
increase from 86,415 in 1881 to probably 170,000 in
1888—and it is growing as rapidly as any city on the
continent, according to the indications of building,
manufacturing, railway building, and the visible stir
of enterprise. It is a very handsome and agreeable
city, pleasant for one reason, because it covers a large
area, and gives space for the display of its fine buildings. I noticed especially the effect of noble churches,
occupying a square—ample grounds that give dignity
to the house of God. It extends along the lake about
six miles, and runs back about as far, laid out with
regularity, and with the general effect of being level,
but the outskirts have a good deal of irregularity and
picturesqueness. It has many broad, handsome streets
and several fine parks; High Park on the west is extensive, the University grounds (or Queen's Park) are
beautiful—the new and imposing Parliament Buildings are being erected in a part of its domain ceded
for the purpose; and the Island Park, the irregular
strip of an island lying in front of the city, suggests
the Lido of Venice. I cannot pause upon details, but
the town has an air of elegance, of solidity, of prosperity. The well-filled streets present an aspect of
great business animation, which is seen also in the
shops, the newspapers, the clubs. It is a place of
social activity as well, of animation, of hospitality.**

There are a few delightful old houses, which date back to the New England loyalists, and give a certain flavor to the town.

If I were to make an accurate picture of Toronto it would appear as one of the most orderly, well-governed, moral, highly civilized towns on the continent —in fact, almost unique in the active elements of a high Christian civilization. The notable fact is that the concentration here of business enterprise is equalled by the concentration of religious and educational activity.

The Christian religion is fundamental in the educational system. In this province the public schools are Protestant, the separate schools Roman Catholic, and the Bible has never been driven from the schools. The result as to positive and not passive religious instruction has not been arrived at without agitation. The mandatory regulations of the provincial Assembly are these: Every public and high school shall be opened daily with the Lord's Prayer, and closed with the reading of the Scriptures and the Lord's Prayer, or the prayer authorized by the Department of Education. The Scriptures shall be read daily and systematically, without comment or explanation. No pupil shall be required to take part in any religious exercise objected to by parent or guardian, and an interval is given for children of Roman Catholics to withdraw. A volume of Scripture selections made up by clergymen of the various denominations or the Bible may be used, in the discretion of the trustees, who may also order the repeating of the ten commandments in the school at least once a week. Clergymen of any denomination, or their authorized representatives, shall have the right to give religious instruction to pupils of their denomination in the school-house at least once a week. The historical portions of the Bible are given with more fulness than the others. Each lesson contains a continuous selection. The denominational rights of the pupils are respected, because the Scripture must be read without comment or explanation. The State thus discharges its duty without prejudice to any sect, but recognizes the truth that ethical and religious instruction is as necessary in life as any other.

I am not able to collate the statistics to show the effect of this upon public morals. I can only testify to the general healthful tone. The schools of Toronto are excellent and comprehensive; the kindergarten is a part of the system, and the law avoids the difficulty experienced in St. Louis about spending money on children under the school age of six by making the kindergarten age three. There is also a school for strays and truants, under private auspices as yet, which reinforces the public schools in an important manner, and an industrial school of promise, on the cottage system, for neglected boys. The heads of educational departments whom I met were Christian men.

I sat one day with the police-magistrate, and saw something of the workings of the Police Department. The chief of police is a gentleman. So far as I could see there was a distinct moral intention in the administration. There are special policemen of high character, with discretionary powers, who seek to prevent crime, to reconcile differences, to suppress vice, to do justice on the side of the erring as well as on the side

of the law. The central prison (all offenders sentenced
for more than two years go to a Dominion penitentiary) is a well-ordered jail, without any special reformatory features. I cannot even mention the courts,
the institutions of charity and reform, except to say
that they all show vigorous moral action and sentiment in the community.

The city, though spread over such a large area,
permits no horse-cars to run on Sunday. There are
no saloons open on Sunday; there are no beer-gardens
or places of entertainment in the suburbs, and no Sunday newspapers. It is believed that the effect of not
running the cars on Sunday has been to scatter excellent churches all over the city, so that every small section has good churches. Certainly they are well distributed. They are large and fine architecturally;
they are well filled on Sunday; the clergymen are
able, and the salaries are considered liberal. If I may
believe the reports and my limited observation, the
city is as active religiously as it is in matters of education. And I do not see that this interferes with an
agreeable social life, with a marked tendency of the
women to beauty and to taste in dress. The tone of
public and private life impresses a stranger as exceptionally good. The police is free from political influence, being under a commission of three, two of
whom are life magistrates, and the mayor.

The free-library system of the whole province is
good. Toronto has an excellent and most intelligently
arranged free public library of about 50,000 volumes.
The library trustees make an estimate yearly of the
money necessary, and this, under the law, must be
voted by the city council. The Dominion Govern-

ment still imposes a duty on books purchased for the library outside of Canada.

The educational work of Ontario is nobly crowned by the University of Toronto, though it is in no sense a State institution. It is well endowed, and has a fine estate. The central building is dignified and an altogether noble piece of architecture, worthy to stand in its beautiful park. It has a university organization, with a college inside of it, a school of practical science, and affiliated divinity schools of several denominations, including the Roman Catholic. There are fine museums and libraries, and it is altogether well equipped and endowed, and under the presidency of Dr. Daniel Wilson, the venerable ethnologist, it is a great force in Canada. The students and officers wear the cap and gown, and the establishment has altogether a scholastic air. Indeed, this tradition and equipment—which in a sense pervades all life and politics in Canada—has much to do with keeping up the British connection. The conservation of the past is stronger than with us.

A hundred matters touching our relations with Canada press for mention. I must not omit the labor organizations. These are in affiliation with those in the United States, and most of them are international. The plumbers, the bricklayers, the stone-masons and stone-cutters, the Typographical Union, the Brotherhood of Carpenters and Joiners, the wood-carvers, the Knights of Labor, are affiliated; there is a branch of the Brotherhood of Locomotive Engineers in Canada; the railway conductors, with delegates from all our States, held their conference in Toronto last summer. The Amalgamated Society of Carpenters and Joiners is a British association, with headquarters in Manchester, but it has an executive committee in New York, with which all the Canadian and American societies communicate, and it sustains a periodical in New York. The Society of Amalgamated Engine Builders has its office in London, but there is an American branch, with which all the Canadian societies work in harmony. The Cigar-makers' Union is American, but a strike of cigar-makers in Toronto was supported by the American ; so with the plumbers. It may be said generally that the societies each side the line will sustain each other. The trade organizations are also taken up by women, and these all affiliate with the United States. When a "National" union affiliates with one on the other side, the name is changed to "International." This union and interchange draws the laborers of both nations closer together. From my best information, and notwithstanding the denial of some politicians, the Canadian unions have love and sympathy for and with America. And this feeling must be reckoned with in speaking of the tendency to annexation. The present much-respected mayor of Toronto is a trade-unionist, and has a seat in the local parliament as a Conservative; he was once arrested for picketing, or some such trade-union performance. I should not say that the trades-unions are in favor of annexation, but they are not afraid to discuss it. There is in Toronto a society of a hundred young men, the greater part of whom are of the artisan class, who meet to discuss questions of economy and politics. One of their subjects was Canadian independence. I am told that there is among young men a considerable desire for independence, accompanied with a determination to be on the best terms with the United States, and that as between a connection with Great Britain and the United States, they would prefer the latter. In my own observation the determination to be on good terms with the United States is general in Canada; the desire for independence is not.

The frequency of the question, " What do you think of the future of Canada ?" shows that it is an open question. Undeniably the confederation, which seems to me rather a creation than a growth, works very well, and under it Canada has steadily risen in the consideration of the world and in the development of the sentiment of nationality. But there are many points unadjusted in the federal and provincial relations ; more power is desired on one side, more local autonomy on the other. The federal right of disallowance of local legislation is resisted. The stated distribution of federal money to the provinces is an anomaly which we could not reconcile with the public spirit and dignity of the States, nor recognize as a proper function of the Government. The habit of the provinces of asking aid from the central government in emergencies, and getting it, does not cultivate self-reliance, and the grant of aid by the Federal Government, in order to allay dissatisfaction, must be a growing embarrassment. The French privileges in regard to laws, language, and religion make an insoluble core in the heart of the confederacy, and form a compact mass which can be wielded for political purposes. This element, dominant in the province of Quebec, is aggressive. I have read many alarmist articles, both in Canadian and English periodicals, as to the danger of

this to the rights of Protestant communities. I lay
no present stress upon the expression of the belief by
intelligent men that Protestant communities might
some time be driven to the shelter of the wider toleration of the United States. No doubt much feeling
is involved. I am only reporting a state of mind
which is of public notoriety; and I will add that men
equally intelligent say that all this fear is idle; that,
for instance, the French increase in Ontario means
nothing, only that the *habitant* can live on the semi-
sterile Laurentian lands that others cannot profitably
cultivate.

In estimating the idea the Canadians have of their
future it will not do to take surface indications. One
can go to Canada and get almost any opinion and
tendency he is in search of. Party spirit—though
the newspapers are in every way, as a rule, less sensational than ours—runs as high and is as deeply bitter
as it is with us. Motives are unwarrantably attributed.
It is always to be remembered that the Opposition
criticises the party in power for a policy it might not
essentially change if it came in, and the party in power attributes designs to the Opposition which it does
not entertain : as, for instance, the Opposition party is
not hostile to confederation because it objects to the
" development " policy or to the increase of the federal
debt, nor is it for annexation because it may favor
unrestricted trade or even commercial union. As a
general statement it may be said that the Liberal-Conservative party is a protection party, a " development "
party, and leans to a stronger federal government;
that the Liberal party favors freer trade, would cry
halt to debt for the forcing of development, and is

jealous of provincial rights. Even the two parties are not exactly homogeneous. There are Conservatives who would like legislative union; the Liberals of the province of Quebec are of one sort, the Liberals of the province of Ontario are of another, and there are Conservative-Liberals as well as Radicals.

The interests of the maritime provinces are closely associated with those of New England; popular votes there have often pointed to political as well as commercial union, but the controlling forces are loyal to the confederation and to British connection. Manitoba is different in origin, as I pointed out, and in temper. It considers sharply the benefit to itself of the federal domination. My own impression is that it would vote pretty solidly against any present proposition of annexation, but under the spur of local grievances and the impatience of a growth slower than expected there is more or less annexation talk, and one newspaper of a town of six thousand people has advocated it. Whether that is any more significant than the same course taken by a Quebec newspaper recently under local irritation about disallowance I do not know. As to unrestricted trade, Sir John Thompson, the very able Minister of Justice in Ottawa, said in a recent speech that Canada could not permit her financial centre to be shifted to Washington and her tariff to be made there; and in this he not only touched the heart of the difficulty of an arrangement, but spoke, I believe, the prevailing sentiment of Canada.

As to the future, I believe the choice of a strict conservatism would be, first, the government as it is; second, independence; third, imperial federation: annexation never. But imperial federation is generally

31

regarded as a wholly impracticable scheme. The Liberal would choose, first, the framework as it is, with modifications; second, independence, with freer trade; third, trust in Providence, without fear. It will be noted in all these varieties of predilection that separation from England is calmly contemplated as a definite possibility, and I have no doubt that it would be preferred rather than submission to the least loss of the present autonomy. And I must express the belief that, underlying all other thought, unexpressed, or, if expressed, vehemently repudiated, is the idea, widely prevalent, that some time, not now, in the dim future, the destiny of Canada and the United States will be one. And if one will let his imagination run a little, he cannot but feel an exultation in the contemplation of the majestic power and consequence in the world such a nation would be, bounded by three oceans and the Gulf, united under a restricted federal head, with free play for the individuality of every State. If this ever comes to pass, the tendency to it will not be advanced by threats, by unfriendly legislation, by attempts at conquest. The Canadians are as high-spirited as we are. Any sort of union that is of the least value could only come by free action of the Canadian people, in a growth of business interests undisturbed by hostile sentiment. And there could be no greater calamity to Canada, to the United States, to the English-speaking interest in the world, than a collision. Nothing is to be more dreaded for its effect upon the morals of the people of the United States than any war with any taint of conquest in it.

There is, no doubt, with many, an honest preference for the colonial condition. I have heard this said:

" We have the best government in the world, a responsible government, with entire local freedom. England exercises no sort of control; we are as free as a nation can be. We have in the representative of the Crown a certain conservative tradition, and it only costs us ten thousand pounds a year. We are free, we have little expense, and if we get into any difficulty there is the mighty power of Great Britain behind us!" It is as if one should say in life, I have no responsibilities; I have a protector. Perhaps as a " rebel," I am unable to enter into the colonial state of mind. But the boy is never a man so long as he is dependent. There was never a nation great until it came to the knowledge that it had nowhere in the world to go for help.

In Canada to-day there is a growing feeling for independence ; very little, taking the whole mass, for annexation. Put squarely to a popular vote, it would make little show in the returns. Among the minor causes of reluctance to a union are distrust of the Government of the United States, coupled with the undoubted belief that Canada has the better government; dislike of our quadrennial elections ; the want of a system of civil service, with all the turmoil of our constant official overturning ; dislike of our sensational and irresponsible journalism, tending so often to recklessness ; and dislike also, very likely, of the very assertive spirit which has made us so rapidly subdue our continental possessions.

But if one would forecast the future of Canada, he needs to take a wider view than personal preferences or the agitations of local parties. The railway development, the Canadian Pacific alone, has changed within five years the prospects of the political situation. It has brought together the widely separated provinces, and has given a new impulse to the sentiment of nationality. It has produced a sort of unity which no Act of Parliament could ever create. But it has done more than this: it has changed the relation of England to Canada. The Dominion is felt to be a much more important part of the British Empire than it was ten years ago, and in England within less than ten years there has been a revolution in colonial policy. With a line of fast steamers from the British Islands to Halifax, with lines of fast steamers from Vancouver to Yokohama, Hong-Kong, and Australia, with an all-rail transit, within British limits, through an empire of magnificent capacities, offering homes for any possible British overflow, will England regard Canada as a weakness? It is true that on this continent the day of dynasties is over, and that the people will determine their own place. But there are great commercial forces at work that cannot be ignored, which seem strong enough to keep Canada for a long time on her present line of development in a British connection.

THE END.